Being a Jett A Girl

BOOK TWO IN THE BOURBON SERIES

MEGHAN QUINN

ISBN: 1505427010
ISBN-13: 978-1505427011

1
"BANG BANG"

Lo

"Uhhhhh, yeaaaaaa. Hmmmm, uh, uh. Heeeee."

There are three different types of men that show up at the Lafayette Club for a good lap dance. There are the men who try to act like your scantily-clad ass dancing across their bean pole is not affecting them even though they are biting their lip while staring at your tits and sweating like a heavyset man in a sauna. Then, there are the men who are so ashamed of asking for a lap dance they don't look at you, don't acknowledge you and don't even breathe until you're done, but their southern friend reaps all the reward as he stands to attention, taking in every last pelvic thrust. And lastly, there are the heavy breathers who communicate to the lap dancer by hissing through their teeth, humming from their throats and gurgling on the foam that has collected in their mouths. Fucking nasty ass men.

I had a heavy breather at the moment.

When I sounded off at the beginning of our presentation for the local Rotary Club, yes, the Rotary Club—do gooders my right tit—I knew right then and there, the man who eye-fucked me as I dropped my ass was going to ask for a lap dance.

We were all wearing gold one-piece bathing suits, blond wigs, gold masks with feathers and a gallon of glitter lotion. My cleavage was so glittery, I was afraid a gaggle of unicorns were going to start sprouting from my nips. Now that would be a show! Torpedo Tits and her Unicorn Breeding Glitter Cleavage. I would pay to see that shit.

"Oh boy, oh boy….heeee, haaa, heee….uhuhuhuhuh." His eyes rolled in the back of his head as the jowls of his face shook.

What.The.Fuck?

The man stiffened under me as my hands were on his knees and my ass was in his crotch. I couldn't see too well but I was pretty sure he just blew his load, all over my lotion bedazzled ass. I looked over at Babs and Tootse who were giving lap dances as well and gave them the thumbs-up. The music died down and our job was done.

Slowly, I got up off the man's lap, trying not to show how repulsed I was as I turned to smile at the heavy breather. When I glanced down at his crotch, I saw a giant wet spot at the tip of his crotch. Minor panic rolled through me as I tried to recall if he just blew a giant load or if I peed on him. I was so caught up in what I was doing that I couldn't remember if I let loose. I did have to pee…

Fuck!

Casually, as I smiled at the man, I ran my hands down my body to give him one last show but really was checking myself. I ran my hand to the front of my body, cupped my Little Lady P and casually checked for drainage. I was clean! Victory, the man was just backed up in the old orgasm department and blew it right there and then. That was when I looked up at him and his eyes were sedated as well as his tongue that was practically hanging out of his mouth.

Eck, gross.

Time to bail.

I squeezed my tits together for him, to give him one last show, patted his knee and went to the back where the other girls were waiting for me.

Francy was still out in the Toulouse Room serving while Pepper sat in the back with Kace, discussing tomorrow night's presentation.

It's been a week since Jett officially made me a Jett Girl and I know it might sound weird, but I couldn't be prouder with myself. I've nailed every single routine since I've been here, with the exception of my first night when some members decided to partake in some alcohol abuse and drench me with their wrong drinks. But we won't go there.

Settling into my new role was pretty easy actually. Now that I was an official Jett Girl, I was able to start looking through what kind of educational classes I wanted to take, I had the chance to help the girls with theming out presentations and Pepper even let me add some moves to her choreographed pieces. I really felt like I belonged, plus, I was fucked by Jett almost every single night.

Currently, I hadn't had sex in three days because Jett has been out of town on business but he was supposed to be returning tonight, or so I thought. I was dying to see him. He still kept his distance, was very closed off but there were moments, when we were in the Bourbon Room together, where he would twirl my hair in his finger ever so lightly or press his palm against my cheek as he stared into my eyes and I knew that was him communicating to me about how he felt.

My relationship with Jett was an odd one, but after he confessed to me that he needed me, there was no way I would be able to leave him because I needed him too. I needed him, I needed the Lafayette Club and the girls and strangely, I needed the brooding Kace as well. I've finally found my home.

I walked through the curtains and ran straight into a tall, muscular wall. I looked up to see Kace looking down at me, with his arms crossed and a stern look on his face.

"If you're trying to be a door, you're failing terribly."

"Cut the crap, what was that out there?" Kace asked, always straight to the point.

"What was what?" I asked as I took off my mask, needing to breathe. The feathers were itching my face all night.

"The little private dance you gave that man afterwards. Don't play dumb with me."

Hmmm...how did I put this eloquently?

"I thought I pissed myself." Not so eloquent but by the look on Kace's face, I did my job.

"You what?"

"When I got off the hisser back there, I saw a giant wet spot and I was nervous I pissed myself. Have you seen the crotch coverage on these bathing suits?" I asked while I squatted and tried to show Kace my crotch as he rolled his eyes and shook his head. "I would have been humiliated so I just kind of wandered my hands down to my—"

"Enough," he said as he turned and walked away.

I looked over at Pepper, Babs and Tootse who all had giant smiles on their faces but quickly removed them when Kace started talking to them.

"Did anyone else think they pissed themselves?"

All three shook their heads no.

Kace turned back to me and said, "Never thought I would have to baby you this much but make sure you go to the bathroom before a presentation, Lo. We don't need you peeing all over our members." He ran his hands over his face and mumbled, "Jesus."

"I didn't pee myself," I said in defense, wanting to make that clear.

"Well, thank God for that," Kace said sarcastically.

"The guy just blew his load," I clarified, making Kace cringe and put up his hands.

"I really don't want to hear about it. You made your money, let's keep it at that."

"You're the one who asked," I reminded him.

"She's right, Kace," Pepper said as she removed her mask as

well.

"We should actually be praising her for doing such a good job," Babs added as she started pouring shots from a bottle of whip cream vodka.

Mmm, I could use some of that.

Not acknowledging the girls, Kace said, "I have a fuck date. Don't be late for the workout tomorrow." With that he started walking away but I chased after him. His phone never chimed with a text and I was curious if Jett was home.

"Kace, wait."

He stopped in the hallway but didn't turn around. His back was tense as I approached him and I chalked it up to him being irritated with me but when I turned him around and looked him in the eyes, I saw pain.

"What's wrong?" I asked, now concerned about him and not caring if Jett was home or not.

"Nothing," he said as he started to walk away.

"Yes, something is wrong. Why won't you talk to me?"

Kace stood inches from my face and said, "What have I told you? We're not friends, Goldie."

So, this has been Kace's motto ever since I became an official Jett Girl. I'm not stupid, I know the man finds me attractive, I've seen the way he looks at me but this total avoidance thing unless he has to speak to me is starting to get on my nerves.

"Who said I want to be your friend," I said defiantly. I mean, I kind of want to be his friend. He seems cool, when he's not mad as hell or yelling at me. Plus, don't friends have the privilege of seeing each other naked? I mean, I see the other Jett Girls naked and we're friends. I think we should all just be naked friends, maybe Kace would be less tense.

Kace guffawed as he said, "Please, don't fuck around with me. What do you want?"

The man was a dick.

Not wanting to play around anymore, I asked, "Is Jett home?"

A small smirk crossed his face making me want to smack him

right across the jaw. The man knew my weakness and I hated it.

"Yeah, he's home."

"He is?" I asked a little too eagerly. "Any, umm…text messages?" I swallowed hard.

That damn smirk still graced Kace's amazingly handsome face as he pulled out his phone and flashed me the screen. It was blank.

I felt deflated. It's been three days and Jett was home, didn't he want to see me? I knew I wasn't supposed to let my heart get involved but who was I kidding, the minute Jett first touched me my heart took off. It was hard not to feel when it came to Jett.

"Must be busy with someone else," Kace said, nailing the dagger in my heart even further.

I nodded, not letting Kace see the deflation in my body from the news and turned around.

"Have a good fuck," I called over my shoulder as I headed back to the girls.

"For what it's worth, he's an idiot," Kace said quietly.

Before I could turn and say anything in return, he was gone. He was such a confusing man.

Once I got back to where the girls were, Babs handed me a shot glass full of the whip cream delight. I threw the drink back and held out my glass for round two. Babs obliged. I took three more shots like that, not even speaking as the girls took them with me.

I was four shots in, in the matter of a minute and ready to go up to my room.

"I'm out, girls. I'll see you tomorrow morning."

"Don't let him get to you," Pepper said as she took another shot, alone. She'd been drinking a lot more lately and it was a little concerning but I wasn't about to say anything, it wasn't quite my place.

"I don't let Kace get to me. I know he's bound to be an asshole at least twice a day."

"Not Kace," Pepper said. "I mean Jett."

Talking about Jett with the other girls was a little awkward

7

because I was the only one Jett called up to the Bourbon Room now. Everyone told me they didn't care and it didn't matter to them but it was still weird.

"Umm, okay," I replied, wanting to drop it. "Thanks for the drinks. I'm off to bed. Have a good night, girls."

They waved to me as I took off toward the back staircase, avoiding all members. As I walked up the curved staircase to my room, I started taking off my heels and wig. I enjoyed dressing up but sometimes, it felt too much. I released my hair and let it fall over my shoulders. It felt good to free everything. We've had a presentation every night since I became official and I was ready for a night off where I didn't have to slap on a layer of makeup and a miniscule article of clothing.

Walking down the narrow hallway where my room was located, I thought about how Jett was home but didn't want to see me. It stung but I tried to convince myself that he must have been tired. I had no clue where he went on business, for all I knew he could have been in a foreign country and he was tired as hell. If I got back from a long trip, I would want to sleep too. Well, unless Jett came knocking at my door, I would peel my eyelids open for that man, that was how good he was.

Damn.

I walked in my room and tossed my heels, wig and mask to the side. I would pick them up later. I was not in the mood to organize.

I looked over at my bed and sighed as I thought about what a great night sleep I was going to get, even if I was a little horny.

I started to walk to my bedroom when I heard a shuffle behind me. I turned around and nearly screamed when I came face to face with Jett.

"Hello, my little one."

Lady wood.

Those four little words, said in his seductively sexy southern voice had not only my heart pounding but my pussy was knocking at the bathing suit I was wearing, begging to be freed.

"Hi," I gulped as he perused my body and licked his lips.

"Do you have something to say to me?"

Fuck yes!

2
"MMM YEAH"

Jett

It was a long three fucking days in New York, trying to square away some property I was purchasing out there and all I wanted to do was get back to the Lafayette Club, invite Goldie up to the Bourbon Room and taste that sweet pussy of hers but when I saw what the girls were wearing, I knew I couldn't let Goldie up into the Bourbon Room, she would get glitter everywhere and I tried to keep the room as pristine as possible. The glitter would have declassed the play room and I didn't want that, therefore, I waited for her in her room.

The girls looked sexy tonight, in their gold outfits and wigs but right now, with her hair down and bare-footed, Goldie had me begging to touch her. I hated to admit it, but I missed my little one. I was growing accustomed to seeing her every night, ready to submit but the past three days left me yearning to get back to my home town of New Orleans and into the Bourbon Room to see her, the one who's been driving me crazy in my dreams.

I could tell she missed me by the way her eyes softened from seeing me and the way her breathing picked up when I asked if she had something to say to me.

I waited patiently as she nodded her head and said, "I'm here to submit to you."

Every time those words came out of her mouth, I instantly got hard. Goldie was by far the sexiest woman I've ever met and it wasn't just because her hair was the color of honey or the fact that even though she was tiny, she had curves for days. No, it was her attitude, her heart, her sass, the way she carried herself that made me so damn attracted to her.

Pleased with her submission, I pressed my palm against her cheek and said, "Did you miss me, Goldie?"

She nodded her head, as her cheek pressed against my hand. "How much?"

"More than I want to admit." Her eyes fluttered close.

"I saw the lap dance you gave tonight. I didn't like it."

Her eyes widened as she looked at me. "Did I not do a good job?"

"No, you did. I just don't like you giving other men lap dances."

A small smile crossed her face from my confession. I was all right with telling her my displeasure for her lap dances on other men because it was true. Normally, I wouldn't divulge such information, I just kept things like that to myself but after her almost leaving me, leaving the club, I realized that I had to confess some things to her if I wanted to keep her in my life. There had to be a little give and take.

She went to touch me but I stepped away. I was in control and sometimes she forgot that. Her face fell from my rejection but I quickly recovered as I said, "Who's in control here, Lo?"

"You are," she said as she lowered her head.

I pushed her chin up with my finger and said, "Lead me to your bathroom."

"Please tell me we're going to have shower sex." She broke her role. I knew it was only a matter of time before she started talking and asking questions. It was typical Goldie behavior. Something I struggled with controlling but I would be lying if I said I didn't enjoy trying to control her wild mouth. It was one of my favorite things.

"I haven't had shower sex in so long. Last time I think was a couple of years ago with this guy named Robert. He was pretty good but he had a crooked dick so it was always weird trying to angle myself so we lined up. Not like you care, you probably don't want to hear about that but it was worth sharing because crooked dicks are odd, don't you think? If one was curved up though, now that would be a dick…"

"Goldie," I said sternly, trying not to smile from her little crooked dick rant.

"Oh fuck, sorry," she said as she covered her mouth. "I'm just so excited you're here!" She jumped up and down and clapped her hands together.

I ran my hand over my mouth, covering my smile as I watched her excitement. Best fucking welcome home I've ever received. Goldie in a tiny bathing suit, jumping up and down, yeah I was one lucky motherfucker.

I held my hand out and repeated, "Show me to your bathroom."

She looked down at my hand, smiled brightly and took it with hers. Her hand was so small compared to mine but I reveled in the feeling of my hand overlapping hers.

As we walked to her bathroom, I watched her hips sway in front of me, enticing me to just toss her on her bed and fuck her right then and there but I had different plans.

When we got to her bathroom, I looked around and almost laughed out loud. The girl was a slob!

Her face cringed as she apparently remembered what her room looked like when she left it.

"It's not normally like this," she said as she quickly turned to face me.

I nodded my head as I took in everything. There were wigs

spread all over the bathroom counter as well as multiple makeup products. Her cabinet that held all her masks was wide open and had masks hanging everywhere. Clothes from workouts and presentations were spread all over her floor and her trashcan was overflowing with makeup cloths.

She fidgeted in place as she looked around and said, "Um, I've been working hard?" Her question/statement had me inwardly smiling.

"I should leave right now, given the appearance of this room…"

She grabbed a hold of my arm and said, "Please, no. I can clean it real quick, see?"

Gathering up her clothes, she started running around in her little bathing suit, throwing things in her hamper and tossing makeup in her drawers.

"Goldie, stop." She stopped in place and turned around as she held multiple masks in her hand. "I should leave, but I'm not going to and do you know why?"

She shook her head no as she placed the masks back on the ground.

"I'm not going to leave because I need a taste of that sweet pussy of yours and I'm not leaving until I get it."

Visibly, I watched her gulp as she nodded her head.

"Strip," I demanded, not wanting to play around anymore. I was hard and I wanted her.

The bathing suit she was wearing was a one-piece but the sides were cut out and the back rode dangerously low on her waistline, showing off her perfect body and curves. I noticed that she had toned up even more since she's been at the club but she still maintained her curves. She was breathtaking.

Being a good little listener, she pulled the straps off her shoulders and pulled the skin-tight suit off her body, revealing her plentiful breasts, bare pussy and toned stomach. Yup, she was about to be fucked…hard.

"You please me, little one."

"That's all I want to do," she confessed while looking up at me through her lashes.

Fuck, I never kissed the girls, ever, but with Goldie, it was different. I couldn't stop myself from kissing her, even if I wanted to.

I pressed her up against the counter, pulled her chin up to mine and pressed my lips against hers as my hand went to the back of her neck and brought her closer to me. I was trying to avoid the attack of the glitter but as her tongue pressed against mine, I didn't give a fuck anymore.

Not getting too deep into our kiss, I pulled away and walked over to her glass encased shower as she was left breathing heavily and pressing her fingers to her lips, like I just branded them. If I needed to bite down on her lips to brand them as mine, I would. I didn't want anyone else touching those delectable lips.

I turned on her shower, set the nozzles to a warm setting, turned on the multiple jets and opened the door for her to get in. She followed my instructions and slipped into the shower. Steam started to incase her as the water slid down each valley and crest of her gorgeous frame. Her hair hung down past her shoulders and her nipples were hard while she looked me up and down for further instruction.

I might have to change my original plan.

"Are you joining me?" she asked.

"No. I want you to wash that glitter off your body."

Her face fell as she realized I wasn't joining her, sending a surge of satisfaction through my veins, knowing that all she wanted was me. It was intoxicating to know that such a beautiful woman would want me.

Watching her fill her loofa up with soap and wash down her body, I thought about how nice it was to have someone actually want me, to look forward to seeing me, to practically begging me to take them. It was a drastic change from the days that I was with Natasha, my ex-fiancée who just so happened to run into the arms of my least favorite person, Rex Titan.

With her back to me, she tilted her head to the side, making her hair fall over one shoulder as she ran the loofa over her other shoulder. Her head turned slightly, catching a glimpse of her face, her long eyelashes fanned which only enticed me more.

Seductress.

"The longer you take washing that fuckable body of yours, the longer you're going to have to wait to feel me inside you."

Her eyes shot open and then the slow seductive movements of her loofa turned into rapid scrubbing as she moved up and down her limbs and rinsed like a banshee on fire. Her antics will never get old.

While she continued to scrub, I took my shirt and pants off, dropping them to the side and opened the shower door. The cold air that entered with me had Goldie turning around abruptly and eyeing my naked torso. I still had on my briefs because, frankly, I wanted her to pull them down with her teeth.

There was a little shelf in the shower that I sat down on and spread my legs as I leaned against the cool glass of the shower wall.

"Are you clean?" I asked as I looked her up and down.

"I believe so," she said as her breath hitched from the obvious erection poking through my briefs.

"Let me see." I held out my hand to her which she took after she hung her loofa up.

I pulled her in close so her stomach was only inches from my mouth. I ran my hands up her sides as her head flew back from the slight graze of my thumb over her nipples. Her breasts were plump and heavy for my hold which I enjoyed. Her nipples were small and pink, just like I preferred. I worked my way back down to her hips and turned her around so I had an up-close-and-personal view of her delectable ass. My hands caressed her backside and ran up her back, pushing on her lower back so she had to bend forward. She easily followed my direction as she bent forward without shame and truly gave herself to me.

Without hesitation, I moved her closer to me and dipped my head into her center to taste her sweet pussy, the one thing I was craving while I was on business.

The moment my tongue hit her sweetness, a moan escaped her mouth as she thrust her hips back making me move faster. I steadied her and then smacked her ass. Her head sprang up so fast I was afraid she was going to get whiplash.

"Ouch," she said innocently. I knew I didn't hurt her, I just startled her.

"Did that really hurt?" I asked, knowing the answer.

"No," she said while rubbing her butt cheek.

"What's your safe word, Lo?"

"Alligator."

"Good, now, if you're not hurt you have two seconds to bend back over and get in position so I can suck on that little clit of yours."

Catching a smile cross her face as she bent over, I shook my head from her defiance. I was never this lenient, ever, but with Goldie, it was different. I liked her defiance, I liked the challenge, I liked giving her empty sexual threats that only made her smile.

After she got back into position, I didn't take my time, I licked her fully as I sucked in her little pink clit, eliciting a violent moan from her. I knew the position she was in, with her head down and her hands resting on her ankles with her ass in the air was rather raw and exposed but I devoured it. I devoured her as I continued to suck on her, making her call out my name. I felt her tense up and right before she fell over, I pulled away. She wasn't going to come on my mouth tonight. I wanted her coming all over my dick.

She cried out as she realized I wasn't finishing her off but I quickly turned her around and looked her in her lust-filled eyes.

"Pull off my briefs." Her hands went to my waistline but I stopped her and said, "With your teeth."

Flames burned in her eyes as realization set in of my command. She knelt before me and ran her hands up my legs, playing her own little game. A long, slow hiss escaped between my teeth as her head bent before me and grabbed a hold of my waistband. Fuck, I was so hard. I was only torturing myself by prolonging the inevitable but I enjoyed watching Goldie struggle with her control as I made her practice patience.

Her nose rubbed up against my stomach as her teeth firmly grabbed a hold of my waistband. I lifted off the bench to help her as she pulled my briefs down. She stopped as my briefs hovered just above my knees and I watched her stick out her little pink tongue and lick the head of my cock.

My cock twitched in excitement, betraying me. I was about to reprimand her when her teeth pulled down the rest of my briefs and tossed them to the side to soak up the shower water.

"Stand up," I demanded and she did as she was told. "That little lick is going to cost you. You can watch me have my own orgasm now." I started to move my hand over my erection as her face fell in disappointment. My heart ripped as her eyes turned from lustful to downright sad. It killed me but she needed to learn a lesson on listening to me.

"Touch your breasts, Lo. Make those perfect little nipples of yours hard. I want you to pull on them."

Her face fell flat as she started pulling on her nipples. I watched as her little buds started to pucker making my erection grow even harder as I continued to pump myself. It was so erotic watching her touch herself but she was lacking in the intimacy I normally demanded from her.

I looked her in the eyes and said, "Little one, come here." I held out my hand and she took it. I pulled her down on my lap so she was straddling me and her pussy pressed right up against my erection. Her chest heaved from the contact as she put her arms on my shoulders. I gripped her hips and made her look me in the eyes.

"I don't like seeing that dejected look on your face."

"I've missed you, Jett, I just want to please you."

"You please me, little one. More than you ever know. You just need to learn how to be a good submissive. I have put up with your defiance for a while, you need to learn now. When I tell you to do something, you do it and don't stray."

"Did you not enjoy me licking you?"

"That's not the point. I like control, I like being able to tell you what to do and I want complete submission from you. That is what you signed up for when you came here."

"I'm sorry," she said as she lowered her head.

Fuck. She was breaking my heart. Where was my fun-loving Goldie?

Lifting her chin to look at me I said, "Do you want this session to end?"

"No!" she said quickly as she scooted closer on my lap, brushing her still wet pussy against my cock. Damn tease.

"Then stop feeling sorry for yourself. You might be a Jett Girl but you're still in training. You still have a lot to learn."

She nodded her head and said, "What can I do to make this up to you?"

"Turn around on my lap and put me inside you," I breathed into her ear as I leaned forward.

With determination, she stood up, grabbed my cock as she hovered over my legs and lowered herself as she slowly inserted me into her heat. Fuck, she was tight and wet and fucking perfect.

"Lean against my chest," I talked into her ear. "And place your head on my shoulder." She did as told and I looked over her body, taking in her beautiful curves.

Running my hands up her body, I grabbed her breasts and said, "Move your hips up and down and tell me how close you are right before you come. I want you to get to the edge but don't you dare have an orgasm without my permission. Do you understand?"

She nodded her head and started moving her hips up and down, using my chest as leverage. My hands wandered her body slowly, one hand focusing on her breasts and the other moving dangerously low to tease her. Once my hand hit her mound, she released a deep moan from the depth of her stomach. It was feral, erotic and everything I could hope for.

The way she moved up and down on me and pressed against my chest had my balls starting to beg for release. It was only three days since I last consumed her but those three days were torture knowing Goldie was sitting at home waiting for me.

"Mmm, God, I missed you," she confessed as she gripped my thighs and started moving faster.

I nipped at her earlobe and brushed my scruff against her sensitive skin. "I missed you," I admitted in the heat of the moment as I felt myself climb to the edge of falling over. I couldn't feel my legs as she continued to pump up and down. I was going to fucking come before her and I couldn't have that, so I ran my hand down her stomach and put pressure on her clit. Her mouth flew open wide as a silent cry escaped her.

"I'm going to come," she announced breathlessly. "Please let me come."

I bit her earlobe and said, "Come for me."

I wanted to edge her out but after not seeing her, being with her for three days, I needed this just as much as she did.

Her cries echoed in the glass shower as she pumped me like a machine. In a matter of seconds, my eyes were shut tight, letting no light in, as my dick was squeezed by her inner walls and I lost everything in me. My heart pounded as I tried to regain feeling back into my legs from the explosive release I just had.

Spent, I lifted Goldie off me, cleaned us both up and then turned off the water. We both dried off and I wrapped a terry cloth robe around her, tying a knot at her waist. She looked up at me with such adoration that I knew I was getting lost in her, easily.

I pressed my hand against her face and cupped her cheek. "Thank you, little one, for trying for me. I know sometimes my style is against your nature, but I appreciate you trying."

"Anything for you, Jett."

I gripped her chin and placed a very gentle kiss on her lips before pulling away.

"Sweet dreams, little one. Get some sleep."

Every time I left her to herself, I saw the pain that crossed her face but that was a pain that I would ignore because even though Goldie was etching a hole in my black heart, I still had my boundaries and sleeping in the same bed was a boundary I wouldn't be crossing. There was a reason why no one but me had seen my bedroom because there is a line in my life that no one is allowed to cross, not even a sassy, foul-mouthed, honey-haired girl, no matter how much she plagued my mind.

3
"POUR SOME SUGAR ON ME"

Lo

"Someone seems to be in a good mood," Babs said as she ran next to me on the treadmill.

Lately, I've been killing it on the workouts and it was oh, so gratifying when the strong and powerful Kace couldn't take me down with his burpees and push-ups. I held right up there with the other girls. Yes, when I got back to my room I soaked in my tub for hours, trying to heal my sore muscles but still, I stuck it to him.

"Jett came home last night," I said, keeping our conversation simple. I still felt a little awkward that the other girls were never called up to the Bourbon Room. Don't get me wrong, I was ecstatic about it but I always felt awkward talking about my...involvement with Jett. It wasn't a relationship, it was just an involvement.

"Ahh, I see. That's why you have some steam to burn off. You're no longer moping around the club because you got some man last night."

"I wasn't moping," I replied, trying to hold on to a shred of dignity.

Babs saw right through me as she said, "Okay, Lo. Nice try. I know you better than that."

I smiled and continued to run my warm-up as the other girls trickled in for our daily workout. We all knew the drill. We did ten minutes on the treadmill and then did whatever kind of plyometric crap Kace planned for us, then ended with either some weights or a little bit of yoga. It was a good hour and a half to two hours that we spent in the gym almost every day. I wanted to complain but when I looked in the mirror and saw how toned I was, I had to admit, well-fucking done, Kace, well-fucking done.

Once we wrapped up our warm-ups, we noticed that the man with the whip hadn't shown up yet which was very strange, he was usually in the gym before any of us.

"Where's Kace?" Tootse asked, confused as she wiped the sweat off her brow.

"No clue," Francy replied as she put a stray hair behind Tootse's ear. They were adorable together and sometimes had me wondering if at some point I should take a tour down Tuna Town because it seemed like they had it going on. I was jealous of their relationship, of seeing how affectionate they could be without a worry or care.

Pepper looked at her watch and said, "Well, he's not here so that means our workout must be canceled. I have some massive school work I have to get done by tonight because I've been procrastinating and dreaming up new choreography so I'm going to peace out girls." She slapped our asses and took off.

"I have some colors to review for my makeup line so I'm going to take off too," Babs replied as she winked and ran out the hallway and up the stairs.

And then there were three.

Tootse and Francy smiled at each other and Francy pulled Tootse into her arms and asked, "Shower?"

A devilish smile spread across her face as she nodded. They entwined their fingers, gave my cheek a little pat and then walked up the stairs together.

"Must be nice," I muttered as I lightly kicked one of the exercise balls in the room.

I had a lot of decisions to make when it came to my school work but I wasn't in the mood to do that and I was only allowed on the third floor when Jett invited me so offering to take a shower with him would be looked down upon, so that left me with one other option that was probably the worst choice but I apparently love walking on the wild side, so I headed to Kace's room.

I knew where his room was located but never actually been there. I was eager to see where he lived, what his room looked like, maybe catch a glimpse of the mysterious man.

Located in the back hallway, on the first floor, where there were no lights and was a little frightening, was Kace's room. The hallway wasn't in the best of shape like the ones upstairs and his door looked like it was made of the cheapest wood available. Talk about a servant's wing, this was it for sure.

A pang of hurt soured through me as I thought about Kace living alone back here. It seemed so dreary, so sad that I kind of wanted to tell him he could move into my room if he wanted. There was plenty of room for him to do so. I laughed to myself as I thought of Jett's reaction to Kace and I becoming roomies, it wouldn't go over well that's for sure.

The image of braiding each other's hair and staying up late, eating popcorn…

"What the hell are you doing here?" Kace said behind me, making me jump right out of my damn bra.

"Jesus Christ!" I yelled as my heart pounded in my chest. "You just can't scare people like that."

"I asked you a question."

I put my hand on my hip and said, "Well excuse me for wanting to check on you. You didn't show up for the workout so I just wanted to make sure you're okay."

Kace stepped into the light and tried to move past me but not before I saw the bloody lip he was sporting and the bruises across his face.

I stopped him by pulling on his arms and said, "Oh my God, what happened to you?"

I went to touch his lip but he pulled away and sidestepped my embrace.

"Leave," was all he said as he blew by me, opened his door and quickly shut it.

Well, that was rude.

My mind debated with itself as I tried to figure out what my next move was going to be. I could leave like he asked me to and go up to my room, maybe paint my nails, do some girly shit or I could do what was in my blood and defy the man and walk right into his bedroom. I never liked straying from being myself...so I puffed my chest, gave myself a quick pep talk and walked in his room.

The hallway that seemed like ghosts were popping out of the walls was a stark contrast to Kace's actual room. His room was so cozy, so welcoming. He didn't have much on the walls but the neutral tones that he used made the whole room feel inviting and warm.

As I looked around, I noticed there really wasn't any kind of personal items hanging or on display. The only thing I assumed was a memento from his life was a pair of boxing gloves hanging on the wall and a picture of him and Jett that was framed and on his night stand. Other than that, it was a pretty bland room.

There was a door open next to the window in the corner of his room so I crept toward it, trying to be quiet. As I worked my way forward, I heard a shower running and stopped in my tracks.

Kace was showering. Kace, the brooding but oh so hot man, was showering! I needed to leave for many reasons but as I told myself that, my feet seemed to move forward rather than backward. My body was so defiant.

Curiosity won out as I walked forward and snuck a peak into his bathroom. It was a little smaller than mine but still updated and nice. There were a few male hygiene products on the bathroom

counter and a green toothbrush but that was about it. My eyes
wandered to the glass encased shower that was steaming up but not
steaming up enough because what I saw had me panting like a
damn dog in heat.

Kace stood in the middle of the shower, naked and totally lost
in the water dripping down his body. His hands were running
through his hair, showing off his well-defined muscles as well as
the tattoo that was still a mystery to me. It was along his rib cage
but was in such loopy cursive that I had a really hard time reading
it. His muscles flexed as he moved with the water and droplets ran
off his skin like the sexiest damn rain I've ever seen.

Cleaning his body with a bar of soap, I watched his hand
run across each curve of his torso, which started a throb in the
center of my core. I held on to the side of the door as my breathing
started to hitch from the soft porn that I was watching.

I looked closer and noticed a deep v-cut in his waist that
had my mouth watering as my eyes ran farther south, very south.

Hello!

Holy fuck, at that moment I realized Kace was seriously
packing, like those are some balls I want in my mouth. He was just
as big as Jett and just as trimmed. I wondered what he might look
like when he was erect. Every nerve in my body was set on fire as I
tried to pry my eyes away but I couldn't, I was fascinated. I was
entranced; I was peeping at a penis that I shouldn't be but yummy
was he hot.

His hand ran down his body even farther and washed the
length of his penis, making it stand slightly to attention from his
touch. I heard a slight groan release from his mouth as his hand
traveled back up his body and across his stomach. Even the little
grunt coming from the steamy shower turned me on. Even though
I knew my heart was saved for Jett, there was still a little part of it
that was saved for Kace and right now, that little part was beating
widely.

Totally fixed on the little show that was playing in my head
where Kace came at me with that giant salami roll he had between

his legs, I missed the fact that the shower had turned off and Kace was now standing in front of me, naked.

"Get a good show?" he asked as he reached for a towel but still not covering up.

I didn't know what to say other than, "Errrr, doye," so I kept my mouth shut.

He wiped droplets of water out of his hair as he continued to show off his now growing erection.

He was turned on, from me staring at him and I was turned on because he was so damn sexy that I didn't have enough confidence to walk away.

"You know, I never stare at you like that so I would hope for the same respect," Kace said as he wrapped a towel around his waist which still showed off his erection.

Shaking my head out of all the amazing and glorious thoughts of Kace, I looked up at him and said, "Just thought I would show you how I felt every night."

"I'm pretty sure the members don't drool," he said while pointing to the corner of my mouth.

I quickly ran the back of my hand across my lips, wiping away the apparent drool that collected during Kace's one-eyed monster show.

"There was no drool," I lied, which made the corner of Kace's lip twitch.

"You forget the fact I have eyes, Lo. There was drool. Now you can tell me what you're doing here or you can get the fuck out."

Always such a moody bastard.

I looked him up and down one last time, taking in his well-defined six pack, the smoothness of his chest and the way his muscles flexed when he got angry. I was working my way back up to his eyes when I spotted more bruising. Automatically, my hand flew to his ribs as I looked up at him.

He flinched from my touch as I said, "What happened to you?"

"Drop it, Lo." He pulled away and walked to his sink.

"I'm not going to drop it when you have bruises all over your body and you missed a workout. Clearly you were in some kind of trouble and you must be embarrassed or something. You can talk to me, Kace."

The momentum of his body startled me as he swung around and pinned me against the wall. He got right in my face and said, "First of all, what did I tell you about being friends? It's never going to fucking happen. Second of all, if I was ever in some kind of trouble, then I would be able to take out whoever came my way." He raised his fist and said, "Do you see this? This will fucking kill a person so don't underestimate my ability to take care of myself ever again."

His tone of voice was so deep, so evil that he was actually scaring me.

"Now, run the fuck along or I'll tell Jett that I caught you sneaking into my room and watching me shower with your mouth wide open and drool hanging out of it."

"You're an asshole! I just wanted to make sure you were okay."

"Well fucking don't. I don't need you, Lo. I was fine before you came here so just leave me the fuck alone."

I wanted to make a snarky comment back to him about maybe thinking about finding a woman to take care of his mood but I was done with him. There was only so much a girl could take and I was at my limit. Kace could suck it.

Not giving him a chance to say anything else, I turned on my heel and walked out of his room. I was going to leave his door open just to be an ass but thought better of it, I didn't want to make my workout even harder than it was probably going to be tomorrow, so I turned around and grabbed the door knob to shut it and that's when I saw it. That was when I saw Kace, sitting on the floor, with his head in his hands, crying.

Wavering between what to do and what not to do, I went against all my instincts and shut the door. Clearly the man was going through some heavy shit and I was the last person in the world that he wanted near him. It hurt to know that after all of the advice and comfort he had lent me in the past, he wouldn't allow himself to rely on me in return.

I walked back up to my room, feeling sorry for the man and upset that he wouldn't confide in me. I wanted to be his friend, I knew we had potential to get there but he just wouldn't break down that wall to let it happen and I didn't know if it was because of the feelings he harbored for me or if it was because he was just that closed off but whatever it was, it hurt like hell.

When I walked in my room, there was a fresh bouquet of flowers waiting for me on my nightstand. There had to be a little leprechaun in the house that kept replacing them because the moment they started to wilt, they were instantly replaced.

I sauntered over to my nightstand and saw a card that was sitting in the arrangement. I sighed as I pulled it out and smiled to myself. Kace might be irritating and hard to understand but at least I had Jett, the all-encompassing Jett Colby.

I pulled out the letter and read.

Lo,

Thank you for last night. After three long days of business meetings, I was pleased to see you, here, in my home, with open arms. I look forward to many more greetings like that.

-J

The man had his grip wrapped around my lady balls. A simple note could take me out to dream land. I was a goner.

4
"BETTER DAYS"

Jett

"In the next two weeks your schedule is really going to pick up, sir," Jeremy, my assistant, said as he started touching his iPad, flipping through whatever the hell he had on there. "You have some meetings and late night events that require your presence."

"What kind of events?" I asked as I stared at my computer, answering e-mails.

"The socials you asked me to book you so you can hob knob with some of the city planners and officials that have a say in Lot 17."

Hob knob...only Jeremy would say that.

"How many?" I asked as I was instantly annoyed about Lot 17 being brought up in conversation.

The property was still up for grabs but my dad was one step further than me in claiming the whole damn thing so he could build his hotel that was going to be very uncharacteristic and an eyesore for the historic and classic city of New Orleans. Plus, the lot belonged to the kids, it should be a park, no question about it but my dad was such an evil fuck that all he could think about was himself. It's a wonder I was able to grow up with such a man.

Jeremy clucked his tongue as he counted on his iPad. "You have about five different events in the next couple of weeks that you have already accepted invitations for."

I peeked over my computer as I looked at Jeremy. "Five?"

"Yes and they all have a plus one with them."

Sitting back in my chair, I ran my hand through my hair as I thought about the events that I so desperately did not want to attend.

"Do I have to bring someone?" I asked as I went through a mental rolodex of the women I could invite.

"It would be best if you did. Many of the men you will be talking to have wives and the wives need to be charmed as well." Jeremy nervously looked up at and said, "You know, Lo might be a very good partner to bring with you—"

"Absolutely not," I cut him off as I pulled out my address book and started flipping through names.

Clearing his throat, Jeremy pushed his luck. "She has the personality that will win people over, she's infectious…"

"She's also a Jett Girl and I don't want anyone to associate her with the club, it would be detrimental to reveal her persona. No, and don't suggest it again."

Jeremy just nodded his head as I flipped through my address book. Most of the women that were in my book were either married or no longer living in New Orleans, had it really been that long since I've actually dated? I thought about it and it had been. I started the Lafayette club a while back and haven't had the need to accompany women since I had them at my disposal in the club. I cringed from thinking about the word, disposal, that was not how I treated them and I chastised myself for thinking of the girls like that. They were by no means disposable…especially Goldie.

"What about Claudia?" I asked looking up at Jeremy.

"She's dating some mogul in Dallas."

"Damn," I muttered as I thought about the long-legged, black-haired woman. She would not have been a hardship to court around the town to these different events.

I flipped through some more names and smiled inwardly. "Keylee Zinc, I know she is not dating anyone and I just saw her a month ago around Jackson Square."

Jeremy did a quick Google search and smiled. "Total country club material. How do you know her?"

"We grew up together. She left New Orleans for a while but I just saw that she moved back. She would be perfect. Find out her number so I can give her a call."

"Give who a call?" Kace asked as he walked in my office without even knocking. The man lacked manners most of the time but then again, we were comfortable with each other enough to not have to knock.

I looked up at Kace and saw that his face was bruised and his posture hung low, it must have been the anniversary. Had it really been an entire year again?

"You look like shit," I said as Kace took a seat in front of my desk. Jeremy eyed Kace with terror and infatuation in his eyes. It was comical to see my gay assistant fawn over my right hand man. Kace had no fucking clue either.

Kace shrugged his shoulders and repeated, "Whose number do you need?"

"I don't believe that concerns you." I turned to Jeremy and said, "That will be all."

Jeremy nodded, smiled at Kace and then took off and shut the door to my office like a good little assistant.

Once the door was shut, I walked over to the buffet in my room that held my bourbon and poured a glass for both Kace and myself. I handed it over to him and sat back down behind my desk.

"When are you going to stop paying people to beat the shit out of you every year? You know you just end up pummeling them without them even knowing what they got into."

Kace didn't answer as he took a sip of his Bourbon. He

stared off past my shoulder.

"Did the girls notice?"

"Just Lo."

"Why just Lo?" I asked as I crossed my ankle over my knee and sat back in my chair.

"She came looking for me in my room."

I automatically sat up and said, "What the hell was she doing in your room?"

"Apparently getting an eyeful," Kace said with a slight smirk. Smug bastard.

"The girls are not allowed back there," I gritted between my teeth.

"I know that but do you really think Lo is going to follow your rules? She barely submits to you when you ask, like hell if she is not going to go snooping around. You know her, once she has her mind set on something, she's going to make it happen."

The fucker was right. Goldie was a loose cannon, a mustang, a hellion, she would do whatever she wanted and there was no stopping her.

"What did you tell her?" I asked, annoyed.

"I didn't. I told her to leave."

"And she listened to you?"

Kace sat back in his chair and smiled over the rim of his glass as he took a gulp of my expensive- as-hell bourbon. Irritable fuck. I hated that Goldie and Kace had some kind of connection, hated it with every damn bone in my hollow body. It didn't slip past me that they shared something, that there was an underlining attraction they had for each other, it was easy to see but what kept me sane was the minute I walked in the room, all of Goldie's attention was drawn toward me. I was the one she truly wanted, Kace was just a little side show for her. I was the God damn main event.

Changing the subject I asked, "When are you going to stop letting people beat the ever living piss out of you? You look like hell."

Kace didn't answer me, he just looked down at his hands. "How does it even help the situation?"

Kace blew out a long breath and said, "You know when you first started the Lafayette club and opened the Bourbon Room? You brought girls up here to forget, to forget and control the pain that coursed through you from Natasha's rejection?"

I winced from the memory but nodded.

"It's completely fucked up on so many levels but this day—" he looked me dead in the eyes and said, "—this day was the worst day of my life. Not only did I ruin any sort of normalcy and future I might have but I destroyed that of a little girl's, of a family's. I killed a man, Jett." I nodded as I watched the pain pour out of Kace. "Getting my shit beat up for a couple of hours relieves the pain that I feel every damn day of my life. Feeling someone's fist connect with my face blacks out the emotions rolling through me, the thoughts that haunt me every day. What if I didn't get drunk that night? What if I didn't let him provoke me? There are so many questions running through my head that paying some dickheads to take me to a back alley and fight me is the only way I can survive this day. It's the only way I can manage the pain."

Kace was all kinds of fucked up and I truly felt bad for my friend. We dicked around with each other most of the time but we had a general understanding for each other and what we have gone through in our lives. We had demons that we were trying to fight everyday but Kace was facing an army of them and it was rare when he talked about them so when he did, I made sure to be there for him.

Watching him sit in front of me with his head hung in shame and his leg jittering up and down had my stomach twisting in knots. I couldn't imagine the pain and torment he went through on a daily basis so even though it didn't make much sense to get the crap beat out of him, I kind of got it. It was a little escape from the reality he had to face every day.

Not wanting to get too deep with him because he would just close off, I said, "You know where to find me and the

Bourbon."

Nodding his head, Kace tipped his glass as a salute to me and then took another sip. Silence fell between us as we soaked in the moment of just being in each other's company.

Breaking the silence, Kace said, "Seriously, what number is Jeremy looking up?"

Sighing because I knew Kace wasn't going to drop the topic, I said, "Keylee Zinc's. I need an escort for some events I must attend in order to get in with the Lot 17 project."

"Keylee? The tiny tart with tits?"

A small smile spread across my face as Kace brought up Keylee's old nickname from school. She was small like Lo but had olive skin and raven black hair that was almost to her waist. Her eyes were a deep gray color and she had a rack that had the guys in high school dragging their tongues around on the ground. She still did have a great rack but now that she was all grown up, she has tightened her body up, graced her neck with a set of pearls and showed a classy display of cleavage. She had just enough class that would work for getting along with the wives of the men I had to impress and just enough sexiness that the husbands would appreciate the arm candy I brought along.

"Yes," I replied.

"Why aren't you bringing one of the girls, like Lo?"

My attention snapped up to Kace as I tried to read his face. He was serious, he wasn't even trying to dick me around.

"You know I can't bring one of the girls, everyone would know that they are a Jett Girl. I will not put them in that position."

"Everyone is going to assume Keylee is one," Kace suggested. I shrugged my shoulders not caring. Keylee's welfare was none of my concern. Yes she was attractive and we grew up together but if it came down to her or one of my girls, I would rather sacrifice her reputation over my girls'.

"Jett, you're going to fuck it up."

"Fuck what up?" I asked, trying to tamp down the anger that was starting to boil. I didn't take well to people questioning me, ever.

"Everything with Lo. If she finds out that you are out with some other woman, she is going to freak out."

The thought crossed my mind but she wouldn't find out, at least I hoped she wouldn't. It wasn't like Goldie gallivanted around with the same people I did. Her friends were locals on Bourbon Street and mine were in St. Charles, they were vastly different.

"She won't and it doesn't matter. We're not exclusive."

"That's bullshit and you know it," Kace called me out. "Lo would be perfect, she would give you the extra help that you would need."

"She has no class," I practically shouted, hating myself for admitting the thought that was hounding me in the back of my mind.

Kace sat back in his chair and eyed me with distaste. Taking the last sip of his Bourbon, he set the glass down on my desk and said, "The only one who has no class is you. That girl has done everything you've asked. Why not give her a shot rather than instantly putting her down? She might surprise you."

"Not going to happen," I muttered as Kace walked away, opening my door where Goldie stood with her head hung low and a defeated stance.

Shit.

5
"CHASING PAVEMENTS"

Goldie

I knew I didn't belong on the third floor uninvited but I was worried about Kace. I wanted to make sure Jett knew something was wrong with Kace just in case someone needed to take care of him. The way I left him, on the floor, crying, was gutting me and I couldn't let it go.

I debated with myself for a while in my room, trying to decide if I should tell Jett or not and my guilty conscience won out so I found myself climbing up the very familiar steps of the third floor. When I reached the door, I heard my name being mentioned so of course, I had to listen in. I was a bit of a rebel and curious at heart so there was no way in hell I was going to pry my ear off the door when my name was being thrown around.

The moment Jett shouted that I had no class, my stomach flipped. It was the one clear thing I heard because he said it loud enough. Everything else was muffled. I heard something about some kind of event Jett had to attend and when he said I had no class, I understood precisely what was going on. Jett was ashamed of me and didn't want me attending any kind of social with him.

Not that I wanted to go to any snooty bullshit party where all you did was drink champagne and ignore the fact that you hated everyone in the room while making pleasantries. No fucking thank you. But the thought of Jett going with someone else was like a dagger to my stomach, I didn't like it.

I didn't want to get caught upstairs, now that it seemed like Kace was apparently all right so I was about to turn around when the door to Jett's office flew open and Kace stood in the doorway. I looked up at him and instead of anger lacing his eyes from seeing me once again break the rules, concern flashed through them. He looked me up and down and tried to read if I heard anything. I just slightly nodded and started to turn around, clearly it was time for me to go back to my room.

"Lo, come in here," I heard Jett call from his office, making me stop in place.

From behind me, I could feel Kace's presence as he mumbled, "You don't have to go in there."

I looked at his battered face and gave him a half smile, even though I should've probably left while flipping Jett off behind my back, showing him that he was right, I had no class, I turned and stared at the man who had captured my heart and twisted it in so many ways that it was almost hard to breathe.

The light from the window behind him cast his body in a shadow as he stood in front of his desk with his hands bracing his upper body on the edge. His hair was slightly disheveled and he was wearing slacks and a button up shirt with the first three buttons undone which only added to his sex appeal. I knew what was under that shirt, what was waiting for my hands to touch, what my body itched for but I blocked those thoughts out of my mind as I walked toward him.

I could feel Kace's judgmental glare as I ignored him and started to close the door. I looked back at Kace just before I shut the door and caught his glare as he shook his head. He was not pleased with me one bit, but I couldn't worry about that now.

The door closed quickly as Jett's body pressed up against mine. His hand was against the door as he hovered over me. His radiant scent filled my senses as I gathered enough courage to turn around and face him. It wasn't easy, to be face to face with such a strong and overpowering man, especially when I was feeling weak and punctured.

"Look at me," he demanded.

Why was he being so rude? He was the one who insulted me. I knew I was technically trespassing but he was the one being mean, he was the one in the wrong.

Gathering my strength, I turned around and put my hands on my hips, causing my business shirt to ride up. I was wearing a pair of black lingerie underneath that you could see through the open buttons up top. After our one and only date, Jett said he wanted to see me in yellow but he must have been bullshitting me because there was never shipment that came in. Made me wonder, did he mean anything that day? I tried not to think about it because it would eat me alive.

There were moments in my "relationship" with Jett that I knew he cared for me, that he wanted me, needed me but there were a lot of times where I couldn't read him. I couldn't tell if I was just another girl to him. I was constantly questioning myself when I was around him and trying to figure out if I was good enough. There were nights that I wondered why I cared so much, why I let a man play with my head but I realized he wasn't playing with me, he was just closed off, he was hurt and he wasn't ready for anything serious. The only thing that kept me coming back for more, that kept me from running away were the light caresses he gave me, the way he called me little one and the way his face lit up when I walked into a room. Those were all signs of a man who cared and that was all I wanted, someone who cared deep for me and I knew Jett did. He captured me and for the life of me, I couldn't walk away.

Looking up at him, I said, "Don't talk to me like that."

"Like what?" he asked as he moved in closer, making my lady

bits start to get excited.

"Like a demanding ass."

Not showing any tells, like normal, he replied, "Are you supposed to be up here, little one?"

"No, but—"

"But nothing. You are out of line."

"I'm out of line?" I pointed at myself as I tried not to be intimidated by his proximity. "You're the one who is insulting me behind my back."

The corner of his eye crinkled, as if he winced but it was quickly gone before I could confirm a reaction from him. The damn man was so stoic.

"You weren't supposed to hear that."

"Clearly." I tried to step away but he blocked me.

"And I didn't mean to say that."

"Bullshit, Jett. I know what you think of me."

"Do you? Please enlighten me about my feelings toward you."

Huffing, I pushed past him and went to his desk where I grabbed a stupid paper weight that was shaped like a little marble globe and tossed it around in my hands. I was fidgety and starting to get wild so I needed something to calm me down.

"You think I'm just some street trash that you found and can fuck for a while and once you're done you can just throw me away, with the rest of the Bourbon street residue."

Okay, I knew that wasn't necessarily true because he cared for me, he took care of me and he told me I was beautiful but I refused to acknowledge any of that right now, I was mad.

"You disappoint me, little one." My heart fell from his words. "I never want you to think of me like that because that is not even close to how I feel."

"Yeah, well, with the way you just stated your feelings about me, how am I supposed to think?"

Jett ran his hand through his hair and blew out a frustrated breath. Ha! I got him. Finally, an emotion!

"I'm sorry." He shook his head as he looked down at the

ground. He loosened his shoulders and then looked back up at me. "I just…fuck, I'm an ass."

I nodded, he was an ass. Good self-assessment.

"We're different, Jett, in many ways and I'm trying on my end. Can you try on yours?"

He continued to stare at me but said nothing.

"Why can't I go to your parties with you?"

Silencing me, he held his hand up and said, "That is non-negotiable. You're not going."

"Because you're embarrassed of me," I stated as my pride started to deflate.

"No." He grabbed my hands and pulled me to his chest. "Not because I'm embarrassed of you, there is nothing to be embarrassed about. I just don't want you to be exposed to those people. You're a Jett Girl, you need to keep your anonymity. I don't want them knowing who you are."

"They won't," I said while pushing the subject. "No one knows who I am on stage so if they saw me in person, they would never be able to tell. I just don't see why you won't give me a chance. I can be classy." I grabbed an empty glass off Jett's desk and held it in front of me and stuck out my pinky finger. In a fake British accent, I said, "Oh why isn't it a charming night in old New Orleans. Did you catch the hobos eating a rat a few blocks down?"

A smile crept over Jett's face as he tried to hold back his laughter. "Not happening," he said more playfully as he pulled me to his chest.

"Just give me a chance. I will go to refine school. I'm sure Kace can teach me a thing or two."

"I don't want Kace teaching you anything," he said with a sharper tone than warranted.

I played with Jett's buttons as I said, "You jealous?"

"When it comes to you, I'm always jealous. You should know that by now. Seeing you interact with anyone but me drives me crazy. I don't think I could stand to take you to any parties with me, there would be way too many people staring at you. I wouldn't be able to take it."

Slipping my hand in his shirt so my hand caressed his bare chest, I said, "Jett, give me a chance. I can be the person you need."

The look on Jett's face was almost comical as he struggled with wanting to say no but also wanting to please me. The man put up a front but like he always said, I held the cards and right now, I could see how much I held them. My other hand wandered down to his waistline and played with his belt. A growl escaped from the back of his throat as he picked me up, threw me over his shoulder and carried me toward the Bourbon Room.

"You will talk to Miss Mary starting tomorrow."

"Who's Miss Mary?" I asked as Jett set me down next to the Bourbon Room Balance Beam. My insides twisted in excitement.

"Your new finishing school teacher," he said as he played with my clothes, eyeing me with desire.

"You're giving me a chance?" I asked in anticipation of hearing the answer.

He nodded his head and licked his lips as he looked me up and down. He stood with his hands in his pockets as he said, "Now, enough talking, do you have something to say to me?"

Boy fucking did I!

6
"I GOT U"

Jett

Sweat glistened off her body as she hung in front of me. My fingers were lodged in her, feeling her damp excitement as my mouth worked its way across her perfect breasts. Her head writhed against the beam as I continued to pleasantly torture her with my tongue against her skin and my skilled fingers in her delectable pussy.

After Goldie walked in and heard me disrespect her in the worst way, guilt washed over me and I saw instantly how I wronged her and everything I believed in. I was here to help these girls, to give them new opportunities that they wouldn't normally have and I was here to protect them. I got so caught up in protecting Goldie because I'm a selfish bastard that I insulted her not only in front of her but in front of Kace as well.

Goldie was different than anyone I've ever met. She was fun, sassy and had a mouth to go along with it but she was sweet and caring as well. There were times that I could see the difference in our upbringings but that never bothered me, I just knew that she most likely wouldn't mesh well with the people I'm obligated to mingle with, not that I cared much about that. I couldn't really give two fucks what those high society snobs thought about me but I didn't want them attacking Goldie and I knew that was exactly what would happen if I brought her around them. They would sense her weakness and tear her apart. Plus, I didn't want her being exposed. My Jett Girls' personas needed to be protected no matter what, no exceptions. If I brought Goldie out to be by my side at these dreadful events, then I would be nervous if people assumed she was a Jett Girl, especially the men. She was a beacon in the club, a favorite and I didn't blame the men, she was absolute perfection.

I wanted to protect her but I wanted to make her happy as well. As she threw her head back with her mouth slightly ajar, I knew that all I wanted to do was please her. So when I said she would be meeting with Miss Mary, she would be. If I was going to take her out with me, the least I could do was prepare her for what she would be getting herself into. I could prepare her and give her the confidence she would need in order to walk around the ballrooms of the pretentious events I have to attend so that if someone does approach her, she will know the exact way to respond without showing one ounce of weakness.

"Oh, God…" She moaned as she continued to writhe against my fingers. "Yes, Jett, yes."

The way my name fell so easily off her tongue in the moment of ecstasy was all the pleasure I needed as my cock jolted against my pants' zipper.

"How close are you?" I asked as I worked my mouth up to her earlobe. I knew how close she was but I loved hearing her tell me.

"So…close." She panted. She was strapped against the balance beam and vertical. Her legs and arms were tied back so she was completely in my hands. She was giving me such a precious gift that I would never take advantage of.

Knowing what she needed to go over the edge, I removed my

fingers from her, eliciting a protesting moan and worked my mouth down her body. I felt her pulse start to kick up as she realized where I was about to go. Her stomach heaved as she prepared for my mouth, waiting for the moment when my tongue reached out and ran along her slick pussy.

My hands gripped the top of her thighs as my head hovered above her mound, itching to give her what she fully wanted. I took one last glimpse at her, our eyes met, sending a bolt of electricity straight to my core. She wanted me, it was evident and damn it all to hell if I didn't want her too.

I took a deep breath, taking in her essence and plunged forward. The moment my tongue met her pussy, her back arched off the beam and she cried out in pleasure. Pride surged through me as she came on my mouth, my name rolling off her tongue. Without even thinking, I tore my pants down, flipped the beam so it was horizontal and plunged myself into Goldie. I couldn't take the pressure that was building up in me anymore, I needed my release, I needed to release myself inside her.

I was normally an emotionless man who never showed a tell. Emotions and feelings were signs of weakness in a man was what I was taught so I kept a straight face but when it came to Goldie, I was lost the minute her blue eyes met mine. It was impossible not to slowly lose myself in her body, in the way she looked at me, touched me, moaned for me. She tested my limits on a daily basis and I would be a lying son of a bitch if I said I didn't like it.

Thrusting into her, my balls screamed as my whole body tensed up for my impending release. My hand reached down and pinched her nipple which erupted an orgasm in her body that clenched my hard length, sending me over with her. We both thrust our hips, inching out every last pleasure until we were spent.

I hovered over her, my arms straddling her little body as I tried to catch my breath. Slowly, her eyes opened and looked up at with me with fondness. It was like a blade to my heart, I didn't want anyone looking at me like that because it meant attachment but I would be damned if I could look away. There was something about this woman, this sassy woman that had me by the balls. She was a man-eater, that was for damn sure.

"Thank you for accompanying me tonight," I said as I looked down at her.

A smile spread across her face and she said, "Thanks for blowing a hole through my pussy with that massive meat sword of yours." She shifted on the table and said, "I'm pretty sure you popped a hole through my bladder."

Trying not to smile, I said, "Did I hurt you?"

"No." She caressed my cheek, something I normally didn't allow but with Goldie…things were different.

"You sure?"

She nodded her head and ran her hand down my chest, making me swell again but I didn't allow for a second round because I knew it was time to part from her for the night. I had some mending to do. I was a shallow ass most of the time but I knew when I was wrong.

I pulled away and fixed my pants, and released her from her confines. Her body was fantastic, every man's dream and she was all for me. I was a privileged man and damn lucky for it.

"Keep looking at me like that and you will find yourself strapped to that bed, waiting for me until I'm ready for you again."

"Is that supposed to be a punishment?" she asked with a straight face.

I leaned over, grabbed her chin with my thumb and forefinger and said, "Yes, yes it is but a delicious one." I pecked the tip of her nose and pulled away completely. "Get dressed, little one. You have a long week ahead of you."

Disappointment fell across her features as I pulled away and walked out the door. If I wanted to, I could spend the whole night playing with her, seeing how many times I could make her scream my name or come on my fingers but I had others thing to do. I grabbed my bourbon, two glasses and headed down the back stairs through the dark hallway that led to Kace's room.

I leaned my ear toward the door before knocking in case he

had a woman with him but it seemed like the coast was clear so I knocked on the door. Kace's voice rang through in a gruff tone, telling me to come in.

His room was dark, besides a light on the night stand that casted a light shade of yellow in the room. Kace was sitting in a chair, facing the window. His feet were stretched out on the sill and he was slouched in his chair as his hand held up his head. His stature was deflated and rightfully so, the man had so many demons to deal with, I didn't know how he went day to day holding his shit together.

"What do you want, Jett?" Kace said without turning around.

"I brought bourbon."

Kace just nodded as I brought up a chair next to him and handed him a glass. I poured us both a generous amount, not really saying anything to each other as we sat in silence, drinking away our problems. This was a tradition we did on this day, this day that changed Kace's life forever. We didn't talk about it, we didn't share, all we did was sit and stare into oblivion. We didn't need to talk, we knew what happened, we knew what we did to cover it up and we knew the effects it had on the innocent people involved. Instead of rehashing everything, we just sat and drank.

We sat for what seemed like hours until Kace broke the silence and asked, "Everything settled with Lo?"

He held out his cup for a refill and I obliged while I responded, "Everything is fine. I was a protective ass that just ended up hurting her."

Kace took a sip from his glass. "If she didn't hear you, would you have changed your mind?"

I thought about his question and answered honestly, "Probably not but seeing the look on her face was enough pain for the day, so I relented."

Kace nodded while he continued to look out his window. "You okay with that?"

"No, but do I have a choice?"

"You used to."

46

I did, I thought as I took another sip of my bourbon. I used to have many choices but now that Goldie has graced me, I find myself with a noose around my neck, not being able to do what I want because the fear of Goldie getting hurt plagues me. I don't want her to hurt…ever. I don't want her to get into trouble or see fear. I want to make everything okay for her which is a big problem because I wasn't expecting to feel that way.

"Don't let her get hurt," Kace interrupted my thoughts. "You have to help her if you bring her into your world."

"No shit," I responded as I shifted in my seat suddenly starting to feel uncomfortable in my skin. "You're the one who pushed the idea of bringing her with me."

"And I meant it but you have to be fucking careful. She's not like everyone else in your world. She has feelings, she has a heart, she can easily be burned, ripped up and spit out by a simple stare from one of your elites. You can't let that happen…I can't bear to see it," he trailed off.

I gritted my teeth from the protectiveness Kace had for Goldie. I hated it, fucking hated it. I was the one who was supposed to protect her, not Kace and every time he showed one ounce of concern for her, it grated on my nerves.

"I won't," I said sternly. "Miss Mary will be starting training with Lo tomorrow so just stay the fuck out of it."

I saw a slight grin spread on Kace's face from the corner of my eye which only irritated me even more.

"You're so far gone," Kace said as he drained the rest of his drink and got up out of his chair. "I need to hit the head and then meet up with Claire."

"Claire?" I asked, a bit curious.

He shrugged his shoulders and said, "She's a good fuck with no intention of being a clinger." Kace walked off toward the bathroom but then turned around before shutting the door. "Thanks for the bourbon…dickhead."

I nodded with a smile. "Anytime, asswipe."

And that was it. That was the extent of our night together.

Silence between us spoke a thousand words. Sometimes conversation was overrated, sometimes, you just needed to sit with another breathing soul, knowing that they understood you, that they felt for you and that they were going to make it through the next day.

Before Kace completely shut the door, I called out, "Next year, just pay me to beat your ass. I would love taking your money."

From the cracked door, Kace called out, "In your dreams, Colby. Any fist fight between us is going to be a guaranteed honest one." With that, he shut the door and I took off for the third floor.

Jeremy, my assistant, met me at the top of the stairs and said, "I found Keylee Zinc's information, sir."

"Put it on hold for now. Call Miss. Mary, she has some etiquette lessons to give."

A smirk spread across Jeremy's face as he typed away on his tablet.

"And wipe that smile off your face. Lo was always my number one choice."

"Yes, sir."

Jeremy took off downstairs as I went back to my office. I set my bourbon down on the bar and walked over to my window that looked over the Lafayette Club lawn and the wonky tress that graced the streets of the garden district. Beads from past Mardi Gras parades still dangled from the trees' limbs and sparkled in the street lights. Pepper was walking to the back entrance, from the street, returning from one of her outings, ones that she had been going on lately. I had a feeling she was fooling around with someone else but honestly, I didn't give a fuck. A girl needed to be fucked and she wasn't getting it from me.

I sighed as I rested my head on the window pane. When did my life become so complicated? It used to be so easy; I worked, I fucked and I protected, now I worried. I didn't want to worry but I didn't have a choice, there were so many new factors in my life that I needed to consider.

Goldie was one of them.

I ran my hand through my hair as I thought about what the hell I got myself into. I was going to bring Goldie out in public, where everyone could see her, could see who she was. It was dangerous, people might even know her, like my dad or Rex Titan but the look on Goldie's defeated face kept outweighing my cons of having her on my arm at my events. At least if she was next to me at all times, I would be able to protect her, to shield her from the cruel and cold world that I lived in.

7
"CRAZY"

Goldie

There is this feeling you have the next morning after an amazing bout of sex, this tingle in your lady area that keeps saying, you were utterly fucked to the hilt of your cervix last night and holy fuck was it good.

As I brushed my hair out for the day, I thought about that feeling that Jett gave me. He was an animal last night, like he couldn't get inside me enough and I agreed, I wish he was able to bury himself deeper. I made a mental note to start stretching more.

Last night, I saw Jett cave, I saw him cave to my needs and once again I realized, I did hold the cards like he always said. Was I insulted last night, fuck yeah but was Jett sincere and honest? He was. He was right, there was a lack of class where I was concerned. I have a dirty mouth and I know how to use it, and I've used it on him so I can only imagine his hesitation when it comes to taking me to some high class society parties but what he doesn't realize is that I can clean up when need be.

It's like going to visit your grandparents, there was a

certain filter you used when talking to them. No fuck this and fuck that and pussy on my shoulder kind of crap. There is a certain innocent poise that you must use with grandparents, like, "Oh the weather was a total dreary mess yesterday." Or "Man, I played a mean game of solitaire last night that kept me up till nine!" Simple as that, when out and about with Jett, I just had to channel my grandparent filter. Shouldn't be too hard, especially since I would be practicing with Miss Mary.

I grabbed my mask and heels and slipped them on since I would be walking through the main house to meet Miss Mary in the dining room. The masks started to feel like a second skin now and when I wasn't wearing one, I almost felt naked. The business shirts that we had to wear were still a little awkward. It was like wearing a dress at all times, which was fine, but fuck I could use a frump day and wear a pair of holey sweats. Heels were heels, I have always worn them so no biggie there.

With my hair in a high ponytail and my Jett Girl attire on, I headed down the back staircase and to the dining room. This would be the first time that I would actually spend time in the dining room. It made me sad that we never really had any formal dinners. The girls and I usually just ate in the back of the Toulouse Room before a presentation. We still had a lot of fun but it would be nice to have something formal, to treat ourselves and have dinner as a "family."

My heels hit the tile of the hallway that led toward the dining room, echoing off the walls. The Lafayette Club was gorgeous and sophisticated, I didn't think I would ever get over the fact that I lived in such a place so instead, I just soaked it all in. Rags to…pretend-riches was my story. They weren't my riches but I lived in them.

I was taking in a picture of Bourbon Street on the wall near the grand entryway when I heard someone walking toward me. My heart flipped as I hoped it was Jett, and even though I saw him for a good portion of last night, I still got butterflies in my stomach just knowing I might see him again. As I looked up to see if it was Jett, I saw a pair of blue eyes but they weren't Jett's or Kace's…they were someone else's.

Standing in front of me, in a well-tailored suit was a light-skinned African American man with a shaved head and piercing blue eyes that hit me in my very soul. I stopped in my tracks as I took in his broad shoulders, his well-defined chest that I could see ripple under his dress shirt and the tight waist that peeked under his sport coat. The man exuded confidence just like Jett and had an air of sophistication that rivaled Jett's.

Umm…fucking yummy.

He smiled at me as he stared at my chest and that was when I realized I was gripping my breast and practically pinching my nipple right in front of the man. I was a horny, horny girl. Quickly tearing my hand away from my breast and hoping my other hand wasn't fingering myself without my knowledge, I nodded at him and continued my trek to the dining room.

I heard heavy footsteps behind me that I recognized as Kace's. The man insisted upon pounding his way through the house.

"Diego, how are you man?" Kace asked with lightness to his voice that I never received. Moody bastard.

"Good to see you, Kace. I'm just fine. Is Jett upstairs?" Diego, I presumed, said in a deep, luscious voice. Oh God, was he hot. Did Jett only know hot people? Was I sucked into some hot man black hole? If I was, I was fucking loving it.

"Yup, he's waiting for you. You can go on up."

I heard footsteps walk away as I held on to the wall of the hallway not minding my own business at all. I was curious and I loved butting into everyone else's business.

"Don't you have refining school to get to?" Kace breathed inches from my ear making me yip in surprise. Apparently the man did know how to be silent when he walked because I didn't hear him coming up behind me at all.

I looked over my shoulder and met his eyes. "I was just taking in the texture of this wall," I replied, trying to pass off my nosiness.

He didn't buy it. "Mind your own business, Lo. How many times do I have to tell you that?" he whispered in my ear, sending goose bumps along my body as I felt his breath caress my skin. My hormones were on overload.

"Probably a couple more," I replied in a cute voice while smiling.

Kace huffed as his eyes blatantly wondered down my shirt that was gaping open at the top. When he looked back up at me, his eyes were blazing with need which only made me gulp.

"Everything okay with Jett?"

Only able to move my head since my throat was dry, I nodded.

"Good. Listen to Miss Mary. She will tell you everything you need to know."

Kace pulled away, allowing me to breathe again, no longer sucking in all the air in my vicinity.

Before I walked into the dining room, Kace called out my name again. I turned to see him standing in the entryway, with his hands tucked into the worn out pockets of his jeans and his plane white T-shirt stretching across his chest. No matter who my heart belonged to, it would always have a special place for Kace…always.

"Thank you…for checking on me yesterday." He looked up through his eyelashes as he talked to me, a modest pose I hadn't seen from him before. Whatever happened to him, hit him hard because he never showed emotion and right now, all I could see was hurt and pain pouring out of him.

"Any time," I replied.

He stepped forward for a second and then shook his head as if what he was about to do would be the biggest mistake of his life. I wanted to go up to him and ask him what was going on but I didn't. I kept the line that was drawn in the sand between the two of us, respected his wishes and entered the dining room with a heavy heart.

***

Learning etiquette didn't seem like it would be very hard to do until I stepped into the dining room and came face to face with Miss Mary. I was expecting to see a little old white lady, with an impressive bouffant and real pearls gracing her neck but instead I was standing next to a six foot tall, rotund black woman with a scarf in her hair and an apron around her belly. Her face read, "Don't fuck with me," and I wasn't going to! I glanced at the ruler that she was holding in her goliath-sized hands and gulped.

"You must be Lo," she greeted.

"Yeah, that's me."

"Yes."

"Yes?" I asked.

"Yes."

"Yes, what?" I asked, confused.

"The proper term is yes, not yeah."

"Ohhh. Yeah, I'm kind of a ditz."

"Yes," she said more sternly, making me realize I did it again.

"Fuck, sorry."

There are times in your life where you realize that you must be wearing a protective shield around your body because the laser beams of pure dragon fire that were spouting out of Miss Mary's eyes would have disintegrated me on the spot from dropping the f bomb if I didn't have that protective shield.

"Oh God." I covered my mouth. "I'm sorry. I didn't mean to say fuck…I mean swear. I didn't mean to swear."

"Sit." Miss Mary pointed to a chair that was pressed up against the wall.

There were no pleasantries, just like the first time I met Kace, we got straight down to business.

Not wanting to see any more scary veins pop out of Miss Mary's forehead, I did as was directed and kept my mouth shut because right now, it was not helping me any.

I sat in the chair, crossed my legs, placed my hand on my knee and sat up properly. There, good posture, legs are closed, chin is tilted up, I look fucking good…I mean, just good.

Miss Mary walked up to me, patting the ruler in her hand as if she were getting ready to pepper my ass with it and observed my stance. I stood tall with confidence even though my insides were quivering.

"Do not move, not even an inch," she said as she stood right in front of me. I didn't know if that meant I couldn't talk but I decided not to risk it so I stayed silent.

She ran the ruler up my arm, up my neck to my chin and said, "Are you better than me?"

"What?" I asked, trying not to move my mouth much because I was afraid I was about to be ruler whipped across the face, that's how scary this lady was.

"Your chin, it's thrust up in the air, which turns your nose up and the only reason someone would have such posture is if you were better than me. So, I will ask you again, are you better than me?"

"No!" I practically shrieked in embarrassment and pushed my chin down so it was threatening to kiss my chest.

"Are you my submissive?"

If ears could pop off a head as they tried to hear someone again, my ears would have been dangling on the damn floor. Is this some kind of fucked up kinky finishing school Jett was putting me through? I looked up at a camera that was in the corner and wondered if he was getting a kick out of this.

"Uh…no?" I asked in a question because frankly I had no clue what the fuck was going on.

"Well, you either are or you're not," she stated boldly.

"I guess I'm not."

"Very well, then your chin needs to be set at an even plain. Too high and you put out the feeling that you are better than everyone, too low and you give the feeling that you are a submissive to everyone and have no confidence." She grabbed my chin and evened out its height. I wanted to scream and tell her she could have just done that in the first place instead of the mind fuck I just went through but knew I was still in freeze mode and she was still holding that ruler.

With the ruler, she ran it up my thigh that was exposed, thanks to the Jett Girl attire I had to wear and stopped where my shirt met my thigh.

"I thought your advertising days were over."

"Advertising?" I asked, not understanding.

"Are you still getting paid for sex?"

"What?! How do you know that?" I asked entirely awestruck and hurt. That was private information that no one else should know besides Jett and Kace.

"Does it matter?" she asked, testing my limits.

"It sure as hell does when you know my private information," I replied, feeling steamed.

"Miss, I suggest you clean up your mouth because your swearing will not be tolerated."

I was about to stand up when Kace appeared in the dining room entry way, with his arms crossed over his chest and an annoyed look on his face.

"Don't even think about getting up," he said with authority.

"I can get the fuck up if I want. What the fuck is this, Kace?"

A loud snap echoed in the room as I felt the swoosh of the ruler hitting the chair I was sitting in breeze by me, sending me into the corner of the chair.

"Fucking Christ!" I screamed as I looked up at Miss Mary who was preparing for another lashing but Kace held her back and whispered something in her ear. Miss Mary nodded and walked out of the room while taking a deep breath as if she was the one who needed a break.

I looked up at Kace and said, "What happened to hiring an old lady with a jittery voice to teach me? I didn't know I would be shaking hands with the devil's dickhole this morning. Fucking hell!"

Kace placed both his hands on the arms of the chair I was

sitting in and leaned over so our noses were almost touching.

"Listen to me carefully, Lo, because I'm not going to repeat myself. You are to do and say everything Miss Mary tells you. You are to learn to be a lady, to control that mouth of yours and to be proper; if you don't, Jett will be taking someone else with him to his social events and I'm sure you don't want that."

"He said that to you?" I asked, feeling a little deflated.

"No, but I know that if this doesn't work out, he has to bring someone and he's not good at giving people second chances. So do as you're told, shut your fucking mouth and get the job done. Got it?"

"Yes," I said meekly as I thought about Jett with another girl.

Kace placed his hand on my chin and made me look him in the eye as he said, "He wants you there, he chose you to be there so don't think for a second that that is not the truth. You just have to prove it to him that he made the right decision, okay?"

"Okay."

"That a girl." His thumb brushed against my cheek for a second before pulling away. "You can do this, Lo, just stop being a stubborn fuck and listen."

I nodded my head as Kace exited and the devil herself walked back in. I got back into position and Miss Mary said, "I'm sorry we started off on the wrong foot and that I offended you by bringing up your past history but before I came here, Kace had to inform me what I was working with and that meant knowing your history." She looked at my legs again and said, "Now, tell me, are you advertising still?"

"No," I said with less bravado.

"Good, then you need to uncross your legs, sit up tall and cross at the ankles, that is how a lady sits."

Last thing I knew, I had a vagina in my pants which made me a lady, despite the way I crossed my damn legs. It was going to be a long-ass day.

8
"ALL THE PRETTY GIRLS"

Jett

"There's the sexiest man I know." Diego's voice rang out as I looked up from the contracts I was reading.

I stood and held out my hand to the man I've known for a while now. "Diego, it's good to see you."

With his free hand, Diego gripped my shoulder and said, "That new girl seems to be doing something good because you're practically glowing," Diego said in a cheesedick voice.

"Fuck off." I smiled as I went to my bar and grabbed small glasses of bourbon for the both of us.

We both took seats in my office as we sipped the amber liquid.

"So, tell me how the club is coming along," I said as I crossed my ankle over my knee.

Nodding his head, he said, "Good, good. Thank you for hooking me up with the lender. He is awesome and I was able to get the money I needed for the renovations."

"Good."

Diego was someone I met from working with the Boys and Girls club. He grew up in the bad part of New Orleans where opportunity to succeed was non-existent. He lived on the streets for ten years which you wouldn't be able to tell now but when he was on the streets, he did anything to earn a dime and that meant he robbed tourists most of the time. It wasn't until he made the mistake of trying to rob me after a night I was working at the Boys and Girls club that he tried to rob the wrong person. Instead of reporting him, I helped him. I gave him an education, gave him a place to live and got him out of the gutter. He was an unofficial Jett Girl which I still joke about. He doesn't take too kindly to it but he's making a name for himself and by the way he was dressed, I could tell he has changed from the inside out.

"When do you start breaking ground on the new place?" I asked, genuinely interested.

"We already have. We have the main room completed and the themed rooms were just started on. The bar they put in is fucking stellar, man."

"I can't wait to see it. Have you decided on the themes yet, or a name for the club?"

Diego and I shared the same interests when it came to the bedroom. We both dabbled in kink and required our women to submit to us and only us. I didn't know much about Diego's lifestyle choice but what I did know was that when he told me he wanted to put together a kink club, I was more than supportive and thrilled about the idea.

"Le Cirque du Diable," he said with pride. "The Circus of the devil is what the club will be called and the rooms I'm still working on, but they will go with the feel of the club. I have some people I still have to hire and then we need to start practicing our shows but I sure as hell know who's going to be the ringmaster," he said with a glint in his eye.

I laughed as I shook my head. "Man, I would love to see you take center stage."

"I didn't take you for a guy lover," Diego teased.

"In your fucking dreams, man."

He laughed and grew serious for a second. "I do need to find someone to paint some designs on my walls."

"Designs on your walls?"

"You know, the club has a vintage circus theme, minus the animals, and I need to add some decorative crap…add a woman's touch, you know? But I need someone I can trust because I don't want the club getting out to the public. It's going to be invite only."

"Yeah, I know what you mean." I stroked my chin as I thought about Diego's dilemma. There was an easy solution that anyone could see and that would be to let Diego borrow Goldie, have her go over there and paint her little heart out but the thought of her being alone in a kink club with Diego gnawed at my gut. It didn't seem like the best idea. I liked Diego but I didn't fully trust the guy either.

"If I think of something, I'll let you know," I said instead, feeling slightly guilty that I already had a solution to his problem.

"Thanks, man." He reached into his pocket and pulled out a piece of paper. "Now, on to the good stuff, I was able to do some…snooping, thanks to some friends that I have and I found out the kind of bid your dad put on Lot 17. It's not a bad bid, man, and he's offering a lot of concessions as well. It's not a formal bid, more of an acknowledgement of what he could offer."

Diego handed me the paper and I took a look at it. The price tag was exactly what I was looking at for myself so that was easily matchable but as I looked at the concessions, I realized that my dad was trying everything in the book to get what he wanted. There were kickbacks from his building that would be given to the sellers for five years, under the table of course and there was also lifetime VIP access into his "gentleman's" club which was just an illegal strip club that I knew of but couldn't quite prove just yet, I was still working on doing some more snooping myself.

I looked up at Diego and said, "Thank you. I appreciate this."

"Anything for you. You changed my life, Jett."

"You changed it, Diego. I just gave you an opportunity." I

finished off my drink and set the empty glass down on my desk. "I'm going to the Fairfield event this Friday. Anyone I need to make sure to shake hands with?"

"Let me check and I will text you later with the information." Diego peeked over at my cameras and nodded toward them, "That the girl?"

I looked up and saw Goldie holding a wine glass and standing in the dining room while having a conversation with Miss Mary. Her posture was straight, she held her wine glass properly and she seemed to exude a little more confidence than normal.

Not able to lie to Diego because he would be able to see right through me, I said, "That's the girl."

Nodding in appreciation, Diego replied, "She's got one hell of a rack, man."

Smiling, he got out of his chair and buttoned his suit coat. It was best he left because his little comment had my rage starting to flare up.

"I'll be in touch. Play nice, Jett."

"I could say the same about you."

Diego threw his head back and laughed. "I never play nice."

And that was what I was fucking afraid of.

***

Jett: Send Babs up

I wanted nothing more than to bury myself deep inside Goldie but knowing that my head wasn't in a good place, thanks to Diego's ribbing and the new found information on my dad and Lot 17, I decided to opt out of the Bourbon Room and call up Babs.

We had a lot to go over and now was the perfect time.

There was a light knock on my office door, alarming me that Babs had arrived.

"Come in," I called out.

Babs walked in, wearing a business shirt over her Jett Girl kit, a pair of thigh high black boots and her hair was a purple bob wig rather than her long blond hair. Her mask wasn't on which I normally would have harped on her for but the club was empty now and she took the back stairs.

"Hey, boss man," she said as she took the seat across from me. "You beckoned?"

"I wanted to go over your makeup line and make sure you were on track for your launch."

Each Jett Girl had the opportunity to gain an education through the Lafayette Club and apply that to real life after they left the club. Babs chose to start her own makeup line. It was a real passion of hers but she needed help getting her business going and working on a marketing strategy so we have been meeting every once in a while to go over her plan. Babs would be leaving soon, my first true Jett Girl to leave, and I wanted to make sure she was fully prepared and ready for her departure. I had to be honest, I was damn proud of the girl.

Babs' face lit up from my interest in her new adventure. She leaned forward, placing her hands on my desk and started talking animatedly. "I just received my test packing in the mail today and I could not be more pleased. I went with a black-and-purple theme, I hope that's okay?"

I smiled. "It's perfectly fine with me."

"I wanted to switch things up, you know? After thinking about it, I really wanted to play off your choice color of purple for justice because this makeup line is my justice. This is my second chance and I want to make sure I take full advantage of it."

"I couldn't be more proud," I said honestly. "Have you opened a business bank account and filed as an LLC yet?"

Babs cringed. "Not yet, but that's next. I hate paperwork and all that business stuff seems too confusing. I'm good at planning and making things but the business side of things is confusing."

"Aren't you taking that business class?" I asked while propping my right ankle over my left knee and sitting back in my chair.

"Uhh, well…"

I looked at her sternly and said, "You're to put everything on hold until you take that class. There is to be nothing else planned, picked out or produced until you pass it with flying colors. You need to know the basics of operating a business if you want to be successful at all. I expected more from you, Babs, you have to set an example."

She cocked an eyebrow at me and then sat back in her chair.

"Oh, I'm sorry. I was only busy helping out Lo so she felt like she fit in, so she was able to prove to everyone that she was meant to be a Jett Girl. Sorry that I took a break from my life to help her out."

My stomach flipped from the mention of Goldie's name and I refused to think about why.

"She didn't have to prove that to anyone, I knew from the start."

"You know that's bullshit. She might not have had to prove it to you but she sure as hell had to prove it to Kace."

"Kace has no authority where I'm concerned."

Babs gave me the "you're full of shit" look.

"Fine, he has a little authority but I overrule him," I conceded.

"Pissing around your territory, Jett? That's very unbecoming of you."

Growing frustrated, I sat up and spoke directly to her. "Stop changing the subject. Everything that is not involved with your makeup line is to desist and you are to sign up for the business class tonight. I'm not doing this to be a bastard like you think, I'm doing this because I want nothing more than for you to succeed and if that means I need to hone you in, then I will. You were right when you said this was your second chance and I'm going to make it my mission that you flourish, all right?"

Babs somberly nodded her head as she looked down at her hands. When she looked back up, there were tears clouding her eyes. Babs never showed emotion, ever. She was just as stoic as I was so to see her eyes brimming with tears was new to me.

"I just want to thank you, Jett."

I didn't do well when people thanked me, gave me credit for things. It was hard to be gracious because all I felt was awkward. I was born into a privileged life and because of that, I made it my mission to help those who weren't privileged, it was my duty.

"You're welcome," I said politely.

"Do you know what I'm thanking you for?"

"I have an idea," I said with a slight smile, not revealing too much, never revealing too much.

"Well, I'm going to tell you anyway. I want to thank you for picking me, for welcoming me into your home and giving me a chance to recreate myself. You gave me a once in a lifetime opportunity and I couldn't be more grateful. You saved me, Jett, you've saved all of us."

I just nodded, wanting this moment to pass.

Babs sensed my uneasiness and laughed.

"God, you just can't handle it when someone passes you a compliment, can you?"

"Nope," I answered honestly. "Now, if you would excuse me, I need to get to bed. You're going to sign up for that class right away, right?"

"Yes, Daddy dearest."

I cringed, making her laugh. "Let's refrain from calling me that."

"You're too easy." Babs got up and started walking toward the door. She turned around in the doorframe and said, "Oh, you might want to go see Lo. I don't think I've ever seen the girl's smile fall so flat since I've been here after I was called up."

I didn't acknowledge Babs because what was going on between Lo and I was our business, I didn't want to encourage the other Jett Girls' advice, especially since they loved giving it so freely.

"Don't you fuck with her, Jett. She is too good for that." Babs apparently didn't care about my silence. Those were her parting words as she walked away and headed back downstairs.

Like I didn't already fucking know that. Goldie was way too good, especially for a heartless bastard like me but because of that lack of heart, I didn't think about the repercussions, instead I just took what I wanted and what I wanted was Goldie.

9
"BREAK IN"

Lo

Another presentation was in the books, making me forget
how many I had under my belt now. I did know that Pepper was
right when she said the original presentations were the best because
I had never felt sexier than when I was wearing my Jett Girl kit that
Jett designed specifically for me. We had a couple of odd
presentations coming up that we have been practicing for so it was
nice to just give a normal one, to dance to normal music and play
out some hot choreography.

Miss Mary and I came to a mutual understanding this
afternoon after butting heads all morning. Basically what it came
down to was that she would stop threatening me with her ruler if I
would put a sugar-coated filter over my mouth. You would think I
had the harder task given the track record of nonsense that flew
out from my lips but I saw Miss Mary glance back at her ruler in
yearning and twitch in need.

I had a couple more lessons lined up with Miss Mary but what
I learned so far was Jett socializes with a bunch of uppity frog
warts and my nights accompanying him were going to be full of

fake smiles and cheesy comments. Frankly, I didn't care because if it meant spending more time with Jett, then I would do pretty much anything. I enjoyed our time more than anything in the Bourbon Room but one of my favorite moments ever was when we were on the Steamboat Natchez, watching the river ripple and being encased by his firm embrace as we watched the big red paddle push us forward. That day was the best date I had ever been on and it was burned in my memory. I only wished he would ask me out again.

I knew that day was hard on him, we both opened up and shared with each other, me more than him, but still, it was the first glimpse I ever saw of the man inside the stoic shell and more than anything, I wanted to get to know that man better because what I did know, I liked a lot and could not stop thinking about.

"Good job tonight, ladies," Kace said as he walked backstage.

All the girls were sitting in chairs, taking their regular shots of the night and discussing the creeps they saw in the room during our presentation. We weren't allowed to talk about them but in our little circle we shared because it was just too good not to.

"Did you see the guy with the neck pube?" Francy asked as she grabbed Tootse's hand and pulled her on her lap. Tootse didn't put up a fight as she succumbed to Francy's demand and placed her head on Francy's shoulder.

"Neck pube?" I asked, trying to recall such a thing on one of the men.

"Yeah, seat six had a giant hair popping out of his neck that practically waved at us as we danced. The damn thing was so distracting."

"How could you see from that far away?" I asked.

"Lo, the damn thing was as thick as a Red Vine and was blacker than burnt shit."

"How black is burnt shit?" Babs asked as she took off her mask.

"Black," Francy replied, very sure of herself.

"I didn't see it but now I wish I did. I was really wondering about the color of burnt shit," I replied with a smile.

"Smart ass," Francy muttered as Tootse gave her a peck on the cheek.

"I'm sure the neck pube was real gross, honey. Yucky!" Tootse added, while scrunching up her nose. "I just don't see why it's so hard for men to stay trimmed. I mean, we keep things clean, would it be so hard for them to trim their neck pubes?"

"Fucking neck pubes," I added to Tootse's rant.

"I'm just grateful I'm a lesbian. Men are nasty," Francy said.

"Not all men," Kace gruffed out as he sat back in his chair with his arms across his chest.

I had to agree with that statement. Not all men was right, especially any of the men that were associated with the Lafayette Club. They were all fine specimens that God graced New Orleans with.

"How was Miss Mary?" Pepper asked as she poured herself another shot. "I remember my first etiquette class with her. I thought she was going to slit my pussy open with the raw edge of that damn ruler of hers. That bitch is terrifying."

I laughed from Pepper's shiver.

"I'm pretty sure she had a crush on me," Tootse said. "All she did was stare at my boobs."

"I don't blame her," Francy added as she poked Tootse's breast with her index finger.

"Stop that," Tootse shoed her away. "We don't want to get Lo all hot and bothered again."

"Shut up," I said while everyone laughed.

"I know lesbian things," Francy joked, quoting me from one of my very intoxicated nights.

"Melons for sale!" Tootse added.

Everyone laughed, even Kace let out a little snicker.

"Ha, ha, you guys are so fucking hilarious. Taking advantage of the intoxicated is a crime, you know."

"No it's not." Babs laughed. "And you wanted all of that, the girls just followed through."

"They enticed me," I said defending myself.

"Yeah and you went with it because you were bi-curious," Pepper said, still laughing, maybe she was slightly drunk.

"Can you blame me? I mean, is it so bad to want to see how the other half lives?"

"We are living the high life, babe," Francy said while kissing Tootse's shoulder again. "Not having to deal with a horny man poking you in the middle of the night, begging you to just spread your legs a little so he can get a little pussy action is something I never have to deal with."

"Yeah, you just wake up with a vibrator shoved between your legs," Babs teased.

"And what a hell of a way to wake up."

Kace's phone beeped, interrupting their little conversation. I didn't move, but waited for my cue to head up to the Bourbon Room. I needed to see Jett after the day I had with Miss Mary. I needed to relax and spend some time with the man who's been clouding my mind.

When Kace looked down at his phone and then at Babs, my heart sank to the floor.

"Babs, you're up," he said, avoiding eye contact with me.

I watched as she nodded, gathered her mask and took off for the back staircase. Putting on a smile, I took another shot, wiped my mouth with the back of my hand and yawned. I needed to get out of this little pow wow because my emotions were about to get the best of me and if I didn't get out of the back room quickly I would soon become a blubbering idiot in front of everyone.

"Hell, I'm tired," I said as I stood up and grabbed my mask. As I looked around, I saw everyone's pity and the way they looked right through my tired act. I ignored them, said a quick good night and headed upstairs.

I wanted to believe the fact that Babs was just going up there to talk to Jett but in the back of my mind, I still had the sinking feeling that I was sharing the man with everyone else. I'm not stupid, I knew the rules that were laid out for me when I signed my contract but I would be lying if I said the truth didn't hurt because the fact that Jett could still call on another girl hurt like a motherfucker.

Once I got to my room, I stripped down and started a bath for myself. I just needed to relax and rid myself of the negative thoughts that were running through my mind.

I scolded my skin with the heated water and bubbles as I sank in deep and rested my head on a folded up towel. I tried to let go of all the thoughts running through my head as I sank deep into the tub and let the water relax me.

I must have drifted off to sleep because next thing I knew, I was freezing cold, most of my bubbles were gone and the towel I was resting my head on was now soaking up the water in the tub. Switching over to the shower, I rinsed off and then dried my body. I quickly put on lotion and headed to my bed where I slipped under the covers, letting the decadent fabric caress my skin.

It was a long day and given the practice line up and lessons with Miss Mary I had scheduled, it was going to be another long day tomorrow.

***

I was in a dream land where ponies talked and rainbows were for eating when I was startled from my slumber by a dip in my bed. Going instantly into defense mode, I raised my arms in a karate fight position and shouted, "One more move and your throat will be knife-handed."

My hair fell in front of my face as I tried to look around so I could catch a glimpse of the intruder. I was fucking ready to slice someone.

A warm hand reached out and pushed my hair behind my ear, which made me jolt back for a second but then I saw the dark shadow of Jett Colby sitting on my bed and I relaxed. Even in the moonlight, he looked more handsome than ever. I didn't think it was fair for a man to look so good but he did, even in his casual clothes.

"Jett, what are you doing scaring the piss out of me?"

He cocked his head to the side and said, "Did you really think you could take someone out with those little hands of yours?"

"I'm tough!" I said while sticking my chin out.

A small smile spread across his face, very small, as he said, "You're gorgeous."

Well, melt my pussy right in half because he was a smooth talker.

"Thank you but what are you doing here?"

He shrugged his shoulders as he looked me in the eyes. "I wanted to make sure you were okay."

"Why wouldn't I be?" I asked while pulling up my covers so Jett's heated gaze would tear away from my nearly exposed breasts.

Jett reached up and grabbed my chin with his thumb and forefinger then lightly stroked my bottom lip.

"I have a lot going on," he said, not answering my question. I just nodded in response because I wasn't quite sure how to respond. "If I don't invite you up to the Bourbon Room, I don't want you to think that I'm not thinking about you or that I don't care about you. I just…" he ran his hand over his face as he paused. I was seeing a side of Jett I only saw once and it was when he asked me to stay with him in the Lafayette Club, and right now, he had the same desired and desperate look on his face. Something must have been going on that I really didn't know about because he looked distressed.

I placed my hand on his cheek and said, "I understand."

"Do you?" he asked as the moon reflected off the side of his face. Dark circles were highlighted under his eyes as he looked at me and that was when I realized that Jett was not just the man that protected me, watched over me and took care of me but there was a whole other side of him that I was soon going to find out about, a side that made him the man he was today.

"I like to think so," I responded, not really sure where any of this was going.

He looked down at his hands while he said, "Friday you are going to be exposed to a group of people who take what they want, when they want it and have zero regard for anyone around them. They are fake and have the ability to tear apart the most innocent of hearts." He looked up at me when he said "innocent" indicating he was talking about me.

"I'm far from innocent," I responded out of instinct.

"You're innocent in this world, despite your past, you're so fucking innocent." Jett shook his head again. He looked like he was in immense pain from having to bring me to his party. I didn't get it.

"Okay, I guess I don't understand. Why is this so difficult for you?"

"Because," he shot off real quick while running his hands through his hair. His chest heaved as he looked up at me and spoke in a calmer tone. "Because I'm exposing you, Goldie. These people are part of a secret society where business is conducted under the table and million-dollar deals are solidified by a hand shake. This isn't a fucking walk in the park kind of event. I have to be on point for every fucking second I'm there and if for one minute I drop my façade, not only will I lose credibility but I will be eaten alive."

"And you're worried that I will distract you?"

"No, I'm worried that I will be too busy trying to protect you."

This whole conversation just seemed so dramatic. It was a stupid social. It wasn't like we were going to a mafia party where the bloods and the crypts were the party honorees. I was pretty sure I could handle some prissy ass debutantes and over compensating men.

I leaned back on the bed, letting the blanket slip dangerously low, like nipples-are-about-to-have-a-party low and pressed my hands behind my head. "Pretty sure I can handle myself, Jett. Thanks for the concern though."

His eyes were no longer looking at me, no, they were eye-fucking my tits as my chest heaved from his glare. I watched as his hand ran up my body, past my stomach and to the edge of my blankets. Just when I thought he was actually going to cover me up, he ripped the blankets off, exposing my naked body.

Without missing a beat, he yanked my ankles down so I was lying flat on the bed and he was straddling my body. He looked me right in the eyes and said, "Say it."

I could not deny this man anything so I licked my lips and said, "I'm here to submit to you."

His lips were on mine, faster than I could blink. He placed both his hands on either side of my head and hovered right above me, not applying too much pressure but just enough to drive me fucking ape shit crazy.

The fabric on his clothes rubbed against my bare skin, sending tingles of excitement through my veins. I knew what was under those clothes and I wanted them…badly.

His lips still continued to move across mine as he lowered down to his elbows and started to caress my face with his thumbs. Slowly, he pulled away and looked into my fucking soul.

"I can't have anything happening to you, little one."

"Nothing is going to happen to me, I promise."

"You don't belong in that world, with those people."

Ouch, that stung a little. I tried to chalk it up to the fact that he meant they were manipulative asshats but there was a little voice in the back of my mind that kept repeating Jett's words over and over in my head, I had no class. I tried to convince myself that his conversation with me was true, that he wanted to protect me and it wasn't him trying to come up with a different reason as to why he didn't want me at his parties.

Instead of responding, I just nodded, even though my heart was feeling a little salty. My body was begging for Jett's touch so I pushed back the pain in my heart and got lost in the feel of Jett's breath against my neck and the way his strong body did make me feel protected.

"Come with me," Jett said as he started to get up.

The abrupt change in his demeanor startled me. He went

from kind and caring, wanting to make sure that I was going to be okay to dominating Jett, the Jett who wanted to fuck me every which way till Monday and at that moment, for the first time since I've been at the Lafayette Club, I didn't want to go to the Bourbon Room. I didn't want to play, I wanted to feel. I wanted to feel the man that just left the conversation, I wanted to feel the protective and sensitive Jett, not the playtime Jett.

He tried to pull me off the bed but I just sat up and hugged my knees. The look of concern that flashed across his face was endearing. Once again, the split personalities of the man looking down at me could be so confusing.

"Is everything okay?"

"I don't want to go up there tonight."

His jaw twitched as he thought about what I said. I could see him waiver between his dominant self, his natural sexual being and trying to be a nice guy. I knew how the game was played, when I submitted I didn't really get an option of anything unless I gave him the safe word but I wasn't ready to cry alligator yet, I wanted to see if he would adjust to my needs.

"This is not up for negotiation, Lo," he responded, using my Jett Girl name. He was going with the dominant man which was disappointing especiallyafter everything that we discussed tonight; I wasn't giving in, not tonight.

I sat up, put on my big girl pants and said, "Alligator."

The room fell silent as utter defeat crossed his features. He turned his back away from me and ran his hands through his hair. A knot formed in the pit of my stomach as I contemplated what I just did, what I just said to him. The tension in the room grew thick as I tried to think of what to say, what to do, how to ease the tension I just so easily put between us by using just one little word.

I didn't want to disappoint Jett at all, but I also wasn't feeling like playing around. I needed human comfort, I needed to know that even though I wasn't the most dignified lady on the block that I was still his first choice, that I was good enough for him.

He turned toward the bathroom and held on to the doorframe

as his head hung low. What the fuck did I do? Did I insult him?

I grabbed the robe that was at the end of my bed, wrapped it around my shoulders and cinched the belt at my waist. I tiptoed across the plush carpet and stood behind Jett. My hand reached out to him but then I pulled back because I had no clue what to do or say. With one simple word did I just ruin everything I built up between myself and this delicious man?

With courage, I lifted my hand back up and gently touched his back. He stiffened under my touch and then turned around. When he looked down at me, the moon shined on his face so I was able to see that for once, he showed an emotion and it was an emotion I didn't want to see because the pained look on his face just absolutely devastated me.

He pulled my hand to make me come closer and he wrapped his arms around my waist, pressing his strong body against mine. He lifted one hand to my face and cupped it as he said, "Please, little one, please tell me what I did wrong."

So he wasn't angry with me…he was sorry, concerned. Would I ever be able to read him properly?

I thought about my needs but how did I explain to a man who was practically emotionally unavailable that I needed to be held, to be touched in a way that only a lover could, that I wanted him but I didn't want the Bourbon Room, the one thing that was non-negotiable. It's not like I didn't always want the Bourbon Room, I just needed Jett, the man Jett, not the dominant Jett.

Taking a deep breath, I responded. "It's nothing you did, it's just something I need."

"What do you need?" he asked as he searched my eyes.

"I need you, Jett."

Slight confusion crossed his face as he thought about what I said. The minute his body language stiffened, I knew he understood what I meant and my heart started tumbling down.

He stepped away from me and said, "You know I can't give you that, Lo."

I hated it when he called me Lo, it seemed so formal. I liked it at first but now I hated it because I knew that when we were intimate, when he was pleased with me he called me Goldie or little one but Lo, that was reserved for everyone in the Lafayette Club, it was reserved for when Jett closed me off and it irritated me.

Growing frustrated from my need, from my feelings, I took off my robe, tossed it to the side and got into my bed. I turned on my side like a very mature person—not—and pulled the covers over my body.

Over my shoulder, I called out, "Make sure to shut the door on your way out."

"Lo—"

"Don't," I said as I tried to hold back all the emotions that were bubbling over. I wasn't good at handling my emotions and right now it was showing. "I get it, all right? I know you don't do attachments but sometimes a girl just needs to be held, not brought up to the Bourbon Room where she will be twisted, tied up, spread out and fucked raw."

There was no response. I was almost positive he left until I heard the clunk of shoes on the floor and a wave of cold air hit my skin as the blanket was lifted.

Jett's hard body pressed against my back and his arms wrapped around my naked torso. Was this really happening? Was I really being held by him? Was he really nestling his head into my hair?

"I don't...do this," he whispered into my ear, sending chills all over my damn body. All the tension and frustration that was taking over my body seconds ago evaporated the minute Jett slid in behind me and held on tight. A small smile spread across my face and I could feel my body melt into his.

"Well you're fucking fantastic at it because I'm pretty sure my little clitty poo is drowning."

"Don't fucking call it that," he breathed into my ear. I was pretty sure I heard him laugh but I could be mistaken.

His hand inched up between my breasts, not in a sexual way but more in a comforting gesture. He pulled me in tighter and spoke directly in my ear.

"Remember when you came up to the Bourbon Room for the first time?"

"Yes." I wished Miss Mary could have heard me answer properly; one day of training was wearing off on me already.

"Remember how I told you I would never do anything you didn't want?" I just nodded, now feeling out of breath from the way his voice caressed my skin. "Well, it's true. I never want to do anything to displease you, to make you uncomfortable or to make you say your safe word. I'm sorry that I can't be that man that you need. I've been..." He paused and my heart ripped out for him. "God, Goldie, you make me say things I would never dream of saying to another person but the moment you said your safe word, I thought my chest was going to explode. I hate that I did that to you. I'm sorry."

Well, now I felt like an ass. It wasn't like he was pinching my nipples to the point of them falling off, I just didn't want to go upstairs with him. Fuck me.

"I'm sorry, Jett. I just didn't—"

"Don't," he interrupted me and pulled me in even closer. "When you first came here, Kace told me you were different, that you needed more than a physical connection, that you needed an emotional one and I knew that going into this. I just chose to ignore that because I'm a selfish prick but I can see that he was right, you do need that aspect of being with someone. I don't do emotions. I'm a fucked-up bastard who has a problem with showing his emotions for many reasons that I won't get into so it's hard for me to give you what you need. I don't know if I ever will be able to..." his voice trailed.

We both lay on my bed in silence as we thought about what was transpiring between us. I could feel him pulling away from me, not physically, no, he had a death grip on my torso but mentally, he was checking out and it was scaring the shit out of me.

"I don't need it all the time, Jett. I just had some bad thoughts in my head and going to the Bourbon Room just wasn't what I needed. I'm sorry."

Why was I apologizing? I heard myself gripping on to any loose end that Jett would throw me and I hated the way my voice sounded, like a desperate woman trying to hang on. But wasn't that what I was? I wanted Jett so fucking bad. There was this undeniable force that brought me to him and even though he says he's an emotionless bastard, I still feel his pain. I didn't want to lose anything we had and right now, it felt like he was minutes from cutting me loose by the way his silence continued. Panic set in.

"Talk to me," I almost demanded. "Tell me what you need, Jett."

He took a second to gather himself before he said, "You, Goldie. I just need you."

My gut twisted. He was so vulnerable, I didn't know what to say. When I tried turning around to face him, he wouldn't let me so instead, I just let him hold me like I wanted but if I were honest, it almost felt like he needed more than anything to hold me at that moment, rather than me needing him.

Instead of talking, we stayed silent and lay in my bed. As Jett wrapped his body around me, my heart tore in two. I wanted this man, more than anything but was he really willing to give me everything? Was he able to give me not just his body but his mind, his soul as well? I wasn't too sure and that realization made my stomach churn from the thought of not being able to keep Jett in my life.

Sleep eluded me as my brain worked overtime and when I woke up the next morning, Jett was nowhere to be found but there was a note on my table. Written in green marker, was a note from Jett.

I will be out of town for a while. Listen to Kace. – J

What the fuck?

10
"WAKE ME UP"

Jett

Canal Street was lit up with lights and tourists exploring the real city of New Orleans. Palm trees flanked the middle of the street where the trolley breezed through. I loved this city. I loved the richness of it, the tradition, the history and the people. I wouldn't want to be anywhere else.

I picked at the plate of gumbo that room service brought up to my suite. I wasn't very hungry. I hadn't been hungry since I left the club, since I practically gave myself over to Goldie.

She told me her safe word. Hearing her say that one little word nearly gutted me. I always considered myself to be a controlled man able to gauge people's feelings, especially the women I brought up to the Bourbon Room but Goldie was different. She was a mystery to me most of the time.

She wanted things I couldn't give her. She wanted a relationship, she wanted someone to hold her and be emotionally there for her but I was too broken after Natasha left me, after she told me I wasn't good enough.

I've worked hard my entire life to be better than my dad, to do good with my money and to give my mom her one wish, to see me settle down with someone, to be taken care of by someone. Knowing that I failed my mom's one wish was almost debilitating. I thought I found the woman I was going to spend the rest of my life with in Natasha but when she told me she wanted more, that I wasn't good enough for her, I changed. She crushed my dreams, my mom's dreams and I've never been the same since.

I'm a confident man in every aspect of my life besides holding on to a relationship, of being emotionally there for someone because how could I do that if I was so fucked up? All I would do is fuck up whoever was with me and that meant Goldie. I wanted nothing but good things for her. She deserved so much, so damn much.

"Did you really think you could hide forever, dickhead?"

Kace.

I turned around in my chair and saw Kace slip a room key into his pocket. The asshole must have fucked the lady at the front desk at one time or another because there was no way they would have given him a key otherwise.

"What the hell do you want?" I asked as I turned back around to stare down at Canal Street.

Heavy footsteps rang in the air as Kace approached me. He walked around the desk I was sitting at and sat on the sill of the window I was looking out of, blocking my view.

"What the fuck are you doing here, Jett?"

I turned away but Kace stopped my chair.

"Don't fucking block me out," Kace said, growing irritated with my child-like behavior.

I ran a hand through my hair as I said, "It's getting too fucking serious. She wants too much from me."

"You're lucky you have an event tonight that's fucking important because I am inches away from punching that dumb ass head of yours."

I looked up at Kace, a little shocked. He was pissed…at me.

"Is that right?" I asked as I brushed off my pant leg, trying to keep calm.

"You're a moron, you know that? You have a woman, waiting back at your club just dying for a little bit of your attention and instead of manning up, you're hiding out like a fucking vagina stuck in a pair of crusty shit catchers."

The man was one with words.

"Why do you care so much?"

"Because, if I was in your position, I would be fucking her every night and holding on to her until the morning. I would bury my head in her hair and inhale her sweet scent. I would revel in the way her soft body feels pressed up against mine and I wouldn't ever let her out on that stage because I would want her to be only for me and me alone."

My heart fucking seized as my hand reached out for Kace's shirt when I stood up out of pure blind rage. I pinned him against the window and said, "You have no right to talk about Goldie like that."

Laughing, Kace shook his head and said, "Why not? You have no claim over her. You treat her like every other girl at the club, you just pay extra attention to her but you have given her no reason to stay, no reason to not stray when she leaves which she will, I guarantee you that. You might have calmed the storm when you gave her a set but without you giving yourself over to her, fully, she's not going to stay, man."

I was still gripping his shirt but it was doing nothing, the man was scared of nothing.

I tossed my hand to the side and started pacing the length of the room.

"I can't, Kace," I stated softly.

"Don't let your past dictate how you live your future," he countered.

"I could say the same about you," I stated as I put my

hands on my hips and looked over at Kace.

"I'm different. I lost my life the same day the man in the bar lost his. I'm done, Jett. You know that. What I care about is seeing you get past your bullshit complex and really living life. One of us has to enjoy life and it sure as hell is not going to be me. Don't throw away something good because you're scared."

"I'm not good enough. I'm not someone she can rely on."

"That's fucking donkey piss. You're the best thing that has happened to that girl. You might be a giant ass but you treat her with respect, you take care of her and honestly, I think you might actually have feelings for her.

Of course I had fucking feelings for her. That was what was terrifying me. I didn't know how to deal with the feelings that were rolling through me. I was a temperamental prick with the ability to snap at anyone who looked at Goldie. I never was like that, even with Natasha, but there was something about Goldie that had set me off. I meant it when I said I think my mom brought us together but dealing with that revelation was a son of a bitch for me.

"Admit it," Kace prodded.

"I really hate you right now," I said in defeat as I sat down in a chair.

Kace threw his head back and laughed. "Dude, you love me and you know it. It's time to move on, man."

"It's dangerous. There are so many repercussions that could happen if I bring her into my life, if I let her in and not just with my fucking black heart but with the people I deal with. They all want a part of me and they will do anything to get it. I don't think I could handle it if something happened to her."

"That's a cop-out. You know just as well as I do that you have the best security team in the damn state and you have me, nothing will happen to her. We won't allow it, especially you."

I nodded my head as I pinched the bridge of my nose, deciding what I was going to do.

"Fuck," I huffed. "I'm a sensitive little bitch." I laughed to myself as Kace laughed out loud. "Fuck!" I shouted again, not being so eloquent.

"I take it you're giving in?"

"I don't fucking want to."

"But you have no choice."

"I know." I looked over at him and the asshat was smirking. I really did hate him. "What if I screw it up, what if I end up hurting her?"

"You're hurting her more by playing fucking mind games with her. It's either going to work or it's not. Might as well give it a chance because I'm sick of dealing with your moody ass and her crocodile tears."

My head snapped up from the mention of tears. "She cried?"

"Dude, seriously? You fucking left her a shady-ass note and haven't been back all week. She thinks you're never coming back, that she did something wrong by asking you to hold her. What kind of dick move is that?"

"The biggest dick move ever," I confessed. "Like I said, I'm a sensitive little bitch."

"Well, time to shave your fucking balls, bud, because it's time to put them on display."

I nodded my head as I thought about how the hell I was going to talk to Goldie, how I was going to let her into my life without getting burned.

11
"ALL IN"

Goldie

"Can you girls just leave me alone? He's not coming so there is no use getting ready."

Babs and Tootse hovered over me, trying to do my hair and makeup for the event I was supposed to go to tonight but I wasn't in the mood and I wasn't going anyway. I hadn't heard from Jett since the morning he left me a note and as far as I knew, he hadn't returned.

I tried to ignore the fact that once again, I was breaking in half, that he was pushing me away, that even though he tried to change the dynamic between us, he still fell back to his old ways of running away.

I didn't think about the way that he made me feel when he was around or the way he talked to me in his sultry southern voice or the way his strong hands caressed my body.

I wouldn't let myself acknowledge the fact that I felt like we were two torn souls brought together to heal each other and there was no way that I was going to allow myself to fall for the man, no way in fucking hell even though the pull between us was so strong that I was drowning in him.

Too bad I was only putting on a front because I did all of those things, every minute of the day he was on my mind. I hated it, I hated that I've become so dependent on the man, that the happiness of my day revolved around him.

"You never know, Lo, he might show up," Tootse said as she wrapped my hair up into a ballerina bun on the top of my head.

"You know I love you, Tootse, but you can seriously be delusional sometimes." Babs came at me with some mascara but I swatted her hand away. "Please, just leave me alone."

"No, you're done sulking. If you're not going out with Jett tonight then you're going to go out with us. We're all going to a bar a couple of blocks away. We have the night off and we're going to take advantage of it."

"I don't feel like going out." I pouted as Babs attacked my lashes. She didn't apply much makeup, kept me real natural which was nice because almost every night of my life since I could remember I was always layering on the makeup. It was nice to feel fresh for once.

"Lo, I hate seeing you like this," Tootse said as she sat down next to me on the bed, my hair pinned and ready to go. "I know it hurts but it's who he is."

"I know," I said defeated as Babs finished up. "That's what everyone keeps telling me and I keep telling myself that but when I'm with him, I feel different. I feel like our souls were made for each other, you know? Like we were brought together for a reason."

Babs and Tootse exchanged glances that told me I was the delusional one and I might just be. I knew Jett's rules going in, to signing a contract with the Lafayette Club but after he offered me a set I just thought things were going to be different, that maybe he would cross that line, go the extra step and fully connect with me, not just physically.

Even though I had the inkling that Jett wasn't going to show up for tonight, I still went to see Miss Mary and learned everything I possibly could from her in the last couple of days. I wanted to make sure that I was trained, that I was ready and on point if I was called up to bat, if Jett wasn't ashamed to be with me.

That's what it seemed like, like he was so ashamed of having me on his arm that he only knew to run away so he didn't have to deal with breaking my heart. He liked me when my legs were spread, behind the doors of the Bourbon Room but that was it. I wasn't stupid, I knew what I was getting myself into, I just wish he didn't lead me on.

Was he leading me on? Maybe I was looking too much into everything? Maybe he really just considered me to be another Jett Girl and was getting his fill. That didn't explain why he wasn't with the other girls though, or why he was so protective, why he didn't want my persona to be revealed.

Fuck, the man was infuriating. One minute I'm flying on cloud nine with my pussy flapping in the breeze waving at all the unicorns and kitties in my dream land and then the next moment, I'm lying low in a gutter full of dragon shit wondering where I went wrong. I liked roller coasters but this was one ride that I was starting to get sick of.

"Are you going to put your dress on?" Tootse asked as we all looked at the hanger that was attached to the top of my bathroom door.

The dress was a pewter gray color made of brocade fabric that was draped to be skin tight on the body and drape loosely past the hips. The top was a classy V-neck but gave a little bit of a show and there was a slit on the side that reached the bottom of my thigh. It looked dynamite on me but I wasn't about to put it on, not when I wasn't going anywhere.

"No, I don't even know why I let you put on this stupid

makeup in the first place." I went to rub it off but Babs grabbed my hands and looked me in the eyes.

She was about to say something to me when someone interrupted her.

"I can take it from here, girls," came the southern voice that haunted my dreams.

In tandem, we all turned our heads and saw Jett standing in the doorway, wearing a black tuxedo, black shirt and black bow tie. My heart beat rapidly in my chest from just the sight of him but with the way he was standing with pure confidence and smoldering eyes, I was about ready to pass out.

He had a little box tucked in his hand as he walked forward with enough swagger to make a woman weak in the damn knees.

Tootse and Babs released me and quickly walked out of the room.

"Shut the door, please," Jett asked, not taking his eyes off me.

His gaze was intimidating, almost too much to handle. The man was a cocky son of a bitch but how could he not be with a strong jaw like his and a stance that just screamed I know how to fuck your clit right off. And he did, multiple times.

Feeling uneasy in my silk robe and the way his eyes were undressing me, I pulled the ends of my robe together and looked up at him with as much confidence as possible.

"What are you doing here?"

Without saying a word, Jett grabbed my hand and pulled me up from my bed. If I wasn't so far gone from the way he looked at me, I would have resisted but I was weak, I was pathetic and I craved him. I craved him so damn bad that I wanted to cry. I hated that he had such power over me, that he could turn me into a ball of mush with just a look.

He placed his hand on my cheek and looked me square in the eyes. "My little one, I'm so sorry that I left you wondering these past couple of days…"

"That's right, you're sorry," I said as I pulled away, getting a little bit of my bravado back. "Do you think it's fun for me waiting for you, wondering where the hell you are or when you're coming back?" I held up my hand before he could talk. "I know we're not in a relationship and I get that, but I'm sorry I just can't sit around after you fuck the ever living hell out of me and then be cool with your disappearance. I worry about you, Jett, I fucking care about you and I think it's real shitty the way you've been treating me. You either like me or you don't, I can't do any more of this wafting around, as if the feelings we have for each other, and I know you have feelings, don't matter. I mean, fuck, Jett. You're killing me! I feel like I'm bleeding when you leave without a word, when you push me away. It fucking guts me."

My chest heaved as I tried to catch my breath from the mini rant I went on. When I looked back up at Jett, his brow was furrowed and the look of disappointment crossed his features.

"Goldie, I'm so fucking sorry. I'm a…uh…" He ran his hand through his hair and then turned his back on me.

He's a what? I wanted to shake him and scream at him to finish his sentence but from the way his shoulders sank and the way his back tensed, I knew whatever he was going to say was going to be extremely difficult for him so I pulled back my anger.

Instead of being a giant dick and walking out, like I should, I walked up behind him and wrapped my arms around his back, giving him comfort. He exhaled sharply and then turned in my grasp. His arms came around my back and pulled me in closer to his chest as he leaned his head down and kissed the side of my temple.

His lips caressed my ear as he said, "I'm a broken man, little one. I was fucked over by someone who I gave my heart to and she stomped on it, broke it in half. She made me feel worthless, used and I haven't been able to get over the words she spouted off as she walked out of my house and out of my life."

"What did she say?" I asked barely above a whisper. I didn't want to scare him away because for the first time since he told me about his mom, he was actually opening up.

Jett shook his head, denying me. Instead of pushing him, I instead rubbed his chest with the palm of my hand and kissed him on the jaw. His body relaxed under my arms and he drew me in even closer.

"You're too good for me, Goldie, but to hell if I can let you go."

"I don't know what that is supposed to mean," I answered honestly.

He pulled away and lifted his hand that was holding a long, flat jewelry box.

"This is for you, my little one." The way he said my name with such sincerity had my stomach flipping in excitement.

I looked at the box and then back up at him with a smirk. "This isn't going to be some Pretty Woman moment where I reach into the box and you snap it on my fingers, is it? Because I have to tell you, you will be sorely disappointed. I have cat-like reflexes."

A small grin peeked at the corner of Jett's mouth as he said, "No, it's not."

With that, he opened the box and revealed a very thin chained necklace made of white gold and in the middle had a very small round gem pendant with a purple center. It was gorgeous.

Not skipping a beat, he pulled the necklace out of the box and unlocked the ends. "May I?" he asked, hovering over my body.

"Yes," I said breathlessly as I turned around and he brought the necklace over my head and rested it on my collarbones as he put it on.

Once the necklace was fastened, the pendant settled right where my neck met my chest and the chain grazed the top of my collarbones. It was borderline choker status but not quite. My hand landed on the pendant as I turned to look at him.

"It's gorgeous, Jett. Thank you so much."

"Do you know what this is?" he asked as his fingers grazed mine so we were both touching the pendant.

"No."

Jett took a deep breath and said, "In my world, a symbol like this would mean that you're mine, that by wearing this necklace day in and day out, you are letting everyone know that you are taken, that you belong to me and only me."

Realization set in as my mouth fell open and I felt the necklace again.

"Is this a...collar?" I asked, almost flabbergasted from the gesture.

Looking a little sheepish, Jett nodded his head as he gripped the back of his neck with his one hand. The man was nervous, actually nervous. Fuck, I could not deny myself any longer.

With one quick jump, I straddled him as he stood, grabbed his head in my hands and placed my lips on his. I didn't take it slow at all, no, I drove my tongue into his mouth, demanding that he reciprocate and he did, he did with a groan.

When I pulled away, I searched his face as I said, "What does this mean, Jett?"

He stroked my face with his thumb as he held me up with the other hand. "This means I want to try, that I want to uh...be exclusive."

"Like a girlfriend?" I singsonged and teased.

He cleared his throat and said, "Something like that."

I hopped off him and placed my hands on my hip. "Something like that? No, that's not good enough. I either am or I'm not. I'm sick of playing games with you, Jett. You said early on that you didn't play games and you know what, neither do I. I'm going to sound like a broken record of a boy band but you need to quit playing games with my heart. I don't deserve to be fucked one night and then dropped off the face of the planet the next. I'm dead serious when I say it's all or nothing with me. I'm done with this guessing game."

Holy shit, I was quaking in my boots. Where the hell did that come from? Even though I was surprised with myself, I realized that I meant it. I truly meant what I said. I was sick of being played with. I was at a breaking point and he either wanted me in his life, fully, or he wanted me to leave forever. I couldn't take this up and down shit anymore.

"Well…" I asked while crossing my hands over my chest.

He looked at me as his hand held on to the back of his head. His pose was sexy as hell and I knew he wasn't doing it on purpose it was just Jett being Jett but fucking hell all I wanted to do was rip his clothes off and take him. Forget about the clothes, I just needed to unzip his pants, I was that fucking ready.

He released his hand and stepped forward. He separated my arms and grabbed a hold of my hands. He brought them up to his lips and he lightly kissed them as he looked me directly in the eyes, stealing my heart, looking into my soul.

"You're mine, Goldie. Are titles that important?"

Were they? Not really but I wanted to hear him say it. I needed to hear him say it but I knew at this moment, I shouldn't push my luck. Even though I was dying to hear the words come out of his mouth, he was opening himself up to me and letting me in. I needed to be happy with baby steps.

"They are to me but I get it, Jett. I get you're scared." I stood up and pressed another kiss to his jaw as my hand caressed his cheek. "I just need to know that since I'm yours, that makes you mine as well. I need to hear you say it."

He nodded his head and without skipping a beat, he said, "I'm yours, Goldie, all fucking yours."

Elation throbbed through my veins as he grabbed the sides of my head and brought his lips down onto mine. His hands ran from my cheeks down to my neck where he caressed my necklace as his mouth explored mine. Waves of nerves and new found feelings rushed through me as he pressed his body against mine, signaling to me that he meant what he said. He was mine.

He groaned and pulled away, leaving me breathless and wanting more. He smiled, fucking smiled down at me and I felt my heart flip upside down from the endearing look on his face.

"As much as I would love to pull that robe off you and

expose that beautiful skin of yours, we need to get you dressed because we have an event to get to."

My eyes lit up from the mention of him taking me out. "We're still going to go?"

"Of course, why do you think I'm dressed like this?"

"To make my clit pop off?"

Jett shook his head as a small smirk crossed his face.

"Oh shit, sorry." I covered my mouth and took a deep breath as I tried to regain myself. "I promise I will be on my best behavior tonight. I've been working with Miss Mary all week to get polished for tonight. You know, in case you did show up."

"I was going to show up."

"I had my second thoughts," I stated as I looked away.

Jett grabbed my chin and made me look him in the eyes. "Listen to me closely, little one. No matter what happens, no matter what comes between us, I will always be there for you. You will always be able to count on me and I don't want you thinking any differently, okay?"

I nodded my head as he lightly kissed my lips.

His hands traveled down to the waist of my robe and untied the tie, revealing my strapless bra and thong.

His gaze wandered down to my flat stomach—thank you Kace—and nodded in appreciation.

"You're exquisite, little one." He frowned as he took in everything. "Where is your gold lingerie? Were you that mad at me to deprive me of such a thing?"

I looked at him confused. "What are you talking about? I never got gold lingerie."

His head snapped up as he looked over to my closet. "You mean to tell me, you never got any?"

"No. Was I supposed to?"

Jett made an indescribable sound as he reached into his pocket and started typing something out on his phone. When he was done, he looked back up at me and then reached for the dress that was behind me on the bathroom door.

"Get dressed, little one. We have a long night ahead of us."

"How is it going to end?" I asked as I grabbed on to his lapels and leaned into him.

"I think you know," he said as he leaned down and played with my necklace. "I can't tell you how much pride runs through my bones seeing you wear my collar. It makes me want to fuck you so hard that you remember who owns you."

"I don't need you to fuck me to know who owns me, Jett. You've owned me since the first day at Kitten's Castle when you ordered your drink with that sultry southern voice of yours."

I pulled away and walked toward the bathroom to put my dress on. As I walked away, I heard Jett faintly say, "You've owned me since the first day I saw you at the cemetery."

When I turned to ask him if I heard him right, I saw him looking at one of my drawings of his mother's grave and decided to let it go. He had enough for tonight. I didn't want to push him any further. I was content with our progress.

12
"YOU REALLY GOT A HOLD ON ME"

Jett

I waited in the grand entrance of the Lafayette Club for Goldie to come down the stairs. My chest should feel constricted right now, I should feel tied down and panicky but I wasn't. I almost felt kind of free, for once, since Goldie entered my life. Was claiming her as mine all it really took?

It was a big step on my part, fucking huge. I've never felt so vulnerable in my entire life but when Goldie allowed me to put my collar around her beautiful neck, I've never felt so much pride before. Pride for myself and pride to have a girl like Goldie on my arm. She was foul-mouthed most of the time and had a hard time submitting and following my rules but I would be lying if I said I didn't enjoy it. That I didn't enjoy the challenge. I never knew what to expect from her and that was one of the best things about being with her, near her and owning her.

When she asked if she owned me, I wanted to laugh. Was it really that hard for her to see? No matter how many times I tried to get her out of my head, I couldn't. She had taken up residence in my brain, my body and my soul. She had me wrapped around that little pinky of hers and I would do anything for her, fucking anything.

I just needed to take baby steps. Being with a girl, with just one girl as more than a lover is overwhelming. There are emotional responsibilities that I need to be prepared for and I'm terrified as fuck about whether or not I'm ready for them. I want to be, I need to be because I can't lose Goldie. She's too damn important to me. I hate to admit it but she has slowly become my world and that bastard Kace can see it. He's laughing his way around the damn club at me. I know he's just itching to say "I told you so," and a part of me wants to shove it up his ass and prove him wrong because that's the kind of ass I am, but I know that won't get me anywhere but miserable in my office with a glass full of bourbon in my hand.

I glanced at my watch and tried to figure out what was taking so damn long for Goldie to meet me downstairs. All she had to do was put on a dress. She was already wearing her undergarments, her hair and makeup were done so she should be good to go.

The thought of her in her black lingerie had me shifting in position so I didn't get too excited about the proposition of seeing her in it again later tonight. One thing I wasn't happy with was the fact that Goldie still didn't have her gold lingerie. I sent a message to Kace about it but he has yet to get back to me. I would be getting to the bottom of that tomorrow.

The faint sound of heels clicking against the hardwood floor brought my attention to the top of the stairs where Goldie was standing. Her hair was no longer in a bun but instead was in long waves cascading down past her shoulders. The gray dress she had on was beyond exquisite, accentuating every beautiful asset of her body.

She glided down the stairs and I felt my heart catch in my throat as I watched her approach me, wearing my collar. She was a sight that could take down any man. Her lips were framed in a pretty light pink gloss that made me want to push her up against the wall and take what I wanted.

"Are you ready?" she asked shyly.

I grabbed her hand and brought it up to my mouth. I kissed her softly and said, "You're so beautiful, little one. So damn beautiful."

A light blush spread across her cheeks as her eyes beamed. "Thank you."

I held out my arm for her to grab, which she did and I leaned down in her ear. "Are you ready?"

"I am," she said while straightening her posture, something she must had learned from Miss Mary. It delighted me to see her try, not that she needed to. Honestly, I would take her any way I could get her. I just wanted her to be prepared for the heinous humans she was about to meet.

I led her to the front door and just when we were about to leave, there was a ruckus of whistles and cheering coming down the hallway. Goldie and I turned around to see the other Jett Girls tossing confetti and blowing on noise makers as they made their way toward us. Goldie laughed and I just stared at them all, a little stunned. Behind them all was Kace, with his arms crossed, leaning against the hallway wall with a slight smirk on his face.

"Finally!" the girls all shouted as they ran up to Goldie and gave her a hug.

"You two are perfect for each other." Tootse clapped as she bounced up and down.

Francy patted her shoulder and then looked at me. "You scored yourself a hot piece of ass, Jett. Don't fuck it up."

"Yeah, don't fuck it up," Babs repeated as she pushed my shoulder.

"Or we will fuck you up," Pepper added as they all started to come at me like a little blonde mafia, besides Francy.

I held my hands up and said, "I may have chosen Goldie but that doesn't mean you ladies can get out of control. Know your roles," I said with a smirk.

All the girls' mouths fell open as Kace threw his head back and laughed behind everyone. I couldn't help it, I let out a little chuckle as well. They were too easy.

"You're lucky you're on your way out," Babs said.

"Give him hell, Lo," Francy added.

I looked down at Goldie who was looking up at me with a devilish glint in her eye.

Without taking my eyes off her, I said, "I have no doubt in my mind that she won't." A small smile spread across her face as I grabbed her hand again. "Time to go." I turned to the girls and gave them all a wink. "Night, ladies. Don't get too drunk tonight."

"Don't worry about us, Lo is the one with the drunken craziness," Pepper said as they all started walking away.

God help the men out on the streets tonight because as their jean-clad asses walked away from me, I knew they were going to cause hell tonight.

I led Goldie out to the waiting limo and held the door open for her. I watched as she hiked up her dress slightly so she could climb in. The slight movement brought the slit up to a dangerous height and the mere thought of what she was hiding underneath had me itching to ditch the event and take her back upstairs.

Fuck me, this was going to be a long night.

I slid in next to her and shut the door. The driver pulled forward as Goldie leaned into my shoulder and rested her head on my chest. I wasn't used to being comfortably intimate with someone but I liked the way she felt against me so I wrapped my arm around her shoulders, allowing her to bury herself deeper into my side.

"Thank you for taking me tonight," she said with not much spunk like usual but more sincerity.

I kissed the top of her head and played with a strand of her hair. "I'm glad I was able to pull my head out of my ass and realize that I needed you."

She nuzzled my chest and said, "Please don't ever stop saying that."

We sat in silence holding on to each other as the streets of New Orleans passed us by. I should feel weird, I should want to distance myself but right now, in this moment, I knew I made the right choice. I just hoped it didn't backfire on me. I wasn't strong enough to get my heart ripped out of my chest again. I liked to pretend I was a strong man and nothing affected me but deep down, I was a hurting son of a bitch with a black hole where my heart should be.

***

"I'm not going to lie, I'm fucking nervous," Goldie whispered into my ear as we rode up an elevator to the top floor where the party was taking place.

"Don't be nervous, I won't leave your side," I said into her ear, trying to still her shaking hand.

"I just have to stand tall, remember not to fucking swear and make sure to keep my chin even."

"Don't overthink it, little one. You'll be just fine." I kissed the top of her head, kind of liking the whole affection thing. "Just be yourself."

She looked at me and gave me that "You're kidding me" look. I shrugged my shoulders and said, "I like you the way you are."

"Yeah, well, you have a special taste for trash..."

What the fuck?!

Blood boiled through my veins as I spun around and pinned her against the wall of the elevator. I held her hands at her sides and got right in her face.

I spoke through my teeth as I tried to contain the anger that was spilling out of me.

"I will not repeat myself, if you ever call yourself trash again or degrade yourself in front me ever again, I promise you this, you won't like the consequences. Do you understand me?"

She gulped and nodded her head.

"I've been one hundred percent honest with you since you've been with me and I'm telling you this, you are the most beautiful, exquisite woman I have ever met. You do something to me, Goldie, that no one has been able to do. You make me open up, you make me feel and for you to call yourself trash is a direct insult to me. Are you trying to tell me I have no taste?"

I was mere centimeters away from her face, studying her eyes intently. I wanted to get it through her thick skull that even though she came from a rough background she was perfect. She was so much better than the people she was about to meet and she could give them a run for their money any day.

"That's not what I'm saying, I just—"

"Good." I cut her off. "Now, you're going to use the training Miss Mary gave you not to change who you are but to give you more confidence. You're so much better than these people, so I want you to show me how you are. Got it?"

She nodded again as her eyes welled up with tears. Fuck. I didn't need her crying.

I leaned in and kissed her earlobe as I spoke gently into her ear, "Steady your breathing, little one. I wouldn't want anyone else on my arm tonight, okay?" She nodded again as I ran my lips along her jawline and found her luscious lips. Knowing we were closing in on our floor, I was going to have to pull away and straighten myself out but I just needed one last taste so I pressed my body against hers and lifted her hands above her head so she was completely at my surrender. With one quick lick of her lips, I plunged forward and tasted her sweetness. She was so damn sweet.

A moan escaped the back of her throat as her hips grinded into mine. Waves of pleasure rolled through me as I reciprocated the motion. She was driving me crazy and I knew I had to put a stop to it but I couldn't, for the life of me, I couldn't stop taking everything from her.

"Ahem." Someone from behind us cleared their throat.

Like a bullet out of a gun, I stood up straight and fixed our clothing. We both wiped our mouths and I tried to hold back the smile that was trying to cross my face from the panic-stricken look Goldie was giving me.

With confidence, I turned around and faced the person who was interrupting our little make-out session in the elevator. There was a bell hop holding open the elevator door for us and right past him was the entire party, standing still and staring at us.

Fuck.

Not the way I wanted to enter the room but I owned it because that was what a pompous and full of himself man did. I learned that from my dad. Goldie on the other hand was shaking so I held out my arm and clasped her hand when she threaded her arm into my side.

I leaned into her ear and said, "Chin straight, little one."

She looked up at me, smiled and walked next to me with confidence.

As we entered the party, the room of attendees parted and watched as we glided across the floor. I led Goldie straight to the bar because she was going to need a little bit of liquid encouragement.

"Jett, I wasn't expecting you to show up with such a gorgeous treasure on your arm tonight," Bernie said as he flanked my side. Putting on my best smile, I turned to him and held out my hand.

"Bernie, what a pleasure to see you tonight." I brought Goldie forward and said, "This is Goldie. Goldie, this is Bernie Butler. He is the vice president over at Citi Bank."

With precision, Goldie held out her hand with just the right bend in her wrist and allowed Bernie to take her hand in his and place a kiss on it. She shied away slightly, working it and then leaned back into me once he was done making her acquaintance. The girl was a fucking pro.

"It's a pleasure to meet you, Mr. Butler."

"Pleasure is all mine, sweetheart." Bernie looked up at me and said, "Jett, where did you find such a delectable creature?"

I focused on not rolling my eyes from his comment and said, "She found me, Bernie," as I looked down affectionately at Goldie.

"I can see that. That was quite an entrance you two had. If I didn't know any better, I would say you two were pretty close."

A fake laugh escaped my throat as I patted Bernie on the shoulder. "You're very observant, Bernie." I looked around the room and said, "Where is Mrs. Butler?"

"Oh, she's in the powder room, she said her face was getting shiny." Bernie leaned forward and said, "I really think she just goes to the bathroom to go gossip like a hen. You know women." He eyed Goldie and said, "Present company excluded."

Goldie smiled politely but seemed a little uncomfortable, like maybe she actually did have to go to the bathroom.

I leaned down into her ear and said, "Do you have to go to the powder room?" She nodded and I responded, "Do you want me to take you?"

"No, I'll be fine." She kissed the side of my cheek and then walked off toward the bathrooms. This was the perfect time to discuss business without Goldie hearing me. That was one thing I was nervous about. I didn't want her to get involved with my business deals, especially when my dad was involved in them. He was an evil bastard and I didn't want Goldie anywhere near him.

Goldie walked away and I turned to Bernie who was watching her hips sway. He had two seconds to pull his eyes off her ass before I clocked the old man in the nuts.

With a perverted smile, Bernie averted his eyes and said, "What a fine woman. Well done, Colby."

This was the part of my life that I hated. When I had to act like what people were saying was okay, that these creepy old men were not perverts and that we were all part of this boys club that got away with murder.

Changing the subject, I said, "So how is the loan business going? I heard there are some changes in the city that are going to be made soon, ones that need a significant amount of money."

A sly grin spread across the evil bastard's face as he brought a toothpick up to his mouth and started chewing on it.

"You're a smart man, Jett." He looked me up and down and then continued. "You want to know if your dad has come to me for money, don't you?"

The bartender handed me my bourbon and I took a sip before answering Bernie. I leaned on the edge of the bar and said, "I don't know how much you could really tell me that I don't already know." I bluffed. I had to make it seem like I knew my shit.

Bernie's eyebrow rose as he looked at me. "Then why bring it up?"

"I just want to make sure you know that I know." I leaned in closer, taking in his musk scent that was straight up revolting. No wonder Mrs. Butler was in the powder room. Fucking hell. "I want you to know that I know what's going on and I'm not afraid to bring it to the city's attention. Illegal deals with my father where he pays you under the table will not go unnoticed."

I took a guess as to what was going on with Bernie and my dad and my guess was right because Bernie's face blanched as he sputtered to cover up his shock.

"I...I, uh, don't know what you're talking about, Colby."

I nodded my head and looked out into the room. "Let's keep it that way, Bernie. I don't play a dirty game and I never will. If someone fucks me over, they're going to pay for it."

I turned back around, looked Bernie in the eyes as I held out my hand. "Always a pleasure."

"As usual," Bernie replied as he limply shook my hand.

It looked like I got my point across from the defeated look on Bernie's face. He was a powerful man but he knew I could take him out in seconds. I had the proof of it. Don't fuck with me because I had video of every powerful man in this city gracing the booths of my club. I could destroy them in the matter of seconds.

BEING A JETT GIRL

Call me the devil but fuck with me or fuck with my girls
and I would take you out before you could zip your pants back up.

13
"JEALOUS"

Goldie

As I walked to the bathroom, I recognized that I actually didn't have to go to the bathroom but in fact, I needed to calm my raging heart from Jett's attack in the elevator. When he said he owned me, he meant it. It was like a light switch went off in him and once he claimed me, he was mine whole heartedly. I wasn't going to lie, I kind of loved it even though our entrance was a little much, especially since I was trying to come across as a dignified woman, not some floozy for the night.

Of course Jett handled the situation with his classic poise which I tried to feed off of but it was hard when my legs were clenching together, begging for more and my body was shaking uncontrollably. That is what he did to me, he turned me into a puddle of mush with just his voice and his glare. He was dangerous but I loved walking on the side of danger, that was why we worked so well together.

The ballroom was grand, I didn't expect anything less. It was on the top floor of a swanky hotel I forgot the name of because I was so wrapped up in Jett's arms in the car. The room was covered in white, floor to ceiling, everything was white. Party goers graced the floor, dancing, laughing and mingling. The whole scene looked like it came from a movie as servers passed through the throngs of people passing out hors d'oeuvres and busying themselves with cleaning while the rich and privileged made back-handed business deals and put on their best showing. Jett was right, this was so not my scene and they were not even close to being my people.

I found the bathroom, after asking two different servers and walked in. There was a seating area in the first room with plush couches and pillows spread across the walls. I walked past the group of ladies who were all huddled together, talking and ignoring anyone who walked in and went straight for a stall that was big enough to fit ten people all together. I carefully lined the toilet with toilet paper even though the seat was probably cleaner then my belly button, lifted my dress and sat down. There was no need for underwear tonight, which Jett would find out later, something to look forward to. After he left, I took them off for...easier access. What can I say, I can be a floozy at times.

I wished I had my phone with me because I would be texting the girls about the party right now but I left it back at the club. I didn't think it was necessary to have especially since I wasn't carrying a clutch which was also a mistake. What if I was turning glossy like Mrs. Butler, I didn't have anything to pat myself down with.

I tried to look at my reflection in the toilet dispenser but couldn't get the right angle while sitting on the john. So not wanting to take my chances, I grabbed a wad of toilet paper and lightly padded my face to remove any excess "gloss." Luckily, the toilet paper felt like it was quilted by nuns because the damn stuff was as soft as a kitten's ass.

With my dress hiked up to my tits and my face being

patted down, I thought about how Miss Mary would so disapprove but at the moment, I didn't care. No one could see me.

I was about to get more toilet paper when I heard some voices travel over the practically blacked out bathroom stalls.

"Did you see that girl? Another flavor of the month must be."

"Yes, but he seemed to actually care for this one. I've never seen him act like that toward another woman, have you?"

"No, but he could be putting on an act."

I tried to tell myself they weren't talking about Jett and me but I had a suspicion that wasn't the case.

"There are a lot of men here tonight that could influence the Lot, he needs to make a good showing. He's probably just dragging that girl around so he can boost his appeal."

"Does he really think he's going to get Lot 17?"

The girl laughed. "He's Jett Colby, he thinks he can get anything."

Just what I suspected, they were talking about Jett. Now if I only knew what they were talking about. What the hell was Lot 17? Was that another club I didn't know about? I thought about the name and liked the way it rolled off my tongue. I would totally rock it out at Lot 17 if that was a club name.

I distracted myself with the possible club name too much as I heard the girls walk away but not before I heard one of them say, "I'm not too worried. Jett and I have a bit of a history. I will be in his club in no time."

What?!

My ears perked up and I quickly stood up and pressed my head against the door of my stall, dress still up around my tits and gloss pad in my hand. Did I just hear her right? She was going to try to get into the club? Was she talking about the Lafayette Club or this Lot 17? Was Lot 17 even a club?

Fuck, I was so confused. I sat back on the toilet and put my head in my hands as I tried to think about what was going on and how to approach it. Did I risk it and straight up ask Jett? We were supposed to be honest with each other but I felt like our new found...relationship was too fresh, I didn't want to push it too far. I needed to take my time and not go full Goldie on him, that would only scare the fuck out of him and I didn't want that.

Realizing I'd been sitting on the toilet for too long, I took care of business, adjusted my dress and exited the stall. Luckily no one was waiting on me and the bathroom was clear. I didn't feel like dealing with bathroom bitches, they were the worst.

Once I was all set, I walked back into the main ballroom and started toward the bar where I left Jett. It was funny walking by everyone because the different fragrances intermingling were quite hilarious. It was like a perfume convention and the person who wore the most was going to win a prize at the end of the night.

I spotted Jett and smiled to myself as I started to walk toward him. It was hard to miss him. He was tall, gorgeous and the most handsome and confident man in the room. He had one hand in his pocket and one hand holding his ever present bourbon. As I walked toward him, I was too busy to notice the raven-haired woman standing in front of him, talking to him and touching him...a little too much.

I shook out of my Jett trance and stopped in my tracks as I saw Jett engage with her. Never touching her but he was listening to her intently and that bothered me. Any other woman near him bothered me.

He smiled gently at her for a moment and then looked up. That was when he made eye contact with me. His polite smile turned into a full on grin as his eyes met mine. With his glass held up, he beckoned me with his finger. The power he had in that index finger of his was unbelievable.

The minute I reached Jett, he pulled his hand out of his pocket and grabbed mine. He brought our connection up to his lips and smiled down at me.

"There you are. Goldie, I would like you to meet an old friend of mine, Keylee Zinc. Keylee, this is Goldie."

I pried my eyes off the delectable man and looked at the

woman with the long black hair. As I took her in, I tried to hide the cringe in my face from the announcement of her name. What the fuck kind of name was Keylee? More like kiwi. I hid the giggle as I took her in and that's when I started to sweat. Kiwi was a fucking bombshell. I gulped as I took her hand in mine and shook it.

"So nice to meet you, Goldie."

Where did I hear that voice before? It was so familiar.

"Jett has not stopped talking about you since I came up to say hi."

Bathroom bitch! Bathroom bitch!

I wanted to shout and point and let everyone know that kiwi was trying to move in on my man but instead, I pulled a number out of Miss Mary's trainings, smiled a gracious smile, hid the devil that was trying to pour out of me and said, "Well, I hope it was all good."

Jett leaned down into my ear and said, "It always is, little one." He gripped my side tighter, making me flush.

Kiwi eyed us up and down and I could see the inner workings of her brain trying to figure out what was transpiring between Jett and me. I fingered my necklace, trying to give her a clue and she took the bait.

"What a beautiful necklace, Goldie." She eyed the damn thing with her laser beam eyes. If I didn't know any better, I would have sworn she was trying to blast it off my neck.

I looked up at Jett with adoration and said, "It was a gift from Jett."

I glanced quickly at the fuzzy fruit and saw a slight glimpse of jealousy pass over her features. I needed to find out about this hooker when I got home. I was going to do a little Goggle magic and the first two searches were going to be Keylee "bathroom bitch" Zinc and Lot 17, possible club/play room for Goldie. Who knew what the hell it was.

Kiwi cleared her throat and said, "Well, Jett, it was nice catching up with you. Maybe we can have lunch one day…to discuss things." She leaned forward, pressed her hand against his chest and kissed the side of his cheek. I stiffened as Jett didn't move. He didn't lean in but he didn't lean away either. I wanted to chastise him but then again, he couldn't cause a scene by denying her a "friendly" goodbye.

"Nice seeing you again, Keylee."

She turned to me and smiled. "Goldie, you're a lucky girl. Take good care of my friend."

The way she said friend made me want to punch her in the throat. I couldn't stand the bitch. It was time for her to go.

Going against the etiquette I learned from Miss Mary, I nodded at the kiwi and then turned my back to her, blocking her off from Jett as I wrapped my arms around him. She must have gotten the hint because I couldn't feel her breathing down my neck with her skank breath anymore.

Jett looked down at me with a questioning eyebrow.

"I don't like that bitch."

Coughing slightly from the abruptness of my statement, Jett composed himself and said, "Care to explain why?"

"She was talking in the bathroom about this new club called Lot 17 and how she was going to be a part of it with you and how you were going to ride off into the sunset fucking each other on a white steed."

Okay, maybe I embellished a little but the bitch needed to be put in her place.

"Wow, that is quite a statement for a little bathroom pow wow."

"I thought the same thing. She was practically talking about names for your kids."

Jett shook his head as he disengaged my arms from around him and led me to the bar.

"This is probably a mistake since you're already losing your mind but let's get you a drink."

"I'm not losing my mind," I said as I pulled my arm away.

In seconds, Jett's gaze lifted behind me and scanned the room for any onlookers and that was when I realized that even though it felt like we were in our own little world, we weren't and we were being observed by everyone.

"Shit, I'm sorry," I mumbled as I straightened myself and took a deep breath.

"We will talk about this later," Jett whispered into my ear as he gripped my arm and led me to the bar.

Double shit.

***

The rest of the night went by in a blur. Absentmindedly, I shook people's hands, smiled and held my chin at the perfect height while Jett laughed and patted his friends on the shoulders. They never talked about anything serious when I was around but when I stepped away for a second to either get a drink or some fresh air, I saw Jett speaking to his comrades intensely but when I came back, they turned back to jovial conversations. Something was going on and I was too fucking curious. I needed to know what all the secretive talk was about but I knew I couldn't ask, not just yet.

The night came to an end and Jett led me out to the limo to take us back home. Like a gentleman, he draped his jacket around my shoulders as we stepped outside. His jacket was entirely too big on me but I loved it. The smell of Jett Colby ran through my senses as I held on to his hand and waited for our limo to pull up. Once it did, Jett held the door open for me and I stepped in. Jett followed immediately and once the door was shut, he pushed me to the floor, pinned me down and hovered over me. I didn't even see him swooping in. He blindsided me.

Fucking stealth move.

My chest heaved as I waited for whether or not he was going to give me a tongue lashing about the little fruit tart or if he was going to take me right there, on the limo floor. My entire body was screaming for the latter, practically begging.

"Tell me what happened," he said as his lips started to

work my jaw.

What were we talking about? What was I supposed to tell him? All my mind was thinking about was dick plus vagina makes me one happy girl.

He stopped his lip magic and said, "You're not talking."

"I'm sorry but it's kind of hard to focus when you're making out with my neck. Not that I'm complaining."

"Why don't you like Keylee?"

"Because she's a skank. Why? Am I supposed to like her?"

Jett let out a frustrated breath as he looked at me. "Why don't you like her and you have to give me a reason."

"I told you," I huffed out. "She was claiming you in the bathroom and was talking about Lot 17, whatever the hell that is and then before she left the bathroom, she was talking about how she was going to be in your club in no time. What the fuck does that mean? Are you going to make her a Jett Girl?"

My gut twisted from the thought of the kiwi coming to work at the Lafayette Club. I couldn't even toy with the idea, it made me sick to my stomach.

"No, Goldie. I'm not. She is part of the elite crowd, she doesn't need the Lafayette Club."

"Oh," I replied as I read his underlining statement. She was too good for it, unlike me who wouldn't survive without the club.

"Don't," he reprimanded. "Don't let one sour thought cross your mind, you got it?" I nodded and tried to keep my facial expressions even as my stomach continued to tie in knots.

"I just don't like her. She was too friendly with you."

"We're friends, you know?"

"You're mine," I shouted, making him jump back for a second, then the most delicious smile crossed his face.

"Say it again," he said in a husky voice as his chest heaved.

"You're fucking mine," I stated as I grabbed his shirt and pulled him down to my lips. His forearms landed on the floor and he encased my face with his strong hands. His thumbs ran circular motions around my cheeks as he kissed me back, with the same force that I was kissing him.

One of his hands ran down my side and connected with the opening of my slit where he guided my dress up a little farther. I waited breathlessly for his next move, for him to figure out my little surprise.

His hand kept moving forward and once it hit my hip, he pulled away from me and looked down into my eyes confused.

"Are you wearing any underpants?"

With a smirk, I shook my head no.

His jaw clenched as he studied me. I waited nervously for his reply.

"When were you going to tell me this?"

"I wasn't," I replied as I moved my hips into his, eliciting a groan from him.

"You've been very naughty, little one, keeping such a secret from me."

"Isn't naughty good?"

"Do you have a response for everything?"

"Almost always," I said with a grin.

He bowed his head and shook it as he tried to regain himself.

The limo came to a stop and Jett looked up to see out the window. He got up off me and pulled me up onto the seat.

He leaned into my ear as the car door opened and he said, "Your time is up, little one. Meet me in the Bourbon Room in five minutes. Stand in the middle, next to the table, wear one of your business shirts and make sure your hair is pulled back into a ponytail. I plan on riding the fuck out of you tonight while I grip that beautiful mane of yours." He didn't give me a chance to reply because he was out of the door in no time.

Holy. Fucking. Hell.

14

"WITHOUT ME"

Jett

I needed to calm my racing heart before I went into the Bourbon Room since it was going about a mile a minute right now. The night was a success for not just business reasons but also when it came to Goldie. Now that she is mine, I'm moving forward with the decision to claim her and I really felt like we made a connection tonight, we had an understanding for each other.

I liked her being jealous about Keylee, it made me feel needed, something that I've been yearning for. Natasha did a number on me and now that Goldie, this strong and attractive woman has claimed me as hers, I've never felt so invigorated before. It almost seemed too easy with Goldie but I wasn't going to think about that too much because she was what I wanted in my life, she was the missing factor I've needed and even though I erred on the side of caution, I was going to enjoy what I was willing to give her right now.

Knowing she's been waiting for me, I took my jacket and tie off and unbuttoned my shirt but kept it on as I rolled up my sleeves and headed to the Bourbon Room, I had some playing to do.

When I entered the room, I was pleased with the purple lighting that lit up the sides of the walls and the lonely light that gracefully shone down upon Goldie who was standing next to the table with her Jett Girl attire on, besides her mask, and her hair pulled back. She was impeccable to look at. The perfect form of beauty was staring right back at me.

Her eyes took in my entire body, starting from the tips of my toes to the top of my head. Heat blazed in her eyes as I walked closer and I could not be happier with her reaction. She was giving me everything I needed, the confidence to approach her and the attraction to pursue such a fine specimen.

When I reached her, I lifted her chin so I could look her directly in the eyes.

"Do you have something to say to me?" I asked, no longer holding my breath for her answer because I knew, the moment I slipped my collar around her neck, she was mine and she would never deny me...ever.

"I'm here to submit to you, Jett."

"Good, now walk to the bathroom," I said while pointing toward a closed door. I knew she was slightly confused since she had never seen that part of the Bourbon Room before but with a nod, she started walking. "But first, unbutton your shirt for me and leave it on."

She lit up as she turned to fully face me and slowly, and like the man-eater she was, she unbuttoned her shirt, inch by fucking slow inch. She was driving me crazy and she knew it.

Once the shirt was unbuttoned I was pleased with the fact that she was naked underneath, even though I didn't ask her to be. It just made my job that much easier.

"You please me, little one. Now, go."

With a smile on her face, Goldie listened to me as I followed close behind. The bathroom was quite large and was all white marble with large mirrors spanning from one end of the room to the other, exactly what I wanted.

I went up behind her and turned her toward the mirror so she could see herself. She pressed her body against mine and tilted her neck to the side to make room for my head. We looked at each other in the mirror as my hands glided up her sides, underneath her open shirt.

"Look at how beautiful you are," I whispered into her ear as my hands found her hip bones.

"You make me feel beautiful, Jett."

"Then I'm doing my job," I replied as I kissed her earlobe. "Grip the edge of the counter with your palms down." Moving quickly, she did as I told her. I pulled her hips out so she was now leaning over, making her breasts hang dangerously close to the opening of her shirt. She was so enticing.

"Now hold still and don't move."

I went into the Bourbon Room, grabbed my iPad and turned on "Without Me" by Fantasia and played it through the bathroom speakers. The beat was slow and methodic, perfect for what I had planned for Goldie.

When I entered the room, Goldie's eyes met mine in the mirror and I could tell at that moment that she was already wet without having to feel her. She was lit up with heat, for me.

"I've been waiting too long for you," she said.

"With patience comes great reward, little one, a lesson that will do you well to learn."

I walked up behind her and gripped the back of her thighs, causing her jaw to clench and her eyes to close from the proximity of my hands. My thumbs ran up her inner thighs and just before they disappeared into her core, I pulled them away and ran them up her backside instead. As my hands ran up her plump ass, I dragged the hem of her shirt up as well, exposing her perfect backside.

Her breathing kicked up as I looked up at her and squeezed her ass. Her eyes traveled down my torso as she licked her lips. Her blatant display of need for me was empowering. I loved her willingness to show me how much I turned her on.

"Do you want me naked, little one?"

"Oh fucking hell, yes!" she breathed out as my hands made slow motions on her ass.

"Before I disrobe, tell me this, are you throbbing for me?"

She squeezed her eyes shut and nodded her head.

"Let me hear you say it."

She was still gripping the counter and leaning over so if I wanted to, I could set a glass of water on her back and it wouldn't teeter over.

"I'm fucking throbbing with need for you, Jett. I'm so wet."

"Are you sure? Should I make sure you're not lying?"

"Please God, yes."

I smirked as I looked down at her and could already see she was wet, I didn't need to test her out and I wanted her to wait.

"No, I trust your assessment."

"For fuck's sake!" she practically shouted.

The outburst warranted a slap to her ass so, I delivered. With a quick snap, my hand made contact to her exposed backside, making her moan out loud.

"Oh fuck me," she said.

"Can I expect any more outbursts from you?" I asked as I held up my hand.

"If it means I get slapped in the ass then fuck yes, because I think I just had an orgasm from that."

I leaned over her body and whispered in her ear, "You better not have because I didn't give you permission, now did I, little one?"

"No, but you can't go and slap my ass while there is a fucking pool between my legs and expect me to act like it has no effect on me."

"You're getting too lippy, little one. You can either mind your manners and keep your mouth shut or I can leave. Remember who runs the room in here."

Realization that she was falling out of her rule crossed over her features and she straightened her position and nodded her head.

"Mmm, it pleases me to see you submit so easily to me, little one. Because you're doing your best, I won't leave you waiting too long."

I pulled off my shirt and tossed it to the side. I watched Goldie the entire time in the mirror as I took off my clothes. Once I was down to just my boxer briefs and a rather impressive erection, I walked up behind her and rubbed my crotch lightly against her bare ass.

Her head dropped as she took a deep breath, trying to control her emotions.

"How do I feel, little one?"

"So fucking good. You seriously have the most beautiful dick I've ever seen."

That made me chuckle even though I knew she meant it as a compliment.

"Thank you. If you were in charge, what would you do with that beautiful dick?"

I continued to rub against her as she answered me, "I would reach behind me and start rubbing you out until I was satisfied with your length, then I would have you fuck me hard from behind the whole time looking me in the eyes in the mirror."

Pleasantly surprised with her ability to read my mind, I said, "It looks like we have the same idea."

I lowered my boxer briefs and let my erection spring free. Her eyes widened as she took in my length. She swallowed hard and then made eye contact with me once again.

"Before I let you stroke me, I have a couple of things I want to take care of first. I moved her so she was just a little farther away from the counter but not too far where she was uncomfortable. Getting on my hands and knees, I crawled below her and looked up to where her tits were hanging perfectly for me.

Reaching up, I was pleased to see her nipples were already hard so with my forefinger and thumb, I rolled her little nubs between my fingers. Her head flew back and she cried out from the pleasure that was shooting through her. As I rolled her nipples, I looked down at her pretty little pussy and noticed how wet she was. I knew I had no choice but to taste her so I scooted my body down and spread her feet with my feet until she allowed my body to scoot between her legs. My one hand stayed and attended to her nipples while my tongue flicked out and made contact with her pussy. Her legs buckled from my touch, making me smile. My hand that was not on her nipples, ran from the edge of her pubic bone and up her stomach lightly. I watched her abs contract from my touch and her breathing hitch from the ministrations I was playing on her body.

With great force, my tongue pressed down on her clit at the same time my hand pinched her nipple.

"Ahh, fuck!" she cried out.

My hand that was gracing her stomach, went around her backside and found her vagina where I inserted two fingers easily, thanks to how wet she was. It was an awkward position for me, trying to keep in contact with everything but I kept up with my fondling and licking because the noises that were escaping Goldie were perfection.

"Oh, Jett...oh, I'm going to come."

With that announcement, I pulled away and stood up behind her. Her breath caught as I left what I was doing. She remained calm though as I came up behind her. I grabbed both sides of her shirt and lifted them up to her back and tied them together so her breasts were exposed for both of us. They were a little pink from pinching them and I loved it.

"You're so fucking hot," I told her as my hand ran up her back and made her ass stick up even farther. "Do you remember what I told you in the car?" She nodded her head. "Do you know your safe word?"

Her eyes shot up to mine and she nodded her head, letting me know that she had no intention of using it which was a relief. I was still reeling over the moment that she said alligator, it would take some time to get over but we've moved on. We were moving on together and I was adjusting for her, so we could possibly see a future.

"Good. I'm going to fuck you, Goldie, and I don't want your eyes to leave mine. Okay?"

"Yes," she responded.

I entwined my hand around her hair so it was wrapped around twice. Her head tilted back slightly and I was nervous I might be hurting her so I asked, "Is this pressure good?"

"It's perfect," she responded.

With that, I didn't take my time. With one quick thrust, I entered her from behind, one hand in her hair and the other pressing against her back. She used the grip she had on the counter to leverage against each thrust of mine so it felt like I was able to go even deeper than ever before.

A hiss escaped my lips as I continued to pump inside her. Our eyes never left each other and I watched as her eyes glazed over from the pleasure I was giving her.

I was close as I felt my balls start to tighten and my jaw tick from trying to hold off but once I saw her mouth open from pleasure, I was fucking lost. I pulled tightly on her hair and fucked her, fucked her hard. Without permission, she screamed my name as her hips slammed into mine. I didn't care because at that moment, when her inner walls constricted around me, an animalistic grunt exploded out of me as I came inside her. It was earthy; everything about our orgasm was and I couldn't believe at the moment that every time with Goldie just kept getting better and better. There was never a dull moment between us and never once was I bored. I only craved her more and more each time.

Once we rode out our wave of pleasure, we paused and just stared at each other in the mirror. She was the first to break our gaze as she lowered her head and tried to regain her breath.

I released her hair, pulled the top of her shirt off so she was naked now and picked her up in my arms. She giggled as I flipped her around so she was straddling my hips and facing me. Her hands graced my cheeks and her lips found mine. Passionately, I kissed her back and pushed her up against the wall, starting to stir another bout of arousal over me.

This was how it was with Goldie, she was a man-eater who turned me into a crazed man who wasn't fully satisfied until I passed out.

It was going to be a long night.

15

"DO I WANNA KNOW?"

Goldie

Light filtered through my curtains as the morning fell upon me. I was sore, really sore but the best sore a girl could be because I was fucked last night in all the right ways. I looked around the room and realized, I wasn't in the Bourbon Room where I passed out but instead, I was in my room.

Disappointment greeted me as I realized that even though Jett might have claimed me as his, I was still not allowed to sleep over. Disappointment probably wasn't the right description, I was more upset. I really thought we made a connection last night, but I guess not if he wasn't even willing to share a bed with me. That was the whole reason why we had a fight, because he couldn't hold me, cuddle me and now that I'm lying here in my bed, naked and alone, I'm realizing that we are back to square one.

A lonely tear fell down my cheek as I tried to rein in my emotions. I tried to focus on the way he stared at me in the eyes with more than just lust last night, how he lit up when I walked into the room and how he made me repeat throughout the night how he was mine, but with all that even added up, I still wished he was able to put aside whatever past he had and move forward with me. It was gut- wrenching to know that he didn't want to share a bed with me.

I rolled to my back and stared up at the ceiling at the same time my hand landed on something that was not a pillow.

Screaming at the top of my lungs, I lunged back and almost fell out of my bed as I gripped the headboard. A head full of untamed, wild hair, popped up and the confused eyes of Jett Colby searched the room as he blinked rapidly from being startled awake.

"Fucking hell," I said as I eyed him.

His hand grabbed the bridge of his nose as he said, "Jesus, Goldie. What the hell are you doing screaming like that?"

"What the hell am I doing? What the hell are you doing?" I asked as I motioned at his naked torso.

Dear God, let him be fully naked.

Jett looked down at himself and then back up at me with such a panty-melting smile that I was instantly turned on and ready for him.

"I'm pretty sure I was sleeping with you until you went and started screaming like a banshee."

"Sleeping with me? When did you start doing that?"

I know I sounded like an idiot and that I wanted exactly what was happening but I was so startled, I didn't know how to react.

Lifting off the bed, Jett grabbed my arm and pulled me down so he was hovering over me, gently caressing my face.

"Ever since I put this around your neck." He thumbed my necklace. "This gives me the right to sleep in your bed, to pretty much do whatever I want."

My insides turned as butterflies floated around in my stomach from his touch. I was falling for the man and it was deadly. In a matter of hours, the man had made me feel more beautiful, needed and wanted more than anyone had ever in my life.

"Oh," I responded, still lost in the way he was looking down at me.

He rubbed my cheek and then looked at me with a questionable eyebrow.

"Were you crying?"

Quickly swiping my cheeks, I lied and said, "No."

"Goldie..." he drawled out.

"Okay, I was."

"Why?" he asked with sincerity.

"It's so stupid but I thought that you didn't stay the night and it seemed like everything we've been through was worth nothing."

Shifting so he was now on top of me, he responded, "Let's get one thing straight, everything we do is worth something, even if it's something as small as a kiss on the cheek goodbye. Everything between us matters and secondly, I know I've been an ass in the past but when I gave you this necklace, I made a promise to you that I'm trying, I'm trying for us."

I nodded as excitement bubbled in me from his words. "I was just thrown off because I was in my room. Why didn't we stay in the Bourbon Room?"

Jett placed a kiss on my forehead and said, "Sweet little one, the Bourbon Room is for playing, not for intimacy. I brought you down to your room to be intimate with you, to hold you, to feel your breath even out as you slept and to wake up to the most gorgeous woman I have ever laid eyes on."

"You're going to make me fucking cry," I admitted as I looked up at him.

"Don't cry." He kissed my cheeks and then my nose. This

was the Jett I wanted, the sweet Jett, the one who didn't mind waking up with me and dealing with my medusa hair and smeared makeup.

"Can I ask you something?" I asked as he kissed down my neck.

"Of course."

"Why didn't we just go to your room?"

I was so curious about what his room looked like, what was in there, how big his bed was, how he decorated it. I wanted to know.

He stopped kissing my neck and pressed his forehead against my shoulder. I shouldn't have asked because I could feel him tense up.

"It's okay," I said while rubbing his back. "You don't have to tell me—"

"No, I do," he interrupted me. "I want to be honest with you, Goldie, so I'm probably going to tell you something you don't want to hear. I need to take this slow, okay? I know you want all of me and I'm trying to give you all of me. I'm there physically but emotionally, I'm working on it. You have to give me time and bringing you into the only world that I have to myself is a big step. I just need some time to figure things out before I do that, okay?"

I nodded my head and continued to rub his back as reassurance. "I understand, Jett. I won't push you, I promise. I'm just so happy that you've decided to even give me this, give me the chance to hold you in the morning. I can't tell you how happy this makes me."

He smiled and kissed my nose.

With my index finger, I pressed the corner of his mouth where he was smiling and said, "This right here, this smile is something that I will never get over. You don't show many emotions, Mr. Colby, and when you do, I feel like my heart twists in my chest. You're so handsome and when you smile, my chest constricts with elation. You make me feel so good. You're mine, Jett, you're so fucking mine."

Smoothing out my hair, Jett leaned down and kissed me. When he pulled away, he said, "You're mine too, little one, all mine."

In one quick motion, Jett flipped me around so he was underneath me and his erection was poking at me, begging for entrance.

"Do you have something to say to me?" he asked as his hands ran up my stomach and started thumbing my nipples. Oh fuck yes, I did!

"Yes, what's for breakfast?"

Jett pinched my nipple, making me squeal in pleasure and laugh.

"Okay." I smiled and laughed. "I'm here to submit to you."

"Ride me then, little one."

I didn't have to be asked twice. I backed up and turned around so my back was to him now. If I was going to ride him, I was going to ride him right. He must have appreciated my spin of his demand because he groaned and started massaging my ass as I positioned myself. I stroked his cock a couple of times and then sat up on my knees and slammed down hard on his erection. We both moaned together as friction started to build between us.

"Your ass is so perfect," he said as I placed my hands on his thighs, bent over and started pumping up and down so he got a great view of what he just claimed was perfection.

"Oh, Jett. Oh fuck, this feels so good."

He didn't respond, instead he grunted some more and started matching my thrusts. Not being able to hold myself up in the position that I was in anymore, I sat up and arched my back so my hands were now balancing behind me. My tits were in the air as I continued to work Jett's cock.

In the midst of pleasure, I heard my door fly open, startling both Jett and I and that's when I saw Kace.

"Ah, fucking Christ!" He threw his hands up as I screamed and Jett yelled.

"What the fuck, get out of here!"

Jett was like a fucking naked ninja as he grabbed a hold of me, flipped me off his dick and covered me up so fast I wasn't sure if Kace even saw anything.

He was shielding his eyes with his arm as he held up his other hand in apology.

"Jesus, I didn't fucking know you were in here," Kace said as he tried to back out of the room.

Jett was out of bed and putting his pants on in no time as he walked toward Kace.

"What the fuck are you doing barging in her room like that? What if she was getting dressed, fuckhead?"

"She's late for practice!" Kace spat back as he straightened his posture and averted his eyes from the bed. In an instant, Kace grew defensive as Jett charged after him. Sparks started to fly between them and the testosterone in the room grew thick.

"That doesn't give you the right to come running in here. It's called knocking." Jett pushed Kace into the door.

Oh fuck. Rage poured through Kace's eyes as he charged after Jett. I was out of bed in no time with the sheet wrapped around my body trying to break up the fight. As I went to stop them, I tripped on my sheet and flung forward so I slid right between them with my hands out as if I was trying to slide into second base. A loud thump and grunt escaped me while I landed on the ground, nipples first.

"Jesus!" Jett shouted as he bent down and gathered my blankets to cover me up and then picked me up. He held me in his arms as he looked at Kace. "This is your one and final warning, don't you ever come fucking charging in here again. This is not your room."

Kace got right in Jett's face and spoke so close that I could smell the fresh soap of his shower coming off his body. I wouldn't mind a Goldie sandwich right about now with these two men. Holy hell, that would be hot.

"Just because your relationship with Goldie is different

now doesn't mean she can let the other girls down."

"Put me down, Jett. He's right," I said as I started to feel guilty. I shouldn't let the girls down just because I was fucking the boss. Well, more than fucking.

"No, I will not put you down," Jett retorted. "I will not fucking stand for the way he's treating you right now."

"Oh fuck off," Kace said as he spun around and headed out the door. Before he left, he turned back around and said, "You know I'm happy for you two but, Jett, there has to be a line. If Lo is going to be a Jett Girl, then you are going to have to treat her like one."

Jett was silent for a second as he pondered what Kace was saying.

"Well, then she's no longer a Jett Girl."

"What?!" Both Kace and I said together.

I tried to wiggle out of his grasp but Jett wouldn't let me go.

"She's no longer a Jett Girl, simple as that."

Kace threw his hands up in the air and said, "Whatever," and took off down the hallway, leaving me with the very overbearing Mr. Colby.

"Put me down." I scrambled until he finally set me down. He shut the door and stood in front of it with his arms crossed.

I told myself not to get distracted by the way his muscles were flexing right in front of me or the way his angry stare was fucking hotter than hell.

"You can't be serious," I said as I gathered my sheet and threw it on the bed. I walked into my closet and threw on some lingerie and a shirt, then went to the bathroom where I started brushing out the rat's nest that was my hair.

Standing in the doorway, Jett crossed his arms again and observed me.

"I'm dead serious. Your show days are over."

"No, they're fucking not," I spat back.

Jett came up behind me and looked at me in the mirror,

bringing up the memories of last night but I pushed them back and didn't let them distract me. Point, Goldie!

Lifting his hand to touch my necklace, he said, "The moment I put this on you meant that you are for me and me only. That means no more showing your body off for members, no more strutting your stuff and no more fucking lap dances."

"You're insane!" I threw my hands up in defense and then spun around to look at him, hair brush hanging out of my hair. "What if I don't want to wear this anymore?" I went to reach to the back to unclasp the necklace when Jett grabbed my hands and spun me against the bathroom wall.

His face was inches from mine as he spoke to me. "This is not a fucking game to me so don't turn it into one. If you take that necklace off, then it means we are over, completely finished. I will not have you using that as a scare tactic, do you hear me?"

I nodded and gulped at the same time.

Taking a chance I said, "Jett, I want to be honest with you so I'm going to tell you something you probably don't want to hear," I repeated his words from earlier, he understood the honesty we were trying to show each other. "You're being a possessive ass right now."

His head pulled away from my words. I tried not to laugh at the confused look he was giving me.

"Just because there is something between us doesn't mean you can control my entire life. I want to be up on stage, I want to be a team with the girls, it makes me happy."

"But I don't want…" I placed my hand over his mouth and stopped him from talking.

"I understand that you don't want other men seeing me, I get that but what if we compromise?" His eyebrow lifted in question but he didn't start yelling so I continued, "What if I take out all lap dances, save those only for you." I winked at him and continued, "And what if I wore more tasteful lingerie like Francy? Stuff that's not as revealing. Would that be okay?"

The tightness of his jaw and the tick of it that was going

off like a firecracker had me nervous but he finally succumbed and said, "Fine, but absolutely no lap dances, that's non-negotiable."

"That's fine," I said while hope sprang through me.

"Fine, but I don't like it."

"I know." I patted his face and kissed him on the lips. "But just think how great the sex will be after a presentation?"

I walked toward the door, to join the girls, when Jett stopped me and said, "The sex will always be great, little one."

If the girls weren't waiting on me, I would be jumping Jett's bones right now. The man was too damn sexy, it was hard to pry myself away, but I did with a kiss blown in his direction and my best hip swag to leave him begging for more. When I glanced over my shoulder, I saw Jett running his hands through his hair as he paced my room. Job well done.

***

When I went to the Toulouse Room to join practice, it was empty so I took the chance and went back to Kace's room to apologize and tell him the new restrictions on my Jett Girl contract.

Like usual, the hallway to his room was dark and creepy so I walked down it as quickly as possible. When I reached his room, I knocked twice and waited. I could hear him shifting around and then he called out, "Come in."

I walked in and saw Kace sitting in a chair with his legs propped up on the window sill. There was a guitar in his hands and he continued to look out the window as I walked in. When did he start playing the guitar? God, his sex appeal was at death con one level. Well, I would give him two, Jett was at one now that he introduced me to his panty-melting smile.

"Hi, Kace."

I wouldn't have thought he was affected by my presence since he didn't turn around from the sound of my voice but I did notice a slight stiffness in his shoulders when I broke the silence.

"What do you want, Lo?"

"I wanted to tell you—"

"Oh shit, Kace, I almost forgot my…" Pepper's voice trailed off as she entered from the hallway and saw me standing in the middle of Kace's room.

Kace stood up instantly and looked at Pepper with a death glare.

"Uh, sorry. Didn't know you were in here, Lo."

"Just talking to Kace about my new provisions."

"Cool," Pepper said as she nodded and looked around, avoiding eye contact, just like Kace.

Umm…this was awkward.

"Do you need to talk to Kace?" I asked as I started to walk toward the door.

"No, uh, I can just, um come back later," Pepper said as she continued to look around.

Her wandering eyes were driving me crazy so I looked around too. What was going on?

Realization hit me when I saw Pepper's purse on Kace's nightstand with her Jett Girl lingerie sticking out of it and next to the nightstand were three opened condom wrappers.

"Oh my God!" I shouted as Kace's hand flung around my mouth and Pepper grabbed her purse and headed for the door.

"I'll take care of this," Kace said as Pepper nodded and ran out the door, closing it behind her.

I tore myself away from Kace and looked at the guilty expression on his face.

"What. The. Fuck?"

Running his hands through his hair, he said, "It isn't what it looks like."

"Oh, is that right? Well, it looked like you fucked Pepper three ways to dawn, am I wrong?"

"Yes, it was four." Kace smirked.

I wacked his chest and said, "Does Jett know?"

"No, and you can't fucking tell him."

"You can't be serious…"

Kace got in my face and said, "I'm dead fucking serious," no more joking around now.

"Why would he care?"

"Because, he would."

Well, that didn't make me feel good. Jett shouldn't care because he was with me now, right? Isn't that how it worked?

"You're not making me feel really good about myself right now," I admitted.

Kace blew out a frustrated breath as he started to pace the length of his room.

"It's nothing against you, Lo. Jett just wouldn't be very fond of his buddy fucking a girl he used to."

"Then why did you do it?"

Stopping mid-stride, Kace turned and looked at me. "I don't fucking know. She was drunk last night, I was…feeling sorry for myself so we fucked."

"Why were you feeling sorry for yourself?" I pressed.

"I don't want to fucking talk about it," Kace snapped as his hands ran through his hair. "Just keep your mouth shut."

"Well, aren't you a ray of sunshine?"

"It's not easy dealing with your privileged ass all the time."

"I'm not privileged."

"Keep telling yourself that, sweetheart."

"You're just jealous Jett claimed me first."

Why the fuck I said that, I had no clue but it hit hard with Kace because he looked up at me and the stone cold man was gone and in his place was a man with damaged eyes.

Instantly feeling regret, I walked closer to him and went to apologize when he held up his hand to stop me.

"You want to know why I was feeling sorry for myself? Because the girl that I'm falling in love with went off with another man, committed herself to someone else."

Love? There was no way he was talking about me, not a fat chance in hell but as I stood there, thinking about what he was saying, his eyes roamed my body and I realized at that moment that

Kace was talking about me and all this time I just thought the guy hated me.

"What?"

"Forget it," Kace said while pushing me out the door.

"Stop! What are you talking about, Kace?"

"I said, forget it."

He opened his door and stood up straight when he saw who was behind me. I spun around to see Jett walking down the hallway with his hands in his pockets. When he looked up and saw me, his jaw tensed and he stopped in his tracks.

"What are you doing down here?"

Still thrown off with what Kace said, I stumbled as I replied, "I, uh, just wanted to tell Kace about my new role."

"I can handle that," Jett said as he came up behind me and wrapped an arm around my shoulders, claiming me right in front of Kace.

Heat blazed through me from the tension that was building up in the hallway.

"I just wanted to make sure everything was clear."

"Everything is, isn't it, Kace?" Jett said in a menacing tone.

"Crystal," Kace said as he pushed past both of us. "Practice in ten, Lo. That's if you want to join us."

With that, Kace walked off and left Jett and me standing in the hallway.

"Why were you down here?" Jett asked, clearly angry.

"I told you, I wanted to make sure Kace knew that I wasn't to do lap dances anymore."

"You don't need to come down here, Goldie. I communicate with Kace every day; I can take care of that business."

"Okay, sorry. I was just trying to help," I said softly as I entwined my fingers together.

I learned too much information in the past five minutes that my mind was spinning. I didn't have enough energy to try to sass Jett right now and stick up for myself. I was still reeling over

Kace's confession. He was falling in love with me? Jett hadn't even said that to me yet and he's had his tongue spread all over every orifice of my body.

Not really paying attention, I was startled when Jett grabbed me and pulled me into his chest. He kissed the top of my head and said, "I don't trust him."

I didn't blame Jett! But I didn't tell him that.

"No need to worry."

"I have issues, Goldie, issues that run deep and I don't like you hanging out down here. It isn't good for my head."

I had no clue what he was talking about but I felt the tension in his back and knew this was him trying to open up so I cleared my head from the past five minutes and focused on Jett.

I grabbed the sides of his head and said, "I'm sorry. I didn't realize this made you uncomfortable." I kissed his chin and continued, "I promise you when I say, you have nothing to worry about. I'm yours, Jett."

He nodded his head and the vulnerable Jett that I was beginning to love pressed his forehead against mine. There was something so special about a powerful man being able to drop his façade and break down in front of you. It made him real and it only made me fall for the man even more.

"You might have to keep reminding me." He pulled away and hit the wall with his fist, startling me. "Fuck, I don't act like this." His vulnerability turned into anger in a matter of seconds, slightly scaring me. "I don't show weaknesses, ever." Hello Mr. Moody.

"It's okay, Jett—"

"No, it's fucking not." He gripped his hair and slouched against the wall until his butt hit the ground. I looked down at him and was introduced to a new man, a deflated man, a confused one and my heart reached out to him.

Taking a chance, I sat down next to him and turned his head to face mine.

"This right here—" I pointed to us on the floor, "—this is

okay. It's okay for you to show me your weaknesses, to show my faults and your defects. That's what makes you human, Jett. You know all about my downfalls in life and you don't judge me for them."

"I wouldn't call trying to survive and provide for yourself after you lost everything a downfall," he responded. "I would call that being a strong individual and not giving up."

Well damn, he could make a girl blush.

"Still, though, Jett. I will never judge you..."

"You can't say that until you know the whole story."

"Then tell me," I practically begged.

He shook his head, making my heart deflate on the spot.

"I just can't. Not now."

"What are you afraid of? Are you afraid that I'm going to leave you?"

"Yes!" he shouted as he stood and started walking away, leaving me completely confused.

Shaking my head, I ran after him and grabbed his arm.

"Don't you dare walk away from me," I reprimanded. "You can't walk away from me. Remember, no fucking games. If I can't take off my necklace then you can't walk away from me. If you don't want to talk about it then fine but do not disrespect me by walking away."

Jett nodded his head, turned around and pulled me into his chest once again.

"I'm sorry," he muttered into my hair. "I'm so fucked up, Goldie."

"It's okay." I rubbed his back. "Just know that I'm not going anywhere."

He tilted my chin up and kissed me lightly on the lips. "Thank you."

Still confused about everything that happened this morning, I held on to Jett in the dark hallway that led to Kace's room. I don't know how long we stood there but what I did know was that I missed practice because as Jett escorted me upstairs, I heard the thump of the Toulouse Room music. I was going to have to make it up to the girls somehow because even though I wanted more than anything to be with Jett, I still wanted to be a Jett Girl and that meant dedicating myself to the girls just as much as to Jett. I wasn't about to give up my new found life for a possible chance with a guy that was quickly stealing my heart.

16
"FIND YOU"

Jett

"Come in," I called out after the peppy knock by Jeremy rang through my office.

"Hello, sir. How are you today?"

I looked up to find the man dressed in Magenta manpris and an orange checkered shirt. He looked like a bucket of sherbet. I shook my head and went back to signing my contracts.

"Fine and you Jeremy?"

"Good. Thank you for asking. I heard the event went well. I'm glad to hear it."

"Who did you hear from?" I asked, curious to know who my assistant has been talking to.

He leaned forward as if he was going to divulge one of the biggest secrets of his life and rested his hands on my desk. I sat back in my chair and studied the excitement rolling off him.

"I joined this Meet Up group in New Orleans—"

"Meet Up group?" I asked not knowing what the hell he was talking about.

"Yeah, it's a website where people who are looking to get out in the community and do things with others meet up, hence the name. There are so many different kinds of groups and they usually revolve around a particular interest like dog lovers or quilters."

"Quilters?" I asked with a raised eyebrow.

"You know, sewing," Jeremy said while making a sewing motion.

"I know what quilters are, I just didn't know there existed that many to form a group."

"You would be surprised at the kind of groups there are out there. Quilters Republic is tame compared to some of the other ones like Swingers and Lovers of Anal Plugs. It can get scary."

I held up my hand, not wanting Jeremy to explain any more clubs. He got the hint and continued with his story.

"So, I started attending one that revolves around personal assistants. It's more for us to network but what everyone mostly does is complain about their bosses and share secrets."

The hairs on the back of my neck tingled as I stood up and hovered over Jeremy who had the fear of God instantly put into his eyes.

"What the fuck are you telling me?" I asked, trying not to lose my temper but finding it quite difficult.

"Before you get all worked up," Jeremy said quickly. "No one knows I work for you. They think I work for some prissy-ass author."

Feeling better, I sat down in my chair and grabbed my glass of bourbon. "Continue." I waved my hand at him.

"Well, I made friends with some assistants to some really important people and was able to get the skinny on what's going down with Lot 17."

A small smirk crossed my face. "Am I going to have to give you a pay raise?"

"You might have to but we can talk about that later," he

said with a wink. "I was talking to Bernie Butler's assistant and apparently you got to him at the event and he turned down the offer your dad offered him. Since he is a member of the club, he didn't want to screw up any kind of relationship he had with you."

"Smart man," I responded, happy with my ability to put fear in another man.

"I also heard that the bidding process has been brought to the attention of the mayor and now that he's running for a second term, he wants to run an honest campaign, meaning, anything he hears that sounds shady, he's going to take it down so your dad's unsolicited bid of Lot 17 has been rejected and he is going to have to go about it like everyone else."

Jeremy sat back in his chair, crossed his legs and smiled at me.

"Wow, I am going to have to give you a pay raise."

"That or a gay cruise, all expenses paid for."

"Don't push your luck," I said as what Jeremy said to me soaked in. "That is great news. Thank you, Jeremy."

"Any time, sir. I feel like I'm just as invested in this program as you are and you know I would do anything for you. If it weren't for you, I would be out on the streets on my ass after my parents disowned me."

I shook off his comments. I didn't care for praise much especially when it came to me helping someone out. It was just a duty as someone who was born into a privileged life.

"Think nothing of it," I responded as I went back to signing more papers. It's all I ever did, scroll my name with ink every damn day of my life.

"Well, that being said, I have you and Lo set up for the Hopkins Social this coming Friday. I have already talked to Tootse about a dress and she is on it. Do you still want to bring Lo?"

"Yes," I said without even giving it a second thought. The past couple of days have really opened up my eyes to a new world which revolved around Goldie. I never thought I would see myself in such a vulnerable position again but I couldn't stay away, she was addicting so now, all I wanted was Goldie near me. It actually pained me to know that she was downstairs practicing and I was up here, signing my life away. I wanted more time with her.

"Oh okay, I wasn't expecting you to answer so quickly." I didn't respond so Jeremy cleared his throat and continued, "I'm not positive on the guest list but so far, neither your dad nor Rex Titan should be there and it's too late to RSVP so it looks like you will be clear to talk to some of the city planners."

For a moment, I forgot about my dad and Rex. I knew there was going to be a time when I would run into them again which wouldn't bother me. What would bother me even more would be running into them with Goldie, I didn't need to show any weaknesses and Goldie was a weakness, she was my fucking Achilles heel.

"Good, if they do show up on the attendee list you are to inform me."

"Yes, sir."

"Is that all?"

"I have one last thing. Kace told me I have to order and I quote, 'a shit ton' of gold lingerie. I'm a little confused."

I sat back in my chair and rubbed the bridge of my nose. Kace was being a total prick these days and it was starting to get on my nerves.

"Don't worry about it," I replied, not wanting Jeremy to get involved. "If that is all, you can leave for the night. Thank you for your hard work."

"Of course."

Jeremy took off and right when he walked out of my office, Kace walked in. He was wearing a pair of jeans, a tight shirt and a black baseball hat. It looked like he was going out which was confusing since he should be downstairs with the girls.

"What do you want?" I asked while flipping on one of the TVs that belonged to the Toulouse Room. An image of the girls practicing popped up on the screen and my mouth watered when my eyes zeroed in on Goldie sliding upside down on a pole. I made a mental note to have her dance for me later. "Why aren't you downstairs with the girls right now?"

"I wanted to come up here and let you know that nothing happened earlier."

"I know nothing happened. Goldie told me, I trust her."

"Well that's awfully big of you," Kace said as he sat in the chair in front of me.

"Is that the only reason you came up here?"

"Just wanted to make sure everything is cool between us."

"It's cool as long as you stay away from Goldie."

"You know that's going to be pretty damn hard when I have to work with her every day."

"You know what the fuck I'm talking about," I gritted out.

The smart ass had the audacity to smile at me.

"Well, Jett Colby, are you falling in love?" There was a bit of a sneer to Kace's voice, letting me know he was in one of his moods.

"Just leave her the fuck alone. I don't trust you."

"You don't trust me in what way? To make sure you don't act like an ass and help you see that perfection is standing right in front of you? To make sure Lo doesn't walk out on your ass because you're a moron? Or to make sure she is protected when you're not watching?"

"I know you like her," I said like a child. "I don't share and never will."

"Yeah, that's old news. I get that."

"Then just stay away."

"I am dickhead. She is the one who keeps approaching me."

From that announcement, my teeth grinded together.

"Don't worry though, she has eyes only for you," Kace said while picking at something on his pants.

"As she should."

Kace looked up at me and stared into my eyes. "She's too good for you. You're a controlling prick with a black heart who can't give her what she needs. You might be able to keep her happy now but she will need more. She always will need more from you, Jett."

Pain ripped through my gut as I thought about how right Kace really was. Goldie was special, a bright light in my dark day that I believed my mom brought to me and to know that I wasn't good enough for her was damaging.

"I know," I said while getting out of my chair. "But I'm going to do whatever it takes to keep her so get that through your thick skull. Stop waiting around for her and move the fuck along."

Kace stood up too and walked toward my door. "I hope you're right."

I didn't respond, I just let Kace walk back down to the Toulouse Room.

I turned to my monitors and watched the girls practice some more. Goldie was such a natural and she got along so well with the girls, she was the perfect fit for the club. She brought a new, revitalized energy that we needed, that I fucking needed.

I sat on my desk and looked at a picture of my mom that I had framed. It was from when she was ill but she still was a beautiful woman. Her face was the same shape as mine and her smile was bright even though you could see in the photo that she was in pain.

"Did you bring her to me, Mom?" I asked as I stared at the picture. "Is this your way of helping me move on? Did you choose Goldie for me?"

I would give anything for my mom to be alive, giving me advice on how to handle my feelings. She would know exactly what to say. Instead, I had an irritable ex-boxer with the hormones of a pre-pubescent teenage girl and a flamboyant assistant trying to guide me.

Jesus, I was so fucked.

17
"YOU MAKE ME FEEL..."

Goldie

"I need some more body glide," I called out as my inner thighs got stuck on the pole. "Oh fucking hell, my pussy is about to rip off."

"Drop off the pole," Pepper said as she came up to me with some more body glide.

"It's too late, there's no use in saving them," I replied as I released the pole and tumbled to the ground. I gripped my thighs and started rocking back and forth.

"You're such a drama queen," Pepper said as she spread my thighs and started rubbing body glide on them.

Placing my hand over my eyes, I said, "I can't look. How bad are they?"

"They're barely red," Pepper replied as she capped off the body glide.

"No way!" I looked down and was surprised to see that she was right. "What the hell? I could've sworn I left some skin on the pole."

Pepper pinched my chin and said, "You have to toughen up, girl." She then looked around and saw that the other girls were doing their own thing so she leaned in and said, "By the way, sorry about earlier. It was a drunken mistake that will never happen again. You can't tell Jett."

Here's the thing, Jett and I said we would be open and honest with each other and I wanted to be open and honest with him but who was I really hurting if I kept this to myself? It wasn't like she was cheating on Jett, because Jett was with me, therefore, it didn't really matter, right?

With the look on Pepper's face, the pleading look, I decided that it would be okay if I kept this to myself. It wasn't that big of a deal. It wasn't like Jett was still fucking Pepper, at least he better not be or else the man was going to be plucking his dick out of his ear once I got done shoving it in there.

"Don't sweat it, Pepper. Just tell me one thing, was it good?"

A smirk spread across Pepper's face. "I think Jett and Kace went to the same school when it comes to dominating in the bedroom because holy shit was he hot."

"I bet."

"Shouldn't you two be practicing?" Kace said, interrupting us and making us stand up straight, guilty as hell.

"Sorry," Pepper said as she walked off to her pole and talked to the other girls.

Before she started the music again, I called out to Kace. "Kace, can I talk to you for a second?"

"Nope." He took off to the back of the room, leaving without another word.

"Well, that was fucking rude," I said under my breath as I got up and followed him.

I was just pulling back the curtain when his hand caught

mine and said, "You don't fucking listen, do you?"

"You don't have to be rude, I just want to talk to you."

He let the curtain fall and he pulled on the brim of his hat as he looked at me. He was hot, like so hot that I wanted to just see him in the shower one more time, just for old times' sake.

"I told you I don't want to talk, can't you just leave it at that?"

"Not when you go and make confessions about—" I looked around and leaned forward, "—about loving me."

"Get over it, Lo. I didn't mean it."

"I don't believe you."

"Then that's your problem. Now get back on the pole and start practicing."

"You're infuriating!"

"And you're a nescient so do us both a favor and leave."

"Ughhhh!" I threw my arms up in the air and stomped away. There was no winning with him.

***

My body was sore, my thighs felt raw and my head was pounding from the constant beat of music that flowed through the Toulouse Room. Practice was rough and we didn't end until well after dinner time. Kace showed a spark of humanity when he brought us all dinner in the middle of practice and made us take a break. Other than that, we were glued to the poles, working on our synchronization and making sure our timing was on spot with every beat of the music.

By the end of the night, we nailed the dance three times in a row and we were happy with the way everything turned out so we said goodnight and headed up to our respective rooms.

I opened my door and was hit by the dim flicker of light coming from my bathroom. Curious, I walked toward the flickering and found Jett, sitting on my counter, wearing a pair of blue jeans and a tight shirt surrounded by tea lights that were lit everywhere.

When he saw me, he hopped off the counter and walked

toward me. He didn't have anything on his feet which made him that much sexier. He grabbed the lapel of my shirt and started undoing the buttons.

"You've had a long, hard day, little one. I had plans for you and me tonight which consisted of you dancing for me and then me fucking you up against the pole in the Bourbon Room but after the hard work you put in today, I decided to save those plans for another night and take care of you."

"What?" I asked breathlessly as he removed the shirt from my shoulders and let it drop to the ground. His eyes engulfed me, made heat crawl through my body.

His hands ran up my sides and went up to my face where he gripped my cheeks. "I want to take care of you, little one. Let me."

I just nodded my head because my throat was too constricted from the unbelievable gesture from Jett. It seemed like a normal thing for anyone to do but for a man who struggled with showing his soft side, with being emotionally passionate, it was a huge step and I could not be happier.

His hands went to my back and with one single flick, my bra was loose and on the floor. Heat poured out of him as he took in my breasts. I could tell his hands were itching to touch me so I helped him. I grabbed his hands and placed them softly on my breasts. A sharp intake of breath escaped him as his hands slowly started to squeeze my chest. My head fell backwards as he rolled my nipples with his fingers and tested their weight.

"You're so damn beautiful, Goldie."

"Thank you," I said, accepting his compliment.

"I need to test the water," he said while pulling away.

I watched as his tight jean-clad ass walked over to the tub and turned on the faucets. There were bubbles already in the tub but the water was only halfway full, I'm sure to save time. As he bent over to make sure the water wasn't too hot, I watched the back of his shirt ride up and show off a little patch of his skin. It was an innocent part of his body but it turned me on as if he took off every piece of his clothing.

I walked up behind him and ran my hands up his back on the inside of his shirt. His back tensed from my touch at first but slowly relaxed as I enjoyed the skin-to-skin contact.

"Did you have a good day?" I asked as I leaned over and kissed his shoulder.

"It just got much better," he said while turning around and placing a kiss on my forehead. "The water is ready." He leaned down and took off my thong, leaving me completely naked.

I could see how difficult it was for him to hold back and I appreciated it.

"Let me help you in," he said as he held out his hand for me.

"Wait, are you joining me?"

"I wasn't planning on it," he admitted honestly.

"Why not? Are you going to go back up to your room?" I tried to hide the hurt in my voice.

Clearing his throat, he said, "Goldie, do you really think I can control myself having you naked and wet in my arms? You should know me better than that."

"Oh." I smiled. "I don't care, I want you to stay. Please."

He shook his head and blew out a frustrated breath. "God, I can't say no to you."

"Good."

I started taking off his shirt and was pleased with the muscles that ripped underneath.

"When do you have time to work out?" I asked, marveled with the fact that he was so cut.

He chuckled and said, "Whenever I get a chance."

"Can I watch you one day?"

A quizzical eyebrow of his rose as my hands wandered around his chest. "You never seize to surprise me."

"That's a good thing."

Undoing his pants, I pushed them down and found that he wasn't wearing any underwear as his erection sprung free, making me gulp. He stepped out of his jeans as he continued to look at me with those devilish eyes.

"Now that was fucking hot," I said as I wrapped my hand around his erection and slowly started to work it up and down. A hiss escaped him from my touch but he didn't stop me, so I continued to work my hand.

In seconds, his length grew to a size that was almost impossible to believe. He was huge and it was all because of me. Talk about making a girl feel good.

His breath became labored as I noticed a sheen of sweat start to caress his skin. At that moment, I realized he was close to coming and just from my hand. Invigorated with a new sense of purpose at the moment, I dropped to my knees, placed my hands on his thighs and wrapped my mouth around his cock. I didn't give him a chance to adjust, I took in his full length until he hit the back of my throat and I pulled back out. His hands found my head and gently massaged my hair as I massaged his dick with my mouth. What he was doing felt so fucking good that I almost forgot what I was doing.

Snapping out of it, I ran my tongue down the underside of his dick and then lightly grabbed his balls with my teeth.

"Aww, fuuuck," he drawled out as he started to sway.

He was so close, so instead of giving him what he wanted, I pulled away from his balls and started to lightly flick my tongue across the underside of his dick all the way up to the tip. Pre-cum sat at the top of his cock and I licked it up with pleasure.

"Goldie…" he breathed as I decided to finally let him go over, even though I was enjoying having the power for once.

I took him fully into my mouth, squeezed his balls with my hand at the same time and sucked as I pulled up and down on his length. With one thrust of his hips, he let loose as a guttural groan escaped him and he lost himself in my mouth. He thrashed about as he lost all control. It was the sexiest thing I've ever seen.

Once he was fully satisfied, he bent down, grabbed my hand and pulled me into his chest. He kissed the top of my head and whispered into my ear, a gesture I was starting to love and count on.

"You didn't have to do that."

"I wanted to."

"Thank you."

He led me into the tub which we had to heat up again and then sat down. He grabbed my hand and helped me in so my head was resting on his shoulder and his arms were wrapped around my waist. I was in heaven. Heaven from being wrapped up in Jett, from being surprised by him and by performing a sexual act with him without having to submit first. Don't get me wrong, I loved submitting to him but it was nice to know that we didn't need to always have the Jett Girl rules hovering over us.

He rubbed slow circles along my lower belly as he kissed my neck.

"How are your legs? I saw that you were using them a lot on the pole today."

"They're sore," I confessed

His hands ran down them and stroked my inner thighs; I cringed from how sore just a light touch was. He pulled away and made me turn to face him.

"Are you okay?" Concern laced his face.

"Yeah, I'll be fine in a couple of days."

"Why did you keep practicing if you knew your skin was starting to go raw?" he asked, now looking mad.

"I can still have sex, if that's what you're worried about."

Now I knew he was looking mad because his eyebrows creased and he looked like he could kill.

"Is that how you see me? Some sex-crazed maniac who is only concerned about getting some pussy?"

"No, not at all. I don't know why I said that." I backpedaled.

"I care about you, Goldie. I respect the fact that you need a break, that you can't have sex with me every night. I get that, so please don't assume that I only care about one thing and one thing only because that is not how I want to be perceived."

He talked to me so business-like, it was strange. I didn't like it.

"I'm sorry. I don't see you like that. I'm just nervous that if I don't have sex with you, you're going to lose interest."

Where the hell did that come from? Was I trying to dig myself a grave? It was true, but I didn't have to go and say it.

His hand went up to my cheek and he pressed his forehead against mine.

"I'm going to be honest with you, little one. When I first met you, when I first saw you, that was all I wanted from you. I wanted your body but once I saw you for who you were, I wanted more. I want your body, your heart and your soul. I want everything. Just because you don't want sex one night doesn't mean that I will get bored, it just means that I get another piece of you that night. Like tonight, I want your mind."

"My mind?"

"Yes, tell me something I don't know."

He spun me around so I was pressed against his chest again and his arms were once again wrapped around me. His chin rested on my shoulder as he waited for me to answer him.

"Well, when I was young, I used to bring my mom's boom box into my room and I would perform my own radio station. I would speak in the attachable microphone and call off what songs were going to play next. I would also pretend to interview people using different voices then I recorded it all on a tape."

I could feel the smile that crossed Jett's face from my confession.

"Fuck, you're so cute," he said while pressing a kiss below my ear. "That turns this black heart a little more pure, hearing things like that."

"You don't have a black heart, Jett. You have such a warm heart, it's just a little scratched right now but it can get better. If you let me in, I would love to help heal it."

Breathing deeply, he said, "I would like that, little one."

My heart tripled in speed as he wrapped around me tighter and held on to me as though if he let go then I would float away forever. His lips pressed against my ear and he spoke softly.

"I'm getting lost in you Goldie and it terrifies me. You broke down a wall that I wasn't willing to let go and you did it so easily." He took a deep breath and continued, still speaking softly. "I can't stand the idea of losing you now."

"You're not going to." I turned my head to look at him but he kept my head forward.

"I want you to know that I would do anything to keep you safe, to keep you out of trouble. I live in a world where anything can happen and I want you to know that no matter what, I will always protect you. Always."

His cryptic message was slightly disturbing because it sounded like something you said before you broke up with someone but I chose to ignore that. There was no way he was going to do that because of the way he clung on to me right now, the way he spoke softly into my ear and sent shivers up my spine. He was opening up and it wasn't very often that he did that.

"You're always doing the protecting, do you ever let someone protect you?" I asked as I leaned back farther into his chest and looked up at him.

He kissed my lips and said, "Yes, right now, I'm letting you protect my fragile heart. All I ask is that you take care of it, little one."

The wind was knocked out of me from his confession. He trusted me enough to admit such a sensitive thing to me that I didn't even know how to respond. I would never do anything to hurt Jett, ever. He saved me when I needed saving, he took care of me when no one else would and he gave me the warm affection that I needed so desperately in my life. If anything happened between us, it was going to be his doing because I wasn't going anywhere.

"I will treat it as if it's my own, Jett."

"That's all I can ask for."

He kissed me again and we spent the rest of the night, holding each other and enjoying the soft silence that settled between us. We didn't have to talk anymore, we understood each other.

18
"GRENADE"

Jett

"Jesus, this thong is really riding up my ass," Goldie said as she lifted off the limo seat and started digging around her backside. "I can't seem to get a good grip. You know, you could order some underwear with just a tad more fabric. How would you like to wear fishing line up your ass all day?"

Shaking my head and smiling to myself, I watched her lift her gold floor-length gown up to her waist and reach behind where she found her thong.

"Sweet nipples, that feels good," she said as she pulled out her thong. "You have no clue what it's like to be a woman, the pain we go through to get a boner out of you."

"You don't have to do much, little one," I responded as I shifted in place. Her underwear hunting left her gown up around her waist, giving me an amazing view of her lower half which only led to my dick wanting to play. It was so easy when it came to Goldie, she really didn't have to do much.

Her head turned to my crotch and her eyes lit up as she looked up at me.

"My, oh my, where did that little guy come from?"

"You know damn well it's not little."

She placed her finger to her chin and contemplated for a second. "You know, I can't really remember. You should whip it out so I can refresh my memory."

"Nice try." I adjusted my pants. "We are almost there. Now put your dress down before the driver comes to open our door and sees something that's only meant for my eyes."

Being the vixen she was, she leaned over and pressed her palm against my crotch, making me shift back in my seat and take a deep breath from her brazenness.

"Do you really want to leave me hanging like this?"

"Like what?" I asked as her breath tickled my neck. She didn't kiss me, she just nuzzled me with her nose, sending chills down my neck.

"Like this." She grabbed my hand and put it inside her thong. She was drenching. My eyes rose in surprise as I looked down at her. She pressed my fingers inside her slick folds and hummed in my ear. "I need you, Jett."

I wanted to give her everything she ever wanted but I knew I couldn't this time. We were so close to the event and we were already late because I found her naked in her bathroom getting ready and I had to take her right then and there, up against the mirror. Her moans rang through my ears as I drove deep inside her. It was erotic, it was sexy as hell and I still wasn't satisfied. I couldn't get enough of her once I gave myself over to her.

Cupping her chin, I brushed a kiss against her lips and said, "I want nothing more than to bury my fingers deep inside that sweet pussy of yours but we are almost at the venue. If we weren't already late, I would ask the driver to circle the block but I can't."

Disappointment fell over her features as she started to push down her dress. My heart split in two from the look she was giving me.

"Please don't think this means I don't want you because fuck, I want you so bad." I pressed her hand against my throbbing erection. "I want you more than anything."

"I know," she said and then shook her head to clear her thoughts. She puffed her chest and cleared her throat. "Okay, sorry. I can just get carried away sometimes."

Needing to show her how much she means to me, I pinned her against the side of the vehicle and took her face in my hands. "When you get carried away, sometimes I feel like I'm the luckiest guy in the world. I look forward to when you get carried away, I just can't right now. I'm sorry, Goldie."

"It's okay, Jett. I understand."

I nodded my head and kissed her lips, lightly. I wasn't into kissing, ever, that was until Goldie came along. It was like her lips were magnets and my lips were metal, I couldn't stay away now that I had a taste.

The car pulled to a stop and I looked out the window, we were here. The Hopkins Social was one of the biggest socials of the year. It was to raise money for women's shelters, something I felt strongly about especially since my mom stayed in one for a while. I did whatever I could to help out the shelters around the city because they not only gave people a second chance but they saved lives. When my mom was first thrown out on the streets by my heartless father, after she gave birth to me, she had no money and nowhere to go. The Hopkins Society helped my mom find a shelter and gave her a place to eat and sleep while she tried to find her way on Bourbon Street.

"Ready?" I asked as I turned back to Goldie who was more gorgeous than ever.

"Ready." She smiled back at me.

Our driver opened our door and I stepped out first, then offered my arm to Goldie to grab on to. She plastered herself to my body as we walked together up the grand marble stairs of the Hopkins House which was also in the Garden District but farther east than my club.

"Wow, this place is breathtaking," Goldie whispered under her breath as we walked in the entrance. She turned to me and said, "But not as nice as the club."

"No need to flatter me, little one. You already have my heart."

Her eyes lit up from my words and she snuggled in closer.

We walked down the hallway to the main ballroom where the social was taking place. The room was lit up in greens and golds which scattered along the walls and the lighting was dim but still bright enough to see everything. The Hopkins Society always put on a beautiful event and they didn't disappoint this year.

"Mr. Colby, what a delight to see you," Marcy Ruttherford said as she stepped toward me, wearing a fake mink around her shoulders and a little too much makeup for a seventy-year-old.

"Ms. Ruttherford, I'm so pleased that you were able to make it out tonight. How are you feeling?" She's been struggling with her weight lately and there was speculation that she had cancer but she wouldn't let anyone in on her personal life so it was always a surprise to see her at an event and looking well.

"Oh, just fine, dear. Who is this beauty with you tonight?" She looked over at Goldie with a genuine smile.

"This is Goldie, my date."

"What a beautiful name, Goldie. It's so lovely to meet you."

Shaking hands, Goldie smiled and said, "The pleasure is all mine, Ms. Ruttherford. This is a spectacular room. The colors are gorgeous."

"Why, thank you, sweetheart. The committee always puts together a wonderful palette of colors and décor for this event." She looked around and waved to someone behind us. "If you will excuse me, I need to go play the part of gracious host."

"No need to play it, Ms. Ruttherford. You are just a joyous

host every year," I replied.

Placing a gentle hand on my cheek she said, "You're such a lovely boy."

She quickly took off and left Goldie and I to finish entering the grand room.

"She was so sweet," Goldie said as we walked toward the bar. The bar was always my first stop at an event. I needed a bourbon to get me through the night, especially when I had plans of talking to the Blarney brothers who were both city officials. I wanted to thank them for putting up an honest bid process for Lot 17. I was still reeling from Jeremy's information, actually I was elated. My dad tried to work his cruel magic and it didn't work. Smug bastard thought he could get whatever he wanted and he was put in his place. I couldn't be happier.

"Jett Colby, what is a sorry son of a bitch like you doing here?" I heard as I put in our drink order. I turned to see Diego standing behind me. He eyed Goldie for a second and then cringed. "Shit, sorry, I didn't know we were in a lady's presence."

"I see that Miss Mary's classes haven't been sticking," I said as I shook Diego's hand.

"It's hard holding your tongue for so long," Diego breathed out.

"I understand," Goldie said, drawing both of our attention. "You have no clue how bad I want to rip this dress off, spread my legs and chug this drink while spouting out fuck in every different language."

Shock crossed Diego's face right before he threw his head back and full belly laughed. He clapped me on the shoulder and said, "Holy shit, where did you find this treasure?"

"Diego, this is Goldie. Goldie, please meet the very well-spoken Diego Muenez."

Grabbing Goldie's hand and kissing the back of it, Diego said, "Goldie, you look awfully familiar." Diego eyed me and at that moment, I knew he knew Goldie was a Jett Girl but where I should be concerned I wasn't because even though Diego had a little too much swagger for my liking, I could trust him, whole heartedly.

Goldie on the other hand, was like a deer caught in headlights, not knowing what to say.

I pulled her hand away and entwined it with mine. "Ignore him," I said into her ear. Turning back to Diego, I addressed him. "What brings you here?"

"Same thing as you, man," Diego spoke honestly. He never met my mom but he heard me talk about her when I was trying to help him move off the streets and start a new life. He would pay his respects when he got a chance and I felt honored that he came tonight.

I nodded in appreciation and surveyed the room. "Anyone I need to look out for?"

"Coast is clear," Diego responded as he looked back at Goldie who was completely confused from our elusive conversation. "Now, how did you get wrapped up with the likes of this guy?"

Looking up at me with adoring eyes she said straight faced, "The tree trunk between his legs tricked me." She was clearly feeling comfortable around Diego and knew she could be herself around him.

Diego slapped his hands together and said, "Damn, I like you."

"Easy," I warned him.

He put his hands up in defense but still smiled.

"What do you do?" Goldie asked, being herself and I loved it. I hated that she had to suppress her personality around the other assholes.

"I'm actually opening up a kink club. We are a couple months away from opening and I couldn't be more excited. Still trying to find someone to help me paint some décor on the walls and I have to train the performers but other than that, we're going to be ready for opening day."

"Wow, a kink club. That sounds like fun," Goldie replied

while she tugged on my arm.

"Don't get any ideas."

Diego laughed and said, "There are private rooms for you two to hang out in if you don't want to do anything out in the open."

"When's opening day?" Goldie asked, at least I thought she did. I was distracted by the tall, dark figure that just walked in the door. My father.

I stiffened from seeing him and prayed that he didn't spot me but as he scanned the room, his eyes met mine and his brow creased in distaste. He pulled on his cufflinks and started walking my way.

Shit, I needed to get rid of Goldie and fast.

"Diego, why don't you show Goldie the paintings over by the garden," I interrupted.

Diego was about to chastise me for interrupting their conversation when he saw my face and then looked behind me. Realization hit him fast as he read in my eyes what I was trying to convey.

With a gentlemanly smile, he put out his arms and said, "Come with me, sweetheart."

Looking up at me in question, I nodded at Goldie and encouraged her to follow him. She leaned up for a kiss but I could see my dad out of the corner of my eye so I instead turned toward the bar for a refresh of my drink. I could feel her eyes burn a hole in my back from my rejection but I couldn't give her what she wanted, not when my dad was watching my every move.

Seconds later, after Diego guided Goldie away from me, I felt my dad's presence step up behind me.

"Jett, what a pleasant surprise."

Turning on my heels, I looked my dad up and down and said, "Wish I could say the same."

His lips pursed as he took in my comment. "That is no way to talk to family."

"I would hardly call you my family."

"Apparently, because I thought I taught my son better manners."

Not wanting to go around in circles, I said, "Is there something you wanted to say to me or can we go our separate ways?"

"I know you have a mole somewhere, digging up my personal business and you're not going to like what transpires from your meddling."

"I don't know what you're talking about."

"Don't toy with me, boy," Leo, my dad, said in a menacing voice. "When are you going to learn not to play with fire?"

I leaned forward and was smacked in the face by his expensive cologne; it had the ability to choke me with one deep breath. Steadying myself, I said, "When are you going to learn that even though you have money and you think you have power, you can't get what you want by bribing people? No one likes you in this town and no one actually wants to do business with you. They only tolerate you because of the status you obtained over the years."

Grinding on his teeth, he looked me up and down and said, "You think you're so smart, don't you, boy? Well, you're not because I have something I can hold against you that can tear you down."

"You have nothing," I replied with confidence. "I run an honest business."

Leo laughed, bordering on crazy as he took a sip of the drink that he was now holding, courtesy of the bartender.

"This has nothing to do with your business and everything to do with that fine little number you brought to this event." Leo nodded toward where Diego and Goldie I presumed were. My back was turned toward them and I didn't want to give my dad the knowledge that I knew what he was referring to.

"My date? What does she have anything to do with this?"

"Everything. I see the way you look at her, the way she was holding on to you. She's everything to you."

With my heart beating out of my chest and my blood

159

pumping at an abnormal rate, I tried to even my breathing as I answered my dad. I didn't want him to make any connection between Goldie and me because he would take no prisoners. I cursed myself as I thought about how I was right at first for not bringing Goldie to these events. I was so fucking right. I knew this was going to happen, that I would run into my dad and he would try to use Goldie against me. I fucking knew it.

Taking a deep breath, I said, "That's where you're wrong. She means nothing to me. She's the one who hit the jackpot tonight and won the honor of escorting me to this event. She is nothing but a cheap whore I found on Bourbon Street."

Leo nodded his head, with a sly grin. "I'm not buying it. I know she stays with you, shares your bed."

Trying not to grow agitated, I replied, "Like I said, she's nothing to me. She is a good fuck that I'm using until I get bored again which frankly I am. She offered herself up to me in the car and I wanted nothing to do with it. She's washed up."

Eyeing me like he was trying to see right through me, I held my stance, showing no tells.

Rubbing his chin with his hand, he said, "You surprise me, Jett. Just when I think that you're nothing like my son, you go and say something like that and I get the sense of pride that you are in fact my kin." He took another sip of his drink and then eyed me. "Either way, stay out of my business or I will find a way to take you down, even if that means taking care of the girls that you're...bored with."

With that, Leo walked away, leaving me with the chance to finally exhale. I ran my hand through my hair and thought about what just happened. Leo was onto me and it was frightening to think about what my dad was capable of when it came to Goldie. He showed no mercy whatsoever and wouldn't show any when it came to taking me down. If he ever got his hands on Goldie, who knew what he would do.

Swallowing a bit of bile that rose from the thought, I turned to look for Diego and Goldie but when I scanned the room,

I didn't see them together, only Diego who was looking around just like me. We spotted each other and started to converge together in the middle of the room.

When we stood in front of each other, I asked, "Where is she?"

"I have no clue. She said she wanted a quick drink and took off before I could go get one for her. Next thing I know, she disappeared."

"Fuck," I muttered as I grabbed the back of my neck and scanned the room again.

Fear pricked my stomach as I thought about where I stood and where the drinks were. Did she hear me talk to my dad?

"Holy shit, I need to find her," I said, forgetting all my manners. I was usually more eloquent but when I had fear pounding against my chest, I lost all ability to be a gentleman. "Where do you think she went?"

We both looked around the room and then turned back to each other.

"Go check the bathroom, I'm going to run a perimeter around the room and then check outside."

Diego nodded his head and we parted. I spent the next half hour searching for my little one in the gold dress but came up short. She was nowhere. I sent a text to Diego to let him know that I was headed back to the club to look for her. The short ride back seemed like hours but once we rolled up to the front gate, I blasted through the door and jogged up the sidewalk. I was about to enter through the front door when I saw a movement from the corner of my eye on the porch. I turned to see if it was Goldie and was slammed up against the wall of the club.

"What the fuck?" I shouted as strong hands pressed against my chest.

"I should be asking you the same thing," Kace's menacing tone breathed near my ear.

Lifting my knee and driving it into Kace's stomach, I was able to release myself from his ironclad grip as he buckled over.

"Where is she?" I asked, not willing to be very patient.

"Where do you think? She's in her room." Before I could move, Kace grabbed me and said, "Did you mean all that bullshit you said?"

"Are you fucking high? Of course not!"

"Then why say it?"

"I was talking to my dad. He threatened to hurt Goldie because he thought she was getting close to me which he's fucking right." Running my hands over my face, I breathed out. "I couldn't stand the thought of Goldie getting pulled into this fucked up mess so I did what I had to do, I made it seem like she meant nothing to me."

"But she does..." Kace stated.

"She means everything to me," I choked out, leaving Kace behind and walking up to her room, praying that she was still wearing her necklace but preparing myself for the worst.

19
"GHOST"

Goldie

My face was buried in my pillow as I cried uncontrollably. Babs was rubbing my back, trying to comfort me but it was no good, Jett's words rang through my head on replay. He actually admitted that he turned me away in the car because he wasn't interested anymore, that I was nothing to him.

I tried to tell myself that he wasn't telling the truth, that he was putting on a front because he's Jett Colby and wasn't used to being attached to someone but still, the words he spat out were so disrespectful, they hurt, no matter what context they were in.

The moment I heard Jett's words, I spun around, ditched Diego and called Kace to come pick me up. He was less than happy to be my personal chauffer because apparently he was in the middle of hooking up with someone but the moment he saw me, his stern face turned soft and he held my hand all the way back to the club, trying to calm my ragged breathing and saying sweet things to me.

When we got back to the club, he walked me up to my room which was where we ran into Babs. They helped me into my bed as I explained to the both of them what happened. Kace's face grew angrier each second and when I was done, he tore out of the room and never returned. I was nervous of what he was going to do, especially to Jett but I didn't care that much because my heart was ripping from my chest.

Once again, I was riding on the roller coaster that was Jett Colby and it just seemed like I kept getting burned.

"I'm going to rip his nuts off," Babs said as she continued to rub my back. I couldn't reply because my throat was too tight from crying. I wasn't much of a crier but when you embarrass me like that, when you insult me, it's hard for me to control my emotions.

"That's not necessary," came that deep southern voice from the opening of my room. I heard Babs gasp but I didn't turn to see who it was. His voice and aura ate up all the air in the room in one fell swoop.

"You have some nerve coming up here," Babs defended me.

"Save it, Babs. You're excused."

"To hell I am. I'm not leaving her with you."

The irritation in Jett's voice grew. "Have you failed to remember who makes the decisions around here?"

"Nope, pretty sure I remember it's a giant dickhead who walks around thinking he's better than everyone."

"Babs, I'm not fucking playing around with you. Leave," he gritted out, sending chills through my bones.

She hesitated before she leaned down to me and said, "I'll have a machete on hold if you want to use it." A small smile played at the corner of my mouth as I nodded my head into my pillow. I might just need that machete after I was done with him.

"Shut the door," Jett said as I felt him come closer.

I coiled up farther, as small as I could go because right now, I didn't want him near me, touching me. His touch was deadly to me. With one touch, he had the ability to make me forget all his past transgressions and do whatever he wanted.

The soft click of my door rang through the room, letting me know that I was fully alone with Jett now. The bed dipped as he sat down next to me, but I continued to look away. I didn't want to see him and I didn't want him to see me like this. I was a pathetic mess.

From the touch of his hand to my back, I recoiled away from him, trying to stay as far away as possible. I needed to avoid his heated touch; it was the only way I would be able to stay away, to keep my distance.

"Goldie, please talk to me."

The only noises escaping me were the little sobs that wouldn't stop, that kept drenching my pillow until it felt like the entire thing was soaked.

"Goldie, please…"

Nope, nothing was coming out, even if I wanted to. I completely lost it. Everything came tumbling down as I cried harder into my pillow. The strong confident woman I once was, was long gone and in her place was a meager woman whose life revolved around a man's touch. There were glimpses of the real me every once in a while but there was something about Jett that made me crazy, that made me into a different person that needed him so damn bad that if I didn't get all of him, I turned into a repressed, pathetic mess.

Jett's weight lifted off the bed and his footsteps retreated. More tears fell as I thought about how easily he was giving up. He could have at least fought a little harder, maybe explain himself. But that wasn't the stoic man's prowess, nope he walked away when things got tough and he never opened himself up so why would he start now?

I sucked in a deep breath as I prepared for a long night of

overthinking everything I did to deserve such treatment and trying to decide what to do in the morning.

Just when I was gearing up for a long night full of tears and heartache, Jett's silhouette stood in front of me and what I could see from my vantage point was he'd lost his tie and jacket and unbuttoned his shirt, revealing his smooth and muscular chest. He wasn't playing fair.

He sat down on my bed, and slid down next to me so our faces were inches apart and our bodies were feeding heat off each other.

His hand gravitated toward my hair and put it behind my ear, revealing my bloodshot eyes. Luckily, Babs was nice enough to wipe my makeup off so I didn't look like a crazed melting lunatic. I was still in my dress but my shoes were on the ground, along with my purse and phone.

"I'm so sorry you had to hear me say those horrible words earlier," he spoke softly, as if it actually pained him for what happened.

Irritated with him, I tried to turn away but his strong hands stopped me.

"Please just listen to me, Goldie."

Not saying anything to him, I stayed still and waited for him to continue. I was actually interested to hear his reasoning, to see how he dug himself out of this hole.

Pressing his hand against my face, he made me look at him and that's when I lost it because I wasn't looking at the strong man who dominated the bedroom and exuded confidence everywhere he went, no, instead I was staring into the eyes of a confused and lost man who looked like his heart was breaking in half.

I squeezed my eyes shut and tried to will the image out of my mind but there was no use, it was engrained in my mind, he was engrained in my mind.

"Goldie." His voice rang out tight, as if a vise was closing in on him. "Please look at me."

Mustering all the courage in my body, I opened my eyes

and stared into his pools of deep blue that were laced with regret.

He exhaled and gripped my face with both hands.

"You're fucking annihilating me right now. Seeing you like this, it's gutting me, little one." I tried pulling away but he stopped and looked down at my neck. His fingers grazed my necklace as he swallowed hard. "You're still wearing it." His gaze went back to my face, showing a broken down man, it was too much to take in.

"Goldie, I want you to know that what you heard was so far from the truth. I can't get into it too much because I will not allow you to get wrapped up in my fucked-up world but that man I was talking to would do anything to bring me down and he saw my weakness, he saw right through me and I had to deflect him, make him think differently."

"Your weakness?" I croaked out, my eyes growing heavy from crying for too long.

"You Goldie, you're my weakness and he saw that."

"How?" I sniffed.

Caressing my face gently, he said, "By the way I held you, looked at you, worshipped the ground you walked on. He saw it all and he fucking called me out on it." Jett pulled away, frustrated with himself.

"What does it matter?"

Turning back toward me, he answered, "Because he is dangerous…"

I huffed and tried to turn away again but he stopped me and pulled me back in his direction.

"I'm not fucking kidding," he warned. "He is a desperate man who would do anything and I mean anything to get what he wanted, even if that meant harming you. He wouldn't think twice about it."

The concern in his eyes made me realize that he was serious and not bullshitting me for his own benefit.

"Does this have to do with Lot 17?" I asked, trying to piece everything together.

"I don't want to get into that right now."

"That means yes," I interrupted.

Ignoring me, he continued, "What I want to talk about is what you heard and how everything about it was a lie. You're everything to me, Goldie. Slowly, you have widdled your heart into mine and have stolen every part of my body. You own me, Goldie, and there is no one that I want more, no one that I want to hold more and no one that I want to wear my necklace more than you."

A stray tear trickled down my cheek as I blinked away others.

"Why is it so hard?"

Rubbing my face with his thumbs, he said, "Because my life is so messed up that I just had to drag you into it because the moment I saw you in the cemetery, I couldn't walk away. So now you have to deal with my bullshit emotions, my inability to be the man that you need and horrible people in my life who want nothing but my money and power."

"You're so much more than that," I confessed, as I watched the strong man I once knew continue to crumble into a pile right in front of me. No wonder he kept this side away from me for so long, it was gut-wrenching to see him so emotionally drained.

Shaking his head, he pulled away a little and looked at something over my shoulder, like he was contemplating. "There is so much you don't know that I'm terrified to tell you and I know you need to know, to understand me, but I can't, I just can't, especially with everything that is going on."

"I understand that but you not telling me is slowly tearing me apart. If you only warned me tonight, I could have been prepared for what you said."

"I didn't think I would run into him there," Jett stated agitated with himself. "He wasn't supposed to be there."

"Well now that I know, I can be prepared for next time."

"There won't be a next time," he stated without hesitation.

I sat up and looked down at him. He avoided all eye contact with me.

"What do you mean there won't be a next time? Don't you have other events you have to go to? Don't you have some more ass kissing you have to do?"

"Yes, but you're not going."

"Because of one asshole?"

The bed rocked as Jett sat up straight and looked me dead in the eyes. "What are you not getting about this? He is a dangerous man, incredibly dangerous and has no problem getting rid of someone to get what he wants. I swore I would do anything to protect you, to keep you safe and I will live up to that. You're not to go to any events and you are to stay in the club until further notice."

"You have got to be kidding me. You can't keep me here like a prisoner."

"I'm trying to keep you safe."

"By secluding me from the world? You can't do that, I'll end up hating you."

His face contorted from my statement, as if I slapped him. "You don't mean that."

Blowing out a heavy breath, I grabbed his hands and said, "Jett, you out of anyone should know that I'm a free spirit, that I need my space, my time with my parents in the cemetery. You can't keep me in here. It's not fair."

Jett rolled on his back and stared up at the ceiling. I could see that he was trying to figure out what to do from the crease in his brow. I took that moment to scan his body. His shirt was parted just enough to show off his bare chest and stomach and his belt was undone, making my mind start to create an image of what was below the fabric of his pants.

"God damn it," he muttered as his hands ran up his face. I watched as his chest muscles flexed with each movement, enticing me.

Wanting to relax, I went to lie down when he wrapped his arm around my shoulders and pulled me into his chest. Reluctantly, I pressed the palm of my hand against his heart, making him intake a sharp breath. His other hand, curled around mine that was pressing against his chest and his lips found the top of my head.

"Please tell me you forgive me, please, little one."

The way his voice cracked made my heart leap in my chest. How could I deny him my forgiveness when he was clearly so torn up about what happened? I couldn't.

"I forgive you, Jett."

Squeezing me tighter, he pressed another kiss against my lips and then looked down at my dress.

"Can you please take that off, I really need to feel your skin against mine."

I lifted up and turned my back to him so he could undo the zipper. He understood my cue and undid the back. Within seconds, I was lying down next to him in only my thong and bra. He saddled me up to his side and ran his hand that was wrapped around me, under my thong and gripped my ass. Not in a sexual way but more in a way that he didn't want me floating away. His other hand entwined with mine and he brought the joining to his lips where he placed a gentle kiss.

My exposed skin pressed against his, where his shirt fell open and we just lay like that as I drifted in and out of consciousness, relishing in the feel of Jett against me.

In the midst of falling in and out of sleep, I heard Jett mutter to himself, "I will find a way, Goldie, no matter what, I'll protect you."

I curled in closer, wrapping my leg over his and gripped him, afraid he would leave in the middle of the night, but he never did. We spent the entire night holding on to each other and borrowing strength from one another as he fought our demons through the night.

20
"DELIRIOUS"

Jett

"Seriously, dude, you need to work on your knee blows. You barely touched me," Kace said as he played with the water bottle he was holding.

"Bullshit, you buckled over and started crying."

"Fuck you, I didn't cry. You wish I did. You were the one on the verge of tears. I saw the glisten in your eyes."

"Glisten? You're such a girl. Now put your damn hands up, I don't have all day."

"Testy today. I thought you made up with Goldie," Kace said as he put on boxing pads and held up his hands. It was our daily workout, one that was always at odd times because of my schedule but I made sure to meet up with him every day when I could because if the girls were working out, I needed to as well. Plus, it was nice to spend time with Kace, even though most of the time we got on each other's nerves.

"I did." We started dancing around the room as I punched Kace's padded hands, throwing upper cuts, hooks and kicks. "I'm just on edge, all right?"

"Have you heard from him?" Kace asked as he continued to move.

"Not yet, but I expect to shortly. It's not like him to wait so long to make contact. I don't think I threw him off too much."

"Right hook," Kace said, instructing me as to what he wanted. "You probably didn't. You haven't been able to throw anyone off since Lo's gotten here. It's been all over your face how much you care about her."

Plastering a sequence of three right hooks in a row, I finished up and then took off my gloves, shucking them to the side.

"I know, fuck. What was I thinking?"

"You couldn't have kept her and hidden her at the same time. You know that. You had to take her out, you had no choice."

He was right, there was no way I was going to be able to get away with being Goldie's and then not take her with me when I had to attend such mind-numbing events.

"I know."

Squatting down and then lying on my back, Kace kneeled next to me and started counting off as I warmed up with some crunches before I got into the heavy stuff.

"So if he does contact you, what are you going to do?"

"I have no clue," I huffed out as I continued to do sit-ups.

"She cares a lot about you," Kace stated as he handed me a ten pound medicine ball then stood in front of me. "Whatever you do, you have to talk to her about it because being the evasive ass you are is not going to fly with her. You can't get away with that now."

"Like I don't fucking know that. I swear to God you just

like to stand there and point out the obvious."

"Isn't that what friends are for?"

"Obviously," I grunted, now tossing the ball at Kace from over my head when I sat up. As I went back down, he tossed the ball back at me.

"Your dad is such a dickhead. He clearly knows that he's not going to get what he wants so now he's using all the options he has."

"Once again, thank you, Captain Obvious."

"Fuck off." Kace chuckled.

Whenever we were working out, Kace was always in his element, he was relaxed and fun. It was when he had time to himself that he started to brood and think about all his past transgressions, the demons that constantly floated above his head.

Once I hit my mark, I sat up and held on to my knees while Kace handed me a bottle of water.

"Push-ups."

"You just love bossing me around, don't you? I bet your old and tired ass couldn't do push-ups anymore."

I knew that was far from the truth but I loved pushing his buttons.

"Get fucking real." Kace tore his shirt off and stretched his arms. Copying the cheesedick, I did the same.

Like clockwork, Kace got into position and nodded to me to do the same. Sucker.

Side by side, we did push-ups, with our shirts off, trying to up the other as we huffed out. Upping the ante, Kace went to one-handed push-ups so I did the same, cringing from how sore I was from the entire workout before the apparent push-up contest. We both switched arms and tried not to laugh at each other. Kace would try to kick my leg when he got the chance and I would do the same but we didn't give up.

It wasn't until we both saw a pair of high heels standing in front of us that we stilled and looked up.

I could pick those legs out from anywhere. Standing in

front of us was Goldie, in her Jett Girl attire and mask. She was sporting a giant smile as she tapped her foot and waited for us to finish.

We stood together and brushed off our hands as we tried to play off what we were doing wasn't a pissing match.

"Oh, please, don't let me interrupt you two," she said as she perused my body with those blazing blue eyes of hers through her mask. It boosted my confidence to know that her eyes were only closed in on my body, especially since Kace was standing next to me with his shirt off as well.

Clearing my throat, I said, "May we help you, Lo?"

Her nose twisted from me using her Jett Girl name. It was weird to me too but around everyone else, that was what I called her, no exceptions.

She held out her arm and handed me a letter. "Jeremy had to bolt so he asked me to give this to you."

Without even having to look down at the note, I knew what it was. Casually, I took it from Goldie and thanked her.

"So, you guys can go back to what you were doing," she said while she licked her lips, enticing me to bring her up to the Bourbon Room. That's what she did every damn day of my life.

"Don't you have some practicing to do?" Kace asked, noticing the letter as well and helping me out because right now, I was seconds away from grabbing Goldie and dragging her upstairs.

"Shock alert, Kace doesn't want to have any fun," Goldie said sarcastically as she waved her hands in the air.

Looking over at Kace, I saw the irritation start to bubble. The man had a short fuse. The tension between Kace and Goldie would get bad if I didn't intervene so I grabbed Goldie's hand, pulled her in for a sweaty hug and gave her a kiss on the head.

"Get out of here, little one, before he explodes," I whispered into her ear, making her chuckle.

Before parting, she looked up at me and said, "God, you're so fucking hot." She kissed me and then took off. I watched her little body walk away from me and was apparently caught up in her man-eating swagger because Kace smacked the side of my head to get my attention.

"Fuck," I said as I held my head and turned to him. "What the hell?"

"Focus, dickweed, what is in the letter?"

If he wasn't such a brother to me, I would be kicking his ass out of here but that would never happen, even though he was an ass, he was the only true family I still had.

Opening up the letter, I shut the door to the workout room, took a deep breath and read the letter out loud.

Jett,

It was an honor to see you the other night. It's always a prideful moment for a father to see their son succeed in life and find someone who can make them a better man.

You can deny it all you want but I know how that girl makes you feel, there is no question about it that she means everything to you, despite what you tried to portray. It's all in your eyes, son.

So, you have two choices, you can either back away from Lot 17 and let me have it, or I can take Goldie for myself. It's only a matter of time until I take her away from you, it just depends on when it is.

Your choice, son, I hope you choose wisely because I would hate to see that pretty little girl in the hands of my associates, or better yet, in the hands of Rex Titan.

Your Father

"Motherfucker," Kace mumbled as his hand drove through his hair.

"Fuck…"

"What are you going to do?" Kace asked, grabbing us both a water.

"The only thing I can do. She needs to leave."

21
"I WILL BE"

Lo

"Are you kidding me? This does not fit me, Tootse. There is no way Jett will let me wear this outside of this dressing room," I said as I stood backstage while Tootse did a fitting for an outfit that I was supposed to wear in two nights.

It's been a week since the "incident." It almost seemed like every couple of days there was an incident between Jett and me but ever since the big one, there haven't been any. He's been more withdrawn and he's been doing a lot of talking on his phone but in a secretive way. I didn't like it. I felt like he was planning something and was waiting to break the news to me.

"Yeah, this fabric isn't as stretchy as I thought it was going to be," Tootse mumbled as pins stuck out of her mouth. "I think I have to scrap the whole thing."

"Do you have time for that?" I asked, trying to make sure my nipples weren't showing.

We had a still life presentation coming up in two nights and we were supposed to resemble trees. We were going to get our bodies painted and Tootse was making dresses that had ivy hanging down them but the fabric underneath wasn't cooperating over my curves at the current moment, making Tootse's life difficult.

"I don't but I can make it work…somehow," she said while studying the dress.

"Ohhhhh gooooood," Babs moaned as she flopped herself on the floor, right in front of me. She was wearing standard Jett Girl gear and was holding her stomach. "I ate way too much."

"A plate of gumbo and two pieces of pecan pie will do that to you," Pepper said as she walked in, wearing the same gear.

"You know I love pecan pie. Chef was tempting me, that evil bastard—."

"Kace is going to kill you," Francy said while staring at Tootse's ass.

"Why?" Babs said while looking up at Francy.

Francy tore her eyes off Tootse to say, "Because, your stomach has grown about five inches in the past hour."

Babs looked down and poked her stomach and laughed. "Fuck, you're right. Oh well. I'm on my way out anyways."

The room grew silent as we thought about Babs' words. It wouldn't be the same without her. We were a family and it would be sad to lose Babs, really sad.

"Ah fuck it, where's the tequila," Babs shot off as she started feeling around the floor, thinking there was alcohol around her.

"I think there is some back here," Pepper said as she started poking around behind the curtains.

"Don't even think about it," Kace's voice sounded off as he appeared as if out of nowhere. "Don't you girls have some studying to do? Pepper, I know you do."

"Yeah, studying of your body," Francy mumbled, causing Pepper to smack her leg and give her an evil glare.

Kace must not have heard her because he seemed unaffected. His eyes scanned the room and when they landed on Babs, his brow creased.

"What the hell is wrong with you?"

Babs lifted her shirt and showed off her stomach. She patted it with pride and said, "About to give birth to two pecan pies and a bowl of gumbo."

Kace gave her a disgusted look as she slowly pulled herself off the floor, saluted us and went off to do who knew what. I tried not to think about it because I was too grossed out. I loved Babs, I really was going to miss her.

"Wow, stare much, "Francy said to Kace. I looked up and saw him tear his gaze away from me and clear his throat.

"Get upstairs, Francy and Pepper, you two have an exam tonight."

"Tyrant," they muttered as two other Jett Girls walked away. Kace was plucking them off one by one.

"Tootse…" Kace said, indicating that it was time for her to leave as well. If I didn't know any better, I would have thought Kace was trying to get me alone.

"Yeah," she called over her shoulder as she continued to pin my dress and study it.

"Don't you have something you have to do?"

"Yeah, it's called what I'm doing right now. I highly doubt Jett would want Lo to do a presentation with only body paint on."

"That's right, I wouldn't," Jett said in his deep southern voice, shocking us all. He never came down to the Toulouse Room so to see him backstage was a little surprising. Looking up at me, he winked and then turned to Kace and Tootse. "No need to continue, Tootse, she won't be needing the dress."

"Ooo, I get to be naked," I said clapping my hands, earning a scowl from Jett.

"No, you're not going to do the presentation."

I turned to Kace who turned to Jett who looked at me with determination. What the hell?

"Okay, soooo, does this mean you're firing me? Because if that's the case, I demand to do a recount."

"A recount?" both Jett and Kace asked at the same time.

"Yeah, you know, from the dick committee. Isn't that where you go to make all your dickhead decisions?" I asked Jett.

Man, I was feeling spicy today. Tootse giggled below me while still pinning my dress, even though apparently I didn't need it.

"Would you mind leaving us alone?" Jett said to Kace and Tootse but kept his gaze on me.

Kace patted Jett's back and said, "Good luck, man, she seems to be in a mood."

"Hey, Kace," I called out as he started to walk away. He turned so I could barely see his face. "Why don't you try calling up that redhead again, it seems like your little dicky doo da needs a red-flamin whoo-ha to warm it up a bit." Like an immature teenage boy, I put my finger at my crotch height and wiggled it around.

The corner of his mouth twitched as he shook his head and walked away.

Laughing, Tootse got up, gathered her things, sent me a wink and left, leaving Jett and me to ourselves.

When I turned to gauge Jett's mood, I couldn't tell what he was thinking. His face was blank of emotion.

"So, catch that football game?" I asked, trying to fill the silence in the room. I hated awkward silences. "Yeah, me either," I continued. "Interesting fact, did you know the Superdome is one of the biggest enclosed arenas in the world? Yeah, weird, huh? It's like the ninth wonder of the world, right in our backyard."

"Eighth," Jett said as he came closer.

"Eighth?"

"Yes, it would be the eighth wonder of the world, if that was the case." He inched even closer.

"No, it would be the ninth. The eighth is sitting in your

pants right now." I shrugged my shoulders and gave him a cheesy smile as I tried to refrain from spouting off a "yuck-yuck" kind of laugh.

His hand found the small of my back and pulled me to him. The smell coming off him was intoxicating as I got lost in his presence, something I found so easily to do.

"Your lips are a little loose today, little one."

"Yeah, well, when you deny me your dick, I start to go crazy. Please impale me so I no longer lose my mind. Your dick is my only cure," I said as I held on to the lapels of his jacket.

"You're never going to get what you want when you ask like that."

His lips ran the length of my jaw, setting my nerves on fire as my toes curled from his five o'clock shadow brushing against my soft cheek.

"Uhh, what?" I asked, forgetting what I was trying to say.

"I need to talk to you." His lips found mine and he gently nipped on them before turning to the other side of my jaw to work his magic.

"Um, talking…what. Ooo, yeah. Is that your tongue?"

Jett pulled away and looked me in the eyes. "It seems like someone is going to put up a fight tonight in the Bourbon Room. You've been rather talkative."

Breathing heavily from his attack on my nerves and the way he pulled away so fast, I said, "I thought we were supposed to talk? I'm so confused. Why aren't you kissing me anymore? More kisses." I puckered my lips and started kissing the air.

A small smile crossed his face as he gave in and pressed his lips against mine. I could not get enough of this Jett, of the affectionate and passionate one. Don't get me wrong, I lived to see the dominant, protective Jett but I could not help but crave his gentle touch as well.

Pulling away again, he pulled me into him and wrapped his arms around my body so I was buried into his shoulder. I felt the tension in his back as I held on to him, drawing concern from me.

"What's wrong?"

Exhaling, he kissed the side of my head and said, "Do you remember Diego from the other night?"

"Yes, is everything okay with him?" I was nervous that whoever the devil man that Jett was talking about the other night might have gotten to Diego. Not that the old man had much of a chance. Diego was grade A man meat with muscles that didn't end for days. Although, old man could have hired someone but then again, Diego would be the guy I would hire to take someone out so I didn't see how he could possibly...

"Goldie," Jett said, interrupting my thoughts. "Please pay attention."

"Sorry."

"Like I was saying, you're going to have to go over there starting tomorrow."

"Wait, what?" I asked pulling away. I missed a big part of that conversation.

"Are you paying attention now?" he asked, growing frustrated with me.

"Yes."

"Diego needs some help with his kink club. He needs someone to help him with some paintings around the club and I knew you would be perfect to help him. It does mean that you're going to have to put your Jett Girl duties on hold and stay there."

"What?!" I shot off him, exposing a tit because the dress I was wearing had no forgiveness. I covered up quickly and put my hands on my hips. "I'm not going anywhere."

"Goldie, this is not up for negotiation."

"To hell it isn't! You can't tell me what to do. I make my own decisions," I said defiantly as I held up my chin and turned to sit on a chair. I crossed my arms over my chest and turned away from him. Yup, I looked like a two-year-old throwing a tantrum.

I could feel the agitation flowing off Jett as he walked toward me, trying to stay calm. I had to give him credit for reining in his feelings. I did a good job of pushing him over the edge and right now was no exception.

Placing both hands on my thighs and squatting down to look at me, he said, "I know you do but I need you to do this. I need you to help him out."

"Just tell me what this is really about. Just say it, you don't want me here anymore."

God, I sounded so whiny.

"You know that's not true so don't go accusing me of such lies."

"Then what is this about?"

"It's about helping someone out for me and…" He trailed off as he grabbed the back of his neck and tried to phrase his next sentence to his liking.

"Just fucking say it." I threw my hands up in frustration. "I can handle whatever you're going to say, I'm not a child."

"You sure are acting like one," Jett said quickly.

"Oh, is that how it's going to be? Well, you're a giant dick."

Groaning, he ran his hands over his face and said, "Can we please have a conversation without getting into a stupid fight?"

"Sure. All you have to do is not be a chauvinistic ass who thinks he can control everyone."

"Jesus!" Jett threw his hands in the air as he stood. "I'm just trying to fucking protect you. Can you let me do that?"

I opened my mouth to shoot back at him but I could visibly see the frustration and pain he was going through so for once, I shut my mouth and walked over to him. His back was toward me so I wrapped my arms around his waist and pressed my cheek against his back.

"I'm sorry. I was just thrown off by the fact that you want me to leave."

"I don't want you to leave," he said while turning around in my arms. "I want to keep you with me at all times, next to me, holding me, whispering in my ear and mouthing off to me." I laughed as he continued, "But I need you to do this, not just for

Diego but for me. Things are starting to get serious and even though I need you, I need to protect you because if something ever happened to you, I wouldn't know what to do with myself."

"What does that mean?"

He took a deep breath and said, "It means, I need to make it look like we're no longer in each other's lives."

"Are you serious?" I asked as tears started to form in my eyes.

Kissing each eyelid, he said, "Please don't cry, little one. I don't want to do this but I don't have a choice in the matter. Please just do this for me, for us."

"For how long?" I asked as I thought about how all of this came out of nowhere.

"Until I get everything settled. It's my number one priority. And it's not like you're going to be alone, I talked to Diego and you'll have a good time painting and being the amazing artist you are. The time will go by quickly."

"No, it won't because I won't have you."

"I will still come to see you. I will try to be there almost every night. There is a back door to the club that will hide my entrance. No one will know. I just need to make it seem like you're not a Jett Girl anymore."

"So you're firing me."

"No, little one. You're just taking a break until I figure everything out." He tilted my chin up and placed a kiss on my lips. "This is all my fault because I couldn't stay away, because I couldn't deny myself these lips and this body." His hands ran up the length of my sides. "I fucked everything up."

"You really did," I said with a chuckle, making him smile.

"I'm sorry."

"You owe me." I played with his tie.

"Can I start making it up to you tonight?"

"Hmm…can I tie you up and have my way with you?"

"Fat chance in hell, little one," he said while pinching my ass and guiding me to the back stairs that led up to the third floor.

22
"FAITH"

Goldie

Silence circulated through the car as I drove with Jett over to Diego's new club with some of my possessions and mainly clothes. I only had two suitcases but it felt like my whole life. This was not what I wanted at all and it all felt like the beginning of the end so to say I wanted to throw up was an understatement. I was sweating, I was terrified, I didn't want to leave him. He was a constant solid in my life now that I depended on and to not have him near me, to have to act like he means nothing to me was like twisting a knife into my heart.

The streets were barely lit and there were still some late night partiers that flanked the streets of New Orleans. Soft lanterns lit up the roads, casting a glow on the trash left over from the night shenanigans. When Jett said I had to leave "tomorrow" he apparently meant first thing tomorrow because we were riding around at three in the morning. He said we couldn't do this in the middle of the day if I wanted him to get me situated which I understood but it was all happening so fast. I didn't even get to say goodbye to the girls or Kace for that matter. Not that I really wanted to say bye to the giant asshole that graced the hallways of the Lafayette Club but it would have been nice to have the option.

My hand was entwined with Jett's as we rode in silence. I knew he could sense my uneasiness so he sat close to me and would occasionally lean over to whisper in my ear or kiss me gently on the cheek.

The car came to a stop as we sat in an abandoned back alley. We weren't on Bourbon Street but we were in the French Quarter and not the nicest part. This was where his club was?

"This is just the back entrance," Jett murmured as if he could read my mind. "The club's front sits on Royal Street and is marked as a plain door. Only the people who are a part of Diego's secret society will know about it."

"Sounds intriguing. Are we near Burgundy Street?" I asked, looking around.

"Yes."

I nodded my head as I was able to place my surroundings. Royal was one street parallel with Bourbon and was considered to be the fancier street of the French Quarter where little boutique's and galleries were located. It was odd, to travel from Bourbon Street where drinkers were pelvic thrusting each other and watching street performers and then walk one block down to Royal where ladies in sweater sets perused the art galleries where pieces of art work were priced well into the thousands. Only in New Orleans.

The car door opened and I reluctantly got out. Our driver grabbed my luggage and led us up the back rickety stairs of Diego's club.

When we reached the top, I saw a dark silhouette standing in the doorway, waiting for us.

"Diego," Jett said as he reached his hand out.

"Jett, good to see you."

"Thank you for helping me out," Jett said quietly.

"Helping you out? Are you kidding me, I will be putting this little girl to work. Come in." Diego winked at me and led the way into his club.

It was nothing compared to the grandiose-ness of the Lafayette Club. It was a step up from Kitten's Castle but I for sure would be slumming it compared to what I was used to now which was ridiculous. I should be happy because Diego's club was beautiful, it just wasn't the Lafayette Club.

We walked down a long, dark hallway that had multiple rooms coming off it. The walls were a deep red with a chair railing halfway up the wall. On the bottom half of the wall, it was painted black and from what I could tell, the floors were black as well. I was really intrigued.

Lights started to ignite throughout the room through gas lanterns, were those allowed indoors? As the light filled the room, I took in my surroundings. We were standing in a circular room with tables lining the outside of it. To the back was a giant curved bar that lined the room and in the ceiling were circular apparatuses like we had at the Lafayette club but there were so many more.

"Welcome to Cirque du Diable," Diego said as he held out his hands.

"Wow," I breathed in as I took in everything.

Long, blood red velvet drapes were cascading down the walls and were tied together where there were doorways. We were standing on a dirt service which was interesting to see in an indoor environment but I was getting the whole vibe. It was like a vintage circus and at that moment, a little bit of excitement blossomed in me.

"Diego, you've really outdone yourself. The place looks amazing," Jett complimented as he looked around.

"Thanks, I owe it all to you, man. Without your help and encouragement, I never would have been able to make this happen."

Jett just nodded, once again passing off his helpfulness as if it was nothing.

"When do you open?" I asked, still taking everything in.

Along with the gas lamps, there were big-bulbed string lights hanging through the ceiling and there were old time typed posters that you would see at a vintage circus, decorating the tables. I wanted to hang out here, it seemed amazing.

"A few months, hopefully. I have to add a few touches with your skillful hand and then practice with the dancers."

"Dancers?" I asked, feeling a little more comfortable.

"Not what you're thinking," Jett mumbled into my ear and wrapped his arm around my shoulder. "Where will Goldie be staying?"

"This way," Diego said, ignoring my question. What was with that? Dancers were dancers, right?

We walked up another flight of stairs which surprised me since the ceilings on the floor we were on were so tall but once we got to the top, I noticed it was an attic space that was converted into a small bedroom and bath. It was quite small but would do. I wasn't going to be a brat about it.

"Where is your room?" Jett asked, looking around.

"On the first floor." Diego chuckled. "Nothing to worry about and look, this door even has a lock so I won't be able to flank her in the middle of the night like the thoughts that are running through your head."

Jett turned to me and smiled. "Make sure to lock up every night."

"I thought you would be staying with me," I said in a whiny tone.

"Here," Diego interrupted, handing Jett a key. "Here are two keys to the room, do what you want with them. I will let you two have a moment. I'm going back to bed. I will see you in the morning, Goldie, well later in the morning."

With that, Diego shut the door and left me alone with Jett. I felt like crying, I didn't want him to leave. Even though Diego was a nice guy and had a pretty cool place, I didn't want to lose Jett. I depended on him and losing him like this, being separated was bringing up horrible feelings of when my parents were taken away from me.

"I hate this," I admitted as I buried my head in his chest.

"I know, little one. I hate it too."

"Then just let me stay with you…"

"You know that is not an option right now, Goldie. Please don't ask again because it's killing me to say no to you," he said roughly.

"I'm sorry. It just seems like I'm losing you and it's bringing up horrible past images of when my parents were taken away from me and I could do nothing about it."

Taking a long, deep breath, Jett gripped me tighter and said, "I'm sorry. Fuck, I'm so sorry this is hurting you. It's hurting me too but please trust me. You trust me right?"

He pulled away to look me in the eyes as I answered. I swallowed hard and nodded my head.

"I trust you, Jett."

"Good."

He grabbed my suitcase and opened it up.

"Wow, you could at least wait to unpack me," I semi-joked.

"I wanted to give you this," he said as he handed me a wrapped present.

"Hey, when did that get in there?" I looked over the suitcase, trying to see if there were any more hidden presents in there.

"Don't worry about it and just open it."

Like a little girl during Christmas, I ripped open the present and gasped when I saw what was inside.

In a green frame, was a picture of Jett and me at our first event together. His arm was wrapped around my waist and he was leaning into my ear, saying something while a giant smile lit up my face."

"This picture was sent to me after the first event we went to. I have the same one on my desk and I wanted you to have one, to put on your nightstand. I want you to remember this moment. I want you to remember the way my arm felt wrapped around you, the way my breath caressed your skin as I whispered into your ear and the way pure elation flowed through your body from it. Memorize it, little one, and carry that around with you because once I leave here, things are going to become complicated and I want you to know that no matter what happens, I will always be yours, always."

"Jett, you're scaring me."

"I'm being honest." He took a deep breath and caressed my cheek. "You're my girl, Goldie. I don't like titles but..." He paused for a second and then said, "You're my girlfriend, you're everything to me and I will do everything in my power to make sure it stays that way. Do you understand me?"

I nodded my head, so confused but understanding the gravity of the situation and having a heavy heart from his confession.

His fingers caressed the frame and he said, "Do you know what the color green means here in New Orleans?" I shook my head no so he continued, "It means faith. I put this picture in a green frame because I want you to have faith that everything is going to work out. Okay? Have faith in us, Goldie, and have faith in the fact that even though you might not like it, I know what I'm doing. I know what's best for us."

"Okay," I responded as a tear dropped down my cheek.

Gently, he took the frame from me and placed it on the nightstand, next to a bouquet of green hydrangeas.

"Did you have Diego put those there?" I asked, trying to be brave and wiping my tears.

"I did. Hydrangeas are tricky flowers, they can mean a lot of things but there is an old saying that a bouquet of hydrangeas means that the giver is grateful of the recipient's understanding." He took a deep breath and continued, "I am grateful for you,

Goldie, and for trusting in my decisions and having faith in the fact that I will be back and when I'm ready and everything has been fixed, you will be with me, fully. You will be back in my club not as a Jett Girl but as my girlfriend, as the one who has stolen my heart."

Not being able to say much from the tightness in my throat, I nodded my head and acknowledged him.

Faith and trust, I could do that. It seemed so simple.

23
"AS WE ARE"

Lo

The smell of coffee pulled me from my bed. Jett made me pack pajamas and made me swear that I would wear them when in Diego's place. I couldn't blame him; I was known to wake up in the middle of the night and venture out, forgetting that I was naked. Jett clearly didn't mind but in someone else's place, he would have none of that.

I tried getting away with packing light camisoles and boy shorts but Jett threatened to make me wear turtlenecks and sweats to bed so we compromised with leggings and a tank top…with a built in bra. The man could be infuriating.

I looked at my nightstand and smiled at the flowers and picture frame that Jett gave me. He had to leave after he settled me in my new room which broke my heart but I understood. I didn't know what was going on and I knew it was dangerous and he didn't want to get me wrapped up in it but I was a little hurt that he wouldn't tell me, especially since I technically was involved now. This would all be so much easier if he let me in but he said the less I knew the better.

I pulled my phone off the nightstand and checked for any messages and was surprised to see one from Jett. Squealing like a girl, I quickly opened it and read it as I sighed to myself.

Jett: Little one, it tore me apart to leave you last night but I know it's a first step to making everything right for us. Don't forget to have faith and trust. When you miss me, hold on to your necklace. I will be in touch. - J

After reading his text about five times, I pulled myself away and walked downstairs. In the morning light, the club actually looked clean compared to what I thought last night. It was such a neat concept. I was excited to see what else Diego had in store and what the dancers were. I didn't forget about that little comment last night. If I was going to be here, I at least was going to make the most of it.

Following the smell of coffee, I was able to find the kitchen. There was a swinging door that I pushed through and was instantly met with Diego's bare chest.

"Whoa," Diego said while holding his coffee and trying to balance the hot liquid from falling over the sides.

I was too distracted by his mocha-colored bare chest and the way that his shorts rode dangerously low on his hips, showing a very attractive line of hair from his belly button to his waistline and a deep V that would make any woman weak in the knees. Fuck, he was hot.

I gulped and looked back up at him. He was now smiling like a damn buffoon from my perusal.

"See something you like?" He wiggled his eyebrows at me.

"Get over yourself," I childishly said as I walked past him and went straight for the coffee. I had no clue where the mugs were so I started sorting through his cupboards. His body pressed up against mine, making me go stiff as he opened a cupboard I hadn't explored yet and pulled down a mug.

He leaned over my shoulder, handed it to me and spoke too close to my ear, "Here you go."

"You're awfully close, you know, especially for someone who gave Jett his word."

Smiling and holding up his hands, he said, "I was just being helpful."

"Too helpful," I said while I pulled away and made myself some coffee. It wasn't the smooth brew I got when I was at the Lafayette Club but it wasn't dirt piss either.

Sitting down at the little kitchen table he had set up, I crossed my leg and said, "I like your place. It's kind of neat. Where did you get the idea?"

He turned around to grab some more coffee and that was when I saw a giant tattoo caressing his back. I couldn't tell what it was because it was covered up by scars and lashings.

"Oh my God, what happened to you?"

His shoulders tensed from my question but when he turned to face me, his face remained neutral.

"How about we get to know each other first before we go diving into some serious stuff, eh?" he suggested while taking a sip of his coffee and sitting down at the table with me.

"Fair enough. Are you from the area?"

"Yup, born and raised, sweetheart. What about you?"

"Yes, I used to live over in the ninth ward until Hurricane Katrina came around."

"That greedy bitch," Diego said, shedding a little bit of humor on a horrific tragedy.

"You could say that. So, where did you get the idea for the club?"

Leaning back in his chair, he looked at me with those gray eyes of his that were not natural for a man of his color but it made him that much more intriguing.

"Well, as you can tell from my choice of club, I enjoy a kinky lifestyle and wanted to open a legit kink club in New Orleans, not one of those cheap knock-offs that bachelor parties go to. I wanted to respect the lifestyle, you know?"

"Sort of. I don't know much about it, I just do what Jett asks and if I don't like it I just say my safe word."

Diego shook his head. "There is so much more to it, Goldie. Maybe while you're here you will learn a thing or two."

I snorted, feeling a little uncomfortable from his gaze. I knew he wouldn't ever do anything because he respected Jett too much but the man had no problem denying his approval of my body that was for damn sure.

"Yeah, we'll see about that."

"I can teach you," he said innocently.

"Ha! Yeah, that will happen the same day Jett Colby lets me tie him up and treat him as a whipping boy."

"You never know." Diego shrugged.

"Why don't we just concentrate on the painting and leave my sex life out of this, okay?"

"Where's the fun in that?" He smiled that sexy smile of his.

The man was one giant flirt, I should have known from when I first walked off with him at the event of "the incident." He was a flirt then, and perused my body too much, like he was doing now, blatantly staring at my chest.

"Seriously, are you going to at least try to be subtle when trying to see through my shirt with the x-ray vision you don't have?"

"How do you know I don't have it? How do you know I can't see your pink little nipples right now?"

Covering my chest and opening my mouth in shock, I turned away from him.

A bellow of a laugh escaped his mouth as he threw his head back and slapped the table.

"Kace was right, you're a pistol."

"Ugh, that explains it. You're friends with Kace."

"That explains what?" he asked while draining the rest of his coffee, intrigued by my statement.

"Why you're an ass."

"Aw, Goldie, you wound me," he said while holding his heart and checking the non-existent watch on his wrist. "And it's only been half an hour and you're already making assumptions about me."

"Well, when you're poking your head in places it doesn't belong and teasing me about my nipples, I'm allowed to make such assumptions."

"Teasing you about your nipples? I don't remember teasing you, I remember saying they were little and pink. That's a compliment if you ask me."

"God, you're infuriating. Do you have a comeback for everything?"

"Pretty much," he said with a smile as he got up and rinsed his cup out. I couldn't help but stare at his back and the scars that laced him, along with the tattoo that seemed like it was pretty but now is deformed.

He must have caught my staring because he started to walk out of the kitchen and said, "We're not that close yet, Goldie. Maybe someday you will hear my story, but not now." He faced me and continued, "I'm going to hit the gym and then take a shower. The first room on the left down the long hallway has directions of what you need to do. You can start whenever you want. The place is yours so make yourself at home."

After his instructions, he left me to wonder how lonely I was going to be. Yeah, Diego was here but he apparently had his own schedule which made sense but ever since I've been in the Lafayette Club, I've been used to having people around me all the time. Not being surrounded by someone was actually kind of sad.

I drank the rest of my coffee, rinsed my cup like Diego did and headed to the room that he was talking about. I pulled my hair up into a ponytail and walked into the room.

I stopped dead in my tracks when I saw the same long cloth-like ribbons hanging from the ceiling as the circular room that I saw last night.

"What the hell?" I muttered as I walked toward them and questioned their texture with my fingers. There were multiple drop downs with loops in all different heights. How did one person even try to begin to get into one of those things? That's what I thought they did at least, get into them.

Taking a quick look around to make sure no one was watching me, I tested the strength of a rather large loop and noticed that it was bolted into the ceiling securely so I took a deep breath and launched myself into the loop. Like Peter Pan on steroids, I flew across the room, locked into the ribbon swing things and flew into the other hanging ribbons at the same time. My limbs flew about as I tried to catch my balance which only made me get tangled up in the other ones even more while I tried to gain my balance.

"Fucking Christ," I muttered as I tried to get the swinging under control. "This was a bad idea."

I wiggled my foot to find out where it was caught but couldn't twist my body because my arms were stuck in multiple loops. Trying to gain any kind of stability to prop myself up was impossible since the damn things wouldn't hold still so instead of fighting it, I stopped moving and finally came to a standstill. Looking around, I assessed the mess I put myself in and started to laugh. Only fucking me.

"You're not even gone for a day and this is how I find you?"

I turned my head to see Pepper staring at me with a joyful look on her face. She was wearing normal clothes which threw my whole life off and she was carrying a small white bag.

"Can you help me?"

"Help you get out or help you get off? I'm not quite sure Jett would be too happy about—"

"Get me out, damn," I said, struggling again.

Laughing, Pepper said, "Hold on one second." She set the paper bag down and busted out her phone.

"Don't you fucking dare," I said, really trying to get out now but only wound up swinging around like a banshee.

"Listen, you can either hold still for a picture or I can record a video of this mess you got yourself in. What's your poison, Lo?"

"Just take the fucking picture."

Laughing, she pointed her phone at me as I flipped her off.

"God, I'm sending this to everyone."

"I hate you."

"Is that right? I guess I'll just leave then," she joked as she started to walk away.

"Get your skinny ass back in here and get me out of these damn things.

As Pepper helped me get out of the ribbons, she laughed the entire time while asking, "What possessed you to get in these?"

"I don't know, I wanted to see if they could hold my weight. Who knew they were going to be tricky little fuckers and take me for a tango I wasn't ready for."

"Maybe next time you wait for Jett."

"Would he use these?" I asked, breaking a rule about talking about sex with Jett but at this point, I didn't care.

Pepper shrugged her shoulders. "He never used them with me."

Silence spread between us as she undid my feet, the last thing that needed to be unknotted before I was able to climb out of the big ribbon.

"Well this is awkward," I joked, trying to lighten the mood.

"Slightly." She chuckled.

Pushing my luck and apparently really wanting to make things uncomfortable, I asked, "Do you miss him? Like...sexually?"

Laughing, Pepper undid the final strap and I hopped

down. "I don't. I mean, I miss the act of sex but that's all it was with him. I didn't have a connection with him like you do. Do I miss the thrill of the Bourbon Room? Yeah, but I can move on."

"Yeah, with Kace." I smiled and jabbed her shoulder.

"Now that was a massive mistake." She looked me in the eyes and raised her eyebrows. "And I mean massive."

"I know, right? When I saw his dick, I was like whoa, man—"

"Hold up—" Pepper held up her hand, "—you saw his dick? When?"

Oh shit, did I say that out loud? Apparently yes, because Pepper's eyes were bulging out of her sockets, waiting for me to answer her.

"Umm, about that…"

"You tell me right now," Pepper demanded, more out of excitement.

"Well, I guess I was trying to see if he was okay and I happened to walk in on him taking a shower and I happened to just stand and watch like a creeper."

Pepper laughed as she covered her mouth with her hands. "Oh my God, I love you. You would just sit there and watch."

"It was hard not to. You've seen the man naked." I looked around and leaned forward so only Pepper could hear me. "I want to ask you something, when I came to the Lafayette Club did I land in some kind of hot guy paradox? Because it seems like every guy Jett knows was made to melt panties right off, including Jett himself. God, he's gorgeous," I said as I thought about Jett and his tender kisses he rained upon me before he left me here.

"I think the same thing sometimes. It's not fair to be surrounded by so many attractive men but it just gives me more ammo for when I bust out the old jack rabbit."

"Jack rabbit?"

"Yeah, my very own Magic Mike." I gave her a quizzical look, making her continue. "You know…dildo, Lo. I'm talking about a dildo."

Laughing, I said, "I know. I just wanted to hear you say it."

"You're a bitch." She smiled as she bent down and grabbed the white bag that she brought with her. "This is for you. It's from lover boy," Pepper carried out, making fun of me.

I snatched the bag from her and opened it up. Inside there was a croissant. I looked up at her with a quizzical eyebrow.

"You're supposed to eat it."

"No shit, but why a croissant?"

"I think there is a note in there."

I grabbed the croissant and saw a note at the bottom of the bag.

For my little one. I know how much you love our croissants, I couldn't bear to think of you waking up and not getting one today. I'm sorry about all of this. Please be patient with me. — J

"He's sweet," I said while taking a bite and pulling away. I nearly choked as I looked on the inside of the croissant. It was bright green. I laughed to myself as Pepper looked at me as if I were crazy.

Swallowing and setting the other piece in the bag, I asked, "So, is that why you came here, to deliver me food?"

"Nope, I'm here to spend some time with you. We're on rotation. Jett didn't want you to feel secluded from the girls or feel lonely so you will be getting a visit from each of us every day while you're here."

"Really?" I asked excited. "Did he tell you what's going on?"

"Not really." Pepper sat in one of the ribbons with ease like a swing. She made it look so simple. "He just told us that he fucked up and that you're in trouble now and he had to remove you to protect you but you were still an item."

"He called us an item?" I said a little too giddy.

"Yes, it was kind of cute. He was shy about it."

My heart melted from hearing that even though I wasn't

around, he still showed how much he cared about me.

"That kind of makes me happy," I admitted.

"You so have him wrapped around your finger. You should have seen the way he lit up when talking about you. It was nice to see him finally find someone to bring him such joy. Before, he was just floating around, but never really feeling and then you come around and flip his whole world upside down. It's kind of awesome." Pepper smiled.

"Yeah, too bad we can't be together right now."

Pepper's face grew serious as she said, "Give it time, Lo. Jett knows what he's doing. He doesn't fuck around. He is doing this for a reason so you just need to be patient."

"It's hard when my pussy is crying for him."

Pepper looked at me for a second and then burst out in laughter. "You're ridiculous."

"Do you know what's ridiculous?"

"What?" she asked while slightly swinging back and forth.

"The fact that you haven't given me details about sex with Kace."

Rolling her eyes, Pepper said, "I'm going to go now."

"No! Okay, we will talk about something else. Tell me, were his balls big?"

"I'm leaving." Pepper got up but I stopped her while laughing.

"You're sucking all the fun out of this."

"Get to work." Pepper nodded toward the sketch Diego wanted me to replicate. I rolled my eyes as she took her seat in the swing again and started studying the instructions Diego left for me. At least I had company **that** was a plus, even if it wasn't Jett.

24
"COOL KIDS"

Lo

"How's it going in here?" Diego asked, startling me from my concentration.

"Don't do that," I said while gripping my heart and checking my lines to make sure they were still on point.

"Do what? Talk to you?"

"No, sneak up on me."

"I didn't sneak up on you. Sneaking up on you would have called for me getting right next to your ear like this and whispering in your ear," he said as he invaded my space.

Swatting him away, I said, "All right, I get your point." I sat back and looked at my work. I was clearly still in the ribbon room since the picture he wanted me to paint was a ribbon-like banner with intricate lettering that said, "Constrain my heart, constrain my soul."

"It looks really good, Goldie."

"Thanks, I'm not done yet, obviously. I still have a lot of shading to do and I want to add an outline to the letters to make them stand out a little bit more but I think it's coming out nicely."

"It is." He surveyed my work. "I like how you made the ribbon look like it was falling and spanned it across the wall. I didn't think of that."

"Yeah, it takes up the wall more so it doesn't look like this tiny drawing on a big space."

"I like it a lot. I'm glad Jett sent you here."

"Thanks. It's been fun painting. Right now I would be practicing my presentations until Kace stopped cracking his whip so it's nice to have a bit of a break."

Diego laughed as he shook his head. "That dude needs to get a woman."

"Right!" I exclaimed. "Thank you! I've been saying that for a while."

"It would do him some good. Too bad his eyes wander to places where they don't belong," Diego looked at me for a second and then turned his gaze to my artwork.

Guilt washed over me as I thought about what Kace said to me in his room a while back. I tried to forget about it, like he wanted to but occasionally it would resurface and I would feel awful. I hated to think that Kace had such strong feelings for me and I didn't reciprocate them. I liked him and hell yeah I thought he was hot as hell, but my heart belonged to someone else, it belonged to Kace's best friend.

"Anyway, are you hungry? It's past lunch and I thought we could get out of here for a bit. Get you away from the paint fumes."

I looked down at my attire and said, "Can I take a two-second shower?"

"Are you one of those girls who says they'll be quick but they really take an hour?"

"No, seriously time me. Give me five minutes."

"Five minutes? No way."

"I'm serious," I said while getting up and wrapping my paint brush in saran wrap since I didn't have to wash them out just yet but didn't want the paint to dry out in them.

Diego held out his watch and said, "Okay, go!"

"Wait!" I shouted, holding up my arms. "You can't start the time until I get up to my room, that's not fair. I don't even know where my room is, I can't remember."

"Ugh, you're so high maintenance," he joked as he walked me to my room. "Okay, when do I get to start the clock?"

I shut the door on his face and yelled, "Go!"

Like a mad woman, I tore my clothes off, turned on the water and brushed my teeth while the water froze my tits right off. With one hand I brushed my teeth and the other I washed my hair like a pro. As I rinsed my shampoo, I washed my body with soap working up a good lather. After I got all the shampoo out, I put in some conditioner and then rinsed my entire body. I was out in less than two minutes. Thankfully, Diego had a heat lamp in the bathroom so I turned that on as I whipped the towel around my body, barely drying off the droplets from my skin. The heat lamp heated up my body as I combed my hair out, threw it up in a bun and then put a little mascara on—I wasn't a barbarian.

Running out to my room, I threw on some denim shorts, skipping the underwear, a bra and T-shirt that read, "Tits" across my chest, stating the obvious, put on some flip flops and then flung the door open where Diego whipped his head around, shocked.

"You're kidding me, that was like three minutes."

"Ha! Told you!" I said while dancing around and giving myself fist bumps.

"Uh, before we go out, you might want to zip your fly."

"What?" I looked down and saw that my fly was undone. Mortified, I quickly zipped it up and tried to pass it off as nothing.

"Nice wax job, damn that was hot."

"Ew! You're a pig!" I said while slapping his shoulder and

heading down the hallway, trying to hide the blush that crept over my cheeks.

"Wrong way," he called out over my shoulder.

I turned on a dime and marched the other way, ignoring him and the infuriating smirk on his face.

***

"What are you going to get?" Diego asked as he looked over his menu at me.

"Is that even a question? We're at the Gumbo Shop, I'm pretty sure I'm getting Gumbo."

Smiling, he said, "Good. I was afraid you were going to be one of those girls who went to a novelty restaurant and got a salad."

"What's salad?" I asked while shoving a piece of bread in my mouth.

"Apparently not." Diego laughed as his phone started to ring. "Excuse me." He pulled his phone out from his pocket and eyed me before pressing it to his ear. "Hello? Out to lunch. Yeah, she's with me."

My heart fluttered as I realized it must be Jett.

"Do you have your phone?" Diego asked me, I shook my head no. I forgot it in my rush to beat the allotted five minutes I gave myself to get ready. "No, she left it at the club. Yeah, hold on."

Diego held his phone out to me and said, "Someone would like to talk to you."

Grabbing the phone and turning away from him so I didn't have to see his snarky face as I spoke into the phone, "Hi."

"Hi." His deep southern voice that made my toes curl rang out. "Are you behaving?" he asked in a teasing tone.

"Yes, I'm behaving." I heard Diego snicker from behind me so I flipped him off.

"Not what I saw. Pepper sent me a little picture of you

testing out some of Diego's apparatuses."

Inwardly groaning and gripping my forehead, I said, "I fucking forgot that she took a picture. God, did she really send that to you?"

"Yes, she did."

"Fuck, that's embarrassing."

Lightly laughing, Jett responded, "I thought it was hot as hell even though you went about it all the wrong way."

"I have no clue how those things work. They're like vines that like to fuck with your mind and claw onto you," I whispered into the phone. "I think they come alive at night."

Laughing some more, Jett said, "I miss you."

It felt like my heart stopped beating for a second, hearing him say such an intimate thing. When I first went to the Lafayette Club, I never thought I would come to this point of my life where I would be talking to Jett Colby on the phone, hearing him say he misses me.

"I miss you, too," I admitted as my face turned red from Diego's staring. I turned to look at him for a second and he was making kissing noises at me. "Don't you have something better to do?" I asked him.

He laughed and said, "I'm going to the pisser."

"Are you talking to me?" Jett asked, a little concerned.

"Sorry, no. Diego was being a dick."

"Do I need to have a talk with him?" Jett grew serious. I loved how protective he was.

"No, nothing like that. He was just making fun of me for saying I miss you."

"He's a jealous bastard. Can you do me a favor?" he asked.

"Of course."

"Can you make sure that you always have your phone on you? I don't like the idea of you being out and about and not having your phone. I need to know that if something happens, you can get in touch with me."

"You're sounding a bit paranoid."

"Goldie, I'm serious."

"I know. I'm just not good with this whole captive thing. I like to have my own freedom."

Jett let out a long breath and I could envision him pinching his nose while looking out the window of his office as he spoke to me. "I know, little one, but right now, we just have to be careful. I have no clue what's going to happen and until I do, I would like you to be as careful as possible. Promise me?"

"I promise."

"Thank you," Jett said, relief washing through his voice.

"Am I going to see you tonight?"

"I don't think so. I have a person tailing me already. I went out earlier and noticed a black unidentified car following me around."

"Are you serious? Jett, are you in danger?" My heart rate started to pick up.

"I don't want you to worry about that."

"Well, I'm fucking worried," I said while raising my voice. "I feel like I barely just got you, I don't want to lose you because some fuckwhit out there has some vendetta over you. Like, get over it, buddy, Jett Colby is by far superior than whoever the hell you are."

Jett laughed in the phone. "If only it was that easy."

"Well, I want you to be safe too. You have to stay in the club, no extra activities after dark and make sure your hand keeps your dick warm at night while thinking about me."

Diego, who just appeared from the bathroom, stopped in his tracks and looked at me as if I was crazy.

"Mind your own damn business," I spat at him.

"Sweetheart, when you're using up my minutes to talk about masturbating with your boyfriend, I'm pretty sure I don't need to mind my own business."

"I should let you go," Jett said with mirth in his voice.

"Fine, I will talk to you later tonight."

"Bye, little one."

"Bye."

I ended the phone call and handed the phone back to Diego who wasn't taking it. "What are you waiting for, my arms to sprout out like Inspector Gadget? Take your damn phone."

"No way, wipe off your face juices first." Diego made a motion with his hand and wiped his shirt with his fake phone.

"I don't have face juices!" I stated while causally glancing at the phone.

Diego erupted in laughter and said, "Yeah, you fucking do."

"You're an annoying bastard, you know that?" I asked while wiping his damn phone and handing it back to him by pushing it across the table, not waiting for him to take it from me this time.

Our food arrived and instead of taking part in a conversation with him, I just buried my head in my bowl of Gumbo. I was irritated not because of Diego, he was actually a good time when he wasn't being annoying but with the situation I was in. I hated being trapped and helpless. Ever since my parents were taken away from me, I've taken care of myself and now that I couldn't do that and was being kept in the dark, I was irritated.

"Man, you need some sex," Diego said while taking a big bite off of his spoon.

"Excuse me?"

"You're so tense. You need to be fucked."

"I've been fucked quite fine, thank you."

"Nah, you need to be fucked until you can't move anymore."

"Oh? I didn't know you were an authority on sex. When did this occur?"

"Last fall," he said with a shit-eating grin.

"Errr, I want to hit you!"

"You're quite violent, you know that?" he said in a calm voice. "One night in one of my play rooms and I would be able to fix that."

"I thought you were Jett's friend."

"I am. Can't a guy lend a helping hand, or possibly a finger…or three?"

"Make it four," I said with a cheeky grin, making him sputter on his gumbo.

"Shocker? You know, two in the pink…" he suggested while making the hand gesture.

"I know what a shocker is and no! God, you're disgusting. Maybe you're the one who needs sex since you talk about it all the time."

"You're right about that," he said while tipping his water glass toward me before taking a drink out of it. "I need a good play time, I just can't seem to find the right girl though."

"What do you mean?" I asked, slightly curious by the semi-serious tone he took on.

"Well, I'm a dom, Goldie. I like to take charge, just like Jett and for a dom like me to be satisfied, I need a willing submissive. Someone who would give me their body entirely without making a sound besides her cries of pure ecstasy. There are girls who will test it out with me but then try to change me, try to push me out of my lifestyle and that's when I send them on their way. There is no changing for me and maybe someday I will find the right girl but until then, I'll just twittle around with you."

"Twittle? There will be no twittling."

Laughing, Diego said, "Relax. I have no intention of doing anything with you. I just like pressing your buttons…or button." He wiggled his eyebrows.

"Seriously! Enough with the sexual innuendos."

"Why? Am I making you hot?"

"You're making me want to slap you around."

"I'm into that."

"Check please!" I called out in frustration as I leaned back in my chair and crossed my arms. Diego just laughed while he patted his mouth clean with his napkin. It was going to be a long fucking couple of weeks at this rate.

25
"SHE KEEPS ME WARM"

Jett

"George, I understand that but I want to make sure we are ready to make a move when we can," I said into my phone as I paced the length of my office.

"Mr. Colby, you just have to be patient."

I wanted to laugh into the phone. Someone telling me to be patient was a joke, I was the most patient man in the world but when it came to finalizing this Lot 17 bullshit, I wanted it completed. I hated being apart from Goldie, now that I had her. The club wasn't the same without her smart mouth and ridiculousness. Everyone missed her, even Miss Mary.

"I'm a very patient man, George, but what is taking so goddamn long? What is the city waiting for? Don't they want to get this over with? Start making some money?"

"They do, but there is a process. Once I hear something, I'll let you know. Until then, make sure your affairs are in order so that when we can put a bid in, we do so in a timely manner."

"You know everything is ready to go, don't treat me like a child." I seethed. I've been working with George ever since I extracted myself from my father and there were times in our lawyer/client relationship where he acted like my father and I had to remind him who worked for who.

"I'm sorry, Mr. Colby. We will get Lot 17. You have good standing in the community and you want to use it for a good reason."

Damn fucking right!

"Thank you, George. I'll be in touch."

I turned off my phone and gripped my desk as I looked out the window of my office. Was this even all worth it? I could find a new lot, some new land. Was I risking too much just because my dad was involved now? I was a prideful man but right now, was my pride getting in the way? I didn't want to lose to my father, but I also didn't want him to destroy the culture and feeling of New Orleans by putting a monstrosity of a building in a place where it doesn't belong, especially when the lot belonged to the children so they could play.

The night had taken over the sky as I was trying to keep my mind off Goldie and figure out my next move. I looked at the time and noticed that it was past ten so I grabbed my phone and walked out to my master suite where I got ready for bed.

My suite was my escape, my only sanctuary and now that Goldie was no longer in the club, sleeping one floor below me, my bedroom seemed so cold and empty. The gray walls seemed large and uninviting as well as the chrome and black furniture that was scattered around my room. I used to find this room to be a place of my own, where I could think and step away but now it almost seemed like a jail cell.

I needed Goldie's arms, her body, her heat. That is where I was comfortable.

As I brushed my teeth I thought about how in a matter of days, I became a pussy whipped man who could barely function without the sweet scent of his girl wafting next to him. I used to make fun of men like me but now that I was in their position, fuck, I wouldn't trade it for anything. I thought I had it all when I was with Natasha but fuck was I wrong. Goldie is having it all, Goldie is peace, she is my heart.

As I chucked my clothes into my dirty hamper, my phone chimed with a text message. Knowing it was my girl, it just had to be, I turned off my lights and got into my cold and empty bed. I pulled my phone out and read the message from her.

Goldie: Hi, handsome. You're probably off gallivanting, trying to save the world but I just wanted to tell you that I had a good day, despite Diego's ribbing and not having you to hold me. I was happy with my painting and felt like I really contributed to something. Tell the girls I miss them and slap Kace in the back of the head for me.

I laughed to myself and typed her back a message.

Jett: Hi, gorgeous. I'm actually calling it a night and headed to bed. I'm glad you had a good day. If Diego gets too lippy, you have my permission to castrate him.

Goldie: That would require me touching his penis. Do you really want me to do that?

Jett: Fuck no. I will hire someone.

Goldie: Overbearing. ☺

Jett: Only for you, little one. Now, tell me what you're wearing.

Goldie: Is this a test? Because if it is, I think I pass…

A picture popped up on my phone and it was a smiling Goldie, lying against her pillow with her hair fanned out around her, wearing a little tank top. She was beautiful. My chest constricted from just the sight of her. I saved the picture to my phone as my wallpaper and then wrote her back.

Jett: You're so damn beautiful. How did I get so lucky?

Goldie: You strolled the cemetery, looking for fresh meat.

Jett: And came out with a sassy, defiant man-eater.

Goldie: I think I eat your manhood pretty damn well, if you ask me.

Jett: You're pushing your luck, don't make me come over there and test your skills.

Goldie: Is that supposed to be a punishment because it seems more like a reward to me.

Jett: The only reward you're going to get next time I see you is a slap to the ass.

Goldie: Once again, it seems like you're trying to punish me…

Jett: Did you think about me all day?

Goldie: Do dogs sometimes eat shit?

I cringed from her foul mouth but just shook my head and laughed. You could take the girl off Bourbon Street but you can't take the Bourbon Street out of the girl, that was for damn sure and at this point, I don't think I would want to. She keeps things…interesting.

Jett: I'm going to ignore that last text and let you try again. Did you think

212

about me all day?

Goldie: Snob! And yes, I did. How could I not? Did you think about me?

Jett: Every damn second. Why are we texting?

My phone started to ring and I smiled as I saw her name pop up on my screen.

"Hi," I answered.

"God, I love your voice. How are you?"

"Much better now," I admitted as I got comfortable in my bed.

"I feel like a teenager, talking to my high school crush right now."

"You have a crush on me, Goldie?"

"I have a hell of a lot more than a crush, Mr. Colby."

"Oh, yeah? Tell me about it."

She laughed and said, "I'm not going to lie here and boost your ego. You know you're hot, you know you own me, no need to repeat myself."

"Sometimes a man likes to hear it."

"You don't need it."

"I do, Goldie," I said weakly. There was something about her that made me weak, that made me feel needy and I couldn't control it.

"Jett, you're such a confident man who knows what he wants and when he wants it, what makes you question my loyalty to you?"

I took a deep breath and thought about telling Goldie about Natasha but found myself unable to speak. She needed to know, it would be so easy to tell her but would she think differently of me?

"Jett, I wish you would talk to me."

"I was engaged once," I said quickly.

"Oh…"

Fear started to prick the back of my neck and my stomach churned. I couldn't do this. Just from her little response, I knew this wasn't a good idea. There was no way I could tell her right now, not when we were so far apart. I would only be damaging what we had.

"Hey, I have to go. I forgot I had to sign a couple of things before I went to bed."

"Jett, don't. Don't you pull away from me."

"I'm sorry, Goldie."

I pulled my phone away and ended the phone call, hating myself for not being man enough to tell her. I was a confident man but when it came to her, I was so fucking weak.

26
"LET LOVE IN"

Goldie

"What the fuck," I said as I looked at the blank screen on my phone. He hung up on me. Jett hung up on me.

Oh hell no!

I got out of bed, threw on a pair of yoga pants and a sweatshirt and grabbed my purse. I was not about to let Jett get away with pushing me away. I didn't care if I wasn't supposed to go out alone. If he wanted me safe, then he was going to have to not fuck around with me and talk. I was growing irritated more every day with his evasiveness. There was only so much a girl could take.

Being as quiet as possible, I stepped out of my room and walked down the stairs to the back entrance. The stairs creaked under my feet and I just prayed that Diego was a heavy sleeper. When I reached the door, I checked the locks first, then opened it as slowly as possible and slipped out of a small crack. I looked behind me before shutting the door to make sure Diego didn't see me. The coast was clear, so I shut the door and walked through the back alley until I hit Royal Street. Bourbon was still roaring with drinkers so I stumbled near my old dwellings and flagged down a taxi.

The ride over to the Garden District was quiet and almost eerie as I passed the wonky trees that lined the roads and the trolley tracks that were vacant of tourists and runners. I didn't travel much at night so it was odd to see the quiet side of New Orleans.

The taxi pulled up to the Lafayette Club which was dark besides Jett's office window on the third floor where a dim light shone through the window pane. The tall, white pillars and dark lanterns seemed intimidating in the dark as I paid the driver and walked to the back of the house where I still had a key to get in.

The driveway was vacant as I walked to the back door and slipped the key into the lock. As I turned, I heard a rustling next to me and my stomach dropped as I tried to unlock the door faster. Fucking spooks.

I opened the door and was about to shut it when someone grabbed my arms from behind. I screamed bloody murder and slapped my purse around to nail the arm grabber right in the head.

"What the fuck?" Kace said as he gripped his head.

Chest heaving and tits blazing, I swatted him in the shoulder and said, "What the hell do you think you're doing sneaking up on someone like that? Christ, only creepy perverts do things like that. Is that what you are, Kace? A creepy pervert?"

Kace looked at me with a menacing look but I held my ground. He could have said something rather than grabbing me.

"Not when I think some psycho is trying to break in."

"With a key?" I held up my key and he examined it, then huffed.

"What are you doing here? Is Diego with you?"

"That is none of your concern," I said while I tried to walk past him but the cinder block wall that was Kace's chest wasn't allowing me to pass.

"It is when you're not supposed to be walking around by yourself, especially at night."

"Oh don't act like you care."

He got right in my face and said, "You know I fucking care so don't test me. Why are you running off by yourself?"

"It's none of your business," I said, growing frustrated now. "I just need to see Jett, okay?"

"Something happen between you two?" Kace asked as his voice softened.

"Not really, he just…I just need to see him. Please, Kace."

"I'm not going to stop you but he's not going to be happy about you being here by yourself."

"I couldn't really give two fucks. Please just let me by."

Kace nodded but grabbed my hand before I walked by him. His thumb ran against the back of my hand as he said, "If you need to see Jett again like this, call me. I'll come get you. I don't want you out there by yourself, okay?"

I nodded and brushed a polite kiss against his cheek. "Thanks, Kace."

The walk up to the third floor had my nerves twisting in knots. Kace was right, Jett was going to be so pissed at me but right now, I didn't care. I just had to confront him, to talk to him. He was not allowed to run away from me.

When I reached the top of the stairs, I saw that his office door was slightly cracked open with a little light filtering from it. With a deep breath, I walked to the door and peeked in. Sitting at his desk, with his elbows on the desk and his head in his hands, pulling at his hair, was Jett. He was shirtless, showing off his glorious muscles that I now knew Kace helped with forming and there was a glass of bourbon sitting next to him.

Pushing the door open, I let myself in. He looked up from his desk and the look of shock on his face made the knots in my stomach twist even tighter until his gaze softened and he pushed back from the desk, showing me he was only in his boxer briefs.

My gut clenched from the sight of him.

"What are you doing here?" he asked, trying to look behind me. "Is Diego here?"

My hands twisted together as I realized I should have been a little smarter about this. He was going to yell, I could feel the calm before the storm.

"He is not."

Stepping forward, I could see his chest start to heave with anger.

I held up my hands and said, "Before you get angry, I want to tell you that I'm mad at you. You can't just hang up on me like that and push me away when things get tough."

"When things get tough?" A sarcastic laugh escaped Jett's mouth as he said, "This is already fucking tough. I have to have you stay with another man because I can't keep you here. I have fear every day that something is going to happen to you, that I'm not doing my job of protecting you. That's what's tough, not some stupid conversation on the phone."

Stupid? Was that what he really thought?

"It wasn't stupid."

"That's not what I meant," he said while pulling on his neck. "There are so many more important things to worry about—"

"No!" I shouted, interrupting him and shocking him a bit. "You're not allowed to decide what's important and what's not important because right now, we don't know very much about each other so when you go and say something like you were engaged, it's important to me to learn about that because I want to know you, Jett. I want to know what makes you tick." I stepped forward and got right in front of him so I could place my hands on his chest. "I don't want to just know this body, I want to know the man too. If this has a chance of working out, I need you to not push me away and open up to me. Are you afraid I'm going to judge you?"

"Yes," he said while holding his head high and not skipping a beat.

Trying not to be thrown off by his confession, I stood back and said, "Well, that kind of stings."

"I don't mean to hurt you."

"Oh, so you were trying to make it feel like kittens were licking my cheeks when saying that?"

"Goldie…"

My pride got the best of me, like it always did and I stepped farther away. "You know what, save it, Jett. God, I'm so sick of this." I threw my hands up and walked toward the door. "I come over here to talk to you, to open up with you and you don't even fucking trust me to do so, so then what's the point? Please tell me what the fucking point in all of this is. Do you only trust me because I signed a goddamn contract?"

He was silent as he looked at the floor.

"Unbelievable. Guess what, Jett, you can go fuck yourself. I'm done. I'm so sick of being thrown around as if I'm just a warm body to fill your nights with. Find another Jett Girl because I'm turning in my set. I'm through."

I pushed open the door as Jett called out to me.

"Don't you dare leave."

I laughed and turned to face him. "Funny thing, Jett. When you're no longer in charge of me, I can do whatever the fuck I want. I don't have to listen to you. Good luck with Lot 17 and whatever other bullshit is going on."

I turned my back and walked down the stairs to Kace's room. With three hard pounds to his door, I waited for him to open the door. When he did, he was shirtless, wearing a pair of Nike shorts that rode very low on his waist and his hair was messed up. I looked over his shoulder and saw a bare leg poking out from his bed. He had company but I didn't care.

"Can you take me to Diego's?"

Without hesitation, he nodded his head and grabbed keys from his bedside table while tossing a shirt over his head. I wanted to make a snarky comment about how he didn't need the shirt but I held my tongue. I wasn't in the mood. I just wanted to leave the club.

We turned and walked down the hallway, in silence, it was the one time I was thankful for Kace's inability to have a conversation. We were about to walk out the door when Kace stopped in his tracks. I looked up to see Jett barricading the door to the garage with his body.

"Goldie, our conversation isn't over."

"But it was over when you hung up on me?" I said over Kace's shoulder, pinning him in the middle of us.

"Can we take this upstairs, please," Jett said in a controlled voice.

"No, I said this was over. Kace, please just take me home."

"Your home is here," Jett spit out.

"No, it's not! I'm living with Diego you...you...douche nugget."

Kace's shoulders visibly shook, I knew he was trying to hold in his laughter so I pinched his side, making him jump to the side.

"What the fuck?"

"Don't laugh at me," I scolded him.

He looked over at Jett who seemed like he was starting to foam at the mouth from anger and then back at me. He put his hands up in the air and said, "I don't want to be a part of this. Sorry, Lo. You're on your own."

"Traitor," I mumbled as he walked away, leaving me alone with Jett.

He looked me up and down and then came after me. He picked me up in his arms and carried me to my room, the whole time kicking and screaming.

"You act like I'm about to murder you," Jett said into my ear as he dropped me down on my bed and then shut my door.

Moon beams filtered through my window and casted a glow on the delicious man standing in front of me. The contours of his muscles looked deeper from the way the light was bouncing off him as he walked toward me. He pressed his body against mine and pushed me against the bed. I wanted to kick and scream but the warmth of his body had me melting into the mattress.

"We're so dysfunctional," I said deflated.

He kissed my forehead and said, "I was engaged when I was young and the girl who I thought was supposed to care about me, to spend the rest of my life with me changed her mind and walked out on me, into someone else's arms. Her reasoning was that I wasn't man enough, I wasn't good enough for her. Ever since then, I've put my heart on hold, not letting anyone get near it, until you."

I was speechless. Who the hell would think that Jett Colby wasn't good enough for them?

"Jesus Christ, was she the princess of a far off planet that has yet to be discovered? Who the hell is too good to be with you?"

Jett chuckled and shook his head. "Apparently her."

"Well, she's a dumb ass because you're the best man I've ever met. You may have your quirks and your overbearing tendencies but you're sweet and kind and care about others. You have a helping and serving heart and even though you don't like to open up much, I can feel your emotions running through me, you're an amazing man and that bitch's bad decision is my good fucking fortune."

He backed away from me for a second and gave me a questioning look. "You're serious."

"Of course I am."

"So you don't think less of me?"

"You're high. Why would I think differently of you?"

"Because—" he shook his head as he steadied his breath, "—because she ran to another man."

"Like I said, her loss, my gain." I stroked his face and leaned in to press a kiss against his lips. "Thank you for sharing, Jett. No matter what you say to me, I will never judge you. You didn't judge me for my past so why would I judge you?"

He looked visibly pained when he said, "I live in a

221

different world than you, Goldie, where forgiveness isn't handed out so easily. It's going to take me a while but I trust you and I want to make this work so even when I'm an ass, you can't give up on me. Please don't give up on me."

I took a deep breath as I closed my eyes and gathered strength.

"Then give me a chance. Don't close me off so easily. Closing me off is only going to lead to me getting mad and my natural tendency is to run when things aren't going my way. It's all I know."

He nodded and then a small smile spread across his face. "God, we really are dysfunctional."

Laughing, I agreed.

His lips met mine and his body pressed against mine, before I was about to tell him I submitted so get down with business, he pulled away and his face grew serious.

"Before this goes any further, I need you to know that I'm serious when I say you're not allowed to walk around by yourself right now. It's only temporary, so please just honor this wish of mine."

I nodded. "Okay."

He looked stunned as he stared down at me.

"What?" I asked.

"I just wasn't expecting you to agree so easily. You usually put up a fight."

I shrugged my shoulders and said, "I still have some surprises up my sleeve."

He hummed in my ear and said, "I can't wait to explore them."

27

"STOLEN DANCE"

Jett

"Dinosaurs are eating my underwear!"

I shot out of bed and looked around in a near-death panic from Goldie screaming at the top of her lungs.

"My undies, my undies!" she cried.

The sheets were all jumbled together and there were lumps everywhere but no sight of Goldie.

"That color is hideous on you, raptor. No, that is my thong," she yelled as she hissed and started swinging her arms, identifying where her whereabouts were.

I sat up and lunged to the bottom of the bed, on the right hand side where her head was hanging off and she was swinging around with her dukes out.

"Jett got those for me, you blasted long neck. Go eat some

leaves, herbivore!"

I was about to shake her awake until she started insulting dinosaurs by calling them herbivores. I couldn't help it, I laughed out loud and from the pit of my stomach, something I didn't do very often.

My laughter must have woken her up because she jack-knifed off the mattress and started swatting at the blanket that was covering her head.

In the midst of laughter, I pulled the blanket off her head to find my little one wearing nothing and her hair falling over her face. Even in her crazy state of delirium, she was still the most gorgeous woman I've ever seen.

"Holy crap!" She breathed heavily as she tried to smooth her hair out of her face.

"Dinosaurs eating your underwear?" I said in a teasing tone.

"What? How did you know?"

"Just screaming in your sleep that's all. I'm pretty sure I almost pissed myself when you woke me up about dinosaurs eating your underwear."

Goldie snorted and covered her mouth as she giggled. "Sorry about that. I don't want no dino messin' with my skivvies. It's an honest request."

"It is," I said while pinching her chin with my thumb. "Now what we really need to discuss is why you're sleeping like a lunatic, horizontally off the bed with your head hanging off the side."

"Was I really?" She looked around and assessed her position. "Well, look at that."

"I don't ever sleep with women so you're going to have to let me know if this is normal behavior," I joked.

She took a second to think and then said, "To save my credibility, I'm going to say that other women usually sleep from the ceiling and stare at you while you sleep so me sleeping with my head hanging off the bed, horizontally, is almost normal."

I laughed, again. It was a foreign thing to me but with Goldie, it started to become a norm.

I grabbed her by the waist and brought her down on my chest as I rested back on the mattress.

"So what you're telling me is that I'm lucky you're not hovering over me at night."

"Pretty much. Consider me a rare breed."

"Oh, I already know you're a rare breed." I kissed her chin before she placed her hands on my chest and rested her head on her hands as she looked down at me.

"I don't want to go back to Diego's. I want to stay here, with you."

I let out a heavy breath as I wrapped my arms around her and held her tight.

"Me neither but we don't really have a choice in the matter. I promise you though, this will be over soon. I have some things in the works and I'm hoping a good distraction will throw some people off."

"You really can't tell me what's going on?"

"Goldie, we talked about this. The less you know, the better, okay?"

"Okay. Can I ask you something?"

"Sure."

"Do you think your mom would have liked me?"

I smiled to myself as I thought about my mom and how she and Goldie would have hit it off, no question about it. My mom was more reserved but she loved to have a good time and that's what Goldie was, a good time. I could picture them ganging up on me during holidays. They would be my two girls.

A pang in my heart started to form as I thought about the loss I suffered and the things my mom was missing out on because she was taken away from me too early.

Taking a deep breath, I rubbed her back and answered her question. "I think she would have adored you, Goldie. No doubt in my mind."

"What about your dad? You never talk about him."

I tensed from her question but tried to show as if the question didn't affect me.

"He's a miserable fuck who doesn't deserve to be talked about."

Silence met us as we both lay there, taking in what I said.

"Did you have any pets growing up?" she asked, not pushing the comment about my father which I appreciated.

Relaxing slightly, I sank into her embrace and said, "No, unless some measly beta fish counted."

"Beta fish? Like those colorful things in a jar?"

"Yeah." I laughed.

"Fuck, that's depressing but for some reason I can picture it. Did you name them things like Mr. Wetherby and Annabell Figglefort?"

Figglewhat?" I laughed some more. "No, I named them fish."

She sat up and stared down at me.

"You named your beta fish, fish?" I nodded and she shook her head and lay back down. "Fuck, that is super depressing."

"I was more interested in being the best in everything I did, rather than worrying about naming something that was going to die in a few weeks anyway."

"Oh, I forgot. Little rich boy problems. Who was the better tennis pro at the club and what kind of white cloth napkins you were going to have at your parties."

"Eggshell."

"What?" she asked.

"Eggshell, that was the best color white."

"Oh my God!" She laughed as she poked my side. "That is so embarrassing that you know that."

"I can throw one hell of a party," I said as I threaded my fingers over her necklace that continued to show up around her neck. Even after some of our worst fights, she still kept it on. It gave me hope.

"Well then, when it's my birthday, I expect you to throw me one hell of a party."

"When is your birthday, Goldie?"

She feigned shock as she said, "Something Jett Colby doesn't know? I'm shocked. You knew my bra and thong size when I walked in this door but you don't know my birthday?"

"I could look in your file." I smiled.

"God, you're infuriating. It's April 24th."

I nodded while I thought about what I would do for her birthday when it rolled around which wouldn't be for a while since it's already passed for the year but it would be something I would want to celebrate, and make a big deal about.

"April is a pretty month to be born in, it suits you."

"Thanks," she said with a bright smile. "When is your birthday?"

"Doesn't matter," I said, hating my birthday. It was never a good day, thanks to my dad.

She sat up and rubbed my chest. "It matters to me. How else would I give you a birthday blow job?"

I raised an eyebrow at her. "Birthday blow job, how is that different than a regular one?"

"Oh it's different." She got excited.

"How so?" I gripped her waist to stop her from wiggling too much, she was starting to get me a little excited.

She sat up and pulled down the sheets, exposing my now growing erection. She looked down at it, smiled and grabbed my cock in one swift movement.

"Fuck," I moaned out as she started to stroke me.

"Little one, I don't believe I gave you permission to be playing down there," I said with less authority than I wanted.

She lowered her head and licked the tip of my cock and then said, "Oh, do you want me to stop?"

The grip she had at the base of my cock was just strong enough that is was pushing all the pressure to my tip, driving me fucking insane.

"No," I grunted out. "But you will pay for your defiance."

"Mmm, I can't wait."

With that, she lowered her head and took me into her mouth, all the way to the back of her throat. She was not playing around, she took what she wanted and ran with it. Her hand ran down, between my thighs and found the weight of my balls. She squeezed them a little harder than normal and then pulled away from my cock, letting it fall to my stomach. I was fucking hard and yearning for her to finish.

"You see, Jett. For your birthday, I wouldn't stop like I am now and instead of squeezing your balls like this—" she gestured, "—I would be putting them in my mouth and swirling them around with my tongue while I run my hands slowly up and down your shaft like this."

Like a mother fucking sloth, she ran her hand so fucking slow up my cock as I hissed out a heated breath. She was torturing me like I tortured her and damn it I was letting her. I couldn't stop her if I wanted to.

"Goldie…" I said in a strangled voice as her hand continued to torture me.

She giggled, fucking giggled and then leaned down so her mouth hovered over my dick, making it twitch in excitement. Her hand continued to handle my balls as she rolled them with sweet, torturous precision while her tongue lightly licked the length of my shaft. Her tongue danced along its length, barely making contact. I was going to explode from her torture, from her teasing.

"Little one, you better get on with it or your punishment is not going to be as pleasurable as you want."

"Tell me when your birthday is and I'll make sure you come like a teenage boy after seeing his first set of fake tits."

"December 20th," I groaned out, needing her to move her lips over my cock.

She pulled away and said, "You're almost a Christmas baby? Aww, why do I find that so adorable?"

"For fuck's sake, Goldie, focus!"

"Oops, sorry. I forgot that your little tippy tip is about to have a bit of a free shower."

I cringed. "God, don't say stuff like that!"

"I just do it to drive you crazy," she said casually as my dick bobbed between us.

I sat up and grabbed the back of her neck and pulled her mouth toward mine. I pressed my lips against her and tongue fucked her to the best of my ability until she was breathless. When I pulled away, I pressed my forehead against hers and said slowly, "If you don't finish me off in the next minute I'm going to make sure I tie you up in the Bourbon Room, bring you to the edge of orgasm and then just leave you there, until I feel like you have paid for the teasing you have put me through today. Don't fuck with me, Goldie, I don't play games."

Her eyes flew wide open and her mouth was instantly attached to my dick, working me like a damn Popsicle. I dropped to the bed as I let myself feel every pull, every lick, every tug of her mouth on my erection. She gave amazing head, like nothing I've ever experienced. I didn't know if it was the way she rotated her mouth or the combination of her hands on my shaft and balls but I was ready.

My toes started to tingle, my gut went numb and my balls seized on me as my back arched off the bed and I groaned a feral sound out of the back of my throat, exploding like a maniac into Goldie's mouth. All the pressure, all the teasing that she built up into me, flew away in one release as my body convulsed and was finally sated.

Her little body climbed over mine and slipped into the crevice of my neck and shoulder. She played with my chest while I regained my composure.

My hand drifted up and down her back as we stared up at the ceiling.

"December 20th, I will make sure to mark that in my calendar. It seems like an amazing day."

I just shrugged, once again not wanting to go into it.

"It seems like you don't like your birthday, which I won't go into, but after this year, you're going to love it. I'm going to make sure of it. You are going to have one hell of a party," she said while kissing my cheek. "Everyone deserves a good birthday."

"I don't need a party. I just need you," I admitted, realizing more and more that my life was happy when Goldie was in it, when I'm holding her and talking to her. Being in a relationship was scary as fuck but with Goldie, it didn't seem as terrifying. It actually seemed doable.

There was a knock on the door and then Kace's voice came from the other side. "Jett, someone is here to see you."

"Tell them I will call them back later," I called out, still holding Goldie.

Kace cleared his throat and responded, "Can't. You have to see them."

The tone of Kace's voice pulled me from a confused Goldie's bed. I put on my boxer briefs from last night and told Kace to come in. When he walked in, I acknowledged him and said, "Please take Goldie back to Diego's, but let her get cleaned up first." Kace nodded his head and went outside.

I turned to Goldie, whose face was crestfallen, making my heart lurch in my chest. I leaned over and pressed a small kiss on her lips.

"I have to go, little one. I'll be in touch, I promise. Please be good and help Diego out."

"When will I see you again?"

"Not sure. I'll call you tonight. Be brave, little one and have faith in me and in us."

"Always," she responded as she kissed the palm of my hand.

I was just about to leave when she called out my name. I turned to face her and was blessed with the sight of her naked body on top of her bed, her hair hanging loosely around her shoulders and her eyes with pure passion beaming from them, only for me.

"Yes, little one?"

"Do I have permission to masturbate to you in the shower?"

I nearly choked on my spit from her question which made her smile.

"No!" I practically shouted. "That pussy belongs to me. You're not allowed anywhere near it."

"You're no fun."

"Be good," I called out.

**

Luckily, I was very quick at taking a shower so I didn't keep my visitor waiting very long. I put on a button up shirt with the first couple of buttons undone and a pair of dress pants. I kept it casual but wanted to make sure I still exuded the business man that I was.

I walked into my office and was quickly hit with a female perfume that was almost too overwhelming. Sitting in a chair in front of my desk was a woman with long, black hair that was curled at the ends. She was wearing a pencil skirt that showed off her tanned and toned legs and black high heels that would make any man melt on the spot.

Clearing my throat to get her attention, she turned in her seat and I was surprised to see that Keylee Zinc was the woman occupying the seat in front of my desk.

"Keylee, what a nice surprise."

The muscles in her legs flexed as she stood and walked toward me with a little more swing in her hip than a normal business associate. She was attractive, really attractive with her contrasting light eyes to her dark hair and her pouty lips but when I looked her up and down, I realized that I had no yearning to take her to bed. She was nothing like Goldie, she couldn't even compare.

Her hand fell to my chest as she looked up at me with bright eyes. "Jett, thank you for seeing me on such short notice."

"Anything for a friend," I said as I removed her hand and

went to the opposite side of my desk but didn't sit until she did. "Please have a seat."

As she sat, her blouse blew open where she had it unbuttoned at the top and showed off a red lace bra that was hiding underneath, propping her ample cleavage up for viewing. I had to admit, she was hot. She had the right curves and if I was in a different situation, I would consider inviting her to the Bourbon Room but even though she was doing her best to display her assets, I had no urge to cash in.

"What brings you here?" I said while sitting back in my chair.

"Well, Jeremy, your assistant actually sent me an invite about the Mayor's Ball and I wasn't sure if you were still considering taking me along with you. I haven't heard anything from you and the event is in two weeks. I didn't know if I needed to find a dress or not."

Fuck, I completely forgot about the Mayor's Ball. I planned on bringing Goldie with me until my dad had to ruin everything. That night I told Jeremy to invite someone else on my behalf, he must have chosen Keylee for me. I made a mental note to talk to Jeremy about running things like that by me before he made a decision. It would have been nice to know who he chose instead of being caught off guard like right now.

"Keylee, I apologize about keeping you in the dark. Things have been a little hectic around here but I would be delighted if you would attend with me."

If I told her she was going to be queen for a day, I don't think she would have been as excited as she was right now.

"Oh, Jett, that is great." She lightly clapped her hands. "I'm so excited. Do you have a plan of what you expect me to wear? I know it's such a stupid question but I don't want to disappoint you, especially since the last girl who was around your arm must have disappointed you since she won't be attending with you."

I didn't feed into her meddling so I ignored her

assumption and said, "Something elegant and form fitting would be just fine."

She bit on her thumbnail, something I found to be very unattractive but for some reason, women thought the nibbling of a fingernail turned a man on so it was a common occurrence when I ran into women, at least in the circles I ran in.

"Can I ask you something?"

"Sure."

"I know you're a very busy man, but do you think you could go look at dresses with me?" She held up her hands and said, "Before you say no, I just want to make sure I look right. I know you have a lot going on in your business world and I want to make sure I do everything right to help you succeed."

Being seen with Keylee outside of the Lafayette Club could be beneficial because she was a debutante of New Orleans and was always seen with paparazzi flocking her. If I wanted to make my dad believe that I was no longer interested in Goldie, being seen publicly with Keylee would be a smart move on my part.

On the other hand, fear tickled my stomach as I thought about Goldie finding out about Keylee and me, especially when she doesn't have all the information. I would keep my distance from Keylee, it would be nothing but platonic, but the media didn't need to know that.

I weighed my options as Keylee waited patiently for my answer. I didn't want to talk to Goldie about what was going on for two reasons, I didn't want to drag her in any further than she was, the less she knew the better and secondly, I didn't want her to know about my father and the kind of man he was. She didn't need to know about what a horrible person I derived from.

The black-patented leather heel bounced on her foot as she waited for my reply, bringing my attention to her legs. Before Goldie, I could see those legs wrapped around me but now, they were just nice to look at.

My eyes ran up her body and found her eyes which were

very pleased with my perusal. Making a decision, I took a deep breath and said, "That would be fine. Schedule a day with Jeremy and I will meet you at whatever store you have planned out."

She leaned forward, showing off more of her cleavage and grabbed my hand with a squeeze.

"Thank you, Jett. I just don't want to look like a fool and you helping me pick out a dress will ease my mind."

"You're doing me the honor of coming with me so it's only fitting that I help you pick out a dress. If that is all, I have some important things to tend to. I will see you out."

Her face fell flat for a second but she slipped in a smile and stood from the chair. "No need, please get back to your work. I will see myself out. It was nice seeing you, Jett. I'll be in touch."

I stood and walked her to the doorway, like the gentleman I was.

"It was a pleasure as always, Keylee."

Catching me off guard, she stood on her toes and kissed me on my cheek, dangerously close to the corner of my mouth.

"Pleasure was all mine, Jett." She patted my chest and walked out of my office, giving me a great view of her backside. I shook my head and closed the door to my office. She was going to have to learn quickly that touching was a privilege, not a right. I wasn't hers to touch and if I was going to go through with this, I was going to have to set some boundaries because even though I was taking her to the Mayor's Ball, she still needed to respect Goldie.

28
"I WILL WAIT"

Goldie

I hate silence, it makes me nervous and I become fidgety and start to get diarrhea of the mouth because an awkward silence between two people is the one thing that will make me break out in hives and lose all self-control. That was why I found myself talking to Kace about an episode of National Geographic where they went into great detail about primates mating.

"So you see, it's just like humans, you know? Bend over and let the man pump his salami right into you. Thankfully, it's not like cats where the males have spikey dicks and can't get out of the feline vaggy until his spikes go down. Could you imagine getting fucked by a spiked dick?" I clenched my thighs together and held on to my crotch. "That's just wrong. I wonder what God was thinking when he designed the cat cock? Was he sitting on his cloud, drawing up sketches and said, 'Do you know what would be fun? Putting pussy ripping spikes on this dick.' Not that God would say pussy, or anything, but still." I shook my head and looked over at Kace. "Fucking cat cocks, right?" I elbowed him, trying to get him into the conversation.

Shaking his head, he said, "You're so fucked up."

"I'm fucked up?"

"Yeah."

"How so?" I asked while crossing my arms.

"You're talking about God 'designing' cat cocks," he said while using air quotes. "That shit is messed up."

I shrugged my shoulders. "I got you to partake in a conversation."

"Next time maybe try talking about the damn weather."

"What's so fun about the weather?"

"It's not fucking cat cocks," Kace said while pulling into the alley that led to Diego's back door.

"God, loosen up." I gripped his arms and tried to loosen his biceps but there was no use, it was pure muscle and was only turning me on.

He just looked at me, as if I was crazy.

"I think I might suck on whoever's tits decides to take you on as their man because they will be a fucking saint to deal with your moodiness. It's called a smile, ever try it before?"

"No," he answered curtly.

"Have you ever wanted to punch someone so hard in the face that your fist blows right through their skull?" I asked while eyeing him up and down.

"No, but I've wanted to fuck someone so hard I would get them out of my system." His heated gaze traveled very slowly from my legs up to my breasts where they lingered and then to my face. A fire lit up inside me from his perusal and I could feel my fists starting to clench from the need to punch him. Arrogant ass.

"Get out of here," he said while turning and facing the

steering wheel.

"I hate you, you're so infuriating." I lied about the hating part as I gathered my things.

"It's better that way, Lo."

"Why? Because you're in love with me?" I singsonged as I opened the door to the car.

I was about to leave when he grabbed my hand and pulled me back down on the seat. His face was inches from mine as he spoke into my ear. His hand was wrapped around my neck, keeping me in place.

"Don't ever belittle my feelings for you again. I might not be the man that you want or the man that deserves you but that doesn't mean you can treat me like the crap that comes out of your mouth. I would do anything for you, Lo, so don't make it seem like I'm some jack off that can only stare at your mouth-watering tits. I'm more than that and you know it."

His nose brushed up against my cheek, making every last hair on my body stand on end. He took in a deep breath and then pushed away, leaving me feeling cold and confused. He gripped the steering wheel of the car and looked out the front window.

"Get out," he said in a menacing tone.

"Kace, I'm sorry—"

"Don't. Just fucking don't."

I sighed, knowing that he shut himself off. Understanding when it was my time to step down, I opened the car door again and stepped out, before closing it, I leaned in and spoke to him one last time.

"For what it's worth, I know your worth in my life and it's invaluable to me."

I closed the door and walked up the stairs to Diego's place feeling sad for the man who needed love more than anyone else that I knew. I just wish I was the one who could give it to him but I wasn't set out to share my heart with two men and right now, my heart belonged to the one and only Jett Colby.

***

"How many more layers do you have to go?" Diego asked as he hovered over me. I was in the second room and this one was more exotic. There was a table in the middle of the room like Jett had in the Bourbon Room but it didn't look as fancy. The room was covered in gold linens, walls and flooring. It was exquisite with the lush fabrics that lined the bench against the wall and the gold and crystal fixtures that hung from the ceiling. It was purely gorgeous.

I was painting a thin damask pattern in a metallic gold that popped off the matte paint of the wall. It was very time consuming and I had to do multiple layers in order for the paint to make its full effect but so far, I was in love with the feel of it.

"Probably one more," I answered while observing my work. "I love this room, Diego. It's bright but romantic. I could see myself in here with Jett."

Nodding, Diego said, "This room is a great reflection of you, I could see you in here as well."

I gave him the "cut the flirting" look and he just laughed. The man was incorrigible when it came to flirting, it was all he ever did. He should be happy Jett wasn't around because I think Jett would have cut off Diego's balls by now. Although, Diego had some kind of street cred that he still didn't share with me so I wasn't sure how far Jett could get when taking down Diego, even Kace for that matter. Diego was fun and easy going but there was a dark side to him that you could see in his eyes, they were experienced, aged far beyond his young years.

"When is lunch going to be ready? I'm starving." It's been two days since I went over to the Lafayette Club and I had seen Jett zero times so I wasn't just starving for food, I was starving for him as well.

I talked to him every night and a couple of times throughout the day but it wasn't the same. It seemed so stupid. We were only living a couple miles apart but it seemed like we were in different states. I hated every second of it but he just kept reminding me that in the end, everything was going to work out.

"Pizza takes time, Goldie. You can't rush it."

"It's Dominos for fuck's sake. It should take ten minutes." I rubbed my stomach and set my paint brush down. I lay down on the floor and looked up at the brocade covered gold ceiling. It was interesting and different to have a fabric on the ceiling but it worked, it just upped the elegance of the room.

"Did you hire a decorator to help you out with all of this?" I asked, wondering how he was able to put everything together.

"No, did everything on my own. I've done a lot of research and made sure to take my time when designing each room. I wanted them to have a reflection of the vintage circus feel without being too cheesy."

"Well it's not cheesy at all. I could see myself squirting a few orgasms out in here."

"You are quite the lady." Diego laughed and shook his head.

"Why circus?"

He took a deep breath and said, "My life has always been kind of a circus, never knowing what the next act is going to be, juggling the good and the bad, so I thought what better way to express myself than finally being the ringmaster and taking control. The key, Goldie, is having control. It's what makes me move, what pushes me. Without that control, I'm lost."

"I know how you feel. When I first lost my parents, all I wanted was a bit of control because it felt like everything was flying out of control. After a while, I just became tired, like I wanted to just give up and that was when Jett walked into my life. He saved me," I whispered.

"Is that why you love him?"

"Love him?" I sat up and looked at Diego as if he was crazy. "I don't love him."

"Ha!" Diego shrieked loudly. "Who are you fooling? It reads all over your face when he calls you or when you talk about him. You love the man."

I bit my bottom lip and lay back down, thinking about Diego's assessment of me. Okay, yeah, I probably loved the man but there was no way in hell I was going to tell him that. That was asking for my heart to get broken. He was slow when it came to our relationship and using the big L word was relationship suicide.

How nice would it be to express my feelings though? The minute I heard Jett's voice at Kitten's Castle, I was pretty sure I started falling for him at that moment. Then he took me into his world, introduced me to some of the best girls I've ever met and gave me a chance to better myself all the while protecting me with the utmost care. How could I not fall in love with the man? He wasn't giving me much of an option.

"Told you," Diego teased as there was a knock on the back door. "Pizza! I'll go pay, you set up the drinks and plates in the kitchen."

He took off and I scrambled to my feet, feeling slightly light-headed from the fumes. My phone chimed in my hands as I walked to the kitchen. I looked down and smiled to myself. It was from Jett.

Jett: Little one, did I tell you that I had a dream last night that you were spread across my desk, arms and legs strapped down so you couldn't move and I had that delectable pussy of yours for dinner?

I gulped as my lady lips started to tingle with need. It's been two days and I felt like I was going to crumble into dust from the strong need I had for him.

Goldie: Hungry? Maybe have yourself a little sandwich to put a dent in that appetite of yours.

Jett: I'll always be ravenous for you.

Goldie: If I didn't know any better, I would say you're trying to flirt with me.

Jett: I don't need to try, little one.

God, a couple of text messages and I was heated up to the point that I was about to head off to my bedroom to take care of my burning need.

Goldie: Do you know how horny I am? It's kind of ridiculous the need for you that is running through me.

Jett: Patience, little one. I promise the wait will be worth it.

Goldie: I'm not a very patient person. When I have something in my head, I want it right then and there and all I can think about is that beautiful cock of yours running up and down my slick pussy.

"I thought I told you to get us drinks," Diego said as he walked into the kitchen, making me jump three feet in the air and drop my phone.

"Jesus Christ!" Holding my heart I looked down at my phone that now had a cracked face. "Great!" I said with sarcasm. "Look at what you mad me do. My phone is broken."

"It's not broken, it's cracked. It just looks ugly now and it's not my fault. Stop sexting your little boy toy and pour us some drinks."

"I wasn't sexting him!" I lied while I grabbed cups.

"Yes you were. I can tell by the way your upper lip is sweating."

Wiping frantically, I said, "It is not."

Clapping his hand together loudly, he laughed as he sat down at the kitchen table and grabbed a piece of pizza. "God, you're too easy."

"You wish. If I was easy then you wouldn't be popping a chubby every time I walked by, you would have me in your bed, panting and screaming your name." I acted out what I would do as

I held on to my breasts and put on a good show, rivaling Meg Ryan in *When Harry Met Sally*. When I straightened up and brushed my hair to the side, I smiled at the dumbfounded look on his face, grabbed a piece of pizza and took a big bite.

"Thank God I was able to record that. I'll be using that later tonight." He wiggled his eyebrows as he shoved his phone in his pocket.

Slapping my pizza back on the box and reaching for his pocket, I said, "You did not get that on your phone." I fondled his pants for his phone as he sat back and let me try to find it.

"A little to the left sweetheart and you'll hit gold." A little to the left would have been his crotch and there was no way I was going there.

"Give me your phone."

He laughed as he handed it over. "I didn't record it. Paranoid much?"

I looked down at his phone and the picture on his wallpaper was of a melted fleur de lis, kind of like the one that was on his back that I saw, at least one of his tattoos.

"What's this?" I asked, showing him the picture.

He grabbed the phone from me and said, "Nothing you need to worry about."

"What, are you part of some kind of secret gang?" I joked.

Not making eye contact with me, he sat back and grabbed another piece of pizza. "Something like that." My phone chimed, letting me know that Jett texted me back. He nodded at my now cracked phone and said, "You might want to see what lover boy wants. I'm going to go work on some things. I'll catch you later."

"You know it's only going to eat you alive by holding it all in," I called over my shoulder.

He turned and smiled at me. "The only thing eating me alive are those killer tits of yours. One flash, Goldie. I promise I won't tell Jett." He held on to his heart.

The serious moment was quickly removed from the air, and was replaced with humor and flirtation, classic Diego. That was his way of telling me to drop the topic because he wasn't going to get into it.

"Get real. I would never give you the pleasure of seeing my tits," I said while grabbing them.

His tongue ran around the outside of his lips as his heated gaze lit me up. "Don't play with fire, Goldie. Cup your breasts in front of me one more time and see what happens. I would never cross Jett but there is only so much a guy can take."

He got turned on from a breast cup? When I looked down, I saw that my shirt rode awfully low and he got a great view of about seventy five percent of my tits, yeah, that would do it.

"Ooops, didn't notice the short neckline." I smiled.

"Like fuck you didn't." He shook his head and walked away while calling out, "You're driving me to an uncomfortable state, Goldie."

"Get a woman!" I called out.

I looked down at my phone and tried to read Jett's text but couldn't see it so instead I called him.

The phone rang once before his smooth southern voice filtered through my ears.

"Hello, little one. What brings me such pleasure of hearing your voice in the middle of the day?"

"God, you're so formal. Who says stuff like that anymore?" I teased.

"Only a true gentleman."

"Is that what you consider yourself? I didn't think gentlemen stuck their heads in between ladies legs and sucked on their clit for hours."

"Hours?" He lightly laughed. "Don't give yourself such credit. You know damn well when I have that little clit of yours in your mouth you're coming in seconds."

Zing, zap, flappity flap flap...my pussy was drenched and calling out for Jett's cock.

"Down girl, self-respect," I murmured as I patted my crotch.

"What's that?" Jett asked.

"Nothing." I covered up.

"Is there a particular reason why you're calling or did you just want to hear me talk dirty to you?"

"As much as I love your sexy voice bringing me to the brink of orgasm, I wanted to let you know that I cracked my phone screen and can't read your text messages so I won't be able to answer—"

"I'll have a new one sent over immediately," he interrupted me.

"No, that's okay. I'll run out tomorrow to get one, I just wanted—"

Not letting me finish he said, "I'm having one sent over right now."

"Is that necessary?" I grew a little frustrated.

"Yes, it is. I want to be able to get in touch with you anytime and anyway possible. I think you fail to realize that hearing from you, even if it is just a text message refuels me. It pushes me to keep moving forward. I crave to hear from you, little one. I need to hear from you in order to keep my head on straight."

"Oh," I said like an idiot. It was hard to follow up with an intelligent comment when he turned my head into mush.

"I'll be sure to have everything transferred over to your new phone."

"Thank you, Jett. You didn't have to. I was more than capable of grabbing a new one tomorrow."

"It's my job to take care of you. When you wear my collar and call me yours, then that means I'm responsible for you no matter what happens. I'm glad you called to tell me. I would have been upset with you if you went out to get your own phone tomorrow. I know it can be difficult at times, but let me take care of you, Goldie. It's all I have that I can truly give you."

My gut twisted from his admission.

"That's not true, Jett. I don't need your money, I don't need your protection, what I need is you. Your brain, your heart, your soul, that is all that matters to me, even if you want to believe differently. I just need you."

"You're so different," Jett admitted as he let out a long pent-up breath. I could just see him now, leaning in his office chair, looking out his third floor window, contemplating what I said. "No one has ever wanted me for just who I am, besides my mother."

"Well, I've been lucky enough to see inside the thick veneer that you cover yourself up with. I've been able to break into it and see you for who you really are and I'm addicted, Jett. I want more of you every day. I want all of you."

"I know, little one. In time, you will have all of me. In time."

I hated that. I hated that I had to continue to be patient. I didn't understand why we just couldn't' be with each other. Because some jack off decided to make it his mission to threaten Jett? What a pathetic person. Like they don't have better things to do with their lives?

Instead of running my frustrations through Jett, I took a deep breath and said, "Well, I'm going to finish my pizza and then head back to the gold room to paint. It's so gorgeous, Jett, it's my favorite room here."

"Gold is your color, always has been," he said. "Please take a picture for me. I would love to see the talented artwork you're putting together for Diego. Your fine artistic touch has always amazed me, from the very first time I saw you."

"I will," I said, flattered.

"Thank you. Be good, little one. I'll call you tonight."

We hung up and I smiled to myself at the luck I had for landing such an amazing guy.

After I finished my pizza, I boxed up the rest and put it in the fridge. I started to head to the gold room when there was a knock on the back door. I looked around for Diego, but he must have been into whatever was going on earlier with him, so I went to the back door and opened it.

A courier held out a package to me and then walked away.

I looked down and saw my name written in green lettering in Jett's chicken scratch. I smiled to myself as I realized the man was on his game.

Inside the package was a new phone but this one had a slim green case on it and a screen protector. The green case was beautiful with encased jewels and was way too much for a phone case but I understood the message Jett was sending. I understood it quite clearly.

29
"WICKED GAMES"

Lo

Music beat through the thin walls of my bedroom as I sat up in my bed. I took a look at the clock on my night stand and saw that it was past eleven. Grabbing my phone, I saw that I had three missed calls from Jett. I must have dozed off after I took a shower. Painting such intricate designs for a long period of time took a lot of mental strength so by the time I finished, I was ready to pass out.

I contemplated calling Jett back but the music flowing through the walls had me intrigued so I set my phone down, put on my slippers and eased out of my bed. I was a curious person at heart and it usually got me in trouble, hence seeing Kace's dingy dong but I couldn't help it. I needed to get in trouble. It's what I did.

I slipped out of my room and followed the music to the main stage where all the acts of the club would be taking place. Diego didn't talk much about the acts or dancers as he put it so my curiosity grew stronger as the music grew louder the farther down the hallway I traveled.

Silently, I peeked around the corner to get a good look at the center stage and saw Diego sitting in a chair, watching something at the top of the ceiling.

When I looked up, I saw crimson fabric wrapped into a cocoon shape dangling from the ceiling. My gaze turned back to Diego who was moving to the beat of the music. He was shirtless, wearing only a vest over his broad mocha chest that showed off the perfect cut of his muscles. He was wearing a pair of black jeans that were open at the waist, displaying a sexy trail of hair that led to his waistline. His abs rippled under the movements he was making with his torso, causing my mouth to water. When I pulled my eyes off his abs, I took in his face and saw that he was wearing black eye-liner, making his gray eyes pop out even more, giving him an almost sinister look. His appearance was pulled altogether with a worn out top hat that sat crookedly on his head. He was liquid chocolate waiting to be licked.

The music picked up and I saw his body tense as he continued to look up. Clearly I was just showing up at the right time for a show, so I sat down in the hallway, which thankfully was dark since the only light that was showing was one spotlight on Diego.

I had a great view that was just close enough to see the glorious bulge in Diego's pants but far enough way to remain undetected. I was in for a treat. I rubbed my hands together and got ready for a show.

With the blare of a bass rocking through the speakers, the lights switched off and red laser beams shone down from the ceiling at the same time the cocoon started to unravel from the top. Multiple pieces of fabric fell down with the cocoon, showering the room with waves of crimson. The lights beamed off the fabric, giving off a dramatic effect, making it almost seem like there was a shower of red falling from the tall ceilings.

Once the unraveling stopped, Diego stood, with his pants hanging low and walked over to where a now dangling woman hung from the fabric.

"Where the hell did she come from," I mumbled to myself as I continued to watch, completely entranced.

She was breathtaking. Wearing only a red bra and thong, she hung with her legs tangled in the fabric, holding herself up with her arms stretched over her head as she dangled right above the floor.

The moment Diego reached the girl, his hand ran from her crotch, across her stomach and up to her bra where with a flick of his fingers, it was undone and her breasts fell out of the tight constraints.

"Holy hell." Her tits were perfect. If I floated down Tuna Canoe River, I would have totally had a lady-gasm from watching her tits sway with the ribbon. There was no way those were real.

Her hair was in a bun on top of her head but that was the next thing to go as Diego's hand fisted her hair and yanked out the clip to release it. Long, brown locks flowed toward the floor and swung with her movements.

Walking slowly around the dangling woman, Diego took his time, taking in every last inch of her. I was so confused as to what I was watching. Was he practicing an act? Or was this some of the kink he was talking about?

When the music changed with a dramatic beat, her hands hit the ground and she did a handstand as Diego snapped the fabric and she was freed. Right then, I knew they were practicing, their movements were too fluid and too on point with the music to not be practicing, unless they had some kind of robot sex. If they were having robot sex, then I was sticking around for that because I wanted to see what kind of freak magic it took to keep up with acting like a robot during sex.

I found my toe tapping to the music as the girl balanced

on her hands, tits falling forward and showing off her ass.

Now standing in front of her again, Diego grabbed one of the drapes and lowered it to her grasp where she gripped it. Diego grabbed two more drapes and when he pulled down on them, the girl's body flew out from under her, causing her to do a summersault while the fabric she was holding on to brought her up into the air. Like a fucking magician, Diego had her legs wrapped separately in two different drapes and in seconds she was hanging from the ceiling, her back to the ground with her legs spread wide apart.

I wanted to clap as they dazzled me with their laser beams and fancy ribbon tricks. I was captivated.

The girl's chest heaved as Diego stood between her legs and moved his hands from her feet to her inner thighs. With one quick pull, her thong snapped off and was thrown to the side like a damn whip sprouting off her body.

An inner pulse started to take place in my core as things started to get intense. Was this what Jett meant by dancer? Was he covering up and not telling me that they were sex-abitionists? Why he would cover that up, I had no clue. Maybe he didn't want me to be intrigued, well, too late because I was.

The music continued to pump as Diego's mouth started to ride up and down her thighs, getting closer and closer to that sweet spot that had me shifting on the floor. Her body writhed to the timing of the music, getting me hotter than I could imagine. I wasn't much to watch porn but right now, this exquisite show of nudity, lights and music had me breathing heavy and aching for one man's hands to find my own.

I watched as Diego's hands ran up the length of her body and gripped her tits. Her back arched to impossible curves, exposing her wet pussy for all to see. It glistened in the reflecting lights and I knew that she was just as turned on as me, probably even more since she had Diego's strong hands running along her body.

With precision, he grabbed her hair from underneath her,

forming her body into almost a circle, she was that flexible and then hovered right above her pussy while he licked his lips and prepared to dive in. From the side, I could see a bit of Diego's erection and I swear I saw his tip poking out the top of his boxer briefs. Was it the tip? I didn't know. I leaned on all fours and reached my neck out to see if I was right. His hips swayed with the music and when he turned my way, I was rewarded with a view that I was expecting. His erection was poking out to say hi.

I started to pant from the scene unfolding in front of me. I leaned forward some more to get a better look, to watch Diego's mouth cascade down upon the girl. His tongue darted out and I waited in anticipation for when it hit the girl's clit, trying to control my erratic breathing and stay hidden.

"Should you be watching this right now, Lo?" came Kace's whispered voice from behind me, making me fall flat on my stomach and stifle a shriek from being startled out of my ever-fucking wits.

He grabbed me by the ankles and dragged my body farther into the hallway so we didn't disturb Diego's practice. When he let go of my legs, I stood up and swatted him in the shoulder.

"What the hell are you doing scaring me like that?"

"What the hell are you doing watching Diego practice? I thought you were told to stay away from that."

"What does it matter? It's not any different from what goes on at the Lafayette Club," I said defiantly as I walked back to my bedroom, still hot and bothered.

"It's very different."

"How so?"

"First of all, that girl was naked. Jett Girls are never naked. Second of all, Diego was about to get naked in about two seconds…"

"Was he?" I spun around to look over Kace's shoulder but he pushed me to my bedroom and continued his speech.

"Thirdly, they were about to have sex up on stage, something Jett would never allow in his club."

"All right, so they're different. I still don't get what the big deal is. It's just sex."

"Jett doesn't want you to be pulled in that direction."

I stared at Kace for a second and then burst into laughter as I walked in my room and flopped on my bed.

"You can't be fucking serious." When he didn't flinch, I laughed some more. "Oh for fuck's sake, I would never want to be prancing my pussy in front of everyone while some guy does me from behind or hanging from some weird contraption. I don't need everyone knowing what kind of sounds I make when I'm having sex or the way my body contorts when an orgasm racks through me, that is only for my man's eyes." I was looking at my nails as I talked to him but when I glanced up to look at Kace since he wasn't answering, I saw the heat that glazed over his eyes.

I cleared my throat and said, "Anyways, why are you here?"

"You didn't answer your phone and neither did Diego so he was concerned."

I sat up in my bed and said, "Was he concerned that I was fucking Diego or was he just concerned about me?" I grew furious.

"No, he thought that someone found out your location and broke into Diego's club."

"Oh, well…I was sleeping and then was woken up by the music so I went to check what was going on. You know how I hate missing out on a good dance party." I started to "throw my bos" in the air while I danced to the drifted-off beat but Kace didn't find it amusing, shock alert.

"You need to call him."

"Can I see him?" I asked, needing his hands more than anything right now. "Will you take me to him, Kace?"

"Lo…" Kace warned.

"Listen, you can either take me to him or you can watch me finger myself from the need burning inside me and then you can explain to Jett later why I came without him near me."

"Jesus." Kace rubbed his face and shook his head. "Get in

the fucking car and lie flat on the seat." He paused at the door and said, "And keep your damn mouth shut. I don't need to hear about cat cocks again."

A smile ripped across my face from the distress in Kace's voice when he mentioned our previous conversation. I might not have the most eloquent conversations with people but at least I make a lasting impression.

***

Jett had his hand fisted through his hair as he leaned over his desk looking at a stack of papers. He was wearing a white button down shirt that was unbuttoned at least three buttons, showing off his gloriously muscular chest and from what I could see underneath the chair, he had a pair of navy blue slacks on. There was a glass of bourbon sitting on his desk next to him as well as a lavender tie that he must have pulled off earlier. I would have loved to see him all business-like and dressed up, he was hot as hell in a suit.

I lightly tapped on the door and stood in the doorway, awaiting his gaze. The minute he looked up at me and recognized me, he dropped everything and stood out of his chair. He was in front of me in two seconds with his hands gripping my arms and looking down at me. The stubble on his face made my mouth water while his eyes searched mine.

"Are you okay?"

"No." He tensed. "I need you, Jett."

"What happened?" he asked while searching my body.

I grabbed his hand, lowered it and slipped it under my thong. I pressed his middle finger into my slick folds and gave him a minute to understand what I was saying.

His confused look turned to dark and sinister as his middle finger lightly stroked me, testing out my wetness. A heat of desire flushed through my body as I moaned.

"You shouldn't be here." He nibbled on my neck as he

leaned forward. "But I'm so fucking glad that you are. Bourbon Room, little one. Wear nothing and stand in front of the tantra chair and wait for your next instruction."

The tantra chair was the wave-like lounge that sat on the opposite side of the Bourbon Room and we only used it once and it was the most amazing sex I might have ever had, thanks to the angles it allowed, so for him to mention the damn thing had me throbbing already.

I nodded my head, quickly tiptoed over to the Bourbon Room and undressed as quickly as possible. I flipped my head over, ruffled my hair and then flipped it back up, hoping I added a little body and sexiness to it. I stood in front of the chair and prayed that Jett wasn't going to teach me a lesson in patience because I wasn't sure how much I could take when it came to waiting. Seeing Diego's act and not being touched by Jett in a couple of days had me yearning to be taken, hard and fast.

Five minutes later, Jett walked through the doors with his shirt undone and his pants unfastened, just the way I liked to see him enter the Bourbon Room. Seeing him like that meant he was ready for business.

Grabbing the remote off the table that sat in the middle of the Bourbon Room, he walked over to me and looked me up and down. Appreciation lit up his eyes as he scanned every last inch of me.

"You're so fucking breathtaking," he admitted right before he turned on what seemed like a remix of some sort. Whatever it was, it was sexy as hell as the beat rolled through the walls, surrounding us with hard bass and soft ministrations.

"Do you have something to say to me?"

"I'm here to submit to you," I answered without hesitation.

Nodding, he took off his shirt, exposing his chest completely. His lightly tanned skin delighted me and made me want to lick his entire body.

"Pull my pants off for me," he demanded as he stood in

front of me. "And don't forget about my briefs as well."

He didn't have to ask me twice. I grabbed both his pants and briefs in my hands and maneuvered them over his hips, slowly. There were only few opportunities when I was getting intimate with Jett that I was allowed some control so when he gave it to me, I soaked it all in.

His chest heaved as his erection was finally released and I lowered his pants all the way. Normally, I would maybe give his dick a little lick or stroke but I learned not to veer from his demands so I restrained myself and let him step out of his clothes.

I kneeled in front of him, waiting for his next command. His hand reached out and played with my necklace.

He spoke in a hushed tone as he said, "It pleases me to see you like this, submitting to me, wearing my collar. It's such a huge turn on," he admitted.

I looked up at him, through my lashes and agreed, it was a HUGE turn on, judging by the way his cock jutted out in anticipation. I was still shocked to see that I had such an effect over such a powerful man, it was empowering.

His fingers pressed against my chin indicating he wanted me to stand up, so I did. He pulled me over to the chair and pressed his hand on my mound.

"How wet are you, little one?"

"So fucking wet." I was ready for this two days ago but I didn't say that, I learned to hold my tongue…at least a little.

Apparently happy with my response, he sat down on the tantra chair so his back was against the big wave and spread his legs so they hung over the sides. His balls sat directly on the chair and his erection stood proudly, just waiting for me.

"I want you to sit on top of me, little one, with your feet pushing against the bottom of the chair. But hover above me until I'm ready for you to take me, not a minute sooner."

Trying to understand his demand, I looked at the chair and tried to calculate how I was going to do this. He must have sensed my confusion because he gently took my hand and pulled me to sit down between his legs so my bottom hit the soft buttery leather of the chair.

His voice touched my ear as he said, "Press your back against my chest, little one, and prop your feet against the second wave in the chair. That will give you strength to hover above me."

My skin tingled from his close proximity, instructing me on how to please him. He could be so soft, so gentle at times it brought me to my knees.

I did as I was told and pressed against this chest with my back. I felt his erection barely rub against my bottom, causing a moan to escape my mouth as my head flew back against his shoulder where I kept it.

His tongue found the column of my neck and he slowly started to snack on me while his hands traveled from the junction of my thighs up to my rib cage where they danced dangerously close to my breasts. My body ignited under his touch, with his slow movements and deliberate licks, making me think of the way his cock would slide in and out of me.

My hands gripped his thighs as I continued to hover above him. Thank God for ab workouts because I was starting to feel the pressure he was putting on my body.

"You're so damn sexy, Goldie. Even though you're not supposed to be traveling over here, I'm so fucking glad you did because I've been dreaming of these perfect tits," he said into my ear as his hands cupped my breasts and toyed with my nipples. "These nipples have been haunting me. I've been wanting to squeeze them for a couple of days now."

My lungs burned as I tried to suck in air from the onslaught of emotions he pulled from me in such a short amount of time.

The slickness of my core rang out, begging for him to let me lower myself. I could feel every last pulse in my pussy as he spoke to me and felt my body with those unyielding hands.

"Jett…" I groaned.

"Patience," he murmured, once again using his go-to

word. Fuck patience, I wanted him to slam into me with all the power he had in his body.

"My legs are getting tired," I admitted, feeling my butt drop lower and lower each second.

"Well, we can't have that, now can we?" His hand pressed against my crotch and pushed my lower half down. My ass enclosed over his rigid cock and I broke out in a cold sweat while I waited for him to move his cock into position.

"I don't know if you deserve my cock today."

"I do," I said breathlessly.

"How so? I heard that you watched Diego's act when you weren't' supposed to. He's very sensitive about them right now and doesn't appreciate an audience."

"He doesn't or you don't?" I asked, mentally slapping myself for starting controversy.

His hand tweaked my nipple and I screamed out loud from the pleasure that ran through my body.

"Don't question me, little one. Another comment like that and I'll be leaving this room, taking your orgasm with me."

Now that would be the worst idea ever so I kept my mouth shut.

"Tell me, what did you do today to deserve my cock?"

I racked my brain to think of something good, something that would guarantee me a good pussy pounding but nothing was coming to mind. My brain went blank and I blamed it on the man who was underneath me, breathing into my ear, making me forget everything I did today, even my fucking name.

"Honestly, I can't think of anything because you have my gut and mind all twisted together from the way your breath caresses against my skin. You make my heart beat faster and my brain slow down, Jett. There is no stopping it when you're around me."

He hummed in my ear and said, "Good answer, little one."

His hand slid down my side and lifted me up temporarily so he could grab his cock and slide it into me. With the first touch

257

that caressed me, I moaned and flew my head back to find his lips attacking mine at the same time. His hand ran down my stomach and started to massage my clit as his tongue danced with mine.

He filled me perfectly but he didn't move his hips, he just played me like a damn instrument instead. His body heat filled my senses and turned me warm to my very core. He was intoxicating and I couldn't get enough of him.

"So fucking beautiful," he murmured as he moved his spare hand across my breasts. "Press against the bottom of the chair, little one, and start moving me in and out of you."

I used my leverage against the chair to thrust my hips and it was so fucking good. Too fucking good. My back arched as I pumped myself and set a pace that was going to get me off in seconds from the pressure of his cock and the way his finger ran against my clit.

"Oh, Jett," I groaned. My hands wrapped around the back of his neck, giving me more leverage and letting me pump harder. His chest tightened under me, letting me know that he was just as close as I was.

His breathing became heavy and his lips were kissing me now on my shoulder, nibbling on me.

A burning sensation started at the pit of my belly and every last nerve ending I had fluttered with a blinding sensation that traveled from my toes to my pussy.

"Jett!" I screamed as I fell over the edge and pounded up and down on top of him. His hands left their stations and gripped my hips. His head flew forward and he bit down on my shoulder as his body tensed and he groaned out his pleasure while rapidly moving my hips up and down.

When he released my shoulder, he lowered his head and I lowered my body over his. His arms wrapped around my waist, not breaking our most intimate connection. His lips found my temple and kissed it lightly.

"It's always so fucking perfect with you, Goldie. No matter what I do, it's always so goddamn perfect."

He gathered me up in his arms and brought me over to the bench where there was a robe for me. He cleaned me up quickly and then looked up at me with the robe in his hands. He was about to put it on when his brow creased and he dropped the robe. His hand went to my shoulder and he said, "Did I bite you?"

A little giggle popped out of my mouth. "You kind of did."

"Jesus, I'm so sorry. Are you okay?" He rubbed my shoulder and examined his bite mark. "God, I don't remember doing that at all."

"I'm fine. I actually kind of liked it."

"You did?" he asked all cute-like.

"I did. It turned me on, not that I needed to be anymore turned on than I already was."

"I'll keep that in mind." He smiled lazily at me as he grabbed the robe and wrapped me up in it. He grabbed one for himself as well and walked me to the door of the Bourbon Room.

"Are you going to send me back to Diego's?" I asked as he grabbed my clothes and tucked them under his arm.

"No, little one. Now that you're here, there is no way you're going back until the sun comes up. You're mine for the night. We're going to your room. I need to feel your skin against mine as we fall asleep. You've turned me into an insomniac when you're not around. I need some sleep."

"Sleep sounds nice, as long as you're wrapped around me."

"As long as you don't start dreaming about panty-eating dinosaurs and are able to sleep like a normal human, I don't think we have a problem with me wrapping my arms around you." He smiled down at me.

I stroked his cheek and gave him a kiss. "You're such a smart ass but I love this side of you. It's refreshing."

"Refreshing?"

"You know…" I puffed my chest out and stood tall, "I'm Jett Colby and I'm serious and can eye- fuck a girl to orgasm," I said in a deep, horrible southern voice.

He laughed, the most glorious laugh ever and then said, "Fuck, I hope I don't sound like that."

"Well, something close to that," I teased as we walked down to my room.

It was moments like this that my defiance came with great reward. I wasn't supposed to visit him and even though I did, I was greeted with a warm and loving Jett. It made my hope for what we were going through grow stronger. He wasn't pushing me away, he really was trying to protect me.

30
"HOLD ON"

Jett

The smell of coffee permeated my office walls as I looked over a couple of bid options my lawyer put together for Lot 17. Everything was coming together and I felt confident in the proposals we had on the table. I had my lawyer put a couple bids together just in case after the Mayor's Ball I found something out that needed to be addressed in the proposal. Right now, we accounted for every little thing that could go astray and wrote up a proposal for each. They were due the day after the Mayor's Ball so we had to be prepared.

I couldn't wait for all this bullshit to be over and to get Goldie back in my arms. Last night...fuck last night was amazing. After we played around in the Bourbon Room, we went back to her room and I held on to her until the middle of the night, she woke me up with the stroke of her hand against my erection which I had no clue I had until she brought my attention to it. I reprimanded her in a good way for not asking permission first and wound up tying her to her bed, making her scream until her voice went hoarse. She then passed out in my arms and was able to contain her crazy sleeping habits and wake up with her head resting on my shoulder. Our blankets might have been swirled around into a rat's nest in the middle of the night but she stayed in my arms.

A light knock came to my office door and a little honey-haired girl popped her head through the crack, making me smile from ear to ear. She did that to me, without even saying anything. Just her presence sent my heart hammering.

"May I come in?"

"Of course," I said as I sat back in my chair.

She was freshly showered and she had a little bag at her side, probably her overnight clothes from the night before. Stopping in front of my desk she twisted her hands as she looked down at me.

"What are you doing, come here," I said as I scooted out from my desk and patted my lap.

Her eyes brightened as she walked over, set her bag down and sat on my lap.

The flowery scent pouring off her was heaven as I took in the smell of her skin, the softness of her hair and the way she felt in my arms.

"You smell divine." I rubbed my nose against her neck.

"I have to go," she announced sadly. "Kace is waiting for me downstairs. I just came up here to give you a kiss goodbye."

We made out on her bed for at least ten minutes before I came up here, making sure I gave her enough kisses to last the next couple of hours so I found it adorable that she wanted to sneak one more in.

I rubbed my thumb against her cheek and said, "Can you hang in there just a little while longer? I hope to have this all settled after the Mayor's Ball which is coming up shortly. After that, this whole mess should be taken care of."

"Really?" She brightened. "Then I can come back here, go back out on the stage and be with the girls?"

"I don't know about the stage…"

"Jett Colby!" She planted her hands on her hips.

"We can discuss that when the time comes."

"I want to be out there," she said defiantly.

"Little one, don't make me raise my voice. I said we will discuss it later."

"Ugh, you're infuriating. Fine, but I'm going to put up one hell of a fight."

"And I look forward to it," I replied while nuzzling her neck.

"I really have to go." She sighed. "Kace is already pissed at me for making him bring me here."

"Kace can suffer while I soak you in for a little while longer."

She wrapped her arms around my neck and brought her lips down on mine. She was soft and gentle with an edge of yearning. Her tongue darted out of her mouth and I tasted minty toothpaste on her lips that ignited a flame deep within. I felt my cock start to grow under her and she noticed too because she pulled away and looked down between us.

"Seriously? You have more in you after last night and this morning?"

"You do this to me, little one," I said as I rested my forehead against hers. "I told you, I need you all the time. I can't control it."

"I need you, too." She took a heavy breath and looked out the window behind me. "I can't wait for all of this to be over, Jett. When it's over, do you think we could, you know, go out in public together? Like on dates?"

The sadness in her voice spilt my heart in two, I hated that our situation made her sad, that I couldn't give her what a normal boyfriend could, that I couldn't even take her out on a simple date like she deserved. She really deserved so much more than me but I was a selfish bastard who wouldn't give her up. She was mine.

"We will have to lay low for a little bit but after the storm passes through, yes, we'll be going out in public together. I would love to take you on dates, little one. Please don't think otherwise, I just need some time to figure this all out."

She nodded and started to get up but I held her down, I had to tell her something that she wasn't going to like very much but I thought I would rather be open and honest with her than she find out another way.

"I need to talk to you about something."

"Okay," she said with hesitation.

"The Mayor's Ball is a big deal and for me to pull off the fact that we aren't together, I need to show up with another date."

"Okay, so are you bringing one of the other girls?"

"No, I don't want to put them at risk. I need someone who is neutral and frankly who I don't care about."

"What are you trying to tell me, Jett?"

"The other day when I had a visitor, that was Keylee Zinc."

"Keylee Zinc, who the hell is…" She stopped her words as realization hit her. "The kiwi?!" She got off my lap faster than I could react and started to pace the length of my office. "You mean to tell me that you're going to the Mayor's Ball with the kiwi who blatantly said she would do anything to become a Jett Girl? Are you trying to deliberately hurt me?"

"What?" I stood up and walked over to her. "No, I would never do that. I'm doing this because it's the only way…"

"That's bullshit. I don't want to hear about how it's the only way. It's not the only way. Take me, take Kace, take Miss Mary for fuck's sake but don't take the one girl who I would rather eat razor blades over seeing socially ever again. Why the fuck would you do that?" I could feel the tension pouring off her, the anger, the sadness.

"I'm not doing this on purpose, Goldie. It's the perfect

distraction. Keylee is well known in the crowd I need to mingle with so if people see us together..."

"They'll think you're together," she finished for me but in a hysterical tone. "I don't want people thinking that."

"Goldie, please think rationally for a second about this."

"I am," she shouted. "I'm the only one thinking rationally. You drive me crazy, Jett. Keeping me in the dark about everything, sending me off to live with some guy who, I'm sorry, has some kind of flirting problem because that's all he knows what to do and then you say you're going to go to an intimate affair with another woman but not just any woman, you're going with the kiwi. Fuck, Jett. You're breaking me in two."

Flirting? I was going to have to talk with Diego because that was unacceptable. No one flirted with my girl but me but I wasn't about to bring that up with Goldie. That would be a separate conversation I had with Diego later.

I grabbed a hold of her arms and made her stop pacing. I forced her to look me in the eyes as I spoke carefully.

"Remember what I told you? Have faith in me, little one. In us." I ran my hand along her necklace. "I gave this to you to let you know that I'm committed to you and you alone. No one else and no one else can step in between that. I might be taking someone else to a ball but you'll be in my heart."

She deflated and shook her head. "I hate this so much. Ever since I met you it's been an up and down roller coaster. I don't know how much more I can take."

Unfortunately, she was right. I've been nothing but trouble for her since she got here. If it wasn't my damn emotional brick walls stopping her from moving forward, it was my father's lack of humanity. I was fucking with her in every which way and I still couldn't be the bigger man and let her go. I kept stringing her along. I didn't want to admit why but in the pit of my stomach, I was pretty sure I knew the reason.

"Please, little one, just hang in there a little bit longer."

Deflating, she nodded her head and looked up at me with

unshed tears. "I just want things to be normal."

"Me too." I wrapped her up in my arms and kissed the top of her head. "Me fucking too."

Instead of sending her on her way, I walked her down to the garage where Kace was waiting and helped her into the car. Before she pressed her body against the seat to hide, she gave me one last kiss on the lips and held on to her necklace.

"Don't forget about me, Jett."

"Not possible, little one. You're on my mind every damn second of the day. Go back to Diego's, relax and enjoy painting. Get lost in the paint and before you know it, you will be back at the Lafayette Club and in my arms."

I kissed her one last time and sent her on her way. It was painful to send her back to Diego, especially since our relationship was rather shaky but I didn't have a choice.

When I got back to my office, my cell phone buzzed against the hardwood of my desk. The number was unknown but I answered it anyway. Given everything that was going on, I was taking just about any call these days.

"Jett Colby," I answered.

"It's nice to hear your voice, it's been a while. Did you receive my letter, son?"

My father. I cringed from the way his voice slithered through the phone.

"I did but there was no use sending it because like I told you, there is nothing going on between Goldie and me."

"That's not what I heard," he replied.

I kept calm as I sat in my chair and fiddled with a pen between my fingers.

"Oh, please enlighten me with what you heard because I can guarantee you that they're wrong. Goldie is no longer a part of my life. She was a decent fuck but after I grew bored of her defiance and inability to submit properly, I dropped her out of my life."

My dad laughed and said, "You always had a problem with

control."

"And you always had a problem with being a decent human," I retorted, not enjoying the father- son conversation he was trying to have right now.

"Life isn't full of candy canes and bimbos, Jett. Take a lesson from me, you have to be cutthroat to get anywhere in this world."

"That's where you're wrong. I've climbed my way to the top using honesty and good business sense. I've never had to bribe anyone or slip anything under the table to get what I wanted."

"Yes, but what you fail to realize is that you never would have gotten to where you are without the foundation I built you and the Colby name. I made you, I launched you into this business world and without me, you would be no one. So don't go and scoff at my techniques because without me, you would be a sorry shit just like your mom."

"Fuck you," I replied, losing my temper.

A maniacal laugh escaped his mouth before saying, "Choose wisely, Jett. Lot 17 or Goldie."

"Do whatever the fuck you want to Goldie, I couldn't care less about her. Why don't you get a fucking clue? It's over between us. She's up for grabs for all I care," I shouted into the phone praying that he didn't read my bluff.

"Good to know. I'll let Rex know she's fair game."

I clenched my teeth and held back the hiss that wanted to escape my throat. "Good fucking luck to him," I said instead.

"See you at the ball," my dad called out and then hung up. I tossed my phone on my desk and leaned back in my chair, rubbing the side of my temples.

I swore under my breath as I thought about my dad's threat and my bluff to throw Goldie under the bus. I just prayed that my father was all talk because if he laid one finger on Goldie, I would lose my ever-fucking mind.

31
"THIS IS HOW WE DO"

Goldie

"Black thong, black bra, black skinny jeans, white tank top and a leather jacket, oh and I can't forget my three inch black pumps."

Jett groaned into the phone. "I think you need to change into a turtleneck and a corduroy jumper."

A laugh escaped my mouth. "How do you even know what a jumper is?"

"My nanny used to wear them all the time. It was her go-to outfit. She had them in every color and texture."

"Classy." I laughed.

"At least there was no chance that as a teenager I would be hitting on my nanny."

"I guess you're right about that. I bet you were a troublemaker."

"Kace and I got into our fair share of trouble but luckily never really got caught. We were able to get away with anything back in high school. No one believed that a Colby would do anything to get in trouble and pair that with Kace's smile that used to melt the pants off all of our teachers, even the men, we got away with all of our pranks."

"Kace knows how to smile?" I asked, acting completely shocked. "I don't believe that one second."

"Well, he's changed," Jett admitted. "The guy's been through a lot in his life and is having a hard time digging himself out of the emotional turmoil that blinds him almost every day."

My heart broke as Jett talked about his friend with such sadness in his voice.

"What the hell happened to him?"

"That's not my story to tell, little one. If he wanted you to know, he would have told you. Just let it go."

"I just wish I could help him," I admitted. Kace owned a little piece of my heart, ever since the day I first met him, even though he was an ass, he still put a hole in my heart and buried himself in it. He helped me through so much and was always there for me, I only wish I could return the favor.

"I do too."

The mood of our conversation went down to an artic level so I tried to spice it up a bit.

"You know, there's still time, you can still go out with us tonight."

The girls were coming over to Diego's and we were all going to go out for a little night on the town, have some drinks on Bourbon Street and do a little dancing. My friend Lyla from Kitten's Castle was going to meet up with us and we were going to take advantage of our night off. Of course Diego and Kace would be trailing us to make sure we didn't happen upon any trouble but I could ignore two beefy bodyguards that took my breath away every time their shirts happened to slip off.

"You know I want nothing more than to spend the night

with you, watching you get sloppy drunk and calling me a cow's vagina but I have a prior engagement I must attend."

"You paint such a beautiful picture of me," I teased. "I still need to see that security tape of that so-called night. I still don't believe you."

"You're saying that I conjured up such a lie?"

I took a second to think about it and then said, "Why, yes. I do think that."

"Little one, it disappoints me that you find it so easy for me to make up such a story about you calling me a cow's vagina. If I made up such a story, I would have at least called me something like a vulture's asshole."

I choked on my spit from Jett's rather rare display of vulgar language.

"Why, Jett Colby, next time I see you I might have to wash your mouth out with soap."

"I know something else you can do with my mouth," he said in his deep southern voice that ran from my ears all the way down to my toes.

"Are you trying to torture me?"

There was a knock at my door as Jett tried to answer me but I couldn't hear him because in a loud wave of cheering came all four Jett Girls with their arms raised above their heads and causing a ruckus.

"Lo!!!!!!!!!" they shouted and all pounced on my bed.

"Who're you talking to?" Babs asked as she smacked her gum and popped a bubble.

"I bet it's Jett," Tootse said as she poked one of my tits.

I swatted her hand away and spoke into the phone, "Sorry, I didn't hear what you said."

"That's okay, little one. I will—"

Before I could hear him finish, Pepper grabbed the phone from my ear and said, "Lo is ours tonight. Goodbye, Jett." And with that, she hung up the phone making the girls cheer and causing my mouth to drop open. Were people allowed to just hang up on Jett Colby like that?

She tossed the phone on my lap and then clapped her hands together.

"Francy, pull it out girl."

Francy stood up and pulled a flask from her purse that was slung across her chest. She then grabbed five shot glasses that she brought over from the club and handed them out.

Apparently we were going to get shitfaced tonight because the dragon fire coming out of my shot glass singed my nostril hairs.

Pepper turned a dance party mix on her phone, set it to the loudest volume and blasted us with a deep beat. We held our arms up in the air and swayed to the music as we counted off.

"To a night with the girls," Tootse said.

"To a night without sweaty, fat man lap dances," Pepper said.

"To a night of no Kace Haywood breathing down our necks," Babs stated.

"To a night of pussies and tits," Francy said.

"To a night of debauchery," I finished.

We clinked our glasses together and chugged them, then held them out for a chaser of...another shot and slammed that as well.

Tootse's face cringed, Francy squealed, Babs shimmied and Pepper thrust her pelvis in the air, we were fucking ready.

Bourbon Street was crawling with tourists, locals, street performers and barely-covered women. I took a deep breath and swallowed the smell of booze mixed with the faint smell of bile...I was home.

Kace and Diego trailed us from a decent distance but always kept an eye on our movements. When Kace showed up, his heated gaze took in my apparel making me shrink from his stare down. Then Diego walked in, wearing a tight V-neck shirt and all bets were off. We had two hot bodyguards and the girls could not be more happy about it. They all were swooning over Diego, I didn't blame them.

"Where to first?" Babs asked as we walked by a duo of street performers dancing on some worn-out pieces of cardboard. The streets were barely lit by lanterns outside of the establishments that flanked the street and bar music and live bands competed with each other, trying to draw in the drunkards to spend more money.

"Daiquiris!" Francy fist pumped the air and took off to a corner bar where there were no doors, just a wall of fifteen different flavored daiquiris that would have you sitting on your ass in less than half an hour if consumed too quickly.

We all followed her and scanned the different flavors that were offered. Flavors ranged from cherry limeade to blue cooler to witches brew.

"Five party animals," Babs ordered for us while slapping down some money on the counter. "And we want the biggest fucking cups you have." She winked at the bartender that was covered in piercings and tattoos. He winked back and started making good on our order.

Francy grabbed my hand and started twirling me in the middle of the bar.

"Time to get loose, baby. You've been too tense lately," she shouted over the music.

"That's what happens when you take me away from my favorite dick," I replied making Francy throw her head back and laugh.

"Thank God I always have my little pussy cat next to me."

We both looked over at Tootse who was bobbing her head to the music and tapping her foot on a barstool. Babs had her arm around her and was twirling Tootse's hair in her finger while Pepper humped the backside of Babs's back. Someone must have started drinking a little earlier than the others.

"Baby!" Francy called out, waving Tootse over to us.

She smiled, grabbed three drinks that were already poured and brought them over to us. The neon cups graced our hands with straws that were almost as tall as the long cups begging for our lips. With one sip of the freezing cold liquid, I knew it was going to be a long, inappropriate night for me.

***

"I'm pretty sure my bra snapped loose a half hour ago," I slurred over the pounding music that was radiating off the walls of a very small and very smelly bar we found. "Look at how jiggly my tits are," I said to Babs as I shimmied at her.

Babs stood up straight and pulled my tank top off my chest and looked down my shirt. She nodded and said, "Yup, you got some free boobies going on there."

"Shit, how did that happen?" I asked as I swayed to the music.

"Probably around the same time you decided to tie your leather jacket around your head like a turban," she said while swatting one of the sleeves that kept dangling over my forehead.

"You have to admit though, it's one hell of a fashion statement."

Babs leaned forward and said, "I'm pretty sure I saw some girls wearing their jackets just like that in the bathroom but couldn't pull it off like you can."

"It's not for everyone," I said as I showed off my turban, framing it with my hands.

"Just gorgeous," Babs encouraged me.

"Ah beh dink ferg, Mama." Tootse came tumbling in sucking her thumb and holding on to her right breast.

"What?" Babs asked. "Was that English?"

I was hammered but even in my drunk state I couldn't translate what Tootse was trying to say.

"I don't think soooo," I said while dancing in a circle.

Francy pulled up next to Tootse and wrapped an arm around her. "Time to say goodnight to your friends. You're drunk, sweetheart, and you can bet your ass I'll be taking advantage of you."

"Aww, lesbian sex," I cooed as my hands started to wave

in the air.

"Just sex," Francy corrected me. "You don't have to put lesbian in front of it."

"But it sounds so much cooler." I continued to sway as I said, "I was a lesbian once, then Jett came and licked my pussy...saddled me right back on the bologna pony express to pleasure Ville."

"I heard that's off Dick Drive and Cunt Circle," Pepper said as she handed out more shots.

"You might want to take her back too." Babs laughed while pointing at me.

"What? Nah! I'm a peach. A damn peach."

"You're a peach all right," Babs retorted.

"Are you going to lick my peach?" Tootse pouted to Francy.

"Christ," she mumbled while pulling her in tight. "I'm taking off ladies. Apparently there is some ripe fruit waiting for me."

"I can't take the visual," Pepper said as she cringed after taking her shot and Tootse's since she was out of commission now.

"I can!" I shouted as I used the now empty shot glass as my telescope. I zoned in on Tootse's cleavage and said, "Ahoy matey, we got here an erect nipple." My finger flicked her nipple, making her squeal.

"That tickled. You tickled my tit." Tootse burst out in laughter. "Tit, my tit. Tit, tit, tit tickler. She's the tit tickler."

"And that's my cue," Francy said as she blew kisses to us and pulled Tootse out of the bar.

"That should be my stage name!" I all of a sudden became excited. I ran to the bar, asked for a pen and grabbed a napkin.

"What are you doing?" Babs asked as she looked over my shoulder.

"Two dots and there!" I said as I held up my napkin.

"Tit Tipper?" Babs asked with a confused look.

"What?" I turned my napkin around and looked at it. "Oh

shit, I meant tickler."

Babs and Pepper burst into laughter. "You're so twisted."

I shrugged my shoulders and put the napkin in my shirt so the writing hung over my breasts. I shimmied at them and said, "Watch out, the tit tipper is going to get you."

"That wouldn't be the worst thing," Pepper said as she motioned to the bartender for more drinks. I wasn't sure how much more I could take, I was at my limit. One more might be sending me down to tile town to meet up with the porcelain gods and that was a visit I really didn't want to make.

"I think I want some water," I said to the bartender who looked me up and down and nodded in agreement. Fucking judger. As If I was the worst thing that crossed Bourbon Street.

I caught my reflection in the mirror behind the bar and instantly understood why the bartender was handing me a tall glass of sober-inducing water.

My hair was sticking out at all ends thanks to my leather jacket turban, my makeup was smeared down my face from sweat and my bra was practically falling out of my shirt from being unattached. The only classy thing about me was the sign hanging out of my chest and that was bordering classy.

"Holy shit, I'm a hot mess," I announced to the girls.

Babs looked me up and down while taking a sip of some kind of red concoction in her hand. "I'm surprised you just noticed that. You were at hot mess status an hour ago when you started pelvic thrusting one of the hobo's dogs on the streets."

My head snapped up to Babs in disgust. "Please tell me it was at least a German Shepard."

"What is wrong with you?" Pepper laughed.

I shrugged and we all leaned against the bar to survey the dance floor.

"A lot of tuna flakes out there tonight," Babs said.

"Tuna flakes?" I asked while sucking down my water.

"A nicer way of saying pussy ass hoes."

"Oh." I nodded as if that made complete sense.

"If they're pussy ass hoes, what does that make us?" Pepper asked.

We stood there for a second until I raised my hand.

"Yes, Lo?" Babs called on me.

"We're a trio of bitch-a-corns."

"Bitch-a-corns?" Pepper and Babs asked at the same time.

"Bitches but by far superior. The most majestic and beautiful bitches you will ever meet. We shit rainbows and fart rainbow dust. Our tits are sparkling orbs and when a man sinks into our pleasure hole, he is touched by a leprechaun's teat, blessing him with multiple orgasms in one night."

"Well shit," Pepper said as she took a sip of her drink. "I had no clue my pussy was so goddamn sacred. I would have wiped it with fucking sheets of gold if I knew the powers it had."

"Common mistake," I responded. "You never know of your pussy powers until one day, you're just sitting and a little man in a green hat pops out of your pussy, waves and pops back in. That was how I found out."

"Yeah, time to call Kace," Babs said as she looked me up and down. "I'm calling it, you're toasted."

"Wait!" I held up my hand. "I need to go to the bathroom. I think I might pee my pants." I held my crotch like a two-year-old and danced around.

Babs shook her head and said, "Go to the bathroom, I'll text Kace to take you home." She patted me on the head and continued, "It's beddy bye time for Lo."

I nodded and took off toward the bathroom. My legs wobbled in the three inch heels I was wearing as I tried to avoid the dancers that kept getting in my way to the bathroom. A couple that was one pair of underwear from being ripped off bumped into me while their tongues massacred each other.

"Blek, gross. Get a room," I said maturely as I pushed them back. They remained unaffected by my assault. Someone else bumped into me, this time it was a frat boy with a neon light-up necklace wrapped around his face.

"Douche bag," I called out as I walked past him, sticking my foot out to trip him which I failed at because what I thought was his leg was actually a bar chair. I stumbled forward from tripping myself and ran into a strong pair of arms.

"Well, hello." I looked up but didn't recognize the man holding my hands. "Ooops, sorry about that tall, dark and handsome." I tried to pat his chest but he wouldn't let go of my hands.

"Your hands are nice and moisturized, mister, but I'm pretty sure we passed that point of accidently holding hands and now we're bordering creepy so if you don't mind letting go…"

Before I could react, the man let go of my hand and lifted his elbow which connected right next to my right eye, pitching me into a plain of darkness. The last thing I remember was falling to the floor while saying, "Captain Throwin' Bos!"

32
"AIN'T IT FUN"

Jett

"Yes, Jeremy. I would prefer to not look like a damn moron at the Mayor's Ball."

"Well, I just figured since you already had three tuxes that you wouldn't want another one."

"Assuming is never a way to conduct business, Jeremy. Have my measurements sent to Armani and make sure the tux is ready by Wednesday in case there needs to be any adjustments."

"Yes, sir," Jeremy said over the phone. "Do you want a town car or limo?"

I mulled over Jeremy's question. Limo sent the sign of high importance but also was more intimate when it came to bringing a date and I didn't want to give Keylee the wrong impression. It was bad enough that I had to go shopping with her for a damn dress. What woman couldn't go shopping by herself? A town car would be less intimate but it was more reserved, less elegant.

"Can I offer a suggestion, sir?" Jeremy asked, sensing my hesitation.

"Please."

"Maybe for appearances, you come in a limo."

Jeremy was right. I was attending the Mayor's Ball to obtain an image and I needed to stick with that. I ran my hand over my face as I thought about the night. It was the last fucking thing I wanted to attend, especially with the clingy Keylee but it was the finish line, the end to this madness.

"That's fine."

"Are you sure, sir?"

"Yes, book it Jeremy."

I listened as he tapped away on his third appendage, his iPad, and waited until he was done.

"Do you want to send over anything to Ms. Zinc before the event?"

"No," I said without flinching. "This is purely business. I don't want her thinking anything else."

"Okay, I just didn't want to be rude…"

"Business, Jeremy, there is nothing rude about it."

"Yes, sir," he said weakly.

"Have you heard anything else about my father's plans for Lot 17?" I've been dying to ask Jeremy for a while but I didn't want to bombard him. He did just start up with his new group and I didn't want him to feel like a spy but I couldn't help it. I had to fucking know.

"Not about Lot 17 but about something else."

"What?" I asked as my muscles tensed.

"According to some of the girls that work with him or for one of his companies, he's started auditioning…women."

"For what?" I was pretty sure I knew what but I wanted Jeremy to confirm.

"He has a new club that he is testing out in one of his hotels. It's locked down security wise. Apparently you have to have some kind of clearance to enter and entry is only granted after a finger print and eye scan."

A burst of laughter wanted to escape me but I kept my professionalism around Jeremy. "You have to be kidding me."

"I'm not. It's of the highest security. No one can get in unless your dad knows about it."

"Interesting." I ran my hand over my chin as I thought about what he was trying to plan.

"According to one of the girls I talk to in my group, he is asking the girls who are auditioning if they would audition nude. There is a privacy clause before they can even speak to your father."

"Nude?" Fuck, he was most likely starting up an illegal sex club. I could only imagine what he had plans for.

"Yes, if any of the girls speak about it, they pretty much can kiss everything they have and all their future possessions goodbye. That's how tight-lipped it is."

"How did your friend find out?"

"She was processing the privacy clauses and happened to glance down at them. She wasn't able to read that much but she got the jest of it all."

I nodded even though he couldn't see me and filed that new information in the back of my head for another day. Right now I had to focus on getting through the Mayor's Ball.

"Thank you, Jeremy."

My phone beeped, indicating I had another incoming call. I pulled it away from my ear to see that Kace was calling me. There could only be one reason why Kace was calling me while he was watching over the girls while they had their fun.

Goldie.

"I will talk to you later, Jeremy. Please arrange those items we talked about." I didn't let him respond as I kicked over to the other incoming call. There was a loud beat playing in the background and a lot of drunk screaming which irritated me instantly because all I wanted was to hear what Kace had to say but I could tell it was going to be difficult.

"What's going on?" I asked.

"Goldie." With that one little word, I felt my heart drop and my pulse start to pick up. I sat up in my chair and placed my head in my hand, trying not to pull out every last strand of my hair.

"What's wrong? Is she okay?"

"She was knocked out by some big guy. I didn't see it coming because he was nowhere near her until she tripped and fell into him."

"What did he do?" I asked, pressing my other ear, hoping it would help me hear Kace better.

"Knocked her in the head, she flew to the side and hit her head on the corner of the bar. Diego is taking her to his place now. She's going to be okay, we have a doctor coming over to check on her and stitch up a cut in her hairline that she obtained when she hit the bar."

I stood up and started for my door when I heard Kace say, "Don't, dude. Sit back down. You can't see her."

"Why the fuck not?" I asked angrily, not liking being told what to do.

"There was a..." his voice cut out.

"What?" I asked while raking my hand through my hair.

"...was a..." he cut out again.

"Fucking Christ," I screamed into the phone. "Get out of the goddamn bar!"

Kace was silent as I listened to the bar music fade out and then the slam of a car door.

"I'm being followed, dickwad," Kace said.

"Shit. Did they know you were with Goldie?"

"I'm pretty sure. When she went down, I kept my distance but I was still in the same bar as her. They could probably put two and two together."

"I knew this wasn't a good fucking idea. Why did I let

them go out there?"

"Because they need to have lives too, Jett."

I blew out a frustrated breath and itched to throw something against my wall but refrained.

"What were you saying in the bar when I couldn't hear you?"

Kace took a deep breath and then said, "There was a note tucked into her shirt."

"What did it fucking say?" I grew angrier every minute.

"It basically issued you a warning. Next time, he won't be as nice. You have to choose, Jett."

"Fuck," I said as I sat in one of the chairs in my office and placed my elbows on my knees and sunk down. "What the hell am I supposed to do now?" I asked dejected.

"Well, you need to stay the fuck away, that's for damn sure. If they see you leave your place now, they're going to know where you're headed and it will blow everything. You need to keep your space."

"I can't keep my fucking space when my girl is fucking bleeding out of her head and could possibly have some kind of concussion. Fuck, Kace!"

"Getting mad is not going to do anything," Kace pointed out. "I know that you're itching to…" Kace cut out for a second as I heard him mumble a curse word.

The sound of shattering glass echoed through the phone as I heard Kace grunt and swear some more.

"One more move and I'm going to blow your fucking head off," came a distant voice. My breathing grew silent as I tried to listen to what was happening. "Tell your friend that his precious little slut isn't the only one we can harm." With that, a gun shot went off, sending a blinding noise through the phone.

A sickening feeling crawled up my spine as I stood and paced my office. I knew better than to start shouting through the phone, in case they could hear me or they picked up his phone. There was a light moan in the phone, indicating that Kace was hopefully still alive.

Bile rose to the top of my throat as my heart sank for the two most important people in my life.

"Fuck," Kace mumbled over the phone. "I'm going to be home late tonight, sweetheart," Kace said in a groan.

"What the fuck? Are you okay, Kace?"

"Bastard shot me."

"Where?" I headed for my bedroom and started pulling out all the dark clothes I had, I was sneaking the fuck out.

"In the arm, grazed my skin but I'll need stitches."

"Christ. I'm coming to get you."

"Stay the fuck where you are," Kace spoke with anger. "I swear to God, Jett, you have to stay there. It's the only way this is going to work."

I sat on my bed and felt deflated, useless, helpless. I was mad at myself, for letting this go too far, for being too stubborn about Lot 17. I should have given it up earlier and then none of this would have happened.

"I'm going to call him. Tell him Lot 17 is all his. I don't want to deal with this bullshit anymore."

"To hell you are," I heard Kace say as his car started. The fucker was going to drive himself to the hospital. "If you do that, you're showing so many weaknesses that now it's Lot 17 but later on it's something else like your club. You can't give him that. I'll make sure Diego takes care of Lo. You hold strong, go to the Mayor's Ball and fuck his shit up afterwards."

"Will this ever stop?" I asked, showing vulnerability.

"I don't know but what I do know is that I can't drive and talk to you with a shot arm at the same time. When I'm done at the hospital, I'll see you later. We'll find a way to pay back that dickhead for what he did to Lo."

For once, I wasn't jealous of the protective instincts Kace had over Goldie because at this moment, I was glad that I wasn't alone when fighting for the one person that could bring me to my knees. I was glad to have someone in my corner.

***

Sleep eluded me as visions of Goldie being hurt ran through my head over and over again. It wasn't until three in the morning that Kace got back to the club. He sent me a quick text that he was just scraped, had a couple of stitches and is bandaged up. I met him down at the entrance of the club and helped him into his room even though he said he didn't need it. The idiot shouldn't have been driving in the first place but trying to control him was like trying to calm a raging bull. He did whatever the hell he wanted.

Because of the pain Kace was going through, we didn't get to talk much about what happened but what he said to me still resonated through my head. It was now four in the morning and all I could hear was Kace saying, "Don't be stupid and let your emotions get the best of you."

How could I not? In a short amount of time, Goldie has wiggled her way into my heart and has planted herself there. A numb feeling crawled through my body, turning my heart cold and my mind black as I continued to keep my distance from Goldie, knowing damn well that she was hurt.

This time, my dad went too far and what I feared the most was that after Lot 17 was acquired, would this all be over? If he didn't get Lot 17 it sure as fuck wasn't going to be over, not after what my dad displayed today.

I pulled on a pair of casual sweatpants as I slipped out of bed. Sleep was no use, I couldn't even begin to fall asleep with so many thoughts running through my head so instead, I paced my room. I pulled on my hair, the back of my neck, I punched my wall a couple of times and finally I couldn't take it anymore. I tossed a T-shirt over my head, grabbed my keys and headed for the passageway that led to the streets of the Garden District without being detected. At least I hoped. If my dad knew about the passageway and informed his minions of it, I was going to be fucked.

Within seconds, I was looking out the window to the underground passageway for any idling cars or anything out of the ordinary. I didn't see anything that seemed concerning so I squeezed out of the small opening and took off toward St. Charles Ave where I had a taxi waiting for me.

I was going against everything I should for the mere protection of Goldie but I couldn't stay away, I had to be near her and I had to see if she was okay with my own eyes.

33
"RED HANDS"

Lo

Warm arms circled around my body as my head pounded to extreme levels. I've been in and out of it but the click of my door and not so smooth footsteps up to my bed woke me up. I stiffened from a man's touch and tried to scoot away in the dazed-like fog I was trying to see through.

"Don't," I mumbled. "I only want Jett."

"Little one, it's me." His warm southern voice caressed the side of my face.

"No, you can't be here," I said while trying to squirm away but his grip was too tight on me.

"I can do whatever the hell I want and if that means coming here to make sure you're okay, then I will."

I turned in his arms and came face to face with the most beautiful man ever. His hair was pulled in all different directions, like he's been stressing over something, his face had a delightful five o'clock shadow caressing his jaw and his eyes carried a lot of worry in them.

My fingers reached out and ran the line along his jaw. His eyes closed from my touch and the grip of his hand on my waist grew tighter.

"You're here," I whispered, almost as if I couldn't believe it.

"Of course I am. I couldn't stay away."

"What happened?" I asked while holding my head. "All I can remember is dry humping Francy's legs, wearing some kind of hat and drinking way too much."

His hands grabbed mine and kissed the back of them. "That seems about right when it comes to you and drinking." A small smile spread across his face but was quickly gone when he searched my eyes. His body leaned over me and clicked on the light that was on my nightstand. Light spread through the small room and lit up the disturbed look on Jett's face.

"What's wrong?" I asked.

His hand reached out and caressed my right eye which made me wince with a shot of pain coursing through my face.

"Ahh, fuck," I exclaimed while pulling away.

"Don't move," he said softly as he climbed above me and straddled my body. His head hovered right above mine as he examined my eye. Pain was flowing through his features as he took his time looking over my apparent injury.

"Let me guess, this isn't from a random person?"

He shook his head no and lowered his lips so they were only a whisper above my eye. He kissed me lightly and gripped the side of my head with his hands as his lips tried to heal my eye.

When he pulled back, I saw the fear that washed over him, the fear of me being hurt, the fear of losing me. My heart wept for him, for the sadness that this stupid and idiotic situation has brought over us.

"I'm so sorry," he whispered before pulling back and

sitting at the edge of my bed with his head in his hands. "This is all my fucking fault and I just don't know what to do."

"What do you mean?" I asked as I tucked myself next to him, both of our legs dangling off the bed.

"What the fuck am I supposed to do? No matter what, you're going to get hurt."

Fear started to trickle down my spine as I felt his body start to retreat, his mood darkened and I could see that he was visibly uncomfortable with what he was about to say so I stopped him.

"I swear to God if you try to break this off with me because you want to 'save' me, I will cut your dick off so fast you will think there was a drive by machete man that just attacked you," I threatened using air quotes.

His face quirked with an eyebrow raised as he looked at me. I was dead fucking serious and he got that when he eyed me up and down. A small smile ticked at the corner of his mouth as he shook his head.

"It's crazy how much I know that's true, that you would really chop my dick right off."

I gripped his arm and rested my head on his. "Don't forget it. Do not give up on me because of a little set back."

His hand ran through his hair as he said, "It's not a little set back. You were hurt on purpose, Kace was shot—"

"What?!" My heart rate picked up as the words, "Kace was shot" ran through my head.

I got up and started looking around for my clothes but was hit by the pounding of my head. I fell to the ground and sat there, with my head in my hands and the threat of tears welling in my eyes.

Jett's strong arms came up from behind me and picked me up. He brought me to the bed and sat down, with me in his lap.

"What the fuck is going on?" I said into my hands, trying to hold back the tears. "Is he okay?"

"He's fine, he just got grazed. He's stitched up and back at the club sleeping it off."

"Sleeping it off? As if he is getting over a hangover? He got fucking shot! Shot, Jett!"

"I'm well aware of what happened," Jett gritted out.

Sensing his anger, I calmed my racing heart and said, "I just don't understand what's going on. What the fuck is Lot 17 and why is it such a big deal? Who is this dickhead who wants to control your life? And why was Kace shot at?"

Taking a deep breath, Jett said, "You and Kace are the closest things to me and the prick who is doing all this knows that. I'm trying to make it seem like that's not the case but I'm apparently not doing a good enough job. I can't go into detail about everything because I truly don't want to get you involved…"

"Well, too fucking late for that," I yelled while holding my head and getting off Jett. "Just tell me already what this is all about."

He grabbed my hand but I pulled away. His shoulders sank in defeat, an act I never thought to see come from Jett. He was such a stoic man that to see him slouch, to show some vulnerability was such a foreign thing to me.

"You trust me, right?"

"Of course I do."

"Then please, Goldie, please let me take care of this. It is killing me inside that I can't take care of you, that…that I'm not man enough to give you what you need."

Our previous conversation about his ex came to the forefront of my mind and I gritted down on my teeth as I thought about the bitch who made Jett so insecure. I wanted to know what was going on because being kept in the dark wasn't working for me anymore but I also wanted to give Jett the opportunity to be the person he wanted to be, the person to protect me so I swallowed my pride and grabbed his hands.

"I want you to know that I have never in my life felt so protected, so cherished and so lusted after in my entire life. You make me feel things I didn't even think were possible so please don't for one moment think that you aren't taking care of me, or that you're not man enough for me, because you are." I kissed him on the cheek and said, "It's just hard right now. I want to help and I get that you don't want to involve me but just understand that this is frustrating for me too, okay?"

Nodding his head, he wrapped his arms around my shoulders and said, "I understand, little one." He kissed right above my bad eye and shook his head. "God, I can't…" His words caught in his throat and his lips nuzzled into my hair as he continued to speak, "I'm losing myself in you. When Kace said something happened to you, I thought the ground fell out from under me. You're more than just another Jett Girl to me, Goldie. You're a bright spot in the dull life that I've been living, you make me feel like I'm not alone anymore and your laugh, your smile, they're so goddamn infectious that I find myself losing every last wall I've built while I'm around you. You're a challenge, you're a little spitfire with a mouth that could bring a sailor to his knees and the best thing about all of this is that for some godforsaken reason, you chose me. You chose to stick through all the bullshit I've thrown at you and you've forgiven me for my insecurities and immature ways of handling things." He gripped my head with both hands as tears fell from my eyes. "I'm falling for you, Goldie, so fucking hard and fast that I can't even catch my breath, find my footing and all want to do is spend my days with you in my arms but I have to deal with this bullshit first. I have some things I need to think about but please know that no matter what, my heart rests in those beautiful hands of yours. You're the keeper, little one."

I was floored. Jett could be an eloquent man of words but what he just said to me, what he just confessed was his way of saying those three little words that I craved to hear from him, that I craved to say to him. He was telling me, in his own Jett Colby kind of way that he loved me and for the love of all dicks and vaginas, I was in love with the man too. From head to toe, there was nothing that I didn't love about the man. He was perfect. From his perfectly styled hair, to the southern voice that rang from his lips, to his insecurities and the stoicism he felt was so important to display.

I may spar with Kace more, I may joke around with Diego but when it came to Jett, he took the cake. His soul was married to mine the minute he asked for a bourbon at Kitten's Castle. We were brought together for a reason and I wasn't going to let that go.

I kissed his lips and let his arms wander up my back, under my shirt and relished in the feel of skin-to-skin, one of his favorite things to feel. I grabbed the hem of his shirt and pulled it over his head.

"Goldie, this might not be the best time—"

"Shh." I put my finger over his lips. "I want to feel you."

I pushed him back on my bed and then took off my shirt and bra that was already unclasped, I chose to ignore the thought that popped up in my mind as to why my bra was undone. Jett's eyes lit with passion and eagerness. He wasn't about to maul me but I knew if I asked, if I encouraged him, he would have me submitting to him in two seconds flat.

Hovering right above him, I pressed my lips to his lips and then pressed my breasts against his bare chest. The feeling was erotic but comforting. My nipples danced across his skin as I positioned myself so I was more on his side and resting my head on his shoulder. His hand that was wrapped around me, caressed my back lightly and his lips found the top of my head. My fingers danced across his chest as we laid in silence, just holding each other, taking a moment out of time to just feel each other and experience.

I nuzzled his chest and said, "Thank you, Jett, for being everything to me. For making me feel again and for making me realize that there really is something to live for."

His only response was a hitch in his breath and a kiss to my head. I knew I caught him in a vulnerable moment so I wasn't going to push him, instead, I fell sleep to the tracing of his fingers against my bare back. All thoughts of the night before vanished and images of Jett and I together clouded my mind as I drifted off into a darkness that encompassed my mind and body.

When I woke up that morning, I was alone to my disappointment but I understood given the situation. I stretched my body and winced when my head throbbed and my muscles ached but not in a good way. I looked over to the side of the bed that Jett was sleeping on and saw that he left his T-shirt that he came in. It was folded on the pillow he was using and I smiled to myself as I grabbed it and threw it over my head.

The smell of sweet and charming Jett Colby washed over me as I hugged my pillow. It was the little gestures that I appreciated, that kept me moving forward. I went to grab my phone to thank him when I saw there was a note on my nightstand along with a bag from Café du Monde. That could only mean one thing. I took a quick look inside and moaned from the sight of three beignets waiting for my consumption. The man was a god.

I grabbed the card that was next to the bag and tore it open. In typical Jett fashion, his chicken scratch was scrolled across crisp white paper in green marker.

Faith, I just needed to have faith.

Little one,

I need you to know that in a matter of a couple of months, you have flipped my world upside down. You're the reason why my heart is set on striving for more because you make me want to be a better man, to give people what they deserve. Your smile, your bright eyes and your quirky mouth bring me so much damn joy every day that at times, I wonder how I became so lucky to have stumbled across you at the cemetery.

These next couple of days are going to be hard. You're going to see and hear things that you're not going to like but I want you to know that it means nothing because in my heart, you're the one who lies there, who has buried herself so far deep in there that I know if you ever left me, it would no longer beat. You're my pulse, Goldie.

Have faith in me and in us.

-J

34
"FREAK"

Jett

My knee bounced up and down as I took a sip of the lousy excuse for champagne that rested in my hand. Never did I ever picture myself at an expensive boutique, sitting on an uncomfortable chair while waiting for some girl to try on dresses but here I was, waiting for a private fashion show from Keylee.

It was the night before the Mayor's Ball and instead of spending it with Goldie in my arms, I was dealing with a stressed out Keylee because I kept canceling our "dates" to pick out a dress. I was hoping that she caught the hint that I really didn't want to go, especially after everything that happened with Goldie and Kace, I just couldn't see myself going out in public and being fake unless it truly mattered, like at the Mayor's Ball but Keylee wouldn't drop it. So that was why I found myself surrounded by cooing women and Keylee's touchy hands.

"Oh I don't know about this one, it seems a little revealing," Keylee announced loud enough that I could hear her through the dressing room. Great, revealing, just what I fucking needed.

I ran my hand over my mouth as I sat back in my seat, might as well get comfortable since it seemed like I was going to be here for a while.

"I think it looks so sexy on you," said the saleslady who was helping Keylee. I was sure she did think it looked good on Keylee. Keylee was about to drop a chunk of change in the shop and the lady would most likely do anything to have that commission.

"I don't know," Keylee said hesitantly. She was a good actress, I didn't buy her shy act one bit. I knew who she was and what she's done in the past. She's a spoiled elite-ess with the ability to make anyone feel for her at the drop of a hat. I was annoyed already and I had to spend the next night with her hanging all over me just to put on a front.

"Let's just show him."

"Okay."

The curtain to the dressing room flew open and Keylee stood in front of me wearing a purple dress made of some kind of shiny fabric. There was a slit on the right that went to mid-thigh which was all right but it was the low cut of the dress that went to her naval that had me adjusting in my seat, not because I was attracted to her but because her chest was popping out so much that I didn't know what to tell her.

"He's speechless!" the annoying saleslady said. I looked at her name tag and cringed. Of course her name was Meghan. Goldie and I talked about meanings of names one day and she introduced me to Urban Dictionary that has a meaning for every name. Meghan came up as a skanky ass ho which pleased Goldie because apparently there was a Meghan at Kitten's Castle that fit the description perfectly and so did this girl.

The memory of looking up names with Goldie one night

brought a smile to my face that Keylee misinterpreted.

"You do like it," she said while sauntering over to me.

Fuck, wrong time to think about Goldie.

"It is revealing," I said while trying to look anywhere else but her cleavage which was approaching me at eye level.

"But not too much, right? And it's purple. I know how that's your color…for Jett Girls and all." She batted her eyelashes as bile threatened to surface.

She stood right in front of me and then without invitation, sat down on my lap. I was so surprised, I didn't have time to react before she wrapped her arms around my neck and pulled me in close.

"You can't tell me that you don't find me attractive in this dress, Jett, that purple isn't my color, that you can't envision me, riding you all night long in your Bourbon Room," she whispered into my ear.

If Goldie was the one in the dress, with her body clinging to mine, whispering in my ear, I would have laid her down on the ground and had her naked in seconds but with Keylee, I was more repulsed then anything. The only thing holding me back from letting her land flat on her back after I peeled her hands off me and got up was the fact that she was the key to getting my dad to lay off for a day or two until the bids were accepted. After that, I would find a way to protect Goldie, a different way and it didn't consist of her living under Diego's roof. That was for damn sure.

I put on a brave face and said, "You look great in purple but I think it might be a little much for the Mayor's Ball."

She smiled and leaned closer, pressing her lips right against my ear as her breasts were shoved against my chest. "I can always save this one for the after party." She winked as she pulled away but not before brushing her hand against my crotch with a suggestive smile.

She must be delusional because there was no way in hell there was going to be an after party with her. After the Mayor's Ball, I planned on spending the night in Goldie's arms, even if it meant sneaking into Diego's place. I was going to need to be refueled by Goldie's gorgeous and beautiful personality after tomorrow night.

"Let's try something a little more tasteful, Meghan. But I want to stick with purple. It seems to work well for me and Jett agrees."

"I have something in mind that will be perfect," the skanky ho said as she winked at me and went off to the main floor to grab another dress.

If another woman winked at me, I was going to jab them in the eye with my damn finger. Irritation was filling up my very soul as I continued to sit in an uncomfortable situation that my father put me in.

"Jett, I need some help," Keylee called out.

"Uh, I think that Meghan girl is going to be back soon."

"Ouch, I think I'm stuck," Keylee said in a panic. "Please, Jett, I need your help."

I rolled my eyes and walked over to the dressing room. Keylee was fidgeting with the zipper of her dress when she looked up at me in the mirror.

"Can you please assist me? Just get it going."

Uncomfortable wouldn't even begin to describe the feeling I was having. I knew damn well that she could wait for the skanky ho but this was her way of getting me to be more hands on. I squelched the growl of anger that wanted to come out of me and grabbed the zipper on the dress. With more force than I needed, I yanked the zipper down at the same time Keylee let the dress drop to the floor by removing her arms.

She stood with her back to me, wearing only a thong and that was it. She had zero modesty because instead of covering up, she thrust her chest out and shook her hair. Her tits were high and perky, definite boob job. There was no way those were real, they were hot, but there was no way they were real.

Turning around to face me, she grabbed my lapels before I could retreat and brought me closer to her. I made sure to keep my eyes trained on hers so I didn't give her the wrong impression. Everything about this moment was so wrong and I didn't want to make it worse by taking a look at her chest. I wasn't interested but I was a man too. It was difficult to not take a look but I kept my eyes focused on the task at hand.

"Put your hands around me, Jett. I want to feel those strong hands on my skin, running up my rib cage and playing with the skin under my breasts. I want to feel your mouth all over my body, sucking on my nipples, playing with me, teasing me. I want to submit to you, Jett. My body is yours to do whatever you want with."

It was rather disturbing how much she knew about me and the Lafayette Club. I didn't know where she was getting her information but I didn't like it. She knew too much.

Keylee was pretty but she wasn't Jett Girl material. She would be in it for all the wrong reasons and she was too privileged. She wouldn't work hard like the other girls. Plus, she was annoying as fuck and I couldn't deal with that.

"Now is not the time, Keylee."

"But there will be a time, right, Jett?" Her hands ran down my chest and gripped the loops of my belt. I kept my hands in my pockets, not wanting to give her any ideas.

"Keylee, this is supposed to be a friends thing, I thought I made that clear. You're beautiful, but I don't want to jump into anything just yet."

"I know but I just want you to know that I see the way you look at me and I see the interest in your eyes. I want you to know that when you're ready you won't have to ask because I'll be so fucking wet and ready for you that you will be able to slip that giant cock into me with ease."

Who the fuck talked like that? Goldie said shit like that but that was different, she was with me. Keylee barely knew me. She was slightly psychotic. Good pick, Jett.

"I'll keep that in mind," I said nicely as I pulled her hands from my pants and set them to her side. I looked at my watch and said, "It's late, Keylee, and I have a couple of proposals I have to work on. I trust your style. I'll be by your place to pick you up tomorrow at eight. Please don't be late."

"But what about dinner?"

I turned around from the slight distance I was able to put between us. "I'll have to reschedule. I do apologize for my rudeness. Will you forgive me?" It took all the strength in my body to be kind to her.

She smiled and said, "Depends on how you plan on apologizing," and with that, she shut the curtain to the dressing room and cut the cord she had wrapped around me. Thank Fuck.

I grabbed the champagne that was on the table, finished off the dog piss and then took off for the front while texting my driver to pull forward. When I hit the front of the store, I was blinded by photographers.

Keylee.

She must have tipped them off. I took a deep breath, put my hand in front of my face to block off the flashes and headed to the car my driver just pulled up.

"Jett, is it true you're now seeing Keylee Zinc?"

"I heard she's pregnant. Is the baby yours?"

"Did you like the way she looked in that purple dress?"

Photographers called out questions as I retreated to the car. Well, I wanted my dad to believe I wasn't involved with Goldie, if this didn't do it, I didn't know what would.

When I was in the car, I pulled out my phone and hit speed dial. I needed to hear her voice, I needed to be reenergized. She answered on the second ring.

"So I have this special ringtone for you and I swear to God, it's like I'm Pavlov's dog or something because every time I hear your ringtone, I instantly get wet."

Now that was what I was fucking talking about, that was what I needed, my sweet little one talking dirty to me.

"Your ability to answer your phone without saying hello is refreshing. What if I was someone else?"

She thought about it for a second and then said, "I guess they would know the kind of effect you have on me."

"And what kind of effect is that?"

"You make me horny," she said without a hiccup.

"Why do I always happen to be in public situations when you get all spicy on me?"

"Where are you?" she asked with innocence.

"In my car, going back to the club."

"Why don't you swing by the French Quarter. I heard there is a girl in a kink club who needs a good spanking."

Groaning, I responded, "You have no idea the kind of punishment I want to give you for making me hard right now but I can't. Soon though, little one, very soon."

"How soon?" I heard her rustling around.

"Are you in bed?" I asked, ignoring her question.

"I might be."

"What are you wearing?" I asked as I gulped and started to get hard, just from the mere thought of her in her bed, talking to me. That is what she did to me, the little man-eater.

"If I said nothing, would that make you come over?"

"It would make me come, that's for damn sure."

"Mmm, Mr. Colby, it sounds like your lips are a little looser these days. It seems like I'm having a bad influence on you."

"I wouldn't say it was a bad influence but it's an influence."

"I hope that's a good thing."

"It's a fucking fantastic thing, little one," I said weakly."

"You sound upset, is everything okay?" she asked, always perceptive.

I ran my hand through my hair, a nervous tendency, as I looked out the window at the pastel houses of the Garden District.

"Yes, I just…" I paused and caught my breath from my pounding heart. I never realized how much I needed Goldie until she was untouchable. "I miss you," I admitted.

"You're killing me," she said as I heard her shift again.

"What are you doing?"

"What do you think I'm doing? I'm giving the old beany boo a tickle. Keep talking, your voice alone will make me come all over my damn fingers.

"Fuck, Goldie. What did I tell you about touching yourself? Whose pussy does that belong to?"

I heard her huff out a breath. "Well, since it's attached to my little v-section here I would say mine but by the tone in your voice, I guess I have to say you."

"You have to say?"

"God, you're demanding tonight."

"Who does your pussy belong to, little one?" I asked between clenched teeth.

"You," she said breathlessly, still shifting.

"Goldie! Are you still touching yourself?"

"What?! No…"

"Do you know what happens to liars?"

"They climax while their boyfriend tells them how much he would love to eat them out?"

I shook my head and held back the smile that was trying to cross my face.

"They're brought to the edge of orgasm while being tied down and then they never fall over because they are left hanging…for the night."

"You wouldn't…"

"I so fucking would so remove your hand from the delicious pussy of yours."

She moaned in the phone as her breath picked up."

"Goldie…" I reprimanded.

"Oh….God…" she breathed out. "I wish you were here, sucking on my hard nipples right now. They're so fucking hard, Jett."

I gripped the back of my neck as I took a deep breath of frustration. Frustration for not being able to be the one who brought my girl to orgasm. My erection from just hearing her breath pressed against the zipper of my pants and I shifted in my seat to get a little more comfortable.

I pressed the intercom to my driver and said, "Drive around until I'm ready to go back to the club."

Thankfully the limo I was in was completely closed off from the public and my driver. I unclasped my belt and pulled down my pants until my erection sprang free.

"Please tell me that was your zipper that I just heard."

"Do you have something you have to say to me?" I asked as I started stroking myself. My head fell back as images of Goldie ran through my mind.

"I'm so fucking here to submit to you, Jett. God, I want you so bad."

"Tell me, little one. Are you naked?"

"I am."

"How do the sheets feel against your gorgeous naked body?"

"Not as good as your hands would feel."

"Where would you want me to touch you?"

Her breathing hitched as she said, "I would want you to play with my nipples. I swear if nipples could have blue balls, mine would have the biggest blue balls known to man. They're just begging for your touch, for your fingers to roll them and then for your mouth to claim them."

A tingling sensation shot up my spine from her words.

"If I was there, I would not only claim your nipples but I would bite them until you moaned my name, then my mouth would travel down your stomach until I hovered right above your pussy. From there, I would tease you with little flicks of my tongue until you were sopping wet. Tell me, little one, how wet are you now?"

Her voice was strained as she said, "So unbelievably wet."

"Where are your fingers, little one? Are they inside, buried deep or are they just teasing that little nub of yours?"

"Teasing."

My strokes started to pick up, envisioning her just stroking herself but never going deep enough, like I do.

"I want you to bury your fingers inside you like I would. I want to hear you moan from the pressure you put on your clit while you finger yourself."

"I don't know how…" she said breathlessly.

"Yes, you do, little one. Just stick two of those beautiful fingers inside you and press down on your clit with your thumb. Do this for me, little one. Please me."

"There's nothing I want more," she said as she moaned out my name.

My cock twitched in my hand from the little mews coming through the phone.

"Oh…God." She panted. "Oh fuck, Jett…"

"Are you going to come?" I asked as my release neared.

"Yes, please, may I come?"

"Pull your hand away," I demanded, trying to stretch out my orgasm.

"What?!"

"You heard me, pull away."

A strangled cry escaped her mouth, indicating her displeasure with my command.

"Tell me, little one, what kind of sensations are rolling around in you right now? If you do a good job describing them to me, I will let you come."

"I'm numb." She breathed out. "My clit is throbbing uncontrollably as my legs tingle with passion. Passion that you gave me, that you made me feel. There is a fire that built up in the pit of my stomach and if I don't come soon I think I might combust. Fuck, if I was a guy, my erection would win a goddamn prize at a county fair. My lady balls are in your hand, Jett, please let me come."

I didn't hesitate because I could feel my balls tighten and my impending release start to come forth as I squeezed the tip of my cock. "You may come, little one."

"Thank fuccccck," she drawled out as her breathing picked up and unintelligible moans flew out of her mouth.

Hearing her come over the phone was my undoing. I leaned over and pumped my hand up and down until every last drop was out of me.

"Holy cock and balls, that was amazing," Goldie said over the phone, making me laugh.

"It could have been better," I breathed out.

"Well, I'll take phone sex Jett over no sex Jett right now any day. Thank you for lending your pussy to me. I hope it had a good time."

I laughed. "Don't make a habit of it. I'm not very good at sharing."

"Sharing is caring, Jethro."

"Jethro?"

"Not your full name?"

I laughed again. "No, it's just Jett."

"Well, that's boring. Are you sure it's not Jethro or maybe Jettispher or Jettonathan."

"You nailed it on the head, Jettonathan is my real name. How did you ever guess?" I said sarcastically.

"I'm just that good," she said in the phone with arrogance.

I told the driver to head back to the club and then sighed as I looked out the window.

"I miss you, little one."

"I miss you more, Jettonathan."

"Let me guess, that's going to stick?"

"Yeah, you're totally fucked. Sorry."

35
"COME WITH ME NOW"

Lo

A loud knocking sounded at my door followed by Kace popping into my room unexpectedly. It felt like déjà vu and as I wiped sleep from my eyes, I could have sworn I was back at the Lafayette Club, late for a practice until I saw the small room that I occupied.

"What the hell?" I said as I tried to make out Kace's body.

"Are you seriously just waking up right now?"

"Are you seriously barging in my room...again? For the love of God, get a hobby."

"It's noon and you're not answering your phone."

"It's noon?" I asked while looking around. "God, that phone sex must have really taken it out of me."

Kace's jaw tightened and that's when I saw the white bandaging that was wrapped around his arm.

My hand flew over my mouth as I stumbled out of bed, he caught me but winced from having to use his arm. Thankfully I got dressed after my little phone convo with Jett or else Kace would have had a handful of naked breasts right now.

"God, I'm sorry." I straightened up. "Are you okay?" I asked while eyeing his bandage.

"Just a scratch. How come you're not answering your phone?"

"Uh, just a scratch? A fucking bullet went through your skin."

"Why aren't you answering your phone?" Kace ignored me...like usual.

I threw my hands up in frustration and went to my phone.

"It's dead. I guess I didn't plug it in last night." I grabbed the cord and plugged the damn thing in. "Why? Do you have a secret you have to tell me? Did you finally lose your virginity last night and you want to talk about it?"

"Cute," Kace said while blowing out a long breath. "Jett was just trying to—"

Kace was interrupted by Lyla, my old roommate flying through my door. Ever since I've been staying with Diego, I've been able to visit her more often. She was out with us the other night when everything went down at the bar but the dumb bitch hooked up with someone and left early.

"Goldie, did you see..." Lyla stopped in place when she slammed into Kace. She looked up at him and her eyes widened. "Oh my God, who's the Adonis?" she said while looking at Kace.

Watching closely, I saw Kace's eyes scan Lyla up and down and a small twitch of a smile tickled the corner of his mouth as he appreciated every last inch of Lyla.

She licked her lips and gave him the same perusal that he did but spent more time looking at his crotch as if she had ex-ray vision. The heat in the room turned up dramatically as they both looked at each other, not saying anything. Holy hell, I was turned on just watching them.

I cleared my throat and said, "Uh, hello. You can eye-fuck each other later. Why are you both here?"

"Kace," he said while holding out his hand.

"Lyla," she said back.

"Oh, so you just give her your name as if it's nothing but I had to agree to be a part of your little gentleman's club world before you told me your name?"

He didn't look at me when he answered, "It's not my club."

My hands went to my hips and I felt like stomping my feet to get their attention. I poked Lyla in the side and said, "Why the hell are you here?"

She slowly turned away from Kace and held out a magazine. "Just delivering the news."

Kace's head snapped as he reached for the magazine but I was quicker than him, for once, since I beat the infuriating man.

"Give me that," he said sternly.

"What are you going to do about it?" I asked as I jumped up on my bed.

He walked over to me, grabbed both of my legs and pulled them out from under me making my ass fall to the mattress and my arms flail about. He grabbed the magazine from my hands, rolled it up and stuffed it in the back of his jeans.

"Hey, that's mine!" I said while trying to gain my balance from tornado Kace that just blew by.

"Call Jett," Kace said then eyed Lyla up and down and said, "Let her call Jett."

"Give me your number and I'll keep my mouth shut."

"Say nothing and I'll think about giving it to you."

"Good enough for me," Lyla responded as she followed Kace out of my door.

"Traitor!" I shouted as they shut my door.

I grabbed my phone but kept it plugged in as I turned my phone on. Sure enough, there were five missed calls from Jett.

I dialed his number and he picked up on the first ring.

"Goldie, why was your phone off?"

"It died, I forgot to plug it in. What's going on, Jett?"

He paused on the phone, making my stomach do a flip. What was so damn bad that he had to take a second to respond?

"There were some pictures taken of me yesterday, and they were published, but I have to tell you, nothing happened."

"What kind of pictures?"

"Pictures with Keylee Zinc."

"The kiwi?!" I shouted into the phone. "What were you doing?"

"I was helping her pick out a dress for tonight. I didn't want to go but I had to, to keep up an image. Please believe me..."

"What were you doing, Jett? What's in the pictures?"

He took a deep breath and said, "It looks so fucking bad, but she asked me to help her get out of a dress she was caught in and before I knew it, she was topless..."

"Topless?" I paused and thought about it. "They're fake, aren't they?"

"Wh-what?" Jett sputtered."

"Her tits, they're fake, right?"

"Um, well I don't know. I didn't touch them if that's what you're asking."

"I'm asking if they're fake, Jett. I don't think it's a very hard question to answer."

"Goldie, please..."

"Are they fake?"

"God...yes, they're fake. Jesus, why does it matter?"

"I knew it. You know, I looked up Keylee in Urban Dictionary and it said bitchy girl with fake breasts."

Jett paused for a second before saying, "Does it really?"

"After I get off the phone, it will."

"Goldie..." Jett breathed out. "Can you please listen to me?"

"I get it, Jett," I interrupted him. "You have to do what you have to do. It's a tough situation you're in and I know that

307

you're doing your best to take care of things. I trust you," I said while trying not to grit my teeth as realization hit me.

Jett would do anything to protect me, even if that meant being caught with another woman. Well, fuck that! I was over this Jett trying to protect me thing. It was time that I took matters into my own hands because right now, the only thing Jett was able to accomplish was push us further and further away from each other. I was done, if we were going to be apart, we were going to at least accomplish something.

"I'm so sorry."

"It's okay, Jett. One more night, right?"

"Hopefully," he responded with not much confidence. And that right there, that was my cue, this was no longer Jett's problem, this was ours.

"Are you coming over tonight?"

"Yes," he said matter-of-factly.

"Good, I will see you then. We can talk about this then."

"Are you mad at me?"

"No, Jett. I'm not. I respect the fact that you're doing the best you can for the both of us."

We talked for a little bit longer but I hung up the phone once my stomach started rumbling. I left my phone to charge and headed down to the kitchen. I was on a mission.

Diego was making a sandwich when he turned around and saw me.

"Hey, sleepy…"

He didn't finish his sentence because in one swift movement, his nipple was my prisoner as I held it in a death grip and looked him dead in the eyes.

"What the fu…" He tried to pull away but I just gripped tighter and spoke sternly.

"You listen closely, you motherfucker. We're going to sit down at this table, I'm going to eat that sandwich you just made and you're going to tell me every last fucking thing you know about Lot 17 or else I will pinch your nipple off so hard that it will look like a goddamn cherry tomato when I'm done with it."

"Jesus Christ," he said as he pulled away.

I grabbed his sandwich, took a big bite and pointed to the table. His hands found his nipples and put up a protective shield when I made a pinching motion at him. I followed him with my pinchers until he sat down.

I took the seat next to him and drank from the cup he had set down for himself.

"Now tell me what the hell is going on."

"Goldie, I told Jett…"

I lunged at him with my fingers and he backed off while saying some obscenities.

"Damn bitch, you're crazy!"

"Test me, Diego. I swear to God, go and test me because you have no fucking clue what crazy is. Try sleeping with me hovering over you with a bloody rat dangling from my hand and a knife in the other."

"Holy fuck," he exclaimed while he scooted back some more.

"Are you going to tell me?"

"Do I have a choice?"

"Not if you like your dick."

His hands quickly went to his crotch as his eyes widened.

"Well…"

"Fine." He took a deep breath and said, "Lot 17 is a piece of property that Jett has been keeping his eyes on for a while, he plans on using it for the local Boys and Girls club and building a park in honor of them and for them."

My heart warmed from that information. Why did he make it seem like it was such a bad thing?

"The only thing standing in his way is his father," Diego added.

"His father?" I asked, confused.

"Yes, the man is in the same business as Jett but he isn't as successful as his son because he's not honest and he's very distrustful. He uses people to get what he wants and he won't let anything stand in his way when he sets his eyes on something he wants, even his son."

"Oh my God, he's the one threatening Jett?"

Diego nodded his head.

"Why wouldn't he tell me this?"

Diego gave me the "are you stupid" look. "Can you imagine how embarrassing it is to have a father who would rather destroy you than love you? He doesn't want to get you wrapped up in that bullshit."

"Too late," I mumbled. "Why does he want Lot 17?"

"He wants to make some kind of high rise in the area that will destroy the atmosphere of the quaint part of the city and it's right next to the Boys and Girls Club and apparently what he has planned for the building is not the most kid friendly situation."

"What does he have planned?"

"Not quite sure on the details but Jett was discussing it with me the other day. It's some kind of sex club, I guess, but an illegal one. I asked around yesterday and he's not the only one who's involved."

"Who else? Please don't say Kace."

Diego laughed. "No, Kace is one hundred percent loyal to Jett."

"Then who is it?"

"Rex Titan."

As if I was in a soap opera, I gasped as I held my sandwich out mid-bite.

"That makes no sense, why would—"

"They have a common goal in life…to take down Jett Colby."

"But…doesn't Jett have enough power to take out Rex and his dad?"

"Not like they have over him. They know about you, you're his weakness and that is just one thing he can't fake."

"But what about Rex and his dad. If his dad is such a bad

person, why doesn't Jett have material to hold over his head?"

"That's what he's working on but Jett can't seem to get anything concrete on him, rather than he said, she said bullshit, which won't hold up in court."

"But—"

Diego cut me off. "That's all I have for you. Can I leave?"

I sat there stunned, wondering what to do next.

"Isn't there a big event tonight?"

"The Mayor's Ball."

"You're going, right?" I asked.

"Yes, I'm going to help Jett."

"You're taking me with you."

A laugh escaped Diego's mouth, a deep and guttural one. "Okay, crazy."

I stood up and charged after him, his hands covered his nipples as he crossed his legs to cover his junk.

Leaning in while reaching for the butter knife behind me, I held it up and threatened him. "Butter knives are much worse when it comes to castrating someone than let's say, something sharp or serrated. I would hate to have to use this in the middle of the night."

Okay, crazy was probably an accurate assessment but I was done. I was sick of people treating me like a goddamn delicate flower. I could hold my own and I was about to. I was not letting anyone push me around anymore. I was going to take care of Jett for once.

"Be ready by eight?" he said. "Wear something fancy."

I patted his face with the flat side of the knife. "Good boy. You're making smart decisions today, Diego. Give yourself a pat on your back."

I tossed the half-eaten sandwich at him and brushed my hands off. "I'll see you around eight."

As I walked toward my room, I thought about how there was some packing I needed to do and some phone calls to make. I had a party to attend and a man to save.

36
"SAY YOU LOVE ME"

Jett

The flowery scent of Keylee's perfume was way too overpowering to be trapped in a small vehicle with her. It was a scent that your grandma would wear on her only fanciest occasions and it was just dreadful.

The dress she showed up in was a deep purple, sweetheart top that hugged her waist and draped over her hips. There was a slip that rode up the center of her legs, showing off quite a bit but concealing just enough that the dress wasn't considered slutty, unless you were sitting next to her in a car, that was a different story.

She crossed her legs and leaned over to me, directing my attention to the slit that rode dangerously close to her underwear, at least I was praying she was wearing underwear. Given her track record, she probably wasn't.

"I'm so excited about tonight." She leaned in and wrapped her hand around my arm. "Is my dress all right?"

"You look very beautiful," I said, trying to keep the little devil calm. Just a couple of hours, that's what I kept telling myself.

"Thank you." She pressed her chest up against my arm.

I refrained from flicking her off me and looked out the window. Life would be so much easier without the complication of my father. Goldie would be in my arms instead of Keylee, she would be going home with me and she would be sleeping with me every night. I wouldn't have this aching feeling that took place in my stomach every night and I wouldn't wake up feeling lonelier than ever.

I took a page out of Goldie's book this morning and talked to my mom at her gravesite. I talked out loud because I thought that maybe if I vocalized my thoughts, she would hear me better. Even though I didn't have her as a present contributor in my life, I still missed her more than anything because just like Goldie, she saw me for who I am, not who society wants me to be. Being without my mom was hard and add the fact that Goldie wasn't in my life either made it that much harder.

It was like the shadow of my father would never really leave. For a while, I was doing fine, I was living my life, free of any kind of emotional worry or care and then Goldie came along and stole my heart right out from under me. She flipped my world upside down and it burned me that I couldn't live my life like I wanted to because I knew the moment that I let my guard down, that I showed Goldie off as mine, my dad would win because he would use my feelings for Goldie against me. Hell, he used my friendship with Kace against me.

The thought of losing Kace was almost as painful as losing Goldie. We might fight, we might call each other some of the crudest names but in the end, we were there for each other. We would do anything for each other and my dad knew that. That was why he went after Kace as well.

My hand ran over my face as I shook my head. What a damn clusterfuck. All because my dad was suffering business wise. He pissed off too many people and was now feeling the loss of those connections. With Lot 17, he was convinced that he would be able to revamp his standing but I knew better. Once you tarnish an image, it's practically impossible to make it shiny again.

Keylee's small hand ran over my thigh. "You're so tense. Do you need me to take care of that for you?" Her hand ran up the inner part of my thigh. I stopped her right before she got too close. She pouted, such a turn off, and huffed.

"What's wrong? Don't you want me to pleasure you, Jett? Isn't that what your girls do?"

"Yes, but you're not my girl, Keylee. You're a friend and I don't think it would be right to cross that line…yet." I added yet at the end so she didn't storm out of the car and leave me hanging. Even though she was a little touchy and pushy, I still needed to dangle a little piece of me in front of her.

"Mmm, I like the sounds of that…yet. Well, if it was up to me I would have that dick of yours in my mouth, sucking you dry."

Jesus.

"We're here," I said as I straightened my tie and sat up in my seat.

The driver pulled up to the drop off zone and came around quickly to our door to let us out. I was by no means ready for this but it was time to get it over with. A couple of hours of kissing ass and then I would be stripping Goldie naked and holding her in my arms.

Lights flashed as I stepped out of the car. I held my hand out to Keylee who eagerly took it and we walked in tandem, down the red carpet that seemed a little extreme, took pictures together and then headed into the grand hall.

The walls were covered in gold and green wallpaper and I couldn't help to think how ironic the colors were given my situation. I needed to take note from my own damn words. I needed to have faith that this was all going to work out, that the honest will prevail. One could only hope.

We made our way through the throngs of people, paid our respects to the mayor who was delighted to see two of the elite pedigree walking hand in hand together.

When we walked through the crowd, it was as if Prince William and Kate were walking through the room. People were delighted, excited and too damn happy to see Keylee and me together.

"Oh, Jett Colby, I knew that was you," came the voice of Mrs. Steevers who was wearing the most god-awful headpiece I had ever seen. It was like she took a dead raccoon, turned it inside out and plopped it on her head.

"Mrs. Steevers, what a pleasure to see you. You look well." I greeted her with two kisses on her cheeks. "You remember Miss Keylee Zinc, don't you?" I asked while pulling Keylee forward.

"Of course I do. I just knew that you two would find each other one day. You're just too perfect together."

"I think so too," Keylee added while wrapping both hands around my arm and pulling in tight.

"How long have you two been dating?"

"We—"

Keylee cut me off and said, "Just off and on for a little bit but just last night Jett pledged his commitment to me. It was so endearing."

Mrs. Steevers clapped her hands in glee as I glared at Keylee for lying. Commitment? To her? The only commitment she would be getting from me was a kick to her lying ass.

"Do I hear wedding bells?"

A sickening cough floated through my throat from the mention of being married to Keylee. Hell no!

Keylee rubbed my back but still spoke to Mrs. Steevers, "Oh, I don't think so yet but we'll see. We're happy enough, that's for sure."

"Excuse me, I need to get a drink," I said while motioning

to my throat.

"Oh please do, dear," Mrs. Steevers said. "It was so good to see you two."

"You too, Mrs. Steevers." I gave her a hug goodbye and made a beeline for the bar. I needed a bourbon and I needed one now.

I heard Keylee trailing behind me, trying to catch up and I made it a point to take a deep breath before addressing her.

The bartender must have known I was coming because he had a glass of bourbon already ready for me. He gave me a wink and I tipped him a twenty.

Once I turned around, I was met with Keylee's glare. "You can't just leave me stranded like that," she said as she popped a hand on her hip.

"I can when you're shooting off blatant lies." My anger took over and I was no longer able to control my temper. I was already on edge, I didn't need Keylee telling the most gossiping hen in the crowd that we were planning on getting married.

"I was just trying to help…"

I leaned forward and whispered in her ear while looking out at the crowd, "If you want to help, be quiet, sip some water and stand by my side without opening that…" My words stopped as my eyes locked on a honey-haired goddess in a black dress that just walked into the party on Diego's arm.

My heart stopped, completely and my stomach bottomed out from seeing Goldie on someone else's arm. Forget that, for even seeing her at the event at all. What the fuck was Diego up to?

"I don't have to take this from you," Keylee said while poking my chest.

Reluctantly, I tore my gaze off Goldie and looked down at her. "You want to be a Jett Girl? Well, that means knowing your role and right now, your role is to be pleasing to the men's eyes while keeping your mouth shut. You think you can handle that?"

Her mouth hung in shock from my directness. I didn't have time to fuck around, to care about her feelings. I needed her to comply immediately.

"You have three seconds to decide," I continued. "Three…two…"

"Okay," she said in a panic. "Just, let me collect myself first. I wasn't prepared for this. May I go to the bathroom?"

Goldie crossed the room with Diego, whispered something in his ear and headed for the bathroom, this was my chance to talk to Diego without Keylee's damn ears dropping in on my conversation.

"Yes, but don't doddle," I commanded.

She nodded, gave me one last look with those damn pouty lips of hers and then took off for the bathroom.

Diego must have sensed my anger because as Goldie crossed the room, he made his way to the bar where I stood. After he ordered a drink, I grabbed him by the elbow, tightly, and swung him around.

With a smile across my face but a menace in my voice, I said, "What the fuck do you think you're doing?"

"Do you think it's smart to be talking to me right now?"

"Don't fuck around with me. What is she doing here?"

The bartender handed Diego his drink and he followed with a tip. Surveying the crowd, Diego stood by my side but never looked at me as he spoke in a light tone, "She made me. I didn't have a choice."

"Are you insane? You're like three times as big as her. Of course you had a choice."

"She really knows how to pinch a nipple, man."

"For the love of Christ. Please don't tell me that you brought her here because she pinched your nipple. I swear to God, Diego, I will take everything away from you that you worked so hard for."

Shaking his head, Diego said, "Low blow, man. Maybe you need to just let her be. She will do whatever the hell she wants, it's about time you realized that."

"You could have stopped her. What if something happens

to her tonight?"

"Nothing is going to happen to her. We're in the middle of the most politically acclaimed event in New Orleans. No one will try anything tonight so stop shitting your pants and do what you're supposed to do. Get the job done, man."

"Fuck," I muttered, trying not to show the distress I was in by having Goldie at the event tonight. With her here, there was no way I would be able to focus on the task at hand.

"Got to go, keep your distance man and for the love of God, don't blow it."

With that, Diego took off and started shaking hands of younger men who Diego grew to know while attending these events. There was a whole secret club of kinky men in the city and Diego knew each and every one of them. They were the only reason why Diego went to these events, so he could network and when he was ready for his club to open, he would have a decent membership.

The next hour flew by in a blur as I watched Diego escort Goldie around, something I should be doing. She made anyone who talked to her laugh and she put a bright smile on their faces. I couldn't blame them, she had the same effect on me.

Through the night, I heard people whispering about the exotic new girl that was wrapped around the elusive club owner's arm. Some people liked them, some people didn't think they belonged but everyone thought she was charming. That she was a breath of fresh air and here I was, with Keylee Zinc acting like a dead fish hanging off my arm. I knew I told her to keep her mouth shut but she took the submissive thing way too seriously. She barely looked up at people and bowed her head most of the time. If anything, she was hurting my image.

Fuck!

The sway of Goldie's hips mesmerized me as she walked across the room, which was why I didn't see my dad step right in front of me until he cleared his throat.

"Who is this treat?" he said while looking at Keylee.

I hated this man, despised him. The fact that he could just walk up to me and act like there was nothing between us made me sick to my stomach.

"This is Keylee Zinc. Keylee—" I swallowed hard, "—this is my father, Leo Colby."

Ever since she went to the bathroom, Keylee finally perked up from the mention of my father and her eyes lit with excitement. She held out her hand and my dad took it in his and placed a kiss on the back of her hand. It was sickening.

"Mr. Colby, what a delight to meet the man who had a part in making this delectable guy." She leaned in and pressed her free hand against my chest.

As if a match snapped, my attitude did a one eighty and I got in the same mind frame as Keylee. Happy couple.

I wrapped my arm around her and leaned in closer. I watched as my father's eyes scanned between us with a grin.

"Well, isn't this a new development."

"New, maybe but I can't tell you how happy we are." Keylee's lies started flowing and this time, I could actually kiss her for turning on at the right moment.

"Is that right?" My father eyed me.

"It is. It's actually embarrassing. The paparazzi caught us in a rather intimate moment yesterday," I added.

"It was rather embarrassing," Keylee said while holding her hands to her cheeks. What a fucking regular old Martha May with her acting skills. Damn.

"That's my son for ya, always had a hard time controlling his needs and desires."

My teeth grinded down, keeping my mouth shut so I didn't say anything too stupid.

Keylee looked between the two of us and sensed the tension because she pulled away and said, "I think I'm going to get a refill. Can I get you anything, baby?"

Baby? Christ.

"I'm fine, thank you."

"Mr. Colby?" She addressed my father.

"I'm good, dear," he said without taking his eyes off me.

Getting a clue, she left us and for good measure, I watched her walk away even though her sway wasn't nearly as impressive as Goldie's.

"She's a nice little number. How much are you paying her to be here with you?"

"Not everyone has to pay someone off for a date," I said while taking a sip of my bourbon.

"So confident tonight, as if you think you've won it all."

"Haven't I?" I asked, trying to be as unflappable as possible. "I have the woman, I have the house and now I will have the property. Cut your losses, old man, and start going after something else."

The corner of my father's mouth twitched as his jaw grew tense.

"I plan on going after something and it's here in this room, dressed in all black and looking absolutely divine."

The moment of truth, my face held still as I took another sip of my bourbon as I said, "And what would that be?"

"Don't play with me, boy."

"I'm sorry that you think I have time to play around with you, but I don't so if you would like to get to the point of this conversation, that would be appreciated."

In the corner of my eye, I could see Goldie approach with Diego chasing behind her.

Not fucking now, please not fucking now. I was holding on by a thread. A bead of sweat trickled down my back as Goldie got closer. Why wasn't Diego stopping her?

My dad's head turned and saw her. An evil grin spread across his face and he finally spoke. "You want to get down to the point, fine. Right here, right now, tell me. Lot 17 or Goldie? You can only choose one."

I knew Goldie heard my father because he spoke loud enough. She stopped in her place as she waited for my answer. I hid the shake in my hand by lowering my glass and set it on a table nearby. My next move would either make or break my relationship with Goldie but I had no choice.

With the flick of my wrist, my hand caressed my jaw, showing off the bright emerald green cufflinks that donned my wrists, trying to portray to Goldie that she needed to have faith.

Without blinking, I cleared my throat and said, "Is there even a choice? No doubt in my mind Lot 17 wins every time."

I saw the slight intake of air out of the corner of my eye from Goldie's chest and the defeat in her shoulders. Without looking back, she turned away from me, grabbed Diego and fled through the crowd.

With all the energy I could muster, I smiled and laughed. "You can't please them all." With that, I grabbed my bourbon and walked away, leaving my father stunned and Goldie broken-hearted.

37
"LOVE OF MY LIFE"

Lo

The bounce of my leg kept my beating heart steady as I sat on my bed and thought about the words that rang from Jett's lips. "Was it even a choice?" I couldn't lie, it fucking stung to hear him utter such words.

Diego tried to calm me down in the car but I ignored him as the street lanterns of New Orleans passed us by in a blur. My mind felt calm, calmer than it's felt in a while because I knew what I had to do.

Without a knock, my door burst open and Jett stood in the doorframe, gorgeous as ever wearing his tux with his tie undone and his hair in a mess from the stress he put himself through tonight. I didn't move, I didn't waiver as he strode to my bed while shutting the door at the same time. He fell to his knees in front of me and clasped his hands over mine.

"Goldie," he choked out, looking up at me with desperation. My hand went to his face and caressed his cheek. "God, I'm so sorry. I hope you know that I didn't mean any of that, that you're always my number one."

"Am I?" I asked with a little bit of emotion lacing my voice.

He sat up and looked up at me. "Of course you are, how could you think that you aren't?"

A part of me wanted to believe him, that I was his number one, that I was the only thing that mattered but that wasn't the case, especially tonight and to be honest I was okay with that because he was a good man and fighting for a good thing. I couldn't hold that against him.

"Jett, you have one of the sweetest hearts I've ever come across. You don't like to take credit but you change so many people's lives. You saved Kace, you gave Diego a second chance, you've sheltered and educated the girls, you're bending over backwards to help the Boys and Girls of New Orleans by sacrificing everything that makes you happy to give them a place to play, a place to grow up in. Am I number one in your life? No, but I'm okay with it because the people, the causes that come before me are deserving of your attention."

"But that's not true," he said but I placed my fingers over his lips.

"It's commendable that you're willing to put everyone before your own needs."

"You're all I need," he said quickly.

Running my hand through his hair, I answered, "I know that but like I said, you put everyone else before you, which means that I get a back seat to everything."

"Goldie, that's not what I want you to think. It's just hard right now. I wasn't expecting to..." He paused as his hands twisted in mine. "I wasn't expecting to fall for you and this all happened in the middle of a deal I'm trying to make."

"And I'm okay with that," I said reassuringly. "I get it, Jett.

I promise you I do but there comes a time where you need to stop trying to protect everyone else and protect yourself. I'm a big girl and I can handle my own against anyone."

"These are dangerous men…"

"I've been through hell, Jett, and you coming into my life was by far the best thing that's ever happened to me and I will forever cherish that."

He perked up and sat down next to me on my bed. "I don't like the way you're talking to me right now, Goldie," he responded seriously.

With a deep breath, I reached behind my neck and unclasped my necklace. I let it fall into my hand as I looked directly into Jett's eyes. The look of devastation crossed his features as he took in the meaning of my gesture.

"Little one…" His throat tightened. "Wh-what are you doing?"

I opened his hand and placed the necklace in his hand and clasped his fingers around it. I bent forward, pulled a suitcase that was packed out from under my bed and stood. My chest burned and my stomach flipped as I looked into Jett's gaze. Tears welled in his eyes as he watched me stand.

My hand cupped his chin and my lips gently kissed his. When I pulled away, my hand gripped the back of his neck as I said, "You've been saving me, protecting me and giving me the chance to live for the past couple of months, it's about time that I returned the favor."

"By leaving? By breaking my fucking heart?" Anger started to sear through his gaze as he clutched the necklace he gave me.

"No, Jett, by taking matters into my own hands. It's about damn time that someone stuck up for you and protected you."

"I don't need to be protected, I just need you, Goldie. This is all over tomorrow…"

"It's not and we both know it. There is only one way to fix this and I'm the one to do it."

I walked toward the door but he stood and clasped his

hand around my wrist, pulling me into him. His lips found mine in a carnal force that I wasn't expecting. The bag I was carrying dropped from my hand and my hands ran up the front of his chest and clasped around his cheeks. Tears spilled over my eyes as my love for the man in my arms encompassed me. I loved him…so damn much that I was willing to do whatever it took to make him happy, to make us happy.

With force, I pulled away and looked up at him. Tears glistened his eyes as well.

"Don't do this, don't do this to me, Goldie. Please, don't' leave me." The vulnerability seeping from Jett was like a knife to the gut, I was two seconds from breaking and giving him what he wanted but knew it wasn't what needed to be done. Instead, I pulled out a box from my suitcase and handed it to him.

"Open it," I said while looking down at his hands that were shaking.

With a deep breath and confused look, he opened the box and a small smile hit the corners of his mouth. He pulled out a watch with a green face and gold numbers.

I placed my hands against his chest and said, "Have a little faith in the power I have, Jett. Trust me with your heart because I promise you that it's the most treasured gift I will ever receive from you." I placed the necklace he gave me in the box and said, "Keep this safe for me for now. When I come back, because I will be back, I will be requesting that you collar me again…that is if you'll take me."

"I always will," he said breathlessly.

I took the watch from him and placed it on his wrist. It was a perfect fit.

I traced the face and said, "Green for faith and gold for power. This watch means that even though we are apart right now, you're mine and you need to have faith in me and in time, the power we crave, the power we have for each other will soon be ours to keep…forever." I kissed him again and said, "This isn't goodbye, Jett, this is only the beginning."

With that, I left the room and took off down the stairs to the taxi that was waiting for me. As the cab drove away, I looked up into the room I once occupied and saw Jett, staring down at me. His hair was tousled and his eyes were wet with emotions. I turned away, not being able to stand to see him in such a state and tried to push back the feelings that were coursing through me. It was game time. I was getting what I wanted and there was only one place to start.

The dark night of New Orleans fell upon me as we pulled up to my destination and then I paid the cabby. With my suitcase in my hand, I took a deep breath and knocked on the front door. Anxiety wrestled with my nerves as I waited patiently for the door to open.

The sound of locks turning echoed through the night and when the door opened, light flooded the entryway. I put on my best smile and puffed my chest out. I could do this for me, but most importantly, for Jett.

A smile met mine as I stepped inside the grand entryway.

"Why hello, kitten. You've just made my night."

Thank you for reading Being a Jett Girl! I hope you enjoyed it. If you did, please help other readers find this book:

1. This book is lendable, so send it to a friend who you think might like it so she can discover me, too.
2. Help other people find this book by writing a review.
3. Come like my Facebook page: Author Meghan Quinn
4. Find me on Goodreads:
https://www.goodreads.com/author/show/7360513.Meghan_Quinn
5. Don't forget to visit my website: www.authormeghanquinn.com

ABOUT THE AUTHOR

Born in New York and raised in Southern California, Meghan has grown into a sassy, peanut butter eating, blonde haired swearing, animal hoarding lady. She is known to bust out and dance if "It's Raining Men" starts beating through the air and heaven forbid you get a margarita in her, protect your legs because they may be humped.

Once she started commuting for an hour and twenty minutes every day to work for three years, she began to have conversations play in her head, real life, deep male voices and dainty lady coos kind of conversations. Perturbed and confused, she decided to either see a therapist about the hot and steamy voices running through her head or start writing them down. She decided to go with the cheaper option and started writing… enter her first novel, Caught Looking.

Now you can find the spicy, most definitely on the border of lunacy, kind of crazy lady residing in Colorado with the love of her life and her five, furry four legged children, hiking a trail or hiding behind shelves at grocery stores, wondering what kind of lube the nervous stranger will bring home to his wife. Oh and she loves a good boob squeeze!

Made in the USA
Las Vegas, NV
06 February 2024

85327122R00184